"S.L. Russell weaves a legal narra... successfully pulling the reader int... fighting to hold on to faith, family, and the pursuit of truth.

Russell writes with such realistic dialogue, readers are sure to find themselves captivated by the strength and determination of Anna Milburn in The Thorn of Truth."

Lauren Brandenburg, award-winning author of *The Death of Mungo Blackwell* and *The Marriage of Innis Wilkinson*

"*The Thorn of Truth is an endearing tale of how life does not always go according to plan. Marriage, career, child-rearing, faith, relationships – sometimes even doing your best may not be good enough.*

But in the midst of all of that, S.L. Russell reminds us why it is always important to do the right thing, despite the risk and the cost... leading to a dramatic conclusion."

Les Cowan, author of the David Hidalgo mystery series

"*S.L. Russell masters the contemporary Christian novel in this beautifully compelling story of the consequences of treading the thin line between heart and conscience.*"

C.F. Dunn, author of *Mortal Fire*

THE THORN OF TRUTH

S. L. RUSSELL

LION FICTION

Lion Hudson Limited
Wilkinson House, Jordan Hill Business Park
Banbury Road, Oxford OX2 8DR, England
www.lionhudson.com

ISBN 978 1 78264 336 4
e-ISBN 978 1 78264 356 2

First edition 2021

Acknowledgments
Scriptures are from the Good News Translation® (Today's English Version, Second
Edition). Copyright © 1992 American Bible Society. All rights reserved.

A catalogue record for this book is available from the British Library

Printed and bound in the UK, January 2021, LH26

ACKNOWLEDGMENTS

So many people have contributed to the making of this story that I am afraid of accidentally leaving someone out. So I will simply reiterate my warm appreciation of all the help I have been given: from family and friends, readers and reviewers, and the team at Lion. I am truly thankful to you all for your support, perspicacity, and patience. One person, however, I must single out: James Rae, Barrister, for his professional knowledge and expertise, and his gracious willingness to share it and put me right when I was wildly off track.

ONE

Leaman.

The name pierced my unshielded memory, unbidden, unwelcome, a teeth-gritting intrusion from a past that wasn't far enough away. It must have been the river – rolling grey, cold, merciless a few metres below me – that sparked the connection to my poor nephew, and then, inexorably swift, to the man who bore the name. Why had I even come to the riverbank that morning? I couldn't say. With an effort I banished the hated image from my mind, called up the dog, and plodded on.

Gordon is eleven years old and should probably know better; but perhaps hope is hard to quench in the innocent heart. My experience of the male sex is not vast, but I am sometimes drawn to the notion that they are – with the probable exception of my ex-husband – more romantic than females. That was certainly the case with my daughter's dog that damp, dreary, early March morning. Gordon is rotund, black, brown, and white in inelegant random patches, odd-eared, short-legged, and sometimes short of breath as well. So he is not exactly a catch, but of course he doesn't know that. All he saw that morning was the dazzling beauty of the graceful female collie that appeared to his popping eyes on a muddy riverbank. He hadn't been too keen to leave his basket when I suggested a walk, but I'm sure in that moment he considered it worth it.

While he and his new friend were sniffing each other,

her feathery tail lazily wagging, his stump revolving like a demented windmill, my eyes were drawn to a woman sitting, head bowed, on a nearby bench. She was dressed in running gear: black leggings and long-sleeved top, serious-looking trainers. I couldn't see her face; she had her hands supporting her forehead. I sensed that there was something wrong and approached cautiously.

"Hello, um, are you all right?" I asked.

She raised her head and looked at me, and I was struck immediately by her eyes: pale blue and piercing. I may actually have taken a step back.

Then she smiled slightly. "Thank you, it's nothing serious." Her voice was husky.

I took in the shadows round those strange eyes and the extreme pallor of her face. "Are you sure? You don't look well."

"I am OK. But thank you." Seeing my doubt, her smile broadened. "I'm pregnant, that's all. A drop in blood pressure, I imagine. Ran too hard and fast."

"Oh."

Then her eyes narrowed and a small frown appeared between her dark brows. "Don't I know you from somewhere? You look... different. But I think we've met."

I looked at her more closely and saw the almost-invisible long silver scar that ran from the corner of her right eyebrow across her cheek, stopping just above her lip where there was a tiny nick. "Yes," I said slowly, memory battling to summon up the time and place. "Yes, you have seen me in court. Wigged and gowned."

Her eyes widened. "I'm sure you were taller." She winced. "Sorry, I don't know why I said that."

Now it was I who smiled. "I always wear high heels in

8

court. As you see, I'm not favoured with height. It can be difficult in my profession to evoke respect when you are female, short, and blonde."

"Of course. You were the defence barrister at Eve Rawlins' trial."

"I was. But I didn't have too much to do." I shrugged. "She refused to let me use any advocacy to shorten her sentence. So it was just a matter of reading out a document we prepared together beforehand."

Suddenly she got up from the bench. She was taller than me by several inches, slim, and lithe. I saw that some colour had come back to her face. She stuck out her hand. "Rachel Wells. I was Rachel Keyte then." She nodded towards the collie. "And this is Dulcie."

I took the proffered hand. "Anna Milburn – and my love-struck mongrel, Gordon." At the mention of his name his stump wagged even more frantically.

Her eyebrows lifted a fraction. "Not Anna Milburn, QC?"

"No. I can't afford it."

She frowned. "What? So being a Queen's Counsel isn't something conferred?"

I laughed. "Like a reward? No, one has to apply. And all the parties and receptions one feels bound to throw cost money. Not to mention that once you take silk, especially in a provincial setting, you are likely to get fewer instructions because you are more expensive. And I need to work. Bills to pay, and all that."

She nodded, obviously pondering what I had said. "I remember the trial. You called me as a witness."

"I was bound to. But it was pretty much a formality. She'd pleaded guilty. It was a serious crime, even though we managed to establish she hadn't actually meant to kill you.

9

And obviously it was traumatic for you. Still, she could have got a shorter sentence, if she'd let me do what I wanted to do."

"That sounds like her," Rachel murmured, almost to herself. She looked at me directly, and again I felt the impact of her eyes. "But I think the jury took pity on her anyway, didn't they? I suppose they would, losing her only child like that."

"Probably. You seem to remember it all clearly." Struck by the seeming thoughtlessness of my words, I continued. "Forgive me, of course you remember. I imagine it'd be hard to forget."

She smiled. "Whereas for you it's vanished in a fog of many other cases, I imagine."

"There've been a few," I conceded. "And it was more than three years ago, I think. But it's not every day I am involved in such a high-profile case. Most of the time now I am battling with custody issues, employment tribunals, nuts-and-bolts stuff. Not many eminent surgeons attacked by a grief-maddened parent! Not too many bloody crimes at all, come to that."

Rachel laughed. "Let's hope that's not prophetic!" She glanced towards the dogs, now chasing each other round the bench. "I'd better get this hound home." She looked at her watch. "I've got to repair someone's aorta this afternoon. Come on, Dulcie. Good to have met you, Anna."

"Yes. You too," I said, and watched her as she jogged slowly away, the collie at her heels. Gordon started to follow, but I called him off. He looked positively woebegone. I reached down and stroked his head. "Never mind, old chap. I think she was probably out of your reach anyway, a classy lady like that." His sigh was heart-rending.

Gordon seemed weary and disinclined for further exercise, and with the damp air beginning to chill my bones as well, I clipped on his lead and made my way back to where I had parked the car. This was not a part of the river I would normally frequent, since I lived towards the other side of the city, but today I had no court to worry about and had decided to stay at home and catch up on some paperwork. My daughter, normally tasked with walking the dog, had needed to get to school early for some reason, so I'd volunteered for walk duty.

As Gordon trudged, disconsolately it seemed, beside me, I thought about that chance meeting and wondered about Rachel Wells. The fact of her pregnancy and her change of name suggested she had married in the time since the trial. I conjured with the name Wells and was rewarded with the image of a tall, quietly spoken man with dark, greying hair and a sombre manner. I couldn't recall what questions had been put to him by the prosecution or myself, but his face I remembered, and his profession. So, injured Rachel had married the plastic surgeon who'd put her back together? That sounded to me too happily-ever-after for credibility, but I had to allow for my own cynicism. As I lifted the boot lid and encouraged Gordon to jump in, which he did with some grunting and puffing, I wondered about Rachel's life. What sort of person was she? What would it be like to have such a friend? I guessed I would never know, since we were as unlikely to meet again as Gordon was to have a chance with Dulcie.

As I drove home, keeping to back streets to avoid the city's manic morning traffic, I thought about friends, in particular the ones I had lost. If I was honest, they were barely friends, more acquaintances, and had been Richard's first, so they had vanished from my horizon with the marriage itself. In hindsight they were no great loss and caused me no real pain. More uncomfortable were the ones I no longer saw or had contact with from Brant Abbey, where I used to worship – much to Richard's mockery. None of them had been especially close, but on the whole they were good, charitable Christian souls and a long way better than nothing. Unfortunately for me, there had been among them a sanctimonious couple who were unkind at a time when I was particularly vulnerable. Clearly, from their lofty vantage point of perfect matrimonial harmony, they blamed me for the divorce, of which they unrestrainedly disapproved. In my more kindly moments, I had to admit that at the time of their censure they didn't know that Richard was already involved with Jenny. In fact, they didn't know Richard at all. That was a painful time in more than one way, and despite the urging of old friends like John Sutcliffe, who is still a steward at the abbey, I have never been back there – or, indeed, to any church.

I did, and do, have one friend, and her I treasure. She is a lifeline, a supporter, loyal enough to tell me when I am going wrong. She is also my clerk at chambers – Janet Clarke. She says whimsically that no other profession seemed suitable with a name like hers, and resolutely refuses to go with the modern way and style herself "Practice Manager". She says it would make her feel like someone running a doctor's surgery. Whatever the case, she does it well, with an efficiency that's almost ferocious, keeping the younger barristers in order and ensuring I get the cases she thinks will suit – most of the time. And she's a friend outside work too. From time to time I take up her invitations to eat with her and her husband, Bob, but since he is a paramedic and works shifts, it is often just Janet and me and a bottle of wine. It's those moments that remind me there's more to life than law, that in the absence of a partner, friendship matters even more.

I was wrong: I did see Rachel again. A fortnight later I'd come from court out of town and I wafted into chambers in the early afternoon. As I dumped my heavy bag on the floor of my room, Janet appeared in the doorway wearing a smart black suit – an image rather skewed by her new, spiky, purple-tipped hairdo.

"Got some instructions for you," she said with her usual brevity. "Nice, short, should be open-and-shut."

I groaned. "That usually means the exact reverse." I regarded her new look. "Nice hair, by the way."

She smiled and patted her spiky locks. "I thought purple would be less offensive than magenta." She paused. "I mean it about the case; it's Hutchins and Phelps, and they're good payers."

"OK, but I need to go shopping," I said. "I'll take a late lunch. I haven't had anything apart from disgusting vending-machine coffee since my half bowl of muesli at seven o'clock. Give me an hour to get some groceries and a sandwich and I'll be back. Hopefully fresh and attentive."

Janet said something under her breath which was probably not very complimentary, then disappeared. I visited the washroom and tried to tame my hair with a brush and some cold water, which lasted about five minutes. There was a sizeable supermarket, not long opened, across the square from Hartington Chambers; I took just my handbag and walked there. In an unfamiliar shop it took me longer than usual to find a few cans of dog food and things I needed for our supper, enough to keep us going for a day at least. I never seemed to have time for ordinary things like shopping and laundry, and the house was never very tidy; what did get done was invariably done in a rush and half-baked. At last I battled through the checkout, bought a couple of carrier bags – even though the understairs cupboard was awash with them – and found my way to the café. I purchased an interesting-looking wrap with something green inside it, and a large cup of coffee, and sank thankfully into a chair at an empty table. The wrap was edible, the greenery turned out to be spinach and avocado, and the coffee was surprisingly good. It certainly beat the dishwater available in most Magistrates' Courts in the backwaters. Having eaten and drunk, and feeling more human, I thought about leaving, but the Hutchins and Phelps stuff wasn't particularly appealing and I sat for a few minutes longer, watching normal people doing ordinary things. Then I heard, somewhere behind me, a vaguely familiar voice muttering something very crossly, and my table was bumped and shaken. "Sorry, sorry!" came the voice. I turned and it was Rachel.

"Oh! Hello, Anna. Sorry for crashing into you."

She was pushing a child's buggy, each of its handles as well as the undercarriage loaded with bulging bags. In the buggy, well wrapped, sat a small child of indeterminate gender, gazing at me solemnly: those same unnerving pale blue eyes.

"Hello, Rachel. Why don't you sit down?"

She almost fell into the chair opposite and groaned. "I hate shopping."

"Not easy with a pushchair," I agreed.

"I normally do it online. Should definitely not have changed tactics. But we were feeling hedged in, needed a change of scene. Didn't we, sweetheart?" She looked down at the child. "This is my son, Jonathan." She reached down and took off the little boy's hat, revealing straight, fine dark hair.

"He has your eyes."

She smiled. "I know. But in all other respects he is a Wells, which is a good thing. Calm and unflappable."

"Would you like me to watch him while you get yourself something?"

"Thank you, that would be great."

"That's if he won't mind."

"No, he won't. Back in as short a time as the queue allows."

She returned in a few minutes with a mug of black coffee. She scrabbled in a bag under the buggy and extracted a child's unspillable beaker of juice and handed it to the little boy, who took it and drank. "Don't throw it on the floor, Jonny. Just give it to me when you've had enough."

"Not working today, then?" I asked.

"No. But believe me, childcare is a lot more testing than surgery," Rachel said. She took a sip of her coffee and flashed me a grin. "How are you? Are you not working?"

"I've been in court this morning," I said. "A dreary Magistrates' Court, a dreary case, and a dreary town an hour's drive from here. And when I get back to chambers my clerk has some new instructions for me which I suspect will be dreary also. Needs must, though."

"Yes. I know what you mean. This little chap needs looking after."

"And soon there'll be a baby as well," I said. "When's it due?"

"October. Shall I sign up for therapy now?" She smiled. "It's fine. It was my choice. We're OK, aren't we, Jonny?" She looked over at me. "And I still get to work a sizeable chunk of the week, thanks to his very accommodating and even-handed father, who is much more of a natural parent than I am." She took the boy's empty beaker and placed it into the rack under the pushchair. "What about you, Anna? Do you have children?"

"A daughter," I said. "Emilia, known as Millie. She turned eighteen in January and guards her adult status with fierce pride."

Rachel nodded. "Still at school?"

"Baccalaureate."

"Bright, no doubt."

"Yes. Plus verbal, obstinate, and frequently contrary, not to mention critical of her mother. Oh yes, and omniscient."

Rachel chuckled. "And I've got all that to come perhaps. What fun."

"Not necessarily. Jonathan looks a peaceful fellow."

"True. And my stepson Jasper, age twenty and a hairy student, was never too horrible."

"Just watch out if your baby's a girl. They're the worst."

"You're right. We should know: we were girls once. And I've had many horrible moments, as I'm sure my mother would agree." She sighed. "I can't stop long, unfortunately. Once I've downed this coffee and the caffeine's taking effect I'll have to get on. You too, I imagine."

"Yes. There's always something, and if I am short of things to do I can always turn out the kitchen cupboards."

"Ha! Last resort." She sipped her coffee. "But perhaps even that would be preferable to the hospital reception I've foolishly agreed to go to this evening. I am rubbish at social events and either say the wrong thing to the wrong person or hug the wall, frozen with boredom."

"And you really must go?"

"No one's saying I *must*," she said gloomily. "But I have avoided quite a few and am feeling twinges of guilt. That's not typical, I assure you! But Michael has to be there, and he often goes to these things alone, so I feel honour bound. At least we don't have to search for a babysitter. My stepson's home for the Easter holidays, and he loves looking after his brother."

"Easter! So it is."

Had she noticed my sudden wince at the mention of Easter? Perhaps. Those eyes were fixed on my face like lasers.

"It's Good Friday this week. Had you forgotten? Maybe these things don't matter to you," she said. "I take it you're not a churchgoer. Oh, what a smug, anodyne word that is! As if we are afraid to say *Christian!*"

I was startled. I hadn't expected this, and it cracked my habitual reserve, just a little. "I used to be. I attended Brant Abbey for years."

Rachel blinked. "I know someone at Brant Abbey. A kind man, who had no small part in teaching me how to be a proper human being." *What did she mean by that?* "Perhaps you know him – John Sutcliffe."

The turn the conversation had taken, entirely unexpected, was bringing back feelings I didn't want to have: sadness at all I had turned away from, defensiveness, cold isolation, grief at the loss of friendship. "John's an old friend. From time to time he tries to encourage me to go back."

"Why won't you?" Rachel said. Then I saw a flush rise in her pale face. "Oh. Sorry. I guess I'm being too nosy, when we don't really know each other. I forget sometimes where the boundaries are."

"So, will you be in church on Friday?" I asked.

"Yes. We go to All Souls – Michael, Jasper, and me. Our

neighbours will look after Jonathan for a couple of hours." At the mention of his name, the little boy started to crow and babble, something incomprehensible to me but not to his mother. "All right, hang on, Jonny." She groped around in the bag again and extracted a toy helicopter which she put into the child's outstretched hand. "There you go, sweetie." She turned back to me. "It's a harrowing service; we all feel very sombre and quiet afterwards. But definitely necessary." She smiled at me suddenly. "Why don't you come? All Souls is all right, lots of nice people." Her smile broadened. "Oh dear, there I go again. It's really not my business, is it? But I am new to being a Christian as well. Much too direct, always saying something that makes people uncomfortable. A few years ago I'd have found that unbearably humiliating, being in a position where I was always making social gaffes. But back then I was extremely stiff-necked, vain, and generally insufferable!"

Since she was being so candid I thought I could be too. "So what happened?"

She took a long gulp of her coffee and laughed quietly. "It's a long story. I wish I could stay and chat; I don't have many people I can talk to so freely. But I must get this shopping in the car, and then it'll be time for my antenatal clinic. After that I have to race home, feed Jonathan, remind Jasper to walk the dog, put the shopping away, warm something up for dinner, and get ready for this tedious reception. It's a shame – I've enjoyed chatting to you." She glanced at her son. "Good lad – he's nodded off." She pushed her chair back suddenly and stood up, narrowly missing an elderly man threading his way through the chairs behind her, holding a tray on which a cup of tea and a plate were sliding precariously. "Must run! Bye, Anna."

After she had gone I sat for a while, wondering about that "long story" she spoke of. When I said I knew relatively little about males, I was speaking of my personal life. In my twenty years as a barrister I had met many men – and women, and children – but that knowledge was superficial. Once our mutual business was done our paths diverged, with little sorrow on either part. But I had never met anyone quite like Rachel Wells, and I admitted to myself that I was sorry we were unlikely to be friends. As she had said of herself, there were few people, with the exception of Janet, I was close to or with whom I could talk unguardedly.

I stood up and gathered my two small bags of shopping. "Oh." On the table, hidden by a crumpled paper napkin, was a credit card. Rachel must have thrown it down when she came back to the table with her coffee. Obviously, I couldn't leave it there. If I left it with the café people it could easily get lost – or even stolen. I put it in my pocket and walked thoughtfully back to chambers.

Janet called to me from her office next to the reception area. At the moment she was alone, her mouse-like assistant, whose name I could never remember, away on some errand round the building. In fact she was rarely there, and I suspected Janet merely tolerated her, preferring to work to her own agenda. I went in. Her desk was stacked high with papers and files, but I knew she had a handle on it all.

"Could you get me the number of the hospital, please, Janet?"

She raised her eyebrows. "You're not sick, are you?"

"No sicker than usual." I explained about the credit card. "I thought I could leave a message with the antenatal clinic. Give them my mobile number for Rachel."

It took longer than I'd anticipated: the woman I spoke to

didn't seem to understand what I was saying. But eventually she had my phone number and promised to find a patient called Mrs Wells. I couldn't think of anything else to do.

I spent what was left of the afternoon at my desk, looking at the Hutchins and Phelps instructions, doing some research, answering e-mails. Then I'd had enough. I shrugged on my coat, picked up my bags, and popped my head into Janet's office. "I'll see you in the morning," I called through. "I'll finish this lot off at home." I waved a folder at her. "Say hello to Bob for me." She grunted dismissively.

As I was unlocking my car, my phone rang. I fished it out of my pocket. "Anna?" It was Rachel. "Thank you so much for rescuing my card – what a numskull I am! I just got your message."

"How can I get it to you?"

"I was wondering," she said hesitantly, "if you're in this evening, and if it isn't too much of an imposition, could we call by after the reception? It won't be late – nine thirty at the latest."

"Of course." I gave her the address. "See you later. Have fun."

"Oh, the irony." She rang off.

As I strapped on my seatbelt I felt a small surge of optimism. It would probably amount to nothing, but I was foolishly glad to be seeing this strange woman again.

Millie is very often prickly, sarcastic, and generally difficult, but clearly this evening she was in a better mood and, having got home before me, had started preparing our supper.

"That smells good, Mil." I sniffed appreciatively. "Thanks."

"And," she said, putting her head round the kitchen door, "not only have I been shopping, but I have also walked the

20

dog and mopped the kitchen floor, which had boot marks all over it." She frowned at me accusingly, and I obediently kicked off my shoes.

I flopped onto the sofa with a sigh, and ran my stockinged foot over Gordon, curled up in his basket. Normally he slept in a corner of the kitchen; Millie must have moved him when she washed the floor. "You have your angelic moments, my love, indeed you do. How was your day?"

She came into the sitting room, wearing a voluminous striped apron and wielding a wooden spoon. "Uneventful. You must have been working hard, judging by your worry-lines."

"I think it's more a case of the ennui produced by dullness."

"There was one brief flash of excitement this morning, though," Millie said. "Someone from my English group came to school in a shiny new red car. New! She's only my age."

I raised my eyebrows. "Do I hear a note of envy?"

"You hear the full concerto, Mother. Why don't *I* have a new red car?"

"Possibly because you are still learning to drive."

She shrugged. "That's just a technicality. I don't think I'm going to get a car even when I've passed my test, let alone a new one. But I'm sure my dad's just as rich as hers. Isn't he?"

I sat up, stretching. "You'll have to ask him that. I no longer know."

"All right, all right. No need to go all frosty. Supper's nearly ready, by the way. Do you want a glass of something to go with it?"

"Yes, please. There's one open, I think. Have one yourself if you like." I got to my feet with a quiet groan. "So, who's this spoilt young person?"

21

"I've told you about her, haven't I? Brassy blonde, surrounded by girls with more bling than brains, not terribly bright, and yes, spoilt rotten. Daddy's little darling – Tiffany Leaman."

If Millie hadn't had her back to me as she stirred something in a bubbling pan on the hob, she would have seen me freeze, steadying myself on the back of the sofa. As it was, I'd collected myself before she turned to the kitchen table with two steaming bowls.

"There you are," she said, and I smiled my thanks. All through the meal she chatted inconsequentially, rather unusually for her, but I hardly registered a word. *Leaman*: there was that name again. I felt rage rise up, threatening to choke me, but I knew there was nothing I could do about it.

Millie had gone to her room to do some schoolwork when the doorbell rang. I shut Gordon in and padded down the hallway to answer it. Standing on the doorstep, wearing a mid-length black coat open to reveal a soft green dress, stood Rachel. She seemed even taller in her black boots.

"Wow," I said. "You're very elegant."

She grimaced. "Another of those 'needs-must' moments. I shall remove it all the minute I get indoors and spend what remains of the evening in my pyjamas."

"Was the reception as dull as you anticipated?"

"Yep."

"Come in," I said. "I'll get your card."

She came in and stood on the doormat. "I won't stop," she said apologetically. "Michael's got the engine running." As I closed the door, I saw the car at the kerb and a dark shape at the wheel.

I fished in the pocket of my coat, which I had hung on a hook in the hall, retrieved her card, and handed it to her.

"Thank you," she said. "My heart did a double-flip when I realized it was missing. Metaphorically, I mean. Hearts really don't behave that way, luckily!" She grinned, then as an afterthought added more seriously, "You know what we were talking about earlier – Good Friday? You should come. Try it out. The service is early – nine thirty."

I shook my head, but I had to smile. "What's this – evangelism?"

"I told you I was rubbish!" Rachel said. "Think about it, though? I'll be looking out for you!" She opened the door and the chill air swept in. "Thanks again, Anna. Goodnight."

As she reached the end of my short front path, the door of the waiting car opened, and the shadowy figure inside raised a hand to me in brief salute.

Being self-employed, I can, in theory, decide when to take my holidays; I just don't get paid if I don't work. (And sometimes even when I do work, or at least not for a long time. Cash-flow is always a problem.) So, I decided to take a long weekend over Easter: Friday to Monday. Maybe I would get to spend time with my daughter, and if she was out with her friends I'd slog on with paperwork, of which I always had a backlog, to avoid loneliness and unproductive television.

On Friday morning I deliberately got up early and took Gordon for a quick race round the local park. Millie was still asleep; before I left the house I wrote her a brief note. Then, I put on comfortable shoes and a warm coat and walked the half-mile or so to All Souls. At nine twenty it was already fairly full. I slipped in, was handed a service sheet, and chose a seat at the back. Already I saw that things were going to be different from what I might have expected at the abbey. For one, children of all ages gave the church a much more youthful vibe: toddlers in pushchairs, small children on beanbags, playing in a corner, even a scattering of adolescents sitting huddled in a group. I didn't see Rachel, but as I discreetly scanned the congregation I saw two men who almost certainly were her husband and stepson: both tall – one broad, the other skinny; the older man dark-haired and wearing a black coat and sober trousers, the younger with long hair tied back in a ponytail, his jaw darkened with a scrubby beard, wearing jeans and a purple jacket.

The service was also very different from the one which would have been unwinding at Brant Abbey, punctuated by unfamiliar hymns and songs. Even today, while the atmosphere was respectful, not a shred of gloom seemed apparent in the generally upbeat tone. To my surprise I felt slightly indignant: *we should be sad today, shouldn't we? Aware of our sins and failings that drove the Son of God to his brutal end?* How strange that my attempt to reconnect with my half-dead faith was awakening in me a regret for today's sombre liturgy at Brant Abbey, where the choir would be singing lamenting psalms and the Passion would be acted out by clergy and selected members of the regular congregation, reminding us – at some length – of that harrowing story. *Harrowing* was the word Rachel had used of this service; I would not have. Maybe it seemed so because on other days it was all celebration, song after song. Today, Good Friday, everything was conducted with sincerity; but it was not for me. I felt the need for much more grieving repentance.

The service came to an end, and as soon as I decently could I slipped away. The woman to whom I returned my service sheet whispered, "There's coffee in the hall." Refreshments *today*? I had not thought myself so conservative, but I felt almost scandalized. I smiled at her briefly, shook my head, and headed briskly outside.

I thought I had got away with it, but as I paused at the top of the steps that led down into the street I heard a voice behind me: a deep voice, full of warmth, but impossible to ignore.

"Ms Milburn?"

I turned to see the tall man in the black coat, smiling faintly.

"It *is* Ms Milburn, isn't it?"

I nodded. "Yes."

"I thought I recognized you from the trial, but you look different, not surprisingly." He held out his hand. "Michael Wells."

I shook his hand.

"My wife asked me to look out for you, and give you a message," he said. "She hoped you would be here."

"Is she all right?"

"More or less. But she's been up most of the night throwing up, so this morning she's feeling very feeble. Sends her apologies." He had a strong and pleasant face, charm without artifice. *Lucky Rachel.*

"Sorry to hear that," I said, meaning it, despite my eagerness to leave. "Please give her my regards." I hoped I sounded sincere.

"Message delivered! Good to have met you, Ms Milburn. Now I'd better go and find my son." He began to walk away, then paused and turned back to me. "She was hoping she might call you sometime. Said she enjoyed talking to you. Would that be all right?"

Of course I said it would be fine, and he smiled and re-entered the church. But I felt strangely uncomfortable. Yes,

I wanted to meet up with Rachel again – but what would I say? She'd been keen for me to come to this service today, and would want to know what I thought, wouldn't she? How would she react if I told her it had made me want to scurry back to the more austere arms of the abbey?

Millie was up when I got home, floating about in fluffy pink slippers and polka-dot pyjamas, her hair, blonde and wavy like mine, tied up in a loose knot on top of her head.

She was cradling a mug of coffee. "You want some?"

"Please."

She busied herself – though *busied* may have been the wrong word, given her languid movements – with my coffee. "So why did you go to All Souls? Not your usual sort of place, is it? A bit lively for you, I'd have thought."

"I didn't know you were an expert in such things."

She gave me a severe look. "I'm not. So?"

I told her about my meetings with Rachel. "I don't really know what made me go today, to be honest. But she wasn't there anyway. Her husband collared me on the steps. Said she was laid low with morning sickness."

"A new friend, then, you think?" She handed me a mug of coffee. "You're not that well off for mates, Mum, are you? Well, there's Janet, I suppose."

I pulled up a chair and sat at the kitchen table. "I've met her – Rachel, that is – before," I said. "And her husband. At a trial. But it was a while ago. And you're right about the mates. Janet's about it, unless you count yourself."

She shook her head. "I hope we're mostly friendly, Mum," she said softly. "But mates? I don't think so. Neither do you, really. Mates are equals, and you still feel the need to boss me about."

"It's called *guidance*, sweetie." I finished my coffee. "I'm going to do some work. I imagine you have some as well, don't you?"

"I'll do it later." As I left the room she said, "Oh, I know what I was going to tell you, Mum. A few days ago, at school, we had to take part in a sort of debate – just your kind of thing. We have to do these extra-curricular things, just to make sure we are 'well-rounded citizens.'" She made a face. "Anyway, it sparked some discussion, and the lovely Tiffany Leaman asked that corny old question you said people ask you at dinner parties."

"Oh, yes? You mean, how can I defend someone I know is guilty?"

"Well, I hope I defended *you*. I told them about everyone deserving representation, whoever they are. That there are places in the world where someone on high decides if you are worthy of defence at all – and we don't want that. OK so far?" I nodded, quietly pleased that she had taken in some of my lectures. "I told her if someone says they didn't do it, then you have to believe them, whatever your private suspicions might be. That the defence barrister doesn't make the decision – whether the accused person is guilty or not. That's for the court." She grinned. "Did I do OK?"

"Impeccably. And thanks for the defence."

I retrieved a bundle of papers and files from my briefcase and went upstairs. My bedroom window overlooks the garden, and when we moved in I put a small desk under it so that I could work at home in peace. Now I sat there, the files unopened, staring out of the window at the small rectangle of grass below, and the wet, weedy borders round it. I'd paid very little attention to this modest patch, but from here I could just see shoots coming up from the earth: bulbs obeying their instincts and the warming weather, someone else's plantings. On the rare occasions that I think about such things, it seems to me that it's we humans that are the transients on our planet.

As I opened a file, my mind drifted. Seemingly at random, *Leaman* had been mentioned twice in as many days. I knew he had to stay buried in a dark corner of my mind if my blood pressure was not to rise to an unhealthy level, but something was conspiring to bring him to my attention, and I squirmed. Of course I was aware that his daughter attended the same expensive private school that my ex-husband had deemed suitable for Millie, but *Tiffany* hadn't been mentioned before. I sighed. Perhaps it was time I well and truly got a change of scenery and a break from work.

Just as I was weighing up my options, my favourite brother, Alastair, rang me.

"Hello, squirt," he said fondly. "Kathryn and I were thinking it might be nice if you came over on Sunday, it being Easter, and had lunch with us. And Millie too, if she doesn't have a better offer."

"Funnily enough, I was thinking of coming over to see you tomorrow. But Sunday would be lovely, if you're sure two extra bodies wouldn't be a burden."

"Not if they're yours and Millie's. Anyway, you don't take up much room."

"All right, enough said! We all know you boys got the height and left nothing for me. I'll bring a pudding if you like, and some smelly cheese."

"Done. See you at one."

Later that evening, after I'd just closed down a website where I was looking up a point of law that I'd forgotten, and was thinking about going downstairs to watch the news, my phone rang again. Millie had gone out, and I wondered if it might be a plea for a lift home. To my surprise it was Rachel.

"Hello, Anna. I hope it isn't too late to call."

"No, not at all. How are you?"

"Better, thanks. I'm sorry I wasn't there this morning. Too green to leave the house."

I thought she would ask me how I had found the service at All Souls; instead she said, "Do say no if you are busy, but I wondered if we might meet up for a coffee somewhere tomorrow. I thought it might be nice to have a more relaxed chat, with no appointments and small children."

"Well, sure... wait, I have a better idea. Why don't you come over here? It'll be horrible in town on Easter Saturday. How's ten thirty?"

She arrived a minute early, flushed and panting, wearing a fetching running ensemble in purple and black and proffering a pack of expensive foreign biscuits. "Thought these might go down well. Left over from Christmas, but not out of date!"

"Goodbye, diet! Thank you, that's kind. Come in."

She kicked off her trainers in the hall. "Why do you need to diet? You aren't in the least bit fat."

"I was. Until about six months ago. Then I decided enough was enough and managed to shed the flab. So I am keen not to backslide. But I'm sure one or two won't hurt and these look exotic." I ushered her into the kitchen. "It's warmer here. How do you like your coffee?"

"Black, please." She looked around while I busied myself with kettle and cafetière. "I like your house. It's quirky."

"*Small* is what it is."

"Less to heat, less to clean. Our place is far too big, but neither of us can face the idea of moving. The position is nice, though, overlooking the river." I put a cup of coffee in front of her. "Thanks." She sipped her coffee, then put her cup down and looked at me with her slightly unnerving directness. "Anna, tell me honestly: do you think I have pursued you? Is that weird?"

"It's unusual, but I don't feel pursued. I get the impression that whatever you do you have a reason. And perhaps you don't like to waste time with more conventional approaches."

She grinned. "You understand. How rare that is." She sobered. "I know a lot of people, but really I only have one friend, and I can't honestly say why she even bothers with me. At least now I have Jonathan we have something to talk about. She has a toddler and a baby. She used to be my favourite theatre nurse, so we have things medical in common, but she's not working now, and I don't feel I can bore her with the details of complex surgery any more. Just lately I've felt the need for another friend, someone who maybe gets me, at least a bit. I'm not even sure why, but somehow you seem different to most. And I don't know any barristers, so your working life has fascination value."

I smiled. "Not as thrilling as you might think, I assure you. Very few cases as interesting as yours, and even that gave me little scope for impassioned advocacy! But I do understand what you are saying about friends. I only have one as well, and she's my clerk at chambers so she's a colleague too, which means we have plenty to talk about, but it's all rather inward-looking. And *I* don't know any heart surgeons. So we're equal. If you're a bit weird, well, so am I, and at least you're honest about it."

At this she almost choked on her biscuit. I topped up her coffee and waited for the fit of laughing to subside.

She wiped her eyes with her hands. "Tell me if you have an appointment or anything. I wouldn't want to outstay my welcome."

"You only just got here. And I have nothing special on. Millie is asleep; the dog is as well. My paperwork is almost under control."

"It's just that I so rarely get to go out on my own. I am probably febrile." She finished her coffee. I hefted the cafetière queryingly and she shook her head. "No, thanks. I may not need to diet, but I do need to watch my caffeine intake." She leaned forward, her elbows on the table. "Tell me about you."

"Such as?"

"Oh, I don't know. We could start with your family. All I know is that you have a daughter called Millie and a dog called Gordon. Then, if we exhaust that we might move on to why you wanted to be a barrister. Not to mention how you got to be a Christian, and why you aren't practising right now."

"I think that would take about a week." I thought for a moment. Much as I valued honesty, I certainly wasn't ready to spill every pathetic detail. "How about a brief biography, up to the age of ten? And then it'll be your turn."

She made a face. "OK, that will have to do."

"Well, one potentially interesting fact about my family is that I have three older brothers, and they're triplets."

Her eyes widened. "Really? Are any of them identical?"

"No, they're fraternal and very different from each other. There are twins in the family, but nothing more, and they came as a big shock to my poor parents."

"Unplanned?"

"Definitely. There was no IVF back in 1971. My parents were very young and had only been married about a year. My dad was in his first teaching job and earning peanuts. My brothers were conceived according to nature's whim and delivered without the assistance of surgery, only about two or three weeks early so all a hearty size. I don't know how my parents managed, but they are made of tough stuff."

"My goodness."

"My mother described it as a featureless whirl of nappies, feeding, crying, laundry, and broken nights – everything new parents normally experience but multiplied by three. And to make matters worse, the boys were only about seven or eight months old when she found out she was pregnant with me. There's just fifteen months between us. But, mercifully, there was only one of me. Grandma helped, and the neighbours were kind, but it was hard. Let me show you something." I pushed back my chair and went into the living room. I opened a drawer and rummaged till I found a handful of black-and-white photos which I had been meaning to find frames for. I came back into the kitchen with one of them and put it in front of Rachel. It showed us all against a backdrop of a Christmas tree decked with baubles, the boys sitting on a bench in a row with my father behind, a restraining hand on the shoulders of the outer two, and my mother beside him and leaning slightly against him, with me aged six months in the crook of her arm. She was managing to smile, but her weariness was plain.

"What do your brothers do now? Do you get on, all of you?"

"Hmm, I suppose we do, more or less. My oldest brother, Mark – daft really, they were born within twenty minutes of each other – he's a financial adviser, lives in London with his family, and suggests ways that wealthy people can get even richer. I'm not averse to comfort and a pleasant lifestyle, but I don't share that level of materialism. Then there's Alastair, my favourite brother. He's a college lecturer here in Brant. Physics. He's clever but modest, a faithful husband and a good father. And then there's Patrick, but nobody calls him that." She raised an eyebrow, and I sighed. "He's an artist, a talented one, so people say who know about such things. Apart from following his creative star, he's never really worked. His devoted wife goes out to work to pay the bills. They don't have children, which is probably just as well. He's always played the part – wild hair, drink and drugs at one time, periods of black mood, a tendency to flaunting. At fifteen he became obsessed with Hieronymus Bosch and wanted us to call him 'Hieronymus' after his idol. We all resolutely declined but being pragmatic agreed to call him 'Ronnie' since he refused to answer to 'Patrick.'"

"Oh! I know nothing about art, but I'm sure I've heard the name 'Ronnie Milburn'. In fact, I'm pretty sure I heard it recently."

"He's up and coming, yes. At least around here. You may have seen an article about him in the local paper. A gathering in the Brant Gallery?"

She frowned. "That does sound familiar."

"I organized a birthday party for my three brothers a few weeks ago – I am obliged to do it every year by some quaint tradition, but to be fair they will do it for me when mine comes round. This year I hired the Brant Gallery, where Ronnie has some of his work on display. It suited Mark as well because there were plenty of well-heeled people among the guests for him to add to his network of connections. The more money you have, the more you have need of a financial adviser, I suppose. And Alastair didn't mind that there wasn't anything specific in it for him. He's a very good-natured man. It involved a catering team, pretty waitresses, and plenty of champagne. Ronnie loved it, Mark cosied up to Brant's elite, and Al and I chuckled over their foibles. All good fun, if you like that sort of thing. Anyway, there you have it. My early life."

"Are your parents still around?"

"Yes. They live not far from here, in the house where we all grew up." I hesitated. Did I really want to tell her about my mother's illness, her galloping dementia, my father having to take early retirement to look after her, now that she couldn't look after herself? I decided I didn't, not yet. It was painful enough without having to rehash it to someone who was, for now at least, still almost a stranger. I think she noted my moment of silence, and she changed the subject.

"So, how does one become a barrister?"

I considered her question. "I don't know how anyone does it nowadays – it seems so much harder, not to mention prohibitively expensive. I was just very lucky." She shifted in her chair and gave me an enquiring look. "My dad has a good friend, Geoffrey," I continued. "They were at college together. Dad went into teaching, Geoffrey trained as a solicitor. Geoffrey married a year or so after my parents, and he and his wife had a son, Charlie. Tragically, Charlie's mother died when he was about five. I don't really remember her. After that Charlie spent a lot of his time at our house, and my mum became something of a substitute mother to him. He's a little older than me but younger than my brothers. Geoffrey was, is, also my godfather, and he always took a keen interest in me, how I was getting on at school, etc. It was down to him that I chose to go into law."

"Do you mind if we find a sofa, Anna? My behind's getting numb."

"Sorry, I forget others are not as well padded as me. Yes, let's go into the living room."

I flopped onto the sofa and Rachel took the easy chair opposite. "OK, so what age have we got to, then?" Rachel asked.

"Ten," I said. "And that's as far as the biography goes, at least for today."

"Did anything significant happen at age ten?"

"Do you really want me to carry on?" She nodded expectantly. "Well, you could say so. It was summer. We were all at Geoffrey's. The four boys were playing cricket in his garden, and they were getting over-excited and rough. Normally I was well able to hold my own – I may have been small, but I had a very loud and accusing voice, so they tell me – but I was going down with something and felt unwell. I was out of sorts and tetchy, and no doubt I dropped the ball once too often. My brothers took no prisoners, though Charlie was kinder. Things became fraught, and you can probably imagine the tears of frustration. Geoffrey took pity on me. He had a collection of films which he'd recorded, and he sat me down in front of *To Kill a Mockingbird*. Did he choose it intentionally? I don't know; now he says he doesn't remember – but he says it with a twinkle. I remember being absolutely mesmerized, even though I didn't understand it fully until I'd seen it about four times and quizzed Geoffrey mercilessly in between. I just remember, that first time, how the sounds of the boys playing cricket, their shouts, the thwack of the ball, simply faded; suddenly I was in Maycomb in the time of the Depression. So I blame the two of them for my career choice – Geoffrey Rowson and Atticus Finch."

Rachel frowned. "Who?"

"The lawyer, the children's father, who stood up to the townspeople when he defended the black guy accused of rape." Now it was my turn to frown in puzzlement.

"Sorry, Anna, I am an almost total ignoramus when it comes to literature. I decided to be a cardiac surgeon when I was fifteen, did science at school, then went to medical school and read nothing that wasn't a medical textbook! Or, more latterly, learned articles. Michael's been trying to educate me and I am gradually becoming more widely read, but there are huge gaps."

"Well, to me, aged ten, Atticus Finch was the epitome of the man of honour, the upholder of the law and decency and neighbourliness against the conventions of his time, a mild-mannered, self-effacing legal hero. I wanted to be just like him – a defender of the powerless. Very idealistic."

"Not any more?" Rachel asked softly.

I laughed. "My work is very different from what I imagined it would be. Nothing like the world of Atticus Finch. Anyway, dear Geoffrey was pretty sure, so it turned out, that I would make a barrister. He said he'd noted my capacity to argue about absolutely anything, tie my brothers in knots, and persuade them that black was white. They say I still can. I suppose I had to – I was younger, smaller, a girl. And there was only one of me against three of them! It was a matter of survival. Geoffrey was a huge help – smoothed my path, introduced me to people he knew, gave me shrewd advice, lent me money. He was – in many ways still is – my mentor. I owe him a lot." I pulled myself up out of my chair. "All this talking is making me dry. I'm going to have more coffee. You sure you'd rather not?" She nodded. "OK, I won't be a minute. Then, like it or not, it's your turn."

When I came back with my coffee she was staring into space, chewing her lip. I sat quietly till she registered my presence.

"Sorry, you caught me thinking," she said. "Am I allowed one more question?"

"Go on, then."

"Can you tell me how you came to be a Christian?"

I laughed. "Just a simple little question, I see! OK, so you'll get a simple little answer, even if it isn't the whole story, not by a long chalk. It all hangs together with my ideas about Atticus Finch – the man, or in my case, woman, of honour. I'd been brought up in a household more or less guided by Christian principles, but again it was Geoffrey's quiet influence which registered with me, and as I grew into my teens I began to apply that concept to Jesus, who seemed to me then the ultimate man of honour, the apogee. There's a whole lot more to it – to him – than that, even if you just consider his human characteristics. But I think that's where it started."

"How extraordinary," Rachel said softly. "I never thought something so important could rest on a character in fiction – Atticus, not Jesus." Her eyes flashed me an amused look.

"But characters in fiction are often archetypes. They resonate across time and space, generations and cultures."

She pursed her lips. "I suppose so."

"You're putting off the evil day, Rachel. I am not fooled, you know."

She grinned. "You found me out. OK. I'll summarize the early bit." She took a deep breath. "Like I said, I decided to be a heart surgeon at fifteen, after I'd watched my father slowly die of heart failure. It took him three agonizing years. He was the biggest influence in my childhood, and I missed him dreadfully. My relationship with my mother was more difficult for many years, though recently it's improved. I worked harder than you can imagine, every hour. Everything got sacrificed to my ambition. Looking back, I see a process of me building a wall around myself, so that never again could I be so hurt. I didn't see it like that at the time, of course. I just set my sights on being the best and I did whatever was necessary to achieve that. I was probably rather ruthless. My plan was to be a consultant by the age of forty. I didn't quite manage it; other things got in the way, and it took a couple more years. But it's no longer the big deal it was.

"You know the bare bones of what happened to me, what Eve Rawlins did." I remembered from the trial what Eve, the grief-deranged mother, had done to Rachel: the sly, sickening threats culminating in the knife attack in the hospital, where she – Rachel – worked. "I don't need to tell you about how I came here to Brant because she hounded me. What she did threatened to destroy me – cutting my hands like that. All I had, all that mattered, was work, and I stood to lose what I lived for. I was hard, narrow, vain, not a very likeable person at all. And angry!"

"Was there absolutely nothing else in your life? Friends, lovers, hobbies?"

"I ran, and I still do – as you know. But then it was just to keep in shape so I could work, and I suppose I also ran off some of the inevitable stress. I had one friend, Beth – I told you about her. And I did have lovers, but they weren't for love, that I can tell you! I took what I wanted, that's all. I did almost get married once, but luckily I came to my senses. The poor man didn't deserve the misery I'd have caused him."

"You are very hard on yourself."

"Maybe." She fell silent for a moment.

"So what changed?" I prompted.

She shrugged. "The damage to my hands shook the foundation of my confidence. I see now that my strong self-belief was built on something shaky, perhaps even unreal. I was in a mess for a while. In a deep, dark hole. But then –" she smiled to herself – "I'd already met Jasper – Michael's son – who for his own inscrutable reasons decided he wanted to be my friend. He was, is, a kind young man. So is his very patient father, who as a surgeon did an amazing job on my injuries but as a human being kept faith with me even when I behaved badly, which was often. It's all mixed up – was he kind to me because he felt sorry for me? Because I was a colleague? Because he was, is, a Christian? At what point did he begin to love me? I don't know, and I don't think he does either. And God was in there too, though I didn't recognize him for a while. Did God lead me to Michael, or did Michael lead me to God?" She shook her head. "I spent some weeks in France with Michael and Jasper – they invited me to help with my healing, both physical and emotional, and it was the happiest time I'd had for years. I suppose I was beginning to be more of a proper human being, more empathetic, and bit by bit they taught me it was OK to trust someone even when, life being what it is, they might be snatched away from you at any moment." She swallowed. When she spoke again it was almost in a whisper. "To be honest with you I am still a bit afraid, even now, when I think about it. Afraid that Michael might die. But I try to summon up my courage and tell myself I would cope. I would have to, for Jonny. And this baby."

I spoke as gently as I knew how. "Your father's death came when you were young and vulnerable. Not surprising it had such a huge effect."

"Yes. I can see that I spent more than twenty years defending myself against the possibility of pain."

"Clearly a great deal has changed, though. In your life, in your head."

Her smile lit up her face. "God, who I've been getting to know little by little over the last four years or so, has been very kind to me as well. And I'm convinced he has a sense of humour. He's encouraged me not to take myself so seriously. His blessing comes in strange, oblique ways, even by tripping you up and making you fall flat on your face, or in my case falling in love with the kindest man on the planet."

"Some accolade."

"Sorry, was that too cheesy?"

"No, not at all. But you're right – the more you have, the more you have to lose, and the scarier it is."

"Yep." She sighed. "We are getting very serious here, Anna. I know what else I wanted to ask you – how did you get on at All Souls yesterday?"

"I thought you might get round to that. And to be absolutely honest with you, it wasn't really my cup of tea."

She nodded slowly. "Everyone needs something different, I think. And it doesn't matter, as long as we bear with one another. For me it was all about welcome and being included, first at the church we went to in France, then here at All Souls. I think Michael would probably like to go to the abbey sometimes, or somewhere different, but now he's settled at All Souls. He knows lots of the nice folk there, and he went there in the first place because his ex did, and they thought it would be better for Jasper because it was lively and there were plenty of young people. And for me, it's where we got married as well."

"There certainly aren't many young people at the abbey,

not as a rule," I said. "My daughter contends there's no one under the age of forty."

"Does she come with you?"

"Not any more." I hardly knew what Millie thought or believed now, and I knew better than to ask. If it came up, if she wanted to, she might tell me. But I was certain that any pressure from me would be counterproductive. Because I said no more, Rachel changed direction.

"So what about Easter Day? Will you go to the abbey service?"

I shook my head. "I probably will go back. It's probably time. Like you, but for different reasons, I've been hiding. But I'll go back to a quieter service, something less public than Easter." I hesitated. "I'm going to have lunch with my brother Alastair and his family."

"Will that be a pleasure?"

"Yes, it will. But a tainted one."

She frowned and shook her head. "You don't have to tell me. Seems like it's a private matter. Maybe I've asked too many questions already."

"Not at all. But we've gone well beyond age ten, haven't we?" For a moment I battled with my anger and grief, considering whether I should continue. My own pain, after all, was nothing compared to the anguish of my brother and his wife. I took a deep breath. "My nephew Sam, Alastair and Kathryn's oldest son, was permanently damaged about two years ago by some dirty drugs."

Rachel's eyes were wide. "That's grim. I'm so sorry." She was silent. "What happened? If you don't mind telling me. If it isn't too painful."

I heaved a sigh. "Sam was fifteen. Doing well at school, no problems there. He was a normal teenager who liked to hang out with his friends. Al and Kathryn were sensible, didn't try to put too tight a rein on him, just stipulated he had to have all his schoolwork done if he wanted to go out at the weekends. He and his friends used to go to one of the clubs here in the city, and sometimes Sam stayed over with a friend instead of going home late. Nothing unusual there. They trusted him to be sensible, but I'm afraid he wasn't. We only found out afterwards just what had been going on, from some of his other friends. Apparently some of them had been buying drugs and enjoying the effects, with nobody any the wiser. As you can imagine, if Al had known, he would have grounded Sam there and then, probably for ever. I'm sure you know that there are a lot of myths surrounding drugs, especially among kids like Sam, that some are purer than others, minimizing what could possibly go wrong. But the fact is that none of them are pure. And some are mixed with some pretty terrible substances. They're all unregulated, the kids have no real idea what's in the pretty pink pill or innocuous-looking powder they're taking, and the dealers don't care as long as they make a profit and don't get caught. Afterwards, Al and I asked some of Sam's friends about the drugs. They talked about something they called 'Molly', and I did a bit of research." I bit my lip, feeling my heart thumping hard in my chest.

"Are you all right?" Rachel said. "Don't go on, if it's too upsetting."

"No, I might as well tell you the whole horrible story now." I paused. "Apparently, Molly is regarded as a 'fun' drug. Fun! Anyway, the friends thought that what Sam and his friend Liam took that night had something in it they called 'bath salts' – very unpleasant chemicals. To cut it short, the effects were not only stimulant, but also hallucinogenic. They were dancing and got overheated. The drugs made them euphoric; they felt they could do anything, and to add to that Sam and Liam had collected a couple of girls and were showing off. The club is by the river, not too far from the hospital, as it happens. There were plenty of barriers, but they weren't impenetrable to determined fifteen-year-olds. The boys decided they'd cool off by jumping into the water."

Rachel's eyes widened. "Didn't they know how dangerous the river is?"

"Oh yes, they knew," I said, hearing the bitterness in my voice, tasting it on my tongue. "But they felt invincible. The girls were probably not doing anything to dissuade them, but I can't really say. No one seemed to know who they were, and we never found out. Anyway, the lads tore off their shirts and shoes and threw themselves into the river. The tide was high, and the invisible currents were strong. Some of their real friends saw what they did, and when they didn't surface they alerted the club staff, who phoned the police."

"Oh, Anna," Rachel whispered. "What a nightmare."

I nodded. "They fished the boys out. Liam drowned. They resuscitated Sam, but his brain had been without oxygen for several minutes. You'll be familiar with hypoxia, I'm sure."

"Yes, unfortunately."

"Well, Al and Kathryn and various health professionals have done their best with Sam, and they've done a good job with rehabilitation and re-education, as far as it goes. But he has cognitive impairment, his motor coordination is all over the place, his memory is patchy, he has poor judgment, and he finds learning difficult. He behaves like a five-year-old. In many ways he's still sweet-natured Sam, but he'll always be a child. He and Millie are almost the same age, and the contrast is devastating." I fell silent then, thinking about what Sam might have been if the events of that night had never happened. After a while I turned to Rachel. "In the course of my law work I've got to know quite a few of the local police force. As you'd expect. They know, and I know – or, more strictly, we strongly suspect – who deals in drugs in this city, or at least some of them. But these people are slippery, and so far only the small fry have been hauled into court. Sam's the chief reason why I have such a passionate loathing of drug dealers."

"Understandable."

"I don't know if Sam might be called lucky, but at least he's still alive. Liam's family have to live with his loss. But for my brother and his wife, it's a tragedy that allows for no healing, because it's always before their eyes."

Rachel shook her head. "I wonder how they can bear it."

"They bear it because they have to, I suppose. He's still their son, and he will always need their support. Anyway, Rachel, I'm sorry to have loaded you with such a horrible story. There's nothing you can do."

"But I will pray for Sam. And your brother." She stretched and pushed herself to her feet. "Look, I have taken up enough of your time. I should go. I just hope telling me about Sam hasn't been too distressing, that's all. It's been good talking to you – I don't talk to anybody like this, except Michael. Do you mind?"

"No, of course not. I've done my share of talking too, haven't I? Splurging, even. Unheard of!"

She smiled. "We will meet again, won't we?"

"I hope so."

She made her way to the hall, and I followed. "Rachel, did you ever wonder about her – Eve, your attacker? What she went through, what motivated her, all that?"

44

She turned to face me. "Yes. Actually, I went to see her a couple of months ago, in prison."

"Oh! What did you hope to achieve by that?"

She paused, standing on one foot as she put her trainers back on. "I'm not sure I can articulate it; I just felt there was unfinished business between us. I knew she was horrified and ashamed at what she had done: that moment of madness, those months of plotting. I wanted her to know that what she did had resulted in some good things. Not just unmitigated disaster."

I couldn't help but wonder what I'd say to the person who'd supplied Sam's drugs – if I ever had the chance. I didn't think I could be so forgiving. "That was a remarkable thing to do."

She smiled faintly. "You think so?" She heaved a sigh. "I must go. Thanks for the coffee – and the talk." She looked up at a sound from the stairs. A rumpled Millie emerged, plodding down the stairs, her eyes closed, swaying slightly to the music from the headphones clamped to her ears.

I raised my voice. "Mil."

Her eyes flew open. "Oh! I didn't know there was anyone here."

"Millie, this is Rachel Wells. I told you about her."

"Yes, you did. Hi, Rachel. Nice to meet you. Sorry I'm still in my pyjamas. Late night."

"Nice to meet you too, Millie. I'm just going. I'll leave you both in peace. Bye, Anna." I opened the door for her, and a fresh gust of wind, laced with rain, blew in. With a wave of her hand she jogged down the front path and was gone.

"So that's your new friend, then, Mum. Lots of interesting chat?"

"Mm. How was your evening? You were late home."

She yawned. "It was OK. Same old, really. Went to a club with Jess and Will, and guess who I met there? Drew Clarke."

"I didn't think clubs were his scene. Last time he was mentioned you were very unimpressed because he'd taken up smoking a pipe."

"I know – twenty-one and behaving like an old man!"

"I expect it's just a passing affectation, Mil."

"Well, whatever else he is, Drew's an old brotherly mate and has his uses. He'd borrowed his mum's car and brought me home."

"I hope he wasn't drinking."

"Not a drop."

"Good. Or I'll shop him to Janet."

Millie shuddered. "Terrifying thought. I'm going to make myself some tea. You want any?"

"No, thanks."

Millie drifted into the kitchen, and I went into the living room and collected the coffee cups. It occurred to me suddenly that among all the exchange of information, some of it very personal and even painful, Rachel hadn't once alluded to my current situation. She must have wondered about Millie's father – whether I was single, widowed, separated; but she hadn't asked. Somehow she had picked up the areas which were just too sensitive at this point in our acquaintance. She was a strange mixture – honesty and diplomacy, strength and vulnerability – and I was intrigued. But whether this beginning would go anywhere I had no way of telling.

TWO

"I want a divorce."
I wonder if I'll ever forget those words.

He stood in the doorway, still almost immaculate in his office suit – dark grey with a faint stripe, white shirt open at the neck, the hated tie in his hand; still ridiculously good-looking for a man in his forties, and if anything he had improved with age. I was sitting at the kitchen table, shoes kicked off, a bundle of papers spread out before me, sipping a cup of coffee and munching on toast.

I looked at him, agape. "What?"

His eyes were narrow, giving nothing away. "Didn't you hear me? I said I wanted a divorce."

That was how it happened: after seventeen years, most of them amiable enough – or so I thought. Perhaps he was a romantic, after all, deciding to swap convenience, a comfortable familiarity, for the hazards of a new relationship with someone younger, fecund and, presumably, adoring. But then, Richard was never short of confident optimism, and perhaps I had ceased long ago to provide any adoration.

Looking back, I felt I had little choice. For one thing I was steam-rollered by the sheer unexpectedness of it. He'd had it all planned and settled in his own mind, and laid out his terms with alarming precision. He would keep the house in which we had lived for the past decade and would buy me out so that I could find somewhere else. Millie would live with me, but he would see her regularly and provide amply for her, including her university fees, if she chose to go that route. We could keep the dog: Gordon had never been other than a risible nuisance to Richard. But for him, our life was over. Risking much, I asked him why. He turned away, a red stain creeping up from neck to jaw. He said he'd found someone else. That was when I realized there was no point in fighting back. If, among all his many infidelities, he wanted to set up home with another woman, he must be in deadly earnest. Keeping my dignity intact, I agreed to his terms. My only stipulation was that *he* would deliver the life-changing news to Millie, since it would be me helping her to learn to live with it. Millie loved her charming dad and he had always been a kind father, if at times a little absent-minded: he was a busy man.

I bought a small house in town, not too far from chambers, and nearer to Millie's school. The three of us moved in. In due course Richard married Jenny, and not long after Millie informed me that her new stepmother was pregnant. Richard had always wanted more children, and now he could found his dynasty. On the surface it all went off in a civilized manner, and we both did what we could, in our separate ways, to make the best of it for Millie. But beneath it all, for me at least, lay a world of bewilderment, resentment, and hurt. At times I would be seething with anger at his dictatorial, high-handed dismissal of our years as a family, however unsatisfactory they had often been. I felt he had robbed me of my say. Perhaps I wouldn't have chosen differently, knowing that he wanted to be with someone else, but I would have welcomed the chance to set my own agenda. For Millie's sake, I said nothing. He would always be her father and to have blackened him to her was unthinkable; she must draw her own conclusions. She visited her old home frequently and, so she said, got on all right with Jenny, who seemed to be making every effort to be nice to her husband's daughter. Millie said little, apart from complaining about the smallness of our new quarters, but I wondered if she felt something of the same sense of rejection, humiliation, and fury that consumed me. I hoped not. Young as she was, and at an age when confidence is so easily dented, she should not have to battle with a poor self-image that was, in her case, undeserved.

To my chagrin I used to dream about Richard from time to time, and sometimes about that evening when he implacably tore our lives up like unwanted paper. Occasionally he would appear in different guises. A plumber up to his ankles in flowing water, shrugging helplessly, or a Victorian headmaster on a tall chair staring sternly down, a monocle in his eye – foolish images, funny in their own dark way, supplied by some dusty corner of my brain – but there was never any doubt in my dreaming mind who this man was. There was the shock of red-brown hair, dusted with grey above the ears and latterly shorn to a manageable crop; the same slightly hooded light brown eyes.

On that Easter Monday morning I woke early, turned off the alarm, and went back to sleep, to be visited again by my ex-husband, a most unwelcome guest. I got out of bed feeling the weight of that time heavily on my bowed shoulders. I wanted Richard as far from my thoughts, both waking and sleeping, as he was now far from my life.

It was not just Richard giving me a sense of wasted time and empty future. I had been to Alastair's the day before – and almost before I was out of the car the front door burst open and Sam galloped down the drive like a very large puppy.

"Auntie Nanna! You're here!"

As I returned his hug I tried not to wince, but to smile, silently wishing that Millie hadn't made other plans. She was always so good with Sam, and her presence somehow took the edge off. If he had been four or five, perhaps "Auntie Nanna" might have been lovable. From a boy with fuzz on his upper lip and a broken voice it gave me pain – as well as feeling like a grandmother goat. As a small child he hadn't been quite able to pronounce "Anna"; now, when he should have been on the cusp of adulthood, he had unwittingly reverted to babyish ways, and it never failed to bring tears to my eyes.

I linked arms with him as we went indoors, holding him close to my side, and noted that he was now three or four inches taller than me – though he would have to be a midget not to outstrip his short aunt eventually, since he had his father's genes. Al is the tallest and thinnest of my brothers and has to stoop to kiss me in greeting. That day he had a corkscrew and an open bottle of wine in one hand which looked about to spill. Kathryn came through from the kitchen, her normally immaculate hair dishevelled from steam, wearing a smart green apron with a pattern of avocados.

"Hi, Anna," she said, pecking my cheek. "Lunch isn't quite ready. The girls are somewhere upstairs, I think. Alastair, don't have any of that wine – you have to pick William up."

"I was just going to pour one for Anna, and for you, bossy," Alastair said amiably.

"Can I help?" I asked. I always ask, and she always pleasantly declines.

"No, it's all under control, thanks. Sam, why don't you show Auntie Anna that new model you made?"

"Yes!" Sam shouted joyfully. "Come on, Auntie Nanna!"

"Hold your horses, Sam. Let me just give these things to your mum." I handed the cheese and the dessert to Kathryn and she smiled her thanks.

"You're funny," Sam said, his smile wide. "I don't have any horses. Just a hamster. Come on, up we go!"

Sam thundered up the stairs, pulling me after him. It was always the way: perhaps Kathryn knew that my partisan feelings for my nephew meant that I would always spend time with him, admiring his toys and listening to his chatter. I wondered if she also knew of the tight feeling in my chest whenever I saw him, a painful mixture of grief and fury. Maybe not. They lived with Sam all the time; I hoped they had found ways to cope. Perhaps they no longer called to mind the boy that he had been.

As always after I visited my brother, my head swam with thoughts of what could have been had Sam not taken drugs that night. In my weary stupor as I readied myself for bed, thoughts of Sam mingled with those of my ex-husband, as though vying for a grim supremacy of which was the more life-altering moment: Richard's blunt declaration on that fateful day or Sam's ill-judged decision.

As I pulled on my dressing gown on Monday morning, yawning and sluggish because I had slept unusually late, I heard my phone vibrate on the desk under the window. I glanced at the clock – it was almost ten, so I couldn't justify the little spurt of irritation I felt.

To my surprise it was Rachel, and she sounded breathless. "Anna, hi. Sorry to bother you, but I could use some help."

"Oh?" I couldn't imagine how this very efficient woman might need something from me, apart perhaps from the opportunity to talk.

"It's Jasper's doing. Yesterday he was going on about how it would soon be Michael's birthday and we should have some event to celebrate because you aren't fifty every day, etc. He said he'd help, and I'm sure he means to, but he'll be back off to uni soon and that leaves me in the frame. Michael wasn't all that enthusiastic but he said if it was OK with me it was OK with him, and, fool that I am, I said I would organize some sort of gathering. Of course I'm happy to celebrate his birthday but I have no experience whatsoever in social things. So I got very cold feet! Then I remembered what you told me about your brothers' birthday party. So here I am, asking for advice."

I thought for a moment, my mind still hazy from sleep. "I suppose it depends what you want. I can tell you about the catering company we used, if you like. You'd have to think about numbers."

"Anna, are you very busy? I wondered if you'd come here so we could chat about it over a cup of coffee. I'd come out, but Jonathan will need his nap and Michael and Jasper are out at some swimming thing."

"Yes, I could do that. Give me time to have a shower – say, in an hour? You'll have to let me know where you live, though."

She told me the address. "It's right by the river where we first met. You can park on our drive. And bring Gordon if you want. He can play with Dulcie in the garden."

Much later, as if from a distance, I remembered that morning almost with nostalgia. The Wells house was big and rambling but not at all discomfitingly tidy. There were squashy places to sit, toys scattered on the carpet, and the smell of coffee brewing. The dogs rambled round the grassy garden, came in and went out as they pleased, bringing mud on their paws, and eventually curled up under the kitchen table, worn out. Gordon, I'm sure, was in heaven. Rachel herself was unnecessarily thankful that I'd come. "I wasn't doing too much else," I admitted. I was curious to see where and how she lived, the atmosphere that surrounded her, and I found it disarmingly normal. I gave her contact details of catering companies I'd used in the past and warned her off some which were less successful. We talked about numbers and food allergies and quantities of alcohol.

"Let other people do the leg work," I said. "You've got enough to think about with a toddler. Otherwise the charming hostess will be grumpy and frazzled."

She pulled a face. "Don't know if 'charming hostess' is in my repertoire. But I see your point. Do you think it's OK just to invite everyone? Do we have to think about who will get on with whom, or can it be more random? I suppose we'll have to include some of Michael's colleagues, at least the less tedious ones. I don't really have many friends. But you'll come, won't you?" She looked suddenly anxious.

"I will, if you invite me and it's not impossible for some reason."

"Consider yourself invited," she said, grinning.

"Who you invite has to be a matter of discussion between you and Michael. You need enough people for a party atmosphere, but not so many it's chaos."

She wrote something in her notebook and tapped her

chin with the pencil. "OK, I suppose I could really have thought of all this by myself," she said. "I probably panicked slightly, which isn't like me at all. I'm not used to this kind of thing. Give me an operating theatre any day."

Then the door banged and men's voices filled the house, or so it seemed. In fact, it was just Michael Wells and his son, who appeared in the living room, still coated and booted, bringing with them a gust of chill air. Although March was almost over, winter that year seemed reluctant to leave the stage.

"Ms Milburn. How nice to see you again." Michael shrugged off his coat and dropped it on the back of a chair. He came over to where I sat and shook my hand.

"It's Anna," I said. "Please, no need to be formal."

"Right. And this is Jasper."

The young man I had seen at All Souls waved from the doorway. His long hair, tied back, was damp and tangled. "Hi, Anna, nice to meet you." He turned his head towards the hall. "I think I hear a little brother squawking. Don't get up, Rachel – I'll go and fetch him."

"He may need changing," Rachel said.

Jasper shrugged. "I'll do it." He bounded up the stairs, whistling.

"Angelic lad," I murmured.

Michael dropped down onto the sofa next to his wife and quite unselfconsciously slid an arm round her shoulders, pulling her close. "I wouldn't say that," he said with a smile.

Rachel turned to look at him. "Anna's been helping me with planning your birthday party. I feel a little less daunted."

Michael shook his head. "You don't have to do this, you know," he said quietly. "I'd be perfectly content with something less challenging."

"No, I said I would, and I must have more courage," Rachel countered, her dark brows contracting in a frown. "Jasper will accuse me of being a lily-livered hermit – again."

I got to my feet. "I must go," I said. "I hope you've got some ideas, Rachel. But call on me if you need to – not that I'm an expert!"

"Oh, no, don't go. Stay and have some lunch. Please, I insist. We're only having soup, but you're welcome."

"I insist as well," Michael said.

"So do I," came a voice from the hall. Jasper returned, his brother in his arms. "And so does Jonathan. I'm not sure what we're insisting about, though."

"Anna staying for lunch," Rachel said, pulling herself free from her husband's arm and getting up. She turned to me with a sly grin. "You did say you weren't especially busy."

Jasper put Jonathan down, and the little boy hauled himself onto his feet by grabbing his father's trouser leg. Michael reached down and set him on his knee. Jonathan looked at me, scowled, and buried his face in Michael's shirt. "In that case I definitely insist," Jasper said. "I want to grill you about all your most fascinating and grisly cases."

"In Brant?" I laughed. "That will be a very short conversation, I'm afraid. All right, you've ambushed me."

I remembered that day with fondness, the atmosphere so relaxed and comfortable, a sharp contrast to what was to come.

I almost didn't see the news item. Millie had left the television on and gone upstairs, and as I passed the living room door on my way to the kitchen, thinking about loading the dishwasher and letting Gordon out for a last visit to the garden, something the newscaster said caught my inattentive ears. The screen showed a dark scene, lit only by arc lights strung high above what looked like a car park. I paused, realizing it was the local news, and something about the image was vaguely familiar.

"A detective from the Brant police department was attacked late yesterday evening," the smartly dressed woman said, her voice grave. "The man was found by the security staff of a neighbouring premises near the docks area. Tragically, Detective Sergeant Miles Winter, who was married with a young child, died at the scene. The police are appealing for witnesses." The screen now showed a tall, slightly stooped figure, and I felt my eyes widen: it was Steve Bryant. His face was sombre, his voice harsh. "Miles Winter was a promising young officer," he was saying, "murdered in the course of his duty. If anyone has any information which might help police with their enquiries, please contact this number." Contact details appeared below Steve's face.

The newsreader switched to an item about football, and I went into the room and turned the television off. Something about this story unsettled me: a murder close to home? The fact that the victim was a police officer, which would mean a huge and intensive investigation? Or was it seeing the face of Steve Bryant, reminding me of an episode I would rather have forgotten?

I opened the back door and shooed Gordon out. Leaving the door ajar, I began to stack our dirty dinner plates in the dishwasher, reluctantly thinking about Steve. About a year ago – clearly, in retrospect, far too soon after the divorce for me to have been thinking sensibly at all – he had asked me out to dinner. We had met on occasion and sometimes indulged in the mildest of flirtation, and I knew him well enough to have heard the rumours that his wife had left him for another man. I felt some sympathy for him because of that and was feeling rather bruised myself; perhaps I thought we might commiserate. Whatever the reason, I agreed to go, and we fixed a date and time. I had no thought of anything that might develop, and it wouldn't have been welcome, but perhaps I anticipated some kind of distraction. Luckily, I was spared any decision. Before the dinner date I heard via the same grapevine that the story of the errant wife was false, that the marriage was in trouble but that the couple were supposed to be working things out. I rang Steve and didn't hold back the scalding disdain I felt. After that, if we happened to meet, we avoided speaking; I felt his behaviour was shabby and he, judging by his black scowl, resented my response.

I put him out of my mind. It was someone else's business, someone else's misfortune. But about a week later I arrived home direct from court to find Millie hovering on the stairs, obviously brimming with news.

"Mum, you'll never guess what," she said, eyes alight. "You know that policeman that was murdered – here, in Brant?"

I dropped my briefcase and hung up my coat. "It's been all over the news," I said. "It would be hard to avoid."

"Well, it was all over school today. They've accused Tiffany's dad!"

"Who?" I blinked stupidly. It had been a long day.

"Tiffany Leaman. I've told you about her. She wasn't in school – too upset, they said. Her dad's in custody!"

I frowned. "Why him?" I was failing to see what relevance this might have, beyond the ripple of excitement among a bunch of twittering girls.

Millie leaned on the stair-rail. "Because of where

they found the body. It was in the yard of Tiffany's dad's warehouse, by the docks. Tiffany said he's got a great big place there, to store stuff he has coming in up the river. It's all surrounded by high fences and barbed wire. I don't know what his business is, but it sounds mysterious."

I took off my court shoes with a small sigh of relief. "It's not mysterious at all, Millie. Tiffany's father imports very expensive cars and boats ordered by private clients."

She goggled. "How do you know that?"

"Look," I said, "if you want to quiz me, come into the kitchen. I'm dry as dust from the foolish wrangling I've had to put up with all day and I need a cup of tea."

She followed me, and I filled the kettle and set it to boil. "I met him once," I told her. "Quite a few years ago. Your father was having some kind of promotional reception and he'd invited a selection of local businessmen. Mr Leaman favoured me with his conversation for about ten minutes before I could make my excuses."

Millie slid into a chair at the kitchen table. "I gather you didn't like him much."

"Not much, no. I thought he was loud and arrogant, but capable of oily charm if he thought it might serve his interests, and he obviously thought cultivating me might help him forge links with your father. He was wrong. Do you want some tea?"

"Please. So why was he wrong? Didn't Dad like him either?"

"Liking didn't come into it." I tossed teabags into mugs a little too vigorously, then added the water. "At the time your father had made a lot of money developing rundown properties all over the city and beyond – as you know. But he was thinking about diversifying into manufacturing and was exploring all sorts of possibilities, seeing what would get him the best profit. I don't think his interests really coincided with Leaman's. To the best of my knowledge they aren't in contact now. And it was the only time I ever met him, thankfully." I took milk from the fridge and added it to our mugs.

Millie took hers from my hand. "I feel sorry for Tiffany," she said. "She's not really my sort of person friends-wise, but it must be horrible if people think your dad's a criminal. A murderer." She shuddered.

"We don't know that he is," I observed. I leaned on the worktop, took a long swig of my tea, and felt slightly revived.

"I suppose," Millie said. She seemed disappointed by my reaction. "Maybe the police are extra keen to get someone in the frame, seeing as it's one of their own." She paused. "I think I'll take my tea upstairs, Mum. Got some revision to do."

When she had gone I found myself wondering. Why, indeed, had they arrested Leaman, just because the body was discovered on his premises? It could have been anyone. Millie had spoken of high fences and barbed wire – didn't he have CCTV too? I wondered about Steve Bryant as well. Was he just a spokesman? Or was he in charge of the investigation? I'd heard he'd been promoted, and this would be a high-profile case, no doubt, needing someone senior to lead it. Whatever, it didn't concern me. Wearily I opened the freezer. What could I find for our supper requiring the least possible effort to prepare?

Later, however, as I lay in bed, my mind circled back to Calvin Leaman. What I hadn't told Millie, partly because I wanted to keep her as far from such things as I could, but also because I didn't truly know whether it was justified, was that Leaman *was* suspected of criminal activity. I'd heard from people I knew in the world of law enforcement that the police were as certain as they could be that he, among others, was behind the various drug rackets that riddled our city. But although undoubtedly wealthy, his legitimate business might well account for the prosperity that allowed the purchase of a new car for his only child, for example. Still, something about this man chilled me. When I'd met him, I felt him to be false. I knew this was no kind of evidence, but however even-handed I tried to be I could not avoid seeing his face in the same frame as that of my sweet, damaged nephew.

The next day things took a turn, if not exactly for the worse, then certainly for the potentially worrying. I was not needed in court, so I planned to spend the morning catching up with e-mails, making phone calls, and setting up meetings. Janet had stuck an alarmingly bright Post-it note to my desk detailing the urgent matters I needed to attend to. I could afford to procrastinate no longer.

I'd been working for less than half an hour when Janet herself knocked at the open door and planted herself squarely before me, impossible to ignore.

"Morning, Janet," I murmured, my eyes on a letter I was trying to read.

"Very, very interesting," she muttered.

I looked up. "What is?" I saw that today she was wearing red: a tight red jumper and a shiny red skirt in a slightly different shade. It hurt the eyes with its clashing – probably intended – but Janet is enviably slim and can carry it off. When I complain how hard it is to keep weight from settling everywhere I don't want it, she tells me I should join her dance class; maybe I should. But the idea of sweaty exercise to loud music in a draughty hall full of writhing bodies is not my idea of fun.

She saw she had my attention. "Hutchins and Phelps again. You're popular, Anna."

"Not a cheque, by any chance?"

"There might be, but I haven't checked the post yet. No, a phone call, just now. Testing the water."

"Don't keep me in suspense."

"The police have got Calvin Leaman for the murder of that young detective."

"I know."

"Hutchins and Phelps are his solicitors."

I looked at her, eyebrows raised. "So?"

"He's asked for us. Actually, he's asked for *you*."

For me? I thought bemusedly. Janet's delivery is usually deadpan. If she said, "The building is on fire," I would probably carry on with what I was doing and say, "That's nice."

Then what she had said hit home. "What? Leaman wants us to represent him?"

"He wants you. Asked for you specifically."

"Why me?" I asked, incredulous.

Janet shrugged. "Says he knows you, apparently. He also says he didn't do it."

"Of course he says that." I took a deep, steadying breath. "Word is he's a slimeball, Janet."

She nodded. "Yep. But, and I quote, 'Everyone deserves representation' – even the Leamans of this world. And maybe he didn't do it. Apart from that, he's very rich and you need the money."

What to do? Could I defend Leaman? *Defend* a man I'd like to see in jail, off the streets, away from the possibility of doing harm?

Janet moved towards the door. "Better think about it, sweetie, like *now*. Hutchins and Phelps want to know. And so, I expect, does Mr Leaman." A moment later she was back. "Forgot to say, there was a call for you from DCI Bryant." She smirked; she knew all about the embarrassing episode. "Perhaps he wants to take you out."

I frowned. "And perhaps he doesn't. I should know better than to tell you anything, especially when we have a bottle on the table. What does he really want?"

"For you to ring him back. Sounded deadly serious. Number's on your pad." She disappeared back to her own cubby-hole of an office.

I sat motionless, trying to call my whirling thoughts to order. Then I silently gave myself a stern talking-to and picked up my phone.

The number was clearly Steve Bryant's direct line; he answered after a couple of rings. "Bryant."

"Good morning, Detective Chief Inspector. Congratulations on your promotion." Try as I might, I could not quite control my tone of voice.

He grunted, sounding slightly embarrassed. "Oh, Anna. Thanks for getting back to me. Maybe you've heard: we've got Leaman for Winter's murder, and I hear from Phelps he wants you to defend him."

"So my clerk told me five minutes ago."

"Anna, we have him. After all these years."

"Look, Steve. I understand; I do. But he's saying he didn't do it, and *someone* will have to represent him."

"Are you telling me you're going to accept the brief?" I could hear it in his voice: the barely contained amazement and disgust.

Janet materialized at my door, saw I was speaking, and

made as if to leave again. I waved at her to stay. She raised her eyebrows and leaned against the wall, arms folded.

"I haven't decided," I said. "I've had no time to think about it. But we shouldn't be having this conversation. Just get Phelps to send me what you've got. I'll be in touch."

"You know what you are?" he spat. "A traitor."

"No, I'm not." I tried not to let my voice betray my anger. "I'm a barrister. And you're a senior police officer. Neither of us should be getting emotional about this."

"A man's dead, Anna. Killed doing his duty. A decent young man with a family. A colleague. Leaman's a snake – you know it and I know it. This is our chance. Whose side are you on, anyway?"

"The law's. I'm a servant of the law. As are you, in case you've forgotten. But I told you, I haven't decided. So you can get off my back."

"Oh, really." When had this man got so vindictive? But he had more in his repertoire, and I regretted having had any personal contact with him, however fleeting. "Perhaps you've forgotten," he said, his voice grating. "Leaman's almost certainly responsible for a lot of wrecked lives in this city. Including, I believe, your brother's boy. You might think of him."

Somehow I bit back my fury. "I'm ringing off now. This has gone far enough." I put the phone down, my hand shaking.

I sat at my desk, motionless, my brain whirling in tight, unproductive circles. I hadn't noticed her disappearance, but a few moments later Janet slid in quietly on her soft-soled shoes and put a cup of coffee in front of me. I came to and I realized this was an epoch-making occasion: Janet didn't make coffee for the barristers. She'd made her position clear on her first day: "*I am your clerk, not your tea lady.*" But Janet was also a friend and a woman of acute perception. Now she said, "Maybe you need some help."

I nodded, picked up the cup, and sipped. The coffee was hot and very strong. Had it contained sugar I would have concluded that Janet believed me to be in shock. I took several more sips, then put the cup down. She was still there, leaning her shiny red-clad hip on the edge of my desk. "Right as always, Janet," I said. "There's a lot going on here. It's not simple."

"I know," she agreed. "And there's no need to be browbeaten by *Detective Chief Inspector* Bryant." Her voice dripped with sarcasm as she said his title. "You're not in court till this afternoon. And it's local. Gives you time to seek a little advice, yes?"

I picked up my phone. "Yes, indeed."

Janet nodded and padded out, closing the door behind her. I dialled and waited. The answerphone cut in. "Geoffrey? Anna. Need some input. Would you ring me back if you're around? I'm in court this—"

Geoffrey's voice broke into my unfinished sentence. He sounded breathless. "Sorry, Anna, I was in the greenhouse elbow-deep in compost. How are you?"

"I'm all right, thanks, Geoffrey. But I need some advice."

"Come over now if you like."

"What about your plants?"

"They can wait."

I lounged on Geoffrey's sofa, a huge, shapeless affair upholstered in mud-coloured corduroy. I'd kicked off my shoes in his hallway and was now playing host to his enormous marmalade cat, Fergus. I'd declined coffee: Janet's restorative, if deadly, brew had already given me a caffeine high. Geoffrey sat opposite me in a matching chair, a china cup and a plate of digestive biscuits at his side. To me he always looked the same, if perhaps a little more elderly as the years passed: a checked shirt and neatly knotted tie, baggy brown trousers, shiny brogues the colour of new conkers; his hair still plentiful, a shock of fluffy snow, and his blue eyes, bright and sharp with wit and understanding. He'd always been smartly suited for work, but he'd retired about five years before and this, today, was how I always thought of him.

There was little debate in my mind about consulting Geoffrey. Yes, I was in breach of confidentiality, but he knew all of that, and I trusted his discretion. It wasn't the first time I'd picked his brains. So, I told him about the offer of the Leaman brief, and now he was thinking, and I knew better than to interrupt. His knowledge of the law was vast, his local experience invaluable; but more than that, he understood the implications. He was my father's oldest friend, the best man at his wedding, my godfather. He'd seen me and my brothers grow up and had been alongside us as the almost-fatal tragedy of Sam had unfolded.

"I see your dilemma," he said finally. "Why do you think Leaman has asked for you by name?"

I shrugged. "Apparently he says he knows me. But he doesn't, not really. We met and had a few minutes of awkward conversation at a business reception of Richard's some years ago, that's all."

"Perhaps what he means is he knows you by reputation."

"Nice of you, Geoffrey, but I'm not sure I have one."

"Well, you're wrong about that," Geoffrey said firmly. "Let's look at this rationally. Your feelings of discomfort stem from your conviction that Leaman, whether or not he is a murderer, is definitely a drug dealer. You have a particular abhorrence of such people, especially because of Sam. Not to mention his young friend, the lad who died, and other young people foolish enough to get involved in these things. That's Anna the family-minded person reacting, the loyal sister, the affectionate aunt. But you've been offered the brief as Ms Milburn, Barrister-at-law – because, my dear, you are good at what you do, and people know that. Besides, he has been accused of murder, not drug-dealing. And he says he is not guilty."

"If he's put away for murder his drug empire – if it exists – will collapse."

Geoffrey sighed. "Maybe, but there'll always be someone else to take his place, I'm afraid." He leaned forward, his brow creased. "Anna, as a barrister you can't afford to go down such a route. I think you know that. Nor should the police be giving in to such ideas, however we may understand their anger at their colleague's death. It isn't honest. And it's probably professional suicide. Whereas, if you defend this man and get him acquitted – assuming he really *is* innocent – it will do your career no harm at all."

"But," I murmured, thinking aloud, "my reputation with the local police will be in shreds, and my brother may never speak to me again. I couldn't handle that, Geoffrey."

Geoffrey shook his head. "If I know Alastair at all, he will see reason, eventually. I think, if you do decide to accept the brief, you need to seek Alastair out straight away, explain your reasons, draw the sting. I have faith in his good sense."

I got up and stretched. "I hope you're right. One thing I'm sure of, though: Kathryn almost certainly won't forgive me."

Geoffrey shrugged and smiled faintly. "Time will tell. Maybe you should invoke the cab-rank rule. But also, maybe you are the most likely barrister in Brant to do a good job for Leaman: the temptation to collude, to see him sent down, would be too great for some." He heaved himself to his feet. "Are you sure you won't have any coffee?"

"No, thanks, Geoffrey. I need to get back to chambers: I'm in the local Magistrates' Court at two." At the sitting-room door I turned to face him. "It may be, you know, that you have far too high a view of my conscience."

"I don't think so," he said. His smile was warm, but there was a little sadness in it. Perhaps he was remembering the distant days when we were all children – my brothers, Charlie, and I. "Remember Atticus Finch."

"I do. But I am not him, unfortunately. And the world has changed. The world of law, the world in general."

"Of course it has. But some things don't change," Geoffrey said. His eyes narrowed. "Speaking of changeless things, isn't it about time you came back to the abbey?"

I paused in the hallway. "Funny you should mention that." I grinned. "Not that you don't mention it every time I see you. I've been thinking; you're right, it's time I summoned up my courage."

"It takes courage to return to your God and your friends?"

"As a treacherous weak-kneed backslider? Yes, definitely."

"A weak-kneed backslider, perhaps. Treacherous, never. And you'll be welcomed."

I took my coat down from the hook on the wall. "Someone else I met recently has been encouraging me to come back as well. Perhaps you know her: Rachel Wells."

Geoffrey shook his head. "I've heard the name, but we've never met. She was a client of John Sutcliffe's at one time, I believe. Maybe it was he who mentioned her, but he would never say anything to break confidence."

I stooped and put my shoes back on. I gave Geoffrey a peck on the cheek, and he patted my shoulder. "Thanks for your time," I said. "Heard from Charlie lately?"

"Oh yes," Geoffrey said. "I speak to him on the phone once every few weeks. Last seen in Hong Kong."

"Give him my love, won't you? I must go and leave you to your horticulture. Bye, Geoffrey."

"Bye, Anna. Don't forget: even if you don't come back to the abbey just yet, there's a higher power with a better view of your problems than mine. Consult him."

"I will. And thank you for caring enough to go on nagging. You'll reel me back in yet."

I walked briskly back to chambers. A fresh breeze caught at my scarf and set it fluttering. April was well advanced but the weather was yet to feel spring-like. As I came to the square where my chambers were, I made a detour into the supermarket where I'd met Rachel and bought a sandwich for my lunch. I was sitting at my desk chewing on it, and reading some papers for the two o'clock case, when my phone rang. To my surprise it was Geoffrey.

"I've been thinking," he said. "After you left, it occurred to me that this brief of yours seems fraught with potential pitfalls. Too many people with an agenda. Anna, my dear, I may be teaching my grandmother to suck eggs, but do be sure you get full disclosure. Don't be fobbed off. You know and I know of too many historic cases where there was a scandalous miscarriage of justice because someone didn't tell all. Sometimes it amounted to sheer incompetence. But there were also occasions when there was deliberate, malicious obfuscation, by officials who should have known better."

I smiled to myself; this was typical of Geoffrey. "It sounds like the title of an avant-garde play – *Malicious Obfuscation*. Not one I'd choose to see."

"Take my point, though," Geoffrey said, mildly enough, but with an edge to his voice.

"I do," I said, sobering. "You're right. Thank you for reminding me."

As sometimes happens, especially when there is something weighing on me, demanding attention, I lay sleepless that night, thinking about what Geoffrey had said. I thought about cases I had avidly studied, cases long before my time of active practice, where there had been a failure to disclose some vital piece of evidence: the Birmingham Six, Judith Ward, Matrix Churchill, all of these happening in my time as a law student; then, during that one heady year when I was a qualified barrister working in London, the case of the newspaper boy murdered in a West Midlands farmhouse came to appeal, revealing staggering malpractice, including disclosure issues, which led to the wrong men being convicted and incarcerated. My memory wasn't perfect, but I knew there had been many more instances of the wrong person losing years of liberty because someone had overlooked or kept back information that would have secured their release.

I gave up on sleep and got up, wrapping myself in a dressing-gown against the cool night, and pulled down books from the shelf on the wall by my desk. For the next hour I flicked and perused, and as I read I found myself thinking, *I can't let that happen to my client*. With a small shock I realized I was already thinking of the despised Leaman in such terms. He wasn't *my client*, and I had yet to be assured of his innocence; but already that combativeness, that desire to win, had surfaced.

I finally slept, but woke very early, the garden birds making their first soft calls. My mind returned to my dilemma – but at some level I acknowledged it no longer was one: I would take the case. The implications were worrying, and not only because of the potential fallout within my family. I was no crusading lawyer taking on the might of the prevailing powers, not like some whose courage had inspired me as a student. I was a provincial barrister who until now had managed to keep a reasonably civil relationship with other law-upholders, including the police, many of whom I knew and, on the whole, respected. I certainly had no wish to fall out with them: we were obliged to work together.

But I also knew that there often existed among them a toxic state of affairs where there was a presumption of guilt – not, as it should be, of innocence. In the case of the Birmingham Six, and others involving terrorist attacks where members of the public were killed and injured, the prevailing atmosphere of fear and hysteria had put even more pressure than usual on the police and prosecution to secure convictions. Might Steve Bryant actually be the Senior Investigating Officer in the Leaman case? That was a worry – he'd already shown me that, instead of considering all angles as he should, he was inclined to follow his instinctive belief that the man they held was guilty. To my knowledge, many a major case had collapsed before it even came to trial, incurring vast unnecessary expense, because something that should have been disclosed at the outset didn't come to light until, in some cases, mere days before the trial was due to start. I remembered the collapse of the Matrix Churchill case when, as a keen student, I had sat in at the Old Bailey. Here it was not the fear of terrorism leading to malpractice, but a government's failure to disclose information – it was claimed, in the service of national security – which was relevant to the defence of individuals facing serious charges. I remembered the Judith Ward case and the words of a senior barrister I'd read in a memoir. He spoke accusingly of the prosecuting agencies' "preconceptions, prejudices, and assumptions" following her acquittal on appeal, after almost nineteen years in prison. Then another piece of legislation was passed – I remembered it well, because it happened the year Richard and I got married, when I was preparing to move to Brant: the Criminal Procedure and Investigations Act – and we were, almost, back to those bad old days. While many, perhaps most, police officers are honest and well intentioned, they are not legally trained. Setting them up as the guardians of disclosure invites the infiltration of prejudice, and the most honest of officers is powerless in the face of what can often be a system-wide culture, following held beliefs instead of strict procedures.

It was just getting light when I went downstairs and made some coffee. My head was aching – but also buzzing. To be offered this case, worrying as it was, seemed to have given me a shot of adrenalin. Geoffrey's warning, and my delving into long-neglected law books, had revived something I thought I had lost. I tried to counter this, reminding myself that I hadn't yet received any details of the investigation, even supposing that it was complete. If it was, it had been remarkably short. Clearly the police were sure of their man. I was keen to find out whether this rested on solid evidence, or whether it was compromised by that presumption of guilt and the desire to put a villain away.

Thinking about Geoffrey, I remembered too his urging to commit my concerns to the God I had sidelined for too long. I hesitated; facing my own failure was a source of deep discomfort. I still believed, I told myself. But did I believe I would be forgiven? Did I really think I would be listened to, counselled, guided? That was another matter.

Despite my lack of sleep, a few hours later I trotted up the steps to the front door of Hartington Chambers and strode into my room as if there were springs in my shoes.

I had barely shed my coat when Janet appeared. "David Phelps has been on the phone."

"Already?"

She gave me a look I knew well: knowing and cynical. "You're going to take the case, aren't you?"

"Maybe. What makes you so sure, anyway?"

She smiled and shook her head. "Working with you. What else? Not to mention the cases you've had in the past few months. Worthy but dull. We haven't had a nice juicy crime for a long time."

I sighed. "No, but I don't suppose Sergeant Winter's widow thinks about it in those terms. All right, I'll ring David Phelps." A thought struck me. "Janet, do you know if Phelps was the attending solicitor when Leaman was questioned?"

"Yes, he was. He acts for Leaman normally. Or at least his dad did before he retired."

"Have you got David Phelps' direct number? It would be nice not to have to run the gauntlet."

"Yep. I'll get it for you."

Soon a sticky note arrived on my desk. When Janet had gone back to her office, I picked up the phone and dialled Phelps' number. He answered almost at once.

"Morning, David. Anna Milburn."

"Ah, Ms Milburn. How are you?"

"All right, thank you. I gather you have a client for me. Accused of murdering a policeman."

I heard him exhale. "Excellent. Mr Leaman will be pleased."

"Where is he now?"

"In Wattisford Prison. I applied for bail, but with no great hope, and it was denied."

"I'm not surprised. David, e-mail me what documents you have and I'll get back to you when I've digested them."

I could almost hear him smile. "Will do," he replied, a little too enthusiastically.

"How much is there?"

"Just the MG5, the Police Case Summary, at the moment. Plus a couple of other bits and pieces. It doesn't tell you much."

"Perhaps enough for now, all the same. Once I've given the brief a look, I'll need to see the client."

David said he would arrange it, and a few minutes after we'd hung up, the brief was in my inbox.

I scrolled down, reading intently. When I had finished, I went back to the beginning and read it all again, this time making notes. Some of it was routine, but some parts – easy to pass over as they were couched in ponderous police-speak – needed closer attention. I was aware of something scratching at the back of my brain, something I couldn't identify precisely: something that didn't hang together, or perhaps something missing… I knew that at this stage I had very little to go on. Later I would be served with the bulk of the prosecution materials, and then I might have a clearer picture. This was just the beginning, but even now it gave me a sense of the form of my defence.

I got up and stretched, flexing my shoulders, and strolled down to the cubby-hole where coffee-making facilities were kept. Janet was on the phone as I passed her open door. She waggled her fingers at me. On my way back, a steaming mug in hand, I popped my head through the door. She had finished the call. "I'm thinking I'll need a junior for this," I said. "Someone keen, bright, ambitious – but not so keen as to want to supplant me. Someone to do legwork without scowling and sighing."

"Hmm. That sounds like young Elizabeth to me. Sharp. Not afraid of hard work."

"Good. And available?"

"We can arrange it. I think she'll be very happy to be getting the experience. Like you, I'm afraid she's been involved in some pretty boring stuff. But—"

I raised my eyebrows. "*But?*"

"There's a way we should play this," Janet said. "I'm surprised you haven't thought of it yourself."

"Go on."

"You are not a Silk."

"OK, so?"

"You are duty bound to offer Mr Leaman the services of a QC. My thinking is, he wants you, not some London hotshot he doesn't know. So, if he declines your offer, as I think he will, he will almost certainly accept Elizabeth as your junior, and be willing to stump up for her as well."

"I can always rely on you to think about payment," I said with a faint smile.

Janet narrowed her eyes. "Someone has to."

"And naturally you've already established that our client is in funds," I said.

"Filthy rich. No worries on that score. And keen to get out of jail. So?"

"Yes, I think you're right. As always."

She dipped her head in acknowledgment. "Anyway, leave it to me." She looked at me sidelong. "Have you read the brief?"

I nodded. "Yes. But there are things that need elucidating. I have to speak to Leaman. If we take his instructions, I can bring Elizabeth along with me and introduce her as a colleague who's assisting me with his case. If he doesn't want me to be led by a Silk, as you suspect, we can upgrade her to junior then. Not that I'm in the least bit interested in the distasteful question of money – I leave all that to you – but it won't hurt to have her on the payroll too. Can you run all this past David Phelps?"

Janet turned back to her screen. "Yep. So you're thinking of a nice spot of prison-visiting? Nothing like it to keep you cheerful."

I grinned. "What – thankful to be on the other side of the bars?"

I heard her soft chuckle. "Well, I wasn't thinking about the décor."

I needed time to digest the brief, to let its contents – its interviews and statements, sketchy as they were at that moment – sink into the brain-layers where processing went on, skirting round the rational part that was loaded down with knowledge, prejudice, and habit. I put on my coat and a pair of comfortable shoes I kept in chambers along with my court shoes, and called to Janet as I passed her door, "Back soon. Got my phone." I walked briskly down to the river and took the path that ran alongside its muddy banks. A few random daffodils nodded in the breeze that ruffled the clumps of coarse grass at its edges. Perhaps spring had decided to come after all. After twenty minutes or so I found myself by the bench where I had first met Rachel.

I needed to talk to my brother – normally a pleasant prospect, today a heart-sinking duty. I sat on the bench and pulled out my phone. Al was almost certainly teaching, so I left him a message.

I wandered on, more slowly now, smelling the slight saltiness on the breeze, carried in on the tide though the sea was miles away. A weak sun glittered on the mud, and I saw that the water was creeping in, masking the rank smell.

Ten minutes later Alastair rang me back. "Hey, what's up? Have you been in touch with Dad? Is something wrong?"

With a twinge of guilt I realized I hadn't even considered he might be worried about our parents. "No, I haven't, not since last week, and no, not that I know of. Sorry to call you at work, but there's something I need to talk to you about – today, preferably. Can we meet up in your lunch break?"

"I usually eat a sandwich at my desk," he said. "Join me if you like. I might even make you some coffee. One-ish?"

"I'll be there."

I put my phone away and turned back the way I had come. Then I heard a soft pounding on the track at my back, and Rachel came to a halt beside me, flushed and panting.

"I thought it was you, but I wasn't sure," she said when she'd recovered her breath. "No dog?"

"No, I'm at work – officially," I said. "Just came out for a bit of air and some thinking time. How are you?"

"Fine," she said. "Got a minute to sit?"

We parked ourselves on a damp bench.

"How's it going with the party arrangements?" I asked her.

She shrugged dismissively. "I took your advice and farmed it out. So as far as I know it's all in hand. I'll get some invitations sent soon." As she turned and looked at me, I wondered what it would be like for a patient seeing those piercing blue eyes above the surgical mask. They certainly didn't convey cosy reassurance. "You look worried," she said.

"Do I?" I sighed. "Maybe I am, a little. I'm not sure if *worried* is the right word, though." I paused, thinking. I couldn't tell her much, in the circumstances. "I've taken on a case which is causing me some stress," I said finally. "I guess you don't have that problem. You don't have to worry about your patient's guilt or innocence. You just do your best to fix their heart, or blood vessels, or whatever it is, and send them back to their life."

She frowned and nodded. "Normally I don't know anything about the patient except their medical history. But surely –" now that fierce gaze was fixed unwaveringly on me – "isn't it much the same for you? Whatever you may think privately, you're not supposed to make moral judgments, are you?"

"True," I admitted. "But the difference is I know quite a lot about my clients, and being human, it's impossible to be completely neutral." I licked my lips. "I've taken on the defence of someone who, I am pretty sure, is what my grandmother would have called 'a nasty piece of work.'"

She raised an eyebrow. "Defending the indefensible?" she asked softly.

"Not exactly, because he may not have done what he's accused of. That's my job – to convince a jury he didn't do it.

Not that he's a decent, upstanding citizen, because I'd bet my paltry pension he isn't."

"But you'll give it your best shot," she said.

"Yes. I have to, because there's a fair bit of hostile feeling out there, and I may need to persuade the jury to put their outrage away and concentrate on the evidence." I smiled, trying to mask the heavy feeling in my chest. "At the moment Anna the human being is at loggerheads with Anna the upholder of the law."

She seemed lost in thought. Then she said, "Isn't there someone you can consult?"

"Oh, I already have. And I know what I'm going to do. But in this case it isn't easy and clear-cut." I stood up. "I'd better get back to chambers. Be seeing you, Rachel."

I sat across the desk from Al. He was leaning back in his chair, his eyes closed. His half-eaten sandwich lay neglected in front of him on a greaseproof wrapper. Looking at his drawn face, almost without colour, and seeing him age instantly beyond his forty-five years, I felt a tight knot of pain in my gut, all the worse because it was I who had dealt my brother another helping of grief. Inevitably, we were both thinking of Sam.

After a while he opened his eyes and tried to smile. "You know I can't keep this from Kathryn," he said, "any more than you could keep it from me." He saw my look. "I'll only share with her what I have to. I understand that you've told me stuff you strictly shouldn't, and I understand why. Obviously you're worried about the whole confidentiality issue. But you'll have to trust my judgment."

I felt a surge of relief, selfish perhaps, simply because he understood. "So you're not thinking I could just have declined the brief?"

He shrugged. "You could. But that just passes the problem on – to someone who may not do as good a job. Someone more likely to duck and dive, someone less conscientious."

"Someone more pragmatic," I murmured. "But thanks for the endorsement."

"This way gives you some control over how it's run," he said. "Maybe not much, but more than if someone else was defending." He sighed. "Tell me, though – how justified are we, really, in seeing Leaman as the root of so much evil?"

I was silent, trying to marshal my disconnected thoughts. "Nothing is conclusive," I said finally. "As soon as you start searching for who's responsible, you find yourself with more questions than answers. And obviously I am not privy to everything the police know, or suspect. I can't say much, Al. But I've read the initial paperwork for this case. He's been on the police radar for years, and they were right behind him. We know – or strongly suspect – he's a big player in the drug scene here. Does that make him responsible for what happened to Sam and his friends? I can't answer that, and neither can you. We'd like to see him out of action, and so would others, I'm sure. But I would want to see that happen as a result of crimes that he's actually committed."

"And you don't think he's a murderer?"

"Al, I can't go into detail. You understand. But I'm concerned, and I think I have reason to be. Let's leave it there." I attempted a smile. "You've asked me to trust your judgment, and I think you trust me to do what seems to be the right thing, but I know I've given you a tricky path to tread. You can't even tell Kathryn everything I've told you. You may understand, but Kathryn won't, will she? And who can blame her, when she has to see Sam every day and think of what he might have been?" I felt again the tearing wrench which always came with thoughts of my nephew. "She'll see it as a betrayal. I just hope she doesn't think that of you, that's all. Especially when you see the need to be cagey."

"Hmm. Well, that's my problem," he said. "It's never easy, is it? I'm glad you told me, though. At least I have it from the horse's mouth."

When I got back to chambers I found a note from Janet stuck to my desk: "Geoffrey rang." Janet's door was closed; either she was on the phone and needed to concentrate, or she had gone out for lunch. I sat in my chair and dialled Geoffrey's number.

"Something else occur to you?" I asked him.

"Not so much," he answered, his tone as usual calm and measured. "I wanted to ask how you were. Knowing you, I felt you would probably accept the brief, so I wondered if you'd spoken to Alastair."

"Just. You were right: I said I would take Leaman on. And Al understood, as you said. He doesn't like it, of course. Frankly, *I* don't much like it. But that's part of my job, and I've chosen to do it."

"Hmm. As far as you can, will you keep me in the picture?"

"Yes, definitely. Your advice is invaluable."

"I'll keep you in my prayers meanwhile."

"I'll be in need of your prayers. I can't seem to pray for myself."

"I'll pray about that as well, then," Geoffrey said, and I heard the smile in his voice.

I called at the supermarket on the way home and got something to keep Millie and me in meals for the weekend.

But when I opened the front door, loaded with carrier bags, an umbrella, and my briefcase, and with a clutch of files under my arm, I found her in the hallway, a small bag on the floor at her side.

"You look loaded, Mum," she said. "Give me something to carry."

Slightly taken aback by her helpfulness and cheerful demeanour, I passed over the two supermarket bags and dropped the rest with a grunt of relief. I followed her into the kitchen, where she was busy unloading and stowing the shopping. "You going out?" I asked, trying not to raise my eyebrows.

"Yes," she said. "Well, it's Friday, and I'm up to speed with school stuff. Jess and I are going to the club."

"Just you and Jess?"

Her smile turned instantly to a scowl. "If she was going with Will I wouldn't be going."

"I thought Will was OK, according to you."

She sighed and shook her head. "It's not Will, although he can be a fool. It's Will-and-Jess that I can't take. It's all got so earnest and starry-eyed! If I ever find a boyfriend I hope it never makes me dump my friends. I hate it when girls do that. Pathetic, mushy, brain-dead morons." She folded her arms and the scowl reappeared.

"She's young," I said. "Love, or whatever it is, can knock you off your feet when you're her age. And yours."

"Please, spare me," Millie muttered. "Anyway, Will's busy, so Jess asked me if I would go with her. Perhaps I should have said no, but I didn't. I'm going to hers to get ready, so I won't need any dinner. I've taken Gordon for a walk and fed him. I can take the bus to Jess's."

"Will you need a lift home?" I asked.

"I don't know yet. Will you be around if I do? It won't be late."

"I suppose so. I just won't have that large glass of wine I was looking forward to while I eat my lonely meal, surrounded by dull legal work."

"Thanks, Mum. I'll make it up to you when I pass my test."

Now my eyebrows did rise. "What, by taking me out? Collecting me from the pub after a riotous evening?"

"Be serious. You wouldn't trust me to drive anyway." She took her coat from the hook in the hall and shrugged it on. "See you later, then. Tonight or tomorrow, depending."

"Perhaps," I said sweetly as she opened the front door, "once in a while you could persuade your father to give you lifts."

She snorted her derision. "As if *that's* going to happen. He's far too taken up with the lovely Jenny and that little bump of theirs. Bye, Mum. Keep the cork in the bottle!"

I wondered, as I filled the kettle to make a cup of tea, if Millie was, in her own elliptical way, expressing her sense of hurt and rejection at no longer being the principal star in her father's firmament, or whether perhaps things were as they seemed and she had accepted the status quo.

In the circumstances I wasn't surprised to hear the phone ring; only that it rang earlier than expected. I'd washed my dishes, closed my files, and had not long switched off the late news, where a couple of solemn pundits were discussing the possible result of a referendum to decide whether Britain should leave the European Union.

If I was surprised that Millie was ringing so early I was also puzzled by the lack of background noise. Normally if she calls for a lift after a night out I have to strain to hear her voice above the din of drunken shouting, singing, and the clinking of glass. There was none of that this evening, Millie's voice sounding unusually quiet and subdued. "Mum, don't worry, you're not needed. I'm staying over with a friend."

Something in her words alerted me. "With Jess?"

"No. Jessica will be lucky if we're on speaking terms after tonight."

"What happened?"

"*Will* happened."

"I thought he wasn't going to be there."

"That's what I thought too. Look, Mum, I can't talk for long. I'm with another friend and I'm perfectly all right. Please don't worry. Chances are I'll be brought home tomorrow. I'll tell you all about it then, OK? Must go."

What is it about the words "Don't worry", especially in the mouth of one's offspring, which absolutely guarantees that worry will be the result? I knew I should trust Millie more; she was normally a sensible girl for her age, but she is naive, obstinate, and inordinately defensive of her adult status. I tried not to wonder where she was and with whom, but inevitably I did. Who was this friend? Had she met someone at the club? Was the friend male or female? Did it matter? Of course it did.

Resisting the urge to text, I knew there was nothing I could do except wait for her to come home, and it was in such situations, rare though they were, that I most missed someone to talk to, to lay out my concerns for my almost-grown-up only child. Richard hadn't been the worrying type and would often dismiss any anxiety of mine, but at least he would listen – usually. My fears were nebulous, not easily expressed; but that didn't rob them of their power.

I found I could no longer listen to political twittering. I

went into the kitchen, pulled an open bottle from the fridge, and poured myself the glass of wine I had earlier been denied. I didn't think it would help, and I was right.

In an attempt to think of other things, the next morning I took Gordon out for a brisk walk to the local park. He met a few of his canine friends there, and with great care and thoroughness checked out the scents that had been deposited since his last visit. As we approached our house on the way back, I quickened my pace: it had just started to drizzle. I saw an unfamiliar silver saloon, gleaming and sleek, pull up outside my door, Millie in the front passenger seat. She got out of the car, leaned in and said something to the driver, then pushed the door shut and stood back as the car pulled away from the kerb. As I came up alongside, I had a brief glimpse of a woman in sunglasses with heavy, dark-blonde hair.

"Who's that?" I muttered to Millie, who was waving at the retreating car.

"Sonia. Mrs Leaman, Tiffany's mother. Said it was the least she could do, even though she doesn't normally get up this early at the weekend."

I felt something cold clench at my guts. *That name again.*

"You went home with Tiffany Leaman? How come? I didn't think she was a friend."

"She wasn't, but after last night I kind of think she is. Or might be. But let's get out of this rain."

Indoors, coats hung up, kettle on, dog fed, we sat at the kitchen table. "So what happened?" I asked.

Millie took a deep breath and slowly exhaled. "It was OK at first. Jess and I had a few laughs getting ready – it was almost like old times. Even at the club, when we finally got there, it was all right. I'd noticed Tiffany was there; I even said hello. She was with three mates I didn't know, not people from school, friends from some dance club she goes to. They were all pretty drunk and very loud." She made a face. "Shouting across at some lads at the bar. Not my business, but they were so loud you couldn't ignore them, even with the music going. Then everything changed. Will turned up with two friends of his, no one I knew, and Jess was all over him like a sudden outbreak of acne, and trying to get me to hang out with these boys who were absolutely not my type – in fact, they were fairly rancid. To be fair to Jess I think it actually was a surprise that he came – I don't think it was a plot or anything – but I might as well not have been there at all. I decided enough was enough and it was time to leave. I went to the loo, and that's where I found Tiffany with her head down the toilet, throwing up and moaning, saying she wanted to die. There was no sign of her three friends, so I helped her clean up. She'd puked everywhere, all over herself, in her hair, all over the floor. I had to go and get the club staff, and they were obviously furious and not all that helpful. I asked her if she wanted me to get her mates and she said no, she just wanted to go home. Apparently she'd driven there in her own car and one of the friends had sworn not to drink so she could drive everyone home, but that wasn't going to happen now. Tiffany was in no state to drive, so I drove her."

"*You* drove? But you haven't even passed your test!"

Millie frowned. "I know, but Tiffany has, and we put her old L plates back on. It was fine. What else was I supposed to do? I couldn't leave her."

"Call a cab?"

"Ha, Mum, you're joking – no taxi driver would have

taken her smelling of vomit! Anyway, it wasn't a problem. I drove her nice, shiny, new red car. She lives in this great ranch-type place outside town, loads of garden, parking for I don't know how many cars, outbuildings, tennis court, massive house, seven bedrooms – for three of them! – can you believe that? The place is a palace. Too flashy for my taste, though. Anyway, Tiffany went off to have a bath and wash her hair, and left me with her mother. It was a little awkward. Mrs Leaman put Tiffany's clothes in the wash and offered me a cup of tea and thanked me for looking after her daughter. She's a funny lady, very skinny, same dark-blonde hair, and loads of jewellery even for lounging round the house. She was very nice but seemed terribly nervous for some reason. Then Tiffany appeared and said I should stay over, and her mum said 'yes, do' and that she'd bring me home in the morning. That's when I rang you.

"Anyway, Tiffany had recovered a little by then and she was very apologetic and grateful for my help. There's a spare bed in her room and she lent me some PJs, and we talked for a while before we went to sleep." Millie paused, her face brightening. "You know what, Mum? I was wrong about her. She's nice, not up herself as I thought. She's not dim exactly, just a bit, I don't know, not very wise, kind of young for her age under all the makeup and the nice clothes. And obviously she has pretty terrible taste in friends." She caught my look. "You think I do too? Jess is all right; she wouldn't abandon me if I was ill; I know she wouldn't. We've been mates for a while and she's basically a good person, just gone stupid over a boy. I hope she'll get over it and see sense. But Tiffany's mates, so-called, are another thing. You know what, Mum? She said she envied me. *Me!* Because I am clever and have real friends, she said. I didn't think she even noticed me most of the time, and then I find it's the other way round! How crazy is that?"

"So what now?" I fought to mask my increasing unease. Millie being matey with Tiffany Leaman was not something I could relish.

Millie shrugged. "I said I'd help her out with some of the schoolwork she's struggling with. Don't worry – I won't neglect my own stuff. You know I don't really know what I want to do, like for a job, but she hasn't got a clue, says she's not clever enough for university. I tell you what, though, she is amazing at art. Her drawings are everywhere, and they are really good. I didn't know that." She was silent, her brows drawn together in concentrated thought. She looked up. "The thing that's weighing on her most right now, though – not surprisingly – is her dad being in jail. She's totally, I mean *absolutely*, convinced he's innocent. I get that – no one would want to think of their parent being a murderer, would they? She seemed to be, I don't know, in awe of her dad. No idea why." She bit her lip. "I feel sorry for her, to be honest."

I wanted to scream. I wanted to warn my daughter not to get involved with this girl, that it was dangerous, however nice the girl herself might be. But I could say nothing. I had to bite back the comments that rose to the surface, and smile. Millie knew her cousin had had a brush with drugs and been badly damaged – of course she knew that. And in some ways she was a great deal more streetwise than I. But as far as I knew, she had no idea whom her elders blamed, let alone his connection with her new friend. Such knowledge, such suspicion, was a pointless burden for her, one from which I wanted at all costs to shield her, as I had sought to protect her from many aspects of my work – quite apart from issues of confidentiality.

But as I fought with my instinctive fears, I also admired her, for her faithfulness and good heart, for her care for someone vulnerable. Her fearlessness, her sense of what was right, were a source of pride – and of terror. In her I saw my younger self: naive, full of self-belief, crusading, ignorant; but the last person I wanted her to be like was me.

That night, unsurprisingly, I lay sleepless for several long hours. Millie and I had been alone for just under two years, and it hadn't always been easy; but this was the first time I'd felt so ill-equipped for the responsibility I carried. My work had crashed into my family life in a way I could not have predicted, and I found myself helpless, at a loss.

I had described myself to Geoffrey as a "treacherous backslider". No doubt that was an exaggeration, but my faithlessness and cowardice made me squirm with shame. Not so long ago my faith, which had kept me company since my teens, would have been a source of strength and guidance. Now I felt I had no other recourse; I had no one else I could turn to.

I rolled over, put the bedside light on, and went to my bookshelf, where my Bible sat, serene and slightly accusing. I slid into a chair at the desk and looked up "judgment" and "justice" in the concordance. There were many references, and most of them didn't really mean justice in the legal sense. Nor did "judges" refer to dignitaries in wigs for whom a courtroom full of people had to rise; they were, I remembered, more like military leaders. But some things did seem to chime across the great chasm of the years. I found this in Psalm 82: "You must stop judging unjustly; you must no longer be partial to the wicked!... You are completely corrupt, and justice has disappeared from the world." And then, in the minor prophet Zechariah, chapter 8: "These are the things you should do: speak the truth to one another. In the courts, give real justice – the kind that brings peace. Do not plan ways of harming one another. Do not give false testimony under oath. I hate lying, injustice and violence."

In a strange way these words gave me comfort. They seemed to be saying to me, *You are doing the right thing. Keep on defending the law, however broken and piecemeal that law, as a human arrangement, may be.* But what of those who were caught up in its grinding gears? What of Millie? If I felt unworthy to ask for help for myself, surely I could do so for her. Tentatively, I prayed – for the first time in a long while – and it was painful. *Lord, I have fallen away. I will come back, if you will have me. I will face my fears and speak sternly to my faint-heartedness. I ask for nothing for myself, because I feel I deserve nothing. But Millie is innocent, and I am afraid she may be in danger, caught in a merciless place, walking blindly, all because she has a kind heart and a conscience. Please, Lord, in your mercy, defend her – because I cannot.*

It wasn't much, and I found to my surprise that the ache in my chest that was always there had translated itself into tears that sprang from my eyes and leaked unchecked down my cheeks; but at the same time the weight that bowed me down lifted, just a little, and eventually I got to sleep.

On Sunday morning I awoke, feeling edgy with a sense of both anticipation and dread, and remembered my resolve: today I would go back to Brant Abbey for the regular ten-thirty service. I had no idea if anyone I knew would be there; part of me yearned to be welcomed back, and another part was desperate to be anonymous. I told myself not to be such an over-thinking self-centred fool and made some efforts to dress a little better than my usual weekend wear. It was all a front.

I feel certain that not every Sunday at the abbey was like the Sunday I returned. There must have been times when I'd felt irritated, jaded, spiritually undernourished, disappointed, or simply dull, quite apart from those times which, by increasing degrees of nastiness, led up to the sugar-coated attack that seemed designed to shred what was left of my self-regard and send me hurtling for cover. That Sunday was as much a blessing and a balm as the bad ones had been like acid on the skin.

As I approached the huge, weathered open door, I saw daffodils in clumps nodding as if in greeting in the little graveyard to the south, and the towering magnolia that leant over them, smothered in pale pink buds about to burst. I walked down the shallow steps into the nave, taking in the familiar scent of old stone, candlewax, and faint incense. A small woman in a red steward's sash came up to me, smiling, her eyes twinkling behind thick-lensed glasses, and handed me a hymn book and an order of service with a quiet murmur of welcome. I didn't recognize her, nor she me, but as I walked up towards the quire (I had come deliberately late and there was no sound but the organ) a tall, stooped figure appeared round a pillar and I heard a loud whisper: "Anna!"

My old friend John Sutcliffe bounded up, put his hands on my shoulders, and planted a kiss on my cheek. "How wonderful to see you! You know your way, of course." His beaming smile disappeared. "There are people here you'll remember, and none you won't want to see. Please don't vanish after the service. Come to the crypt for coffee."

I had to smile. "Go the whole hog, John? I'll see what I can do. Good to see you too."

As I found a space to sit, heads turned towards me and familiar faces smiled. There was no time for more: now the choir was processing in. From then on the service wound its familiar way, words and music laying peace on my spirit. The hymns were familiar as well, and although my voice was rough and cracked from lack of use, I made an attempt to join in wholeheartedly. Many things in that service spoke to me; it was as if someone other than myself had chosen that particular Sunday for my return. The collect spoke of God "... whom truly to know is everlasting life" – a life I had been denying myself for almost two long years. "Grant us so perfectly to know your Son Jesus Christ to be the way, the truth and the life, that we may steadfastly follow his steps in the way that leads to eternal life..." Three times I heard "life" and knew that here, in my neglected discipleship, was where I might seek and find it. And from the true life of God inevitably sprang joy, something that I had been short of in recent times.

The choir broke out in Psalm 148, calling all creation – the heavenly armies, stars and moons, the earth and its elements, the panoply of living creatures and every human being – to praise and glorify the God who had made it all happen and sustained its existence, in an exuberant chant that rang round the heads of the worshippers. Soon after, there came a reading from Revelation, and the vision of the new heaven and the new earth. It seemed that a theme was developing, and had it not been so solipsistic, I might have heard the voice of God saying, "Let's make sure this errant soul is inspired and uplifted!" But then the Gospel reading came from John, soberly exhorting the believers to love one another. "By this everyone will know that you are my disciples." This, I thought, was how it must be: from the heights of exaltation to the everyday. There was much to hope for as we lifted our eyes to heaven and the future, but also much to do, to follow and to grow, as we lowered our eyes to our necessary tasks, infused, if we could hold on to it, with that same light and warmth that comes from the heart of God. Like an old, forgotten friend, a simple truth gently lodged itself into that empty space I'd tried so hard to ignore: that living this life was never going to be easy, but we would always have help.

I stayed in the pew for a while, listening to the organ's closing voluntary, barely aware of people moving, shuffling, murmuring greetings to one another as they left. Slightly dazed, I descended from the quire, hesitating at the top of the worn shallow steps that led down to the crypt, only to be jerked out of my reverie by a hand on my elbow. I turned to see a face I knew and liked. "Anna! You're back. How lovely. Come and have some coffee. You'll see some changes down here – they've made it like a café." The hand on my elbow guided me firmly down and I found myself in a well-lit space, tables and chairs dotted about, steam rising from an urn, the comforting clatter of cups, the buzz of chat and laughter.

A cup of coffee appeared on the table in front of me. People I'd dearly missed without wanting to admit it said they were pleased to see me; no one said "Where have you been?" except one elderly lady who asked if I had been away on business. I smiled inwardly; she made it sound as if I had been securing trade deals in the Far East or travelling with a diplomatic mission. She never had really understood what my profession entailed, so I replied simply, "Yes, in a way."

When he was released from his stewarding duties, John planted himself in the chair opposite me, a cup of coffee in one hand and a custard cream biscuit in the other. "So," he said with a broad grin, "I hope this means you are really back. No more hiding."

"I hope so too, John." I caught his expression. "Yes, that's the idea."

He looked suddenly serious and lowered his voice. "You know those people don't come any more. You weren't the only person they upset."

"I should have been more robust."

He leaned forward. "I don't think that. It was a difficult time and you were vulnerable. But you should have trusted us more, your brothers and sisters."

I heaved a sigh. "You're right; I know you are. That's what I've felt this morning – it's like a homecoming. Except that one's actual relations aren't usually so tactful!"

He chuckled. "That's what we all decided would be best – your friends. If you came back, to welcome you and say nothing."

I was surprised. "You've all been discussing me?"

"Wouldn't *you* be worried if someone just vanished like that, obviously hurt?"

I took a deep breath. "Yes, I suppose I would. I see how much I have missed, in many ways."

As the chatter buzzed around me, I relaxed and realized once again what I had been missing all this time. Dunking a rich tea biscuit in my coffee, I told John that I had found a new friend, someone he also knew.

He nodded thoughtfully. "Hmm, yes, unusual woman, Rachel Wells." He looked at me sideways. "As are you. Perhaps you will be good for one another. Michael was my

93

friend first, and I met Rachel as a client, but that was just for the course of counselling she came to me for. Now she's a friend too. You know, I'd never have put those two together. It was a surprise."

"I don't know them well, but they seem pretty united."

"They are very different people: Michael is reserved and cautious, and Rachel – well, Rachel can be direct, even fierce!"

"Seems to me that if people are willing to learn from each other that can be a workable formula – rare, though."

He nodded. "There, I think, you have it. Michael's had tough times too. They've not just made him careful but given him insight. He's open-minded. And I know from my fairly intensive meetings with Rachel how keen she was to learn a different approach to life. I don't think that counts as a breach of confidentiality, does it?"

"Even if it did, you know it's safe with me."

"Yes, I know. Anyway, they seem to have found a way to appreciate one another's particular gifts, and that often takes longer than three or four years, or however long it's been." He paused, obviously thinking. "It took Jean and me a lot longer than that! But they are both clever people."

"I gather that there may have been some matchmaking activity from the stepson."

John laughed. "Ah, yes, Jasper! Perhaps he was wiser than he knew. Did you know I'm Jasper's godfather?"

"No, I didn't. But I have a very high view of the role, as you can imagine. I didn't see Geoffrey here today."

"He sometimes comes to Evensong."

"So he does. I'd forgotten. By the way, Rachel persuaded me to go to All Souls – on Good Friday."

John's eyebrows shot up. "Did she? How did that go?"

I smiled and sipped the last of my coffee. "Let's just say that I'm glad to be back at the abbey. They were good people there, but this is more my spiritual home."

I walked back to my earthly home that spring morning fortified. I remembered the source of strength that had nothing to do with my own abilities or acquired wisdom and told myself that I would not neglect to tap into it. Somewhere beneath all these positive thoughts I had a vague, quiet notion that I was going to need the grace of God and the support of my Christian family – but at that moment, I had no idea how pitilessly, and how soon, my resolve would be tested.

I opened my front door to the sound of girlish laughter floating down from upstairs. My first thought was that Millie and Jess had made up their quarrel, but though I recognized Millie's voice I realized the other didn't belong to Jess, who had a tendency to be gruff, her laugh throaty. This girl's laughter was light and giggly. Before I had even shed my coat, a door opened onto the landing and Millie came clattering down the stairs, dressed for the outside world, and followed by another figure I didn't recognize.

"Hi, Mum," Millie said with uncharacteristic brightness. "This is Tiffany."

Unease spread through me like a cold tide, but I smiled and returned the girl's tentative wave. "Hello, Mrs Preston," she said quietly. This threw me off balance too – I was almost never referred to as "Mrs Preston", but how was this girl to know? She'd simply used her new friend Emilia's surname. "Hello, Tiffany," I managed. "Nice to meet you." She was a small, slight girl, her face pale and without any arresting features, but she had beautiful hair: thick, shoulder-length, heavy, and dark blonde, expertly cut. Millie had mentioned Tiffany's haircuts cost £80 a time, and I had shuddered.

"Tiff's invited me over for lunch, Mum," Millie said. "That's OK, isn't it? She's even said I can drive her car again!" She sighed. "I'm getting a taste for it!"

Tiffany smiled, revealing perfect teeth. "Least I can do, after you rescued me from the club and those pretend friends."

"Oh, all right," I said. My voice sounded faint. "How are you getting home, Millie?"

"Don't worry, Mrs Preston," Tiffany said, her expression earnest. "I'll bring her home. And I won't have had any alcohol. After that night I decided it's not worth it."

"Better not be too late," I said. "You have school tomorrow. And no doubt revision for both of you."

Tiffany turned to Millie. "Isn't that what we're supposed to be doing this afternoon? At least some of the time?"

Millie hooted, full of wicked humour. "Allegedly. On the other hand, we might just eat chocolate, lounge around, listen to music, and gossip about anyone we can think of! Much more fun."

"Millie, be serious!" Tiffany pleaded. She glanced at me, a little worried mouse. "We're going to do some work – you said so. You promised to help me finish that project thing."

"I will. I was just mucking about. You both look so funny – you panicking, Mum disapproving." She turned to me, the gleam in her eye reminding me of her father in one of his dare-anything moods. "Bye, Mum. Have a nice afternoon. Try not to miss me!"

Bags banging on their shoulders, they were gone. Tiffany tried to say something polite to me but Millie had her by the arm, dragging her, laughing, down the path. A short way down the road the red car was parked by the kerb; I'd noticed it but somehow hadn't registered whose it was. Now the girls clambered in, jostling and giggling. There was a roar as Millie revved the engine, and then they were round the corner – far too fast – and lost to view.

I took my coat off and hung it up, then walked into the kitchen. I felt half-conscious, as if something had hit me hard on the head. My earlier mood had completely evaporated, replaced by something heavy, dank, intractable, a gnawing uneasiness. I could tell Millie nothing, and I had no doubt that for now she knew nothing of my connection with Tiffany's father. Would he tell his daughter I was acting for him? Would he even have the opportunity? Would he let her visit him? I had no way of knowing. I was fairly sure that Millie knew about the need for discretion, but that was no guarantee of sensible behaviour, especially now that, as I suspected, she wanted to impress her new friend; nor could I hope that Calvin Leaman and his family would keep their counsel. Was the whole thing compromised? I hardly knew. And there was not much I could do, certainly not at this moment. All sorts of clichés came to mind, most vividly among them a terrifying vision of thin ice, cracking away from my feet, revealing the freezing irresistible torrent beneath.

THREE

We were due to see Leaman at the prison at ten thirty. That morning I went into chambers early and had asked Elizabeth Merchant to meet me there, before even Janet was in residence. We sat each side of my desk, a cup of coffee for me and a herbal tea for Elizabeth, steaming gently among the spread-out papers.

"There's not much, is there?" Elizabeth commented. "Not really what you might expect from a murder investigation."

"No. Especially when the victim is a police officer. I've been through this stuff many times, and something here doesn't sit right. But I'd like you to go through it, see what you think. I won't try to influence you."

I reread the reports and handed each one to Elizabeth. It took her about half an hour of silent concentration, sipping her tea as she read and turned the pages. I hadn't had much to do with her before; she was relatively new to chambers. Janet seemed to think well of her, and I suspected that her quiet demeanour, her youthful good looks and neat appearance – brown hair scraped back into a knot, dark suit and white shirt, clear skin and bright eyes – hid a steely intelligence. She finished her tea, flexed her back and neck, and looked up.

"On a first reading, it's not what's here so much as what isn't," she said with a slight frown. "They seem to be relying very heavily on the victim being found on Leaman's property and Leaman's watch being found by the body. Despite Leaman apparently having an alibi and an explanation for the watch."

"Yes, that was my thought too. But you have to take into account their belief that Leaman is a villain. They'll assume he's lying."

Elizabeth nodded knowingly. "Janet filled me in a bit with that. He's suspected of dealing in drugs in a major way, yes? Does that make him more likely to be a murderer?"

"Maybe some might think so."

"Do we know who's prosecuting?"

"Palace Chambers. Not sure who yet. Possibly Clive Stephenson, but if it is him I suspect they'll go for some high-flying counsel from London to lead him."

"Do you know of him? I'm new to Brant so the name means nothing to me."

I pushed my chair back and stood up, stretching to relieve my stiff muscles. "I know him slightly, professionally and socially. I'm surprised, to tell you the truth. I'd have thought he'd see the holes in this lot." I waved a hand towards the scattered papers. "But he's a busy man and maybe he's relying too heavily on the police investigation being as thorough as it should be. We all know how overstretched the CPS is, and the underfunding of the police as well. But I have the uncomfortable feeling that this whole case is resting on a presumption of guilt. I need to find out who the SIO is." I started to gather up the files. "David Phelps should know."

Elizabeth glanced at her watch. "He'll be here soon. I'll get myself organized." She paused in the doorway. "The police had an unmarked car watching Leaman's premises that evening. They must have been expecting something to happen."

"Probably a delivery. I don't know, but I'm guessing they had some intelligence that Leaman was waiting for the arrival of merchandise through the port. Maybe they think that's how he brings in drugs from overseas. My view is that he's much too canny to go by that route: it's too obvious. That's why we need Leaman's instructions, rather than relying on the police investigation. I hope I'm wrong, but it seems to me it's seriously flawed. Admittedly we don't have much at this stage."

We were both waiting in reception when David Phelps' black Mercedes glided to a halt in one of chambers' precious parking spaces. He got out of the car to greet us, a sober-suited, slim man about my own age. I introduced him to Elizabeth and they shook hands.

"David, I'll sit in the front with you," I said. "I've a few questions for you as we go."

"How far is it?" Elizabeth asked as she climbed into the back seat.

"About a forty-minute drive if the traffic's not too unkind," David said.

For about ten minutes we travelled in silence while David found his way out of the city in the full early-morning throb and roar of engines. Once we were on the ring road, we were able to move more freely and we were soon cruising in the outer lane. David drove with his usual watchful precision.

"So, what do you want to know?" he asked me.

"Who the SIO is."

"Someone from out of town. I don't recognize the name."

I turned to look at him. "Not Bryant?"

"No. He's been named deputy. I think he was seen as too newly promoted to take on the job, but he's the local man, so in practice he'll have been heading up the investigation and reporting to his chief." He returned my glance briefly. "You know Bryant, I think."

"Yes. And from what I know of him he'll probably be resentful he wasn't given the top job. I'm concerned, though. This has been his patch for a number of years. It was probably his idea to stake out Leaman's premises on that evening, so I guess he was getting close, or so he hoped."

"It would certainly be a coup for him to get someone of Leaman's reputation and slipperiness put away," David murmured.

I thought for a moment. "David, did the police take his computers?"

"Yes. He was arrested at home in the small hours of the morning after the body was found. And because the crime was committed at the warehouse, they took a computer and paperwork from there as well. My feeling is they won't find anything. Mr Leaman is no fool. But we can't expect anything definite for a while yet. Once they serve the bulk of the prosecution materials, you'll have more of an idea. All the forensic should be there, including from the computers, plus a transcript of the defendant's interview and the psychiatric reports." David indicated and took the slip road off the motorway. He cleared his throat. "I guess you know, somewhat to my embarrassment, my family has had dealings with Leaman."

"I did wonder," I said, trying to sound neutral. "Was it from him that your father acquired his boat?"

"I'm afraid so," David said. "Sailing somewhere in warm seas as we speak, probably drinking with his cronies."

I nodded, remembering Lionel Phelps, who had headed up his firm for many years before taking retirement and leaving it to his son. I had never much cared for him; he had made the mistake of patronizing me when I first moved to Brant. A bluff, cigar-smoking, string-pulling incautious man, he'd assumed that because I was young, short, blonde, and female I must of necessity be a lightweight. David was by far the better solicitor and someone to respect.

"So I know first-hand," David continued, "that Leaman keeps tight accounts, with everything above board. Whatever else he is, as I say, he is not stupid."

"He wouldn't have survived this long if he was," I said. "OK, so between us we know quite a few of the pieces in this puzzle. But that's why I want to talk to Leaman himself. His story will help us, or at least that's my hope."

"He's saying he wasn't there," David said. "And he's furious that he's in jail at all, but I couldn't get him bail." He slowed and turned off the road onto a long approach. "We're almost there."

Elizabeth leaned forward. "Can I ask something? Presumably Leaman's a wealthy man. I'm wondering why us? Why Hartington? He could have hired a QC either here or in London. Of course I'm not saying Ms Milburn won't do a good job, but from his point of view…"

"He says he knows me," I said. "We have met. I wouldn't call it any kind of acquaintance. And speaking personally, I didn't like him."

"But," David said quietly as he parked the car, "whether you know it or not, you have a reputation, Anna. For an even-handed view. For adherence to the letter and the spirit of the law."

"Thank you, David," I said. I felt a familiar heaviness settle on me; I was not looking forward to seeing Calvin Leaman again. "I hope I can rise to that expectation."

The room they set aside for us, where we were to speak to Leaman, was the usual drab, institutionally featureless setting normally provided by prisons. Following a taciturn prison officer, we tramped down an echoing corridor which felt cold and damp, and into a room which offered the barest minimum of accommodation: a rickety table and a stack of plastic chairs. A high, grubby, uncurtained window let in pale spring light.

After a few minutes' silent waiting, the door opened and another prison officer came in, ushering Leaman before him. He indicated a chair opposite the three of us, on the other side of the table, and Leaman sat down. "There's a bell if you need anything," the man said, addressing David, and indicating a buzzer on the wall behind us. His voice was gruff, his tone uncompromising. "I'll be just outside the door."

While these arrangements were being settled, I studied Calvin Leaman. He had changed since that first meeting years ago: his hair had thinned and was stretched across his scalp. His skin had a greyish tinge, as if he had been living underground too long with nothing but artificial light, but two red spots stood out on his cheekbones. He didn't look well; but then, he had been in prison, subsisting on prison food. He smiled, and I had an immediate mental image of a snake. I gave myself a little irritated shake. Clearly I was allowing my prejudices to colour my judgment, and that wouldn't do. Leaman leaned across the table, his hand outstretched. David Phelps shook it very briefly.

"David. Good to see you. Hope you're well."

I'd forgotten Leaman's voice, which hadn't changed at all. Hearing it spun me back through the years to the first and only time I'd heard it, and it had the same effect, somehow mesmerizing: a local accent, not at all cultured, but deep and persuasive. Try as I might to maintain objectivity, everything about this man smelled of falsehood. Now his gaze swivelled to me, and the grin broadened. "And Ms Milburn. How do you do? Good to see you again. It's been a while." He did not offer his hand.

I nodded curtly. I saw he wasn't going to wrong-foot himself by suggesting we go by first names, because I would have cut him off with all the frostiness I could muster. I indicated Elizabeth. "This is Ms Merchant, who is helping me with your case."

"Very pleased to meet you, Ms Merchant." His eyes, I saw, didn't leave her face; a lesser man might have been tempted to let his gaze drift down to where her knees were clamped tightly together, slightly shiny in expensive tights.

"Mr Leaman," I said, trying for an even, unemotional tone, "before we begin on today's business, in the circumstances I am duty-bound to offer the services of a QC – which I am sure you know I am not."

Leaman shook his head and waved a dismissive hand. "I'm not bothered about titles. I asked for you because I've lived in Brant a good many years, and I've kept my ear to the ground."

"Then, if I am to take your instructions, I propose Ms Merchant as my junior, if you are willing."

Leaman shook his head briefly, as if disposing of tedious

trivialities. "Ms Milburn, you are aware I am not a poor man. Whatever it takes, whatever you need."

"In that case, let's make a start. I have come here hoping to hear your version of the events on the night of Detective Sergeant Winter's murder."

"Yes," Leaman murmured. "Poor young man. Leaves a widow and a son, I believe. I wonder what he was doing at my premises."

"The police would have us believe that he saw someone – you – let himself into your warehouse yard. That DS Winter, and DC Fuller, had been tasked with keeping watch on those same premises. We are not told precisely why, merely that it was part of an ongoing investigation. Can you shed any light on that?"

Leaman shrugged. "The police do watch me. If you want to know why you'd have to ask them."

I changed tack. "Tell us about your business, if you will. If I am not mistaken you import speciality vehicles and vessels, often from outside the EU, for specific clients. Why do people want foreign cars and boats, would you say?"

He smiled again, revealing mismatched teeth. "That's easy. Take boats. In the US they're a third cheaper, even half the price of anything you can buy here. It's particularly true of motorboats, but sailing yachts as well: bigger, better, cheaper."

"Even with all the shipping costs?"

"Yes, even then. And that's what they pay me for. To deal with all that. The rules are pretty tough. I know all the legal requirements that show a product complies with EU directives. All kosher and watertight. David knows that, don't you, David?" David nodded reluctantly. "And with older craft, the last ten years or so there've been even more rules about engine noise and exhaust emissions. Bit of a minefield, but after all these years I've got all that at my fingertips." As if demonstrating he spread his hands on the tabletop. "See, my clients are often very rich people. They get a notion they want something special. Show off to their friends. They see something in a magazine. Perhaps something some famous name has got. But they don't want all the bother of the paperwork, the legal stuff. That's my part of it, and my services don't come cheap.

"Then there's the cars. It's not just the legalities. I know the dealers, I keep my eye on the exchange rates. Some motors you just can't get here. A couple of months ago I had a lady wanted a Mustang Shelby GT for her old man's birthday, and it had to be green. I got one for her, and she shelled out the necessary and went away happy." He gave a small, sly grin. "So, if you wanted something a bit different, I'm your man."

I quelled an inward shudder and thought of my serviceable but very ordinary car: good enough for a teenager to practise in, but definitely not the flashy model this man had acquired for his daughter.

"And this importing of cars and boats is your only business?" I asked.

"It keeps me busy. No time for anything else, not even hobbies. Not even holidays. But it's all above board, every penny of profit. You can ask my accountants." He named a large and respectable firm in the city.

"All right, Mr Leaman. The question of why the police are interested in you will have to remain unanswered for the moment. Perhaps you can tell us your movements on the evening that DS Winter was murdered."

"Sure." He took a deep breath. "I left work early. My daughter'd asked me and her mother to go to an event at her school – a fashion show for local charities, it was. Tiffany likes to follow fashion, and I'm happy to support charity. Putting something back into the community, seeing I've had my share of the good things in life." I tried not to cringe at his bare-faced hypocrisy, his self-righteousness. He looked at me under stubby lashes. "You probably got an invite too, I dare say. Don't our girls go to the same school?" Suddenly, I could hardly breathe. Then he said, "Perhaps they don't know each other that well."

I felt a momentary rush of relief; then I knew, with cold certainty, that he was lying. He was probably aware exactly how well Tiffany and Millie knew each other. The dread that I had been suppressing all day rose up, threatening to choke me. Somehow I managed to swallow it down. I leaned down to where my bag sat at my feet, took out a pad and pen, and scribbled a note, simply to regain my composure. When I looked up he was staring at me with an expression of studied innocence.

"So you attended a charity fashion show. What time did it begin?"

"Six o'clock. My daughter went earlier, as she was involved, and her mother went with her. Plenty of people saw me there."

"You were there for the whole thing?"

"Yes. It ended about eight thirty. I chatted to some people I knew for a few minutes. I'd arranged to meet my old friend Billy Telfer at the Duke of York in Clevedon Street. Tiffany was staying on to help clear up and then she was taking her mother home in her car. That was the last I saw of them that evening; by the time I got home they were asleep."

"Your meeting with Mr Telfer was purely social?"

Leaman leaned back in his chair and sighed. "In a way.

Billy used to work for me, way back when. In the early days. Sad thing is, Billy's an alcoholic. Can't hold down a job for love or money. Always broke. I've tried to help him over the years, but it's hopeless. Anyway, I like to keep an eye on him from time to time."

"And do you always meet in that particular pub?"

"Usually. Sometimes at the Feathers in the town centre. But that's got a bit rowdy since the students discovered it. The Duke's a lot quieter."

"You were with Mr Telfer all evening?"

Leaman nodded. "Yep. Said cheerio about eleven."

"And then?"

He shrugged. "Billy staggered off to wherever he dosses these days. I drove home. And no, I wasn't over the limit."

"Where was your car parked?"

"Down the end of the street. No... round the corner. There was a removal van in the space I normally park in."

"Do you happen to know, by any chance, whether there is CCTV at the Duke of York?"

Leaman frowned. "Yes, I'm pretty sure there is. At the front, over the door, I think. I wouldn't know about anywhere else. I've only ever been in and out of the front door."

I made a note to double check that point. "All right, so what happened then?"

"I went home, made a cup of coffee, watched the late news, went to bed. And then the local law banged on my door at 3 a.m. and arrested me for murder." His voice rose in pitch, resentful and querulous. "Why would I even be sneaking round my own warehouse? I can just let myself in whenever I want, no need to creep around. But I wasn't there. The police don't believe me, because when they moved that copper's body they found my watch underneath him."

"You agree it was your watch?"

"Yes – it's got my initials engraved on the back: C.A.L. But like I told the police, that watch was nicked."

"Can you tell me about that?" Even though I'd read the report of the police interview, I wanted to hear it from Leaman himself.

He paused, as if collecting his thoughts. "We've got a little washroom at the warehouse – just a toilet and a washbasin. But we were having some trouble with the plumbing. Water everywhere. I arranged for a plumber to come, but he couldn't do anything straight away. The other blokes weren't too bothered, but I've got a thing about hygiene – ask my wife. So I hired one of those temporary cabin things, got it put down one side of the warehouse. It's still there. I'd been checking over one of the cars that had come in through the port, and I got my hands dirty. Went and washed them. I always take my watch off, roll up my sleeves, do a thorough job. Someone called me, said I had a phone call. I was distracted. Not usual for me, but I left the watch on the side of the basin. Answered the phone, got talking to one of the lads in the warehouse, so it was half an hour or so before I realized, but when I went back it wasn't there.

"I went ballistic, accused the guys who work for me of nicking it. They all denied it. And to be fair, it could have been someone else. We were in and out, stock was being delivered, the gates weren't locked, and the cabin was on the outside. But I don't believe it. Too much of a coincidence that someone would just come in on the off chance, the only time I've ever left my watch off. It's worth a bob or two, that watch, and my blokes would have known that. I couldn't prove anything. But I reckon I know who did it."

I let this go for the moment. "All right, Mr Leaman. Tell me about the men who work for you on a regular basis."

He shifted in his chair and folded his arms. "There are four or five lads I employ, not always the same ones, mostly for prepping the cars and boats before they're sent on, so they arrive nice and shiny. Can't even remember most of their names. One's called Ricky, I think, and there's a Paul... I'd have to check my payroll. You might like to know that most of them are bad boys – or they were. Been in and out of trouble with the law, all set for a career in crime, most probably. They're no age, these lads – most of them around nineteen or twenty, and one or two have been inside already. I take them on, give them a proper job to do, sponsor them, if you like. Give them a chance. Up to them if they take it. Some of them don't last long, and there's no more I can do for them, but I've seen some of them go on to be better citizens. Anyway, they're not always the same lads, so I don't keep tabs on them too much. I leave all those nuts-and-bolts things to my number two – Vince Priddy." He spoke the name with a sneer. "It's got to be him that nicked my watch. I sometimes think he hates me – especially the way he's been recently."

"Why's that?"

"Because he's a hateful bast— Sorry; I mustn't use bad language. I've thought about getting rid of him, but then I think it's better if I've got him in my sights. At least then I know what he's up to." He pursed his lips, and his tone spoke of undeserved injury. "I've done a lot for him, gave him a job when he got out of jail, when nobody else would, just for old times' sake. His dad, John Priddy, was good to me when I was starting in business. When they let Vince out, old John asked me to take him on, and I did it because I felt beholden.

But Vince is a loose cannon. Sometimes I think he's actually a bit unhinged. Got into too many fights when he was young, maybe did something to his brain. Was sent down for GBH when he was a lad, spent a few years inside. That's where he got his nickname: they used to call him Prettyboy, the other cons, because of his name, but also because he's got the ugliest mug you ever saw. He hates it when anyone calls him that, makes him mad as a bag of rats." He looked at each one of us in turn, almost, if you could credit it, pleading to be believed and vindicated. "Now there's a violent man – he's got a record for it. Whereas I've never gone in for anything physical. Not me. I haven't got a violent bone in my body."

"And yet you keep him on," I murmured.

"Like I said. I like to know what he's up to. Anyway, he keeps the lads in order. They look up to him, like he's one of them. And he's good with cars. There's not much he doesn't know." He paused again, his gaze flicking over us, a small smile stretching his lips. His attempt at appearing harmless, even winsome, was sickening. He turned to me. There was nothing positive in his demeanour that warranted it, and maybe I was imagining it, but despite his earnest tone, his attempt at sincerity, I had the clear sense that he was holding us all up to ridicule. For a man accused of murdering a policeman, this was breathtaking hubris. I reminded myself sternly that I was there to defend him against a charge I considered far from proven, even massively improbable – not to stand in judgment on his moral failings; but it was a battle.

"Ms Milburn," he said, with a show of humility that would have deceived no one. "Do you think I have a chance of getting off?"

I put away my pen and pad with deliberate slowness.

Elizabeth, I realized, had been taking notes all along. David had been sitting with his arms folded across his chest, staring at a point somewhere behind Leaman's head. "I'll do my best for you, Mr Leaman," I said coldly. "More than that I cannot say. Is there anything else you think we should know before we leave?" He shook his head, sullen now. I got to my feet. "Well, if anything does occur to you, you will need to contact Mr Phelps." I gathered my files. "Goodbye, Mr Leaman."

Unusually, that morning we were the only legal outfit visiting a prisoner at Wattisford, so apart from the usual checks we were not unduly delayed. Presumably to avoid the time-consuming palaver of having to repeat the searches many times over, prisons seemed to have a policy of letting all the lawyers out at once, so sometimes visitors had to wait a long time. We were all quiet on the way back to the city, and that suited me: I had plenty to think about. David dropped us off at chambers with barely a mumble of goodbye.

"What's got into him?" Elizabeth asked.

I opened the door into reception. "I don't think David enjoys prison visits much. If he had his way he'd probably stick to conveyancing. He inherited Leaman from his father, but he doesn't have to like him."

"That I can appreciate."

"Come into my room a minute, will you," I said. "There are things I want to ask you."

We hailed Janet as we passed, and closed my door behind us.

We sat each side of my desk, and I leaned my elbows on it, feeling suddenly weary, in need of coffee. "What do you make of Leaman?" I asked.

"He's not exactly lying," Elizabeth said. "But there's a whole long story behind the story we're being told, it seems to me. He's a paradigm of insincerity and posturing. Manipulative. Other than that, an angel." She grinned briefly. "But that's not really the point, is it? This case has more holes in it than a sieve. We know that Leaman claims he and Telfer shook hands outside the pub at eleven o'clock. Once we get to see some more of the backup material – including any CCTV footage they deign to let us have – we can confirm that. But according to the police Leaman had time to leave by the back door, walk back to his car, and drive to his premises, where presumably he parked out of sight – why, if he was on legitimate business? We know someone entered the yard, opening the gate with a key, went into the warehouse, but didn't turn on any lights, and the coppers say they saw the CCTV wink out. So, apparently, our friend is inside a darkened warehouse, sees DS Winter nosing about, comes out with a handy piece of timber, and clobbers him. Why? Because he has something inside he doesn't want them to know about? We don't know yet with certainty what they have found on those computers, but if David Phelps is right they won't find anything incriminating. We can be reasonably certain when Winter died, because DC Fuller heard a yell at nine-forty, the security man from the place next door corroborates that, and anyway that was the conclusion reached by the doctor who certified the time of death. The security man also says he saw a figure in black creep round the side of the building and disappear out the back. So the police are right in a way – it could have happened the way they say it did. But where's any reference to the CCTV of the rear of the pub? Everywhere has it these days – we're the most looked-at and checked-up-on country in the world, so I've read, and it's cheap enough to install. And if Leaman is right about Priddy, why wasn't he grilled more thoroughly?"

"Because he has an alibi."

"But it's no more convincing than Leaman's! He says he was with one of the other workers, Paul Fleetwood, at Fleetwood's flat, drinking beer and watching a film. Very convenient for both of them."

I thought for a moment. "Let's allow things to simmer for a while. Once we get the rest of the material the prosecution is depending on, we'll go through it with the proverbial fine-tooth comb and see if we still detect gaping holes."

"And if we do, we may need to ask for the rest of the unused material. What if they say there isn't any?"

"They will. So we ask again. It's inconceivable the police didn't think to get the CCTV from the back yard of the pub – that's if it exists. You know, I read of a case recently where a barrister consulted a judge when the police held out on him. The judge agreed, and miraculously the missing CCTV appeared and the case fell apart."

Elizabeth's eyes widened. "Do you think it will come to that?"

"No." I smiled at her frowning face. "We'll take things one step at a time. Wait for the rest of the prosecution material to arrive. See what we think. If this case is as full of holes as we think it might be, I'm hoping a phone call to Clive Stephenson might be all that's required."

Elizabeth walked over to the window, apparently looking out, but as there was little to see apart from an alley I assumed she was thinking.

"Ms Milburn—"

"Anna, please."

"Oh, right, Anna – I've been wondering… with so much against it, with the feeling against Leaman seemingly so general, why did you accept the brief? You'd seen very little of the paperwork then. You stood to make yourself very unpopular."

"I still do. I'll tell you what it was – a phone call from one Detective Chief Inspector Bryant, who we now know is deputy SIO for this case." I told her what Bryant had said. "I also took some advice from my godfather, who's a retired solicitor and a wise man. I came to the reluctant conclusion that Leaman could get sent down for something he didn't do. And I can't have that, however much I'd like him to be put away for the things he probably has done, and might still do. It goes against everything I've believed in and worked for. I don't need to tell you, of all people, that we have to defend our system of law, because as flawed as it is it's there to defend the innocent, as well as punish the guilty. It's not for me, or you, or Steve Bryant, to decide cases in advance."

"Principles like that can land you in hot water," Elizabeth said quietly. "Of course I agree with you, but fortunately it doesn't happen very often that we have to stand by them quite so publicly. It could get rough."

"Maybe. We'll face that one if we need to. Incidentally, do you remember if there was anything in the paperwork about keys?"

"Keys?"

"Yes. Was Leaman asked who, apart from himself, had a key to his premises?"

"I'll look again and check, but I seem to recall he kept a spare in his desk in the office at the warehouse."

"A bit careless, that. Someone could have copied it."

She nodded slowly, and a smile appeared briefly on her serious face. "So they could."

"One last thing, Elizabeth, then I'll let you go. What's your instinct here? Is Leaman a murderer?"

She shook her head. "I don't think so. It's possible he could have done it – just. But what strikes me is that nothing incriminating was found, either physically hidden in the building, in the rather fancy boat that was there waiting to be collected or sent on, or, so we suspect, in his computers and in his accounts. Obviously Leaman knew that, so why would he need to murder a snooping policeman? If he was there at all, why wouldn't he just say, 'Good evening, Officer. Can I help you?' Whereas someone else, not just the police, might have suspected there was something to be found and was looking for it for his or her own reasons. To me it seems most likely it could be someone on the inside of the operation. It's not instinct, Anna – I don't think I have much of that. It's more like logic. Leaman wasn't there – I imagine he really was in the Duke of York. But if he *was* there, he had nothing to gain, and everything to lose, from bashing a policeman over the head. He presents himself as an honest businessman. We may not believe that, but murder doesn't fit the image."

"Thank you," I murmured. "I was thinking along those lines too, but it helps to have someone else lay it out."

"Whereas," Elizabeth mused, "supposing it was Priddy who was creeping about that night, as Leaman seemed to be hinting. That might be a more fruitful line of enquiry."

"Mm, perhaps. But that's not for us to pursue."

Elizabeth walked to the door and paused. "Can I ask you something? Why aren't you a QC? Why don't you style yourself Head of Chambers? It seems to me you are, in effect."

I smiled. "Well, if I am, it's probably because I've been here the longest of anyone. We're a small set – at the moment I think there are about thirty-five of us, but people come and go so I may be a bit out there. If I don't give myself titles, it's because I don't see how it helps anything, except my ego, which doesn't need any encouragement. And I do have one advantage, which I didn't actually seek, but which has sort of evolved – the impeccable services of our chief clerk. All the other clerks – and she rules them with steely discipline, in case you haven't noticed – are relegated to various hidey-holes around this warren of a building, and they're good enough for all the other barristers. As for not being a QC, someone else asked me that very thing recently. I gave her the same answer – too expensive, too many tiresome social gatherings at my expense with people that don't give a hoot, and then I'd be too expensive myself for the average citizen to afford, so I'd be waiting for jobs, and my cash-flow wouldn't like it. I have an eighteen-year-old daughter, always in need of something, as you can imagine." I saw Elizabeth smile. "However, I may have to knuckle down soon."

"To what?"

"Our beloved Janet tells me I should be thinking about my old age – in other words, a pension. If I am to get anything remotely adequate, I will probably have to think about a judicial appointment. Our overlords at the Ministry of Justice like to get at least twenty years' service out of their judges, so I'm told. If I must, I must, but I'm not keen. Apart from anything else, there are exams! More work, more eyes crossing from reading legal tomes late at night."

"Hmm, yes," she said. "I'd feel the same. If I had to sit another exam, I think I'd probably need counselling. But for what it's worth, I think you'd make a great judge."

"Thank you."

"It's not a huge commitment, is it?"

"I'm not sure of the exact requirements these days, but if I took on a Deputyship in the first instance it'd mean sitting about twenty days in the year, I think."

She turned to leave, her hand on the door-handle. "When I think about some of the judges I've come across…" she said, almost to herself. She turned back to me with a broad grin. "Let's just say you could only be an improvement."

"Mum!" Millie loud-hailed from the top of the stairs as I closed the front door behind me that evening. "Geoffrey rang about half an hour ago. Something about Granny and Grandpa. Said could you ring him back?" I bit back a word inappropriate to be using to my daughter – if I wanted her not to swear, I could hardly be doing it myself. But I felt both dread and frustration, plus a dose of guilt that I had neglected my parents over the past few weeks. "OK, thanks. I'll make myself some tea first, then I'll do it. You all right, Mil? Reasonable day at the treadmill?"

She waved an expressive hand. "I'll be down in a minute. Got something to tell you."

I dumped my bag, heavy with files, on the kitchen table, shrugged out of my coat, and set the kettle to boil. Gordon heaved himself out of his basket, lumbered over, and sniffed me thoroughly, then took himself back to bed. While the tea was brewing, I called Geoffrey's number. Before he answered, my gaze fell on the shelf by the door where I kept current bits and pieces, and I saw the bright purple card inviting me to Michael Wells' birthday party, which, I realized with a small shock, was no longer a distant prospect. I'd sent Rachel a brief e-mail accepting her invitation soon after I'd received it, knowing otherwise it would be forgotten. *It's been a while since we were in touch. I should call her – she might like to know how I got on at the abbey.* Then Geoffrey answered. I held the phone between ear and neck while I disposed of the teabag and added milk to the mug.

"Hello, Geoffrey. How are you?"

His voice was grave. "I am all right, thank you, Anna, but things aren't so good with Jem and Nan. I went to see them yesterday. Your father's coping heroically, but some things are getting out of control, and he's always hated a muddle."

"Are the carers still going in?"

"Yes, but they are short-handed, the cleaning lady has gone on a month's cruise, and it's all Jem can do to keep Nan fed and clean and reasonably happy. He's run ragged, Anna. He can only attend to domestic matters when Nan's asleep. I did what I could, but I thought you should know. He'll never ask."

"No, you're right. Thank you, Geoffrey. I'll have a word with Al and Ronnie, but I'll go over there myself tomorrow. I should have phoned Dad long since."

"It's hard. You are all busy. But I'm sure he'd welcome a call. How's the Leaman case unfolding?"

"I went to the prison to see him today. Once they serve me the rest of the materials they're depending on, I'm thinking I'm going to have to present a humdinger of a defence statement – point by point, a demolition job. What I really want is to persuade Clive Stephenson his case is made of wet cardboard. I don't even want this to go to trial at all if it can be avoided."

"Hmm. I can see why. A jury of local people might not be inclined to set evidence above prejudice. Depends on the judge too, of course. Well, keep me posted, as far as you can."

As I ended the call I saw Millie in the doorway, standing on one leg in a characteristic pose, her arms in trailing sleeves wrapped around her slender torso. "Do you want some tea?" I took a sip of my own.

"No, thanks, I already had some." She slid into a chair at the kitchen table. "Lots of work to do?" she said, eyeing my bulging bag.

"Hmm. Lots of thinking. Complicated case."

"Why do you do it, Mum?"

"Do what? Go to work?"

"No, lug lots of heavy files around. Couldn't you do it on your computer?"

"I do a lot there, as it happens. More now, since the Digital Case System is being rolled out across every Crown Court as we speak." I caught her frown. "All it means is that we have to upload stuff, essentially. But I like to work from paper files as well. Computers have been known to crash. Vital information gets lost."

"We'll both be working hard tonight, then. But I wanted to tell you what Tiffany told me."

I raised my eyebrows, hoping I looked only mildly interested. "Oh yes? You two still best buddies, then? No reconciliation with Jess?"

Millie snorted. "That won't happen, not while she's entwined with Will. I can hardly get a sensible word out of her, not that I've tried very hard. And actually, Tiffany is a much nicer person than I thought. Yeah, loads of money, nice clothes, flash car, etcetera, but she's actually rather lonely, I think. And it's nice to be around someone who reckons I am amazingly clever! Anyway, she told me today about the night her dad was arrested."

"Really?" I was curious, but at the same time I was

screeching inwardly even while knowing I could say nothing, and even if I could, it would be useless: *Millie, keep away!*

"Apparently two police cars came roaring up her drive in the middle of the night when they were all asleep and banged on the door demanding to be let in. Everyone woke up and Tiff and her mum were terrified – you can imagine. But her dad was calm, apparently – let them in, only complained a little about the unsocial visit, said they could have found him at a more reasonable hour! A cool character, don't you think? Anyway they took away his computer and searched the house, which took a long time. Tiff and her mum couldn't get back to sleep, so they just sat in the kitchen drinking coffee, and then the police arrested Mr Leaman and accused him of murder! Tiff's mum kind of fell to pieces at that, but the police were hard as nails, wouldn't give anything away, just hauled her husband off. One of them took pity on her, stayed behind for a minute and said what had happened – that a police officer had been found dead in Mr Leaman's yard down by the docks and there was potentially incriminating evidence. Tiff still doesn't really know what's going on. Her mum's been to see her dad in the prison and she knows more but I think they're trying to keep Tiffany out of it. Poor girl. I think she'd rather know. Well, maybe I say that because *I'd* want to know if I was in her position. So you can see right now she really needs a friend."

"Yes, I see that." I really believed it, but at that point I would much rather my daughter was involved with anyone other than Tiffany Leaman. "Just don't let all this keep you away from schoolwork, though. It's too important a time."

"I know, I know," Millie said, scowling. "They never stop telling us at school. Anyway, I'm helping Tiffany as well.

If anyone's got an excuse to fall behind, she has. And she struggles with some of it."

It was already late, and I found myself still sitting at the desk in my bedroom that overlooked the garden – now completely dark. I hadn't drawn the curtains, but there was nothing to see, just trees swaying in the wind. I was not so much thinking as brooding. Thought implies logic, perhaps with a quantifiable outcome; mine was more like suppressed panic. My parents needed help, in a situation for which there was no solution, except the saddest. Calvin Leaman could get sent down for murder if I didn't succeed, and if I did it could have unthinkable repercussions within my family. Tiffany Leaman needed a friend, and my own child had to be it. To be responsible and helpless at the same time was hard for one body and brain to bear. I rested my head in my hands, thinking I should really go to bed, but doubted the possibility of sleep. There was really only one course open to me, and because I had neglected it for so long it felt strange. I took a deep breath.

Sorry, Lord. Sorry I am such a flake. Sorry I am weak, proud, in denial, all of it. Sorry I'm coming to you because of this extremity, when it's something I should be doing every day – because you have given us this privilege for our benefit. You don't need to be told what's going on and how it's put me in this tangle. Please, help me to be a better daughter, sister, mother, lawyer. Help me cope. Show me the sources of help – apart from yourself, of course. Help me to know what is right, and to have the courage to pursue it. But please, please, defend Millie. The last thing I want is for her to be caught up in this, but she is, and I can't stop it, and I'm scared.

I rose from my chair with a quiet groan, feeling at least

the beginnings of something like peace. Randomly, it seemed, I remembered Michael Wells' party. I slid open the door of my wardrobe and looked critically at my clothes. There weren't many – I had given a lot to charity shops at the beginning of the year, but there was a dress I liked, and I had some shoes to go with it that weren't too excruciating but gave me a bit of height. I didn't know if I could get into it any more, because it was a few years old, and the weight that I'd lost was probably creeping back on. As I peeled off my day clothes to put on pyjamas, I caught sight of myself in the mirror and pulled a face at the flab that was beginning to bulge around my middle. Something had to be done.

I decided to take a shower then, to save time in the morning, and as I stood under water that was just slightly too hot I made a mental list. Phone chambers and speak to Janet – get tomorrow morning's workload passed on to someone else. Phone my dad, tell him I'm coming over, get an idea of the situation, and phone my brothers. Spend the morning helping my parents, getting in some groceries, doing some cleaning. Bring their laundry back, maybe. By the end of this week, maybe sooner, go to the gym. I'd signed up with one a few months back and had only actually gone about three times, but I remembered that although my muscles protested for a few days it did actually make me feel better. Perhaps foolishly, I felt the need to get into some kind of training for the slings and arrows that were to come.

For once my plan operated smoothly. Janet looked at the diary for everyone at chambers and in her usual high-handed but efficient style gave a deadly piece of work to someone too junior to complain, who needed the experience. Normally, in the service of equitable dealing, I try to do my share of the donkey work, but today I was needed elsewhere, and seniority has some benefits. "Yep, that's all covered," Janet said. "Will you be back this afternoon?"

"I hope so," I said. "And thank you for recommending Elizabeth. She's very good."

I had rung my father early. I didn't ask – I simply told him I was coming and asked him to ring me back with a shopping list. I decided to put off ringing my brothers until I had something concrete to tell them. As I hauled carrier bags out of my boot, my father came to the door, and I felt an actual pain in my chest when I saw him. He seemed to have shrunk and lost all colour; even his hair, still abundant, looked dead.

I gave him a hug; he felt thin. "Dad. You look wiped out."

He heaved a deep sigh. "That does about sum it up," he said with a faint smile. "Come in." He led the way, carrying the bags. "I'll stow this lot, then I'll get the kettle on. Your mum's in the front room."

If my father hurt my heart, my mother broke it into small pieces. She was clean and cared for, her hair neatly brushed, but she was dressed in clothes that would, in better days, have made her howl in derision: a loose floral skirt, a pink cardigan, fluffy slippers. When I entered the room she turned and smiled, and stretched out her arms to be hugged – but she did this, I knew, for everyone. I could have been the postman for all she knew. I returned her embrace, trying to smile. My father came in quietly behind me.

"Nan, it's Anna. Our daughter."

"Anna." It was just an echo, as she was an echo of the woman she had been: the woman who had raised four children on a teacher's salary and done it with imagination and aplomb.

We drank tea together quietly, the three of us, my father

holding a cup for my mother and feeding her morsels of digestive biscuit. Then he turned on the television and we left her smiling, nodding, sometimes singing to herself.

In the kitchen I said, "She seems happy enough, Dad. But what about you?"

He shrugged. "This is it, love. What I've got now. Till one of us snuffs it." He smiled. "But enough of that. Buckle on your apron, because there's work to do. You might as well, now you're here."

I spent that morning cleaning their place in a way that I hadn't managed to do at my own. I scoured the sink and mopped the floors, scrubbed the bathroom, vacuumed and dusted, stripped the beds and changed the towels and piled the linen in rubbish sacks. "I'll take these home and wash them, Dad, and bring them back in a few days. Shall I get you some lunch ready for later?"

"No, love. I can do that. Sit down, tell me what's been going on in your life. And what about Millie?"

I told him about my work, and how Millie was doing well. "She's got important exams coming up, as you know. When they're over we'll come and see you together."

After I left them that morning I went straight to the gym. I worked on the cross trainer and the treadmill, then finished off with twenty lengths of the pool. At the end of it I was exhausted, breathless, aching, but I had somewhere among it all expunged the sense of hopelessness that had trailed me all the way from my parents' house. I showered and sat in the gym café with a bowl of soup, letting my hair dry, uncaring that it would be a mass of tangles. I phoned Al and Ronnie, but everyone was out, so I left messages. Then I got back into my car and drove slowly across town to chambers.

A few days later I received an e-mail with several attachments. I scanned most of them briefly, dismissing the police-speak that told me what I already knew. As we had expected, forensic evidence was scanty. No worthwhile fingerprints had been found on Leaman's watch, which had lain in a shallow puddle under Winter's body. Nothing incriminating had been found in any of Leaman's computers, nothing that related to business other than his innocent importing of foreign cars and boats. Psychiatric reports gave nothing of consequence. Then I came to what I was looking for. I was told that CCTV showed Leaman and Billy Telfer shaking hands on the pavement outside the entrance to the pub and parting at eleven ten that evening. There was no mention of any other CCTV, nor did it appear in the Unused Material Schedule.

I leaned out of my door and hailed Janet. "Come to my room when you can, please, and bring Elizabeth with you if she's not engaged in something vital."

Ten minutes later both of them arrived, Elizabeth carrying a tray with two cups of coffee. She put one of them on the desk in front of me.

"Thanks," I said. "Take a seat." When they were settled I took a deep breath. "I've just been served the prosecution materials," I said. "While I haven't studied them minutely, I can tell you there is no mention of any CCTV from the rear of the building." I saw Elizabeth and Janet look at each other. "I will draft my defence statement on the basis of what I have been given," I continued. "As I should. But if you two agree, I propose a little unconventional research. Janet, as someone who knows everything, are you acquainted with the Duke of York?"

Janet shook her head. "No. But my Drew knows it. He

used to go there a fair bit at one time with his mates. I think he knows the landlord quite well."

"Could Drew go there for us and check out whether there actually is any CCTV at the back of the premises? He'll have to be discreet; the landlord might be twitchy after being interviewed by the police."

"I think that might be arranged," Janet said with a sly smile. "I'll ring him now. See what he knows." She fished her own phone out of her skirt pocket and dialled. Elizabeth and I waited; the silence seemed charged with unknown possibilities.

"Drew? What, you were still in bed? Lazy boy. Look, Drew, you used to hang out at the Duke of York, didn't you? In Clevedon Street. Do you remember if there was CCTV there?" She listened. "What about at the back?" Again, a pause. "OK, son, I'll get back to you."

She switched off her phone. "Drew is certain about the front. He thinks there's CCTV at the back as well, and maybe even in the dead-end alley at the side, where there's a gate to the pub's back yard. But he's not sure. He said if I gave him some cash and the loan of my car he'd go round there tonight and find out for sure."

Elizabeth leaned forward. "Should we really be doing this? Aren't we exceeding our responsibility?"

"Officially we aren't doing anything," I said. "I'm going to look at the prosecution materials again to make sure I'm not missing something important. Then I'll draft the defence statement on that basis – what we have been given, not what we haven't. But it won't hurt to know where we stand. And Drew is perfectly entitled to go out for a pint at one of his old haunts. If he has a chat to the landlord about the unusual recent events, so much the better."

Janet got up. "I'll see to it."

Elizabeth also got to her feet. "I understand what you're doing," she said. "I'm not saying anything against it, but it makes me a little anxious."

"Don't be. It's my responsibility. And I'll note your reservations."

She nodded and left the room, closing the door quietly behind her.

Drafting my defence statement took me the rest of the morning, and I was meticulous. When I was satisfied, I sent copies to Elizabeth and Janet, and to David Phelps to take to the prison, because strictly speaking it was Leaman's statement and he was obliged to sign it. Elizabeth and Janet came back to me, approving what I had done. By the end of the day I had it back, because David Phelps with admirable foresight had already booked a visit to the prison so was able to take it for Leaman to sign. I uploaded it to the Digital Case System and sent it on its way. I should have had the sense of something completed – but I knew there was more to come.

The next morning I arrived at chambers early and fortified myself with a cup of strong coffee. Then I booted up my computer and cleared my e-mails. A short while later I heard voices in the corridor, and Janet put her head round my door. "Can I come in?"

"Please do."

"Elizabeth is here too."

"Good, but can you ask her if she wants to be part of this?"

Janet frowned. "Why wouldn't she?"

"Humour me, Janet."

Moments later both of them came in. I wished Elizabeth good morning and said nothing more. She was present;

presumably she had squared away any misgivings she may have had.

"My son did a good job last night," Janet said, wriggling in the hard chair till she achieved some degree of comfort. "He didn't have to use much discretion either – the landlord was only too happy to chat. He remembered Drew from when he and his mates used to frequent the pub, and it was a quiet night, so he brought Drew up to speed with all the recent happenings. I suppose it's not every day a place like the Duke of York gets a lot of police attention. I don't know if that sort of notoriety's a good thing or a bad thing for trade; maybe it's always quiet these days – maybe people are staying away. Anyway, Drew got all the lowdown without any effort on his part apart from a few grunts between pints. Turns out the landlord – Des, I think his name is – didn't tell the coppers everything when they interviewed him. For a start, he knows Leaman and Billy Telfer very well. He almost, but not quite, said the two of them meet there regularly and he – Des – knows why, but he turns a blind eye. There's got to be something in it for him. That's Drew's feeling, anyway. He told the police he didn't notice what Leaman was doing all evening – he couldn't be absolutely certain he didn't slip out – but he was there jawing to Telfer for a good couple of hours at least and all they drank was fruit juice. So much for Telfer being an alcoholic. Anyway, once the police had finished with Des they took all the CCTV stuff for that night. Front, back yard, side alley. I guess they had to let us see the results for the front, but they've kept very quiet about the back, considering they're claiming Leaman could have sneaked out that way."

I nodded. "This is brilliant, Janet. Perhaps we should employ Drew!"

Janet snorted. "I'd be very happy if he could get a job, but preferably one that's nowhere near me."

I turned to Elizabeth, who had been sitting quietly, listening to everything Janet said. "Elizabeth, could you please go and ring David Phelps from Janet's office? Ask him to search out the rest of the unused material. If he comes back claiming that there isn't any, tell him we'll take everything – even if they consider it irrelevant. Even if it's just bread-and-butter stuff like how a constable disposed of his rubber gloves. Then come straight back here. I'd like your input. We can leave the door open to hear the phone ring. I want this call to come from Hartington, not from me personally."

Elizabeth nodded and left the room.

Janet eyed me with her usual sideways look. "It all looks a bit dodgy, doesn't it?"

"Mistress of the understatement, as ever."

"What?"

"It's more than a bit dodgy, Janet. I can't make up my mind whether it's carelessness, over-confidence, or incompetence. I hope it's not worse than that. Whichever way you look at it, this investigation's slipshod. I can't understand why the prosecution even considered it worthy of pursuing – that's what's worrying me. Clive Stephenson isn't stupid or inexperienced. Someone's persuaded them they have a chance of winning. But the evidence against Leaman is flimsy."

"Which suggests that Stephenson hasn't got all the evidence either."

I shook my head. "I don't know."

Elizabeth came back into the room. "He says he'll do it straight away. We should hear from him in a few minutes."

She slid into her chair and picked up her coffee cup from the floor. "What are you thinking, Anna?"

"We'll see what David comes back with. I suspect we'll get put off with some nonsense. In which case I'll ring Clive Stephenson himself, ask after his wife, and very pleasantly tell him I think he's been sold a line. If he's got any worries of his own, that'll add to them. I'll press him as hard as civility allows. The system we've got, with prosecution and defence in a sort of game, where each side claims it's got the better chance of winning, can lead to this cat-and-mouse bluffing. But behind it all is deadly serious stuff, with someone's liberty at stake."

"He'll have read the defence statement by now," Elizabeth said.

"I know." I groaned quietly. "I just hope I've pulled it off."

We heard the phone ring from Janet's office, and Elizabeth went to answer it. She was away only a few minutes and came back shaking her head. "Just as you predicted – they're saying they've served us with everything germane to the defence."

"Ha! We'll see about that." I said. "All right, you two, you might as well go and get on with whatever I dragged you from. I'll ring Clive Stephenson later today. I'll let you know how it goes and what comes next."

Elizabeth nodded and made a swift exit. Janet paused in the doorway. "I didn't get a chance to ask you yesterday. How did you get on at your parents'?"

I shook my head. "No change, I'm afraid. Except that my father's not coping so well. I did a spot of cleaning, took him some supplies, brought washing back. It's little enough. My brothers will have to step up too, even if it's just some practical help and encouragement. It must be a lonely life for Dad. He's only sixty-eight, but he looks eighty."

"Never thought of putting her in care?"

"He won't hear of it. We've suggested it a number of times – we've said we'll share the cost, especially now that she doesn't seem to know where or who she is. But he's adamant that while she's comfortable and content at home, he'll do his utmost to keep her there. It's his decision."

"Hmm. Your dad's a hero, for sure. I wonder if Bob would do the same for me. No telling, is there?"

I shuddered. "Perish the thought it should ever be necessary, Janet. We need you here, with every brain cell firing."

She smiled enigmatically and disappeared into her office.

I had decided to leave it almost to the end of the working day to phone Clive Stephenson. He would be expecting me to call, after the initial approach from David. I wanted to sow a seed of doubt, if one was not already germinating, but he hardly needed any word from me to consider his own and his chambers' reputation. Although I did not know him especially well, I seemed to remember he was a cautious type, but few barristers are immune to the desire to win – almost at any cost.

It was almost five o'clock when my phone rang. I'd meant to call Clive Stephenson by then, but obviously I had made him sweat long enough, because he was ringing me.

I feigned surprise. "Oh, hello, Clive. How are you? How's Felicity?"

He made a few remarks about the health of his family, and politely enquired after me and mine. Then he said, "I had a call from the CPS earlier. The Leaman case."

"Ah, yes."

"Apparently you think we have some material we haven't served you."

"I'm sure of it, Clive."

"Bryant assures me there's nothing else."

"He would."

"What do you mean exactly?"

"Without wishing to impugn anyone, I think Bryant is desperate to put Leaman away. Understandable, when he's been after that gentleman for a long time. He may not have been completely upfront with you. But that's as may be. I'm certain there's more, and if I don't get it by the end of this week I'll do whatever it takes. I don't want to put unnecessary pressure on you, Clive, but I'll be frank: it's my belief this case shouldn't even go to trial. It'd be a waste of public money."

"Not go to trial? You're that convinced? Or is this some kind of bluff, Anna? We all know how it works, after all."

"No bluff, Clive, I assure you. The thing is, I understand that the police took all the CCTV from the Duke of York. So why is there only reference to the front? Why isn't the CCTV from the back and the side on the MG6C?" There was silence from his end. "Of course," I continued, "I can't guarantee outcomes – no one can. But within those parameters…"

"I'll speak to Bryant. I'll be in touch as soon as I can." Did he sound, under the calm delivery, just a bit rattled? I hoped so.

"Thank you."

Lying sleepless in bed that night – it seemed to be the norm for me in those days – I felt that the case had come to a natural hiatus – probably brief, but that was out of my hands. Until I had something from Stephenson, I could only wait. It gave me space to breathe, and ponder. I thought about Bryant and wondered if he was worried. In general I have a lot of sympathy for the police, and believe that they do a tough, unenviable job, often in difficult circumstances and facing unrealistic expectations. But, for everyone's sake, I couldn't let dishonesty or incompetence go unnoticed. The same applied to juries: on the whole the system had worked well for many years, and continued to do so, as long as the individuals concerned leant on the evidence and not on their prejudices; and any judge worth his or her salt would seek to direct them to that end. But in some cases – and I thought this might well be one – I was afraid the public perception of Leaman and his ilk might colour the whole proceedings, however unfairly, and however strong the judge's direction. It was often the same in cases of sexual misdemeanours: such was, and is, the emotional reaction to the crime and the revulsion against the accused. A jury is a random selection of citizens, and no one can guarantee their fair-mindedness. If I could persuade the prosecution that this case was fatally flawed, they would, I hoped, drop it. It would mean that Leaman would be back at large; it may mean that the police would have to start their investigation over again, because there would still be a murderer to catch. As far as the lawyers were concerned, it would deny both sides the opportunity of flaunting their adversarial and interrogative skills and their command of their native language. A shame, I thought with an inward smile: but so be it.

FOUR

I should have known not to offer any unnecessary challenges to my daughter. Sometimes it had to be done; but it should never be on a whim, and this started as a whim, even though it developed into something different. Perhaps, in a way, I had known all along that some higher cause was at stake, justifying my gauntlet.

She'd put her head round my door as I was battling with a pair of tights. "Party time, is it, Mum? Aren't you a bit late?"

"Yes," I grunted. "Michael Wells' birthday. At least I was spared having to find a gift for a man I barely know who probably has everything he wants. He said firmly 'no presents'. But we can contribute to some charity or other if we like. And yes, I am late. Pressure of circumstances." I looked up, and a spirit of mischief seemed to appear from nowhere. "The invitation says I can bring a friend. Want to come?"

She grimaced. "Do me a favour. It'll be all old people I don't know."

"Pretty much. There won't be many people I know either.

135

Just Rachel and Michael – and John Sutcliffe. But there's one young person at least, and he's nice-looking. Jasper – he's only twenty or so."

The look of disgust she gave me should have been warning enough. "I thought you were all in favour of me being a total hermit until my exams are over. Anyway, I already know Jasper Wells."

This was a surprise. "Really? How come? You never mentioned meeting him."

"If I had, what would you have said?" she shot back, all challenge and righteous indignation. "Something about concentrating on work? Not getting mixed up with someone because it's *oh, such a frightfully important time*?"

I finally won the battle with the tights and stood up. "I didn't say anything about you being *mixed up* with anyone." I spoke as mildly as I could muster. "I just wondered where you'd met Jasper, that's all."

She scowled, and I was reminded of a much younger Millie. Some things didn't change. "Actually, if you really want to know, it was at the club, that night I took Tiffany home. He was there with some friends. I didn't know him, but when he saw me bringing Tiff out of the loos he asked if he could help. And he came outside with us and waited with Tiff while I got the car. He was nice." Her scowl darkened. "But you don't have to read anything into that."

"Millie, for goodness' sake," I said, beginning to feel a level of exasperation. "I am reading nothing. As you love to remind me, you are an adult now. If you were engaged in a torrid affair with Jasper Wells I couldn't do a lot about it."

"Do me a favour, Mum," she growled. She turned to leave. "Anyway, I'm going over to Tiff's."

I took my chosen outfit off its hanger. "At the risk of

making myself even more unpopular, you do seem to be spending an inordinate amount of time with Tiffany."

Immediately she was all bristle and narrow eyes. "So? What's wrong with Tiffany?"

"Nothing. She seems a nice enough girl. But are the two of you actually working?"

"You don't have much faith in me, do you?" Millie said bitterly.

"I have every faith in you," I said. "But anyone, however clever, however well intentioned, can be distracted."

"So that's what Tiffany is, is she, just a distraction? Couldn't you maybe believe she's a real friend? And one that needs some help?"

From the thinning of her lips and the flaring of her nostrils, I should have known I was digging a deep hole for myself. I should have kept my peace; but I stumbled on. "That's another thing. It's right and proper to help people, I know that, but I don't want you neglecting your own studies."

"Just listen to yourself, Mum. *Right and proper*. You sound like some crusty old headmistress. Of course it's right. You do it all the time, don't you? Don't you ever risk your own benefit for your clients? I know you do. Why's it different for me?"

I floundered. "Because, Millie, you are only eighteen. You don't know yet what you don't know."

"What? Well, you're only forty-three, and you don't know what you don't know either." Her voice was rising dangerously.

"I just don't want you to mess up your exams, that's all."

She folded her arms, and her eyebrows were a solid line of fury. "Exams! Is that all you can think of? There are

137

other important things in life. Don't you know that? Like friendship. Or maybe," her voice dropped to a hiss, "you don't want me to mess up my exams because you don't want me at home for another year! Is that it?"

"For heaven's sake, Millie! You're being ridiculous."

"Am I, Mum? Am I really? Well, it makes no difference. Tiff will be here in a minute. Have a nice evening with all those old people." She closed the bedroom door behind her with a deliberate click.

If the evening had begun badly, I probably had myself to blame in large part. I told myself this as I brushed my hair and dabbed a spot of perfume in my cleavage. There were ways of handling Millie, and I had bungled. But I felt I had to air my disquiet, even if, for her, it smelt of hypocrisy. I sighed. Finally dressed and ready, I heard the doorbell clang, and then Millie was gone. From the head of the stairs I saw her go out and say something to Tiffany; I saw she had her school bag on her shoulder, and it looked heavy – I suppose that was something. But I was not in a party mood as I shrugged on my coat and went to my car.

It took twenty minutes to get to the Wells place on the other side of the river; the Saturday evening traffic was its usual snarling, slow-moving self. There were already several cars parked on their gravel forecourt, but I found a space between two heavyweights and teetered across to the front door. My shoes, while suitable and matching, were potentially a death-trap on the uneven surface.

The door was wide open and as I approached I heard the pleasant hum of conversation, sprinkled with female laughter and the hearty baritone of the men. I felt a sense of dread, as if I were Millie and not myself walking into that

138

gathering, knowing I was quite out of place. I told myself sternly that I was no self-conscious adolescent, and adopted a beaming smile.

"Anna! I'm so glad you're here." Rachel looked as I had never seen her before. I am certain she didn't for a second consider herself beautiful, but this evening she was fabulous in a sleek sky-blue dress which clung to her long, slim frame and moulded itself round the gentle swell of her developing pregnancy. Her eyes were all the bluer for her dress, and something in a deeper blue sparkled round her throat. Even her hair was relatively tame. "I've been looking out for you. Playing Mrs Charming is getting tougher by the minute." Her grin was impish. "Let me dispose of your coat."

I took off my coat and gave it to her, and she disappeared into a small room by the door.

"Now," she said, closing the door behind her and taking me by the elbow, "please, join the merry throng and be my backup. I'm counting on you."

"First I must wish your husband a happy birthday."

"Well timed – here he is. Michael, Anna's arrived."

Michael Wells turned from the man he had been speaking to, laid an apologetic hand on his arm, and shook my hand. He, like Rachel, had scrubbed up well: he was resplendent in a white shirt and black bow tie; his silvering dark hair was brushed back, and he smiled warmly. "Glad you could come, Anna," he said. "Now perhaps Rachel will feel she has an ally."

She gave him a look. "Anna, come and get a drink. I will have one too – just one. I can't believe one small glass of very weak white wine will damage my infant beyond repair, whatever they say."

We threaded our way through the throng. "You're a doctor," I said. "You're supposed to be stern about such things."

"I'm a surgeon," she said, grinning. "Which is a totally different matter."

"And I'm a barrister," I said. "Middle Temple's my alma mater and barristers from Middle Temple used to have a reputation for drinking unequalled in the western hemisphere. But since I drove here tonight, I shall have to be just as abstemious as you."

We arrived at a table laden with bottles and glasses. She took one for herself and handed me another. "We actually have a handful of very young waiters and waitresses with trays," she whispered. "Terribly posh." She sipped her wine. "I will probably have to play my part," she murmured. "But I'll come and find you when I can."

"Don't worry about me," I said. "I've just spotted our old friend John Sutcliffe. I'll go and say hello. You look amazing in that dress, by the way."

She gave the dress a tug; it was clinging to her thigh. "You think so? Thanks. I feel loads better these days, now that the puking phase seems to be over."

"I think you have entered the glowing phase."

She chuckled. "There may be all manner of reasons for that." Did I imagine the glance she flashed at her husband across the heads of the guests? "You look pretty good yourself, I have to say. John's seen you – he's waving. I think he may be keen to be rescued from that very large lady who looks as if she is asking for a free psychiatric consultation, judging by her expression – and his."

"What – tonight?"

"You'd be surprised," she said. "As soon as people know

what John does for a living, they are spilling their symptoms. I told him he should say he's a garbage collector."

"Yes, I suppose that's true," I said. "I've been collared in social situations by people asking for free legal advice."

"Whereas I am rarely told someone's heart issues," she said, her eyes lighting up with wickedness. "I've perfected an expression of grave concern. And the art of dazzling with the most terrifying and abstruse medical jargon I can think of." She gave my arm a little pat. "Go and rescue John. I'll catch up with you later."

John did indeed seem relieved when I joined him. He introduced me to the lady who'd been bending his ear, and whose name I forgot almost immediately. My concerns for Millie, and for the Leaman case, with the uncertainties rife in both instances, seemed to be fogging my brain. I made what I hoped was pleasant enough small talk with the large lady, until she smiled and slipped away to more congenial conversations.

John smiled down at me. "How are things with you, my dear Anna? And the lovely Millie?"

"I don't know how lovely Millie is." I told him a version of our little altercation, and he laughed.

"You are very alike," he said. "Maybe that's the trouble."

"Are we? And isn't that rather conventional wisdom for a shrink?"

He looked round the room furtively, as if he feared being overheard. "Please, don't you start too."

John and I chatted inconsequentially for a while. Safe and comfortably insulated in the company of an old friend, I began to relax. I made my small glass of wine last and declined the offers of very young servers when they timidly approached. The room began to fill, and as the evening grew dark I saw Rachel close the front door. The servers began to appear with delicacies on trays and I accepted some.

"I think there'll be something more substantial later on," John said.

"I hope so. I haven't had anything to eat for hours. Even this drop of wine is going to my head."

"Just as long as you don't fall over and embarrass yourself."

"Be sure to catch me if I wobble, OK?"

We were chuckling quietly at the prospect of me swooning gracelessly into John's elderly arms when the doorbell rang, and I saw Rachel go to answer it. A tall, elegant, blonde young woman embraced Rachel, who submitted, looking startled. When the young woman straightened up, shedding her voluminous coat, I saw that she was very pregnant. *So much fecundity!* But then my sour thought was swallowed up in horrified shock, because through the open door behind the tall blonde, a protective hand under her elbow, came my ex-husband.

I suppose I had never really dealt with the fallout from my divorce in any meaningful way. If I had been asked what I now thought of Richard, our seventeen years of marriage, my answer would have been different depending on my mood. Maybe that was why seeing him, for the first time in almost two years, was so horrible. We had occasionally spoken on the phone, but necessary communication had otherwise been transmitted via Millie, or by e-mail. That evening, when I pulled back from the brink of that dizzying shock, I realized I had forgotten what a handsome man Richard was. Perhaps he seemed more florid now as he entered his middle years, but his coppery hair was still thick and only lightly dusted with grey, his skin was tanned, and if he had put on a little weight it suited him, adding somehow to the aura of success and prosperity that he wore with ease.

John finally noticed what I was staring at, and I felt his steadying hand on my shoulder, but it was no use. I found I could not stay in that room. Richard's presence, and that of his young, fertile, smooth-skinned, new young wife, was unbearable. To my own surprise, I had no resources sufficient for any contrived social meeting, for the slippery lies that must be uttered for the sake of our hosts.

"John," I muttered. "Say nothing. I am going to find a loo. As soon as I can I am going to get my coat and slip away, hopefully unnoticed. Please, will you do the honours? Apologize for me to Rachel and Michael. Say I am unwell. Say anything." I looked up at him; his expression was all concern. "Please." I felt as though my skin was crawling with unseen insects.

He nodded. "Let me help—"

"No. Stay right where you are. Smile as if nothing untoward is going on. As soon as it is remotely possible, I must go."

I ducked behind him and made for the bathroom that I had seen people going in and out of, down a short corridor at the back of the room. As I slipped inside, I saw Richard and Jenny melt into the crowd. After a few minutes I flushed the unused toilet and sidled out. As I passed I smiled at John. It must have been a ghastly smile, judging by his frown. I made it to the front door and collected my coat. No one remarked on my passage. Soon I was out in the cool spring night, tottering across the gravel to my car. Inside, I kicked off my shoes, started the car, reversed carefully and, driving in my stockinged feet, hurtled towards home.

I parked the car outside the house, barely registering

my unusual luck in finding so close a space, and ran up the path, clutching my bag and shoes. I unlocked the door and slammed it behind me, panting as if I had run a hundred-metre sprint. I wanted to sit quietly, with no sound but a snoring dog and a ticking clock, and think: why had seeing him, and her, so turned me inside out?

I threw my foolish shoes on to the stairs and padded into the kitchen, filled the kettle, and set it to boil. Gordon raised his head blearily from his basket and greeted me with a lazy wag. I leaned on the counter, chewing my thumbnail, waiting for the kettle. What was it? Was it Richard himself? Was it all that he had that I didn't have and that he had stolen from me? Was it something he represented? My failure, perhaps? But how had I failed? I had done what I should, according to my rights, and it was no worse than many. What should I have done this evening? Carried it off with a light word, as if it were of no consequence? Mastering myself would have been some kind of public victory, but it would have been a sham, and I felt, fiercely in that moment, that I was done with falsehood.

The kettle boiled and switched itself off. At some level I realized that I was functioning erratically, that I needed to be calm. I put a teabag into a mug and poured the boiling water carefully, even though my hand was shaking. I realized that what I felt was anger, anger at what Richard had done to my life, anger at myself that I couldn't seem to get past his treachery and rejection, and that I had been hiding from this knowledge for the past two years.

When accidents happen, so often they change our circumstances so quickly that we almost believe they can be undone. In my stockinged feet, holding a brimming mug of tea, I failed to notice the puddle on the kitchen floor that my dog had deposited in my absence. One foot slithered forward, the other swiftly followed, sending the mug of tea flying into the air. I hit the floor hard on my back, and scalding tea cascaded down the side of my jaw and onto my neck. I cried out with pain. The mug crashed to the floor and shattered, and as I tried to break my fall the jagged edge slashed the pad of my thumb. And it all happened in the most fleeting of seconds.

For a moment I lay on the floor, dazed and whimpering. My back twinged if I tried to move, the floor was awash with cooling tea, my scalded neck stung like snakebite, and my injured hand dribbled bright blood onto the tiles.

Somehow I managed to get onto my hands and knees. I could barely see for the tears of pain brimming in my eyes. My head hurt – had I cracked it on the floor when I fell? I couldn't remember. What to deal with first? I didn't know. The capacity to think seemed to have vanished. Had I actually passed out? Where could I find help? I was alone.

Grunting and moaning with the effort, I tried to pull myself up, but a wave of nausea knocked me back. The floor was a mess. My handbag was on the worktop, its handles hanging down. I grabbed it and fumbled for my phone. Who could help? Millie was probably staying over at Tiffany's. Blinking to clear my eyes I keyed in my contacts. Janet's number was at the top, and I dialled it.

"Hello? Anna? Aren't you at the party? Is something up?"

My thoughts wouldn't stand still, and I heard how odd my voice sounded, like a drunk's. "I was, but now I'm at home, and I've had an accident."

Her voice sharpened. "Are you hurt?"

"Yes. Scalded. Back hurt. I fell in the kitchen. Cut hand."

"Do you need A and E?"

"I think – I don't know. Maybe. Probably. I banged my head – think I passed out."

"I'll come now. Do you still leave a key under the flowerpot?"

"Yes."

I think I must have dropped the phone. I guess the pain was really beginning to hit then: back, head, neck, hand, in waves of intensity.

When I came back to awareness Janet was there, gabbling into my phone. I seemed to be lying on the floor, the ceiling undulating above me. Tears of pain and shock were dribbling down my face, and then Janet was squatting beside me, mopping my cheeks, muttering reassuring words that I couldn't understand, and then more people appeared in the kitchen, big people who smelled of fresh air, and I must have passed out again.

There were moments when I was conscious: strapped down in a jolting ambulance, Janet holding my good hand, then a stretcher, a white cubicle, someone doing things to my neck, cleaning and bandaging my hand. Someone rolled me over and I screeched with pain. A voice said something about an X-ray and I was wheeled away again, but not before I threw up.

Finally it was over. Janet was still there, looking frazzled, grey smudges under her eyes – weariness or makeup? I couldn't tell. I was in a white bed, propped up. My hand was bandaged, and there was a cool dressing on my neck. Janet slumped into a chair beside me. "You going to tell me what the heck happened?" she said.

I swallowed. My voice was a rasping croak. "Gordon must have peed on the floor. I didn't have any shoes on. Slipped over. Just made tea. That's all."

"What were you doing back home at nine o'clock anyway?"

"Don't ask." I turned to look at her, and my head clanged. "Have I broken anything? My head hurts. My back hurts."

"Seems not. The X-rays came back – you're badly bruised is all. A deep cut on your hand, and a nasty scald on your neck. You did a thorough job, but they patched you up. You'll probably live."

"Thank you for helping." I still sounded slurred.

"They're going to keep you in overnight, just to keep an eye on you. They've given you some strong painkillers, so you'll probably sleep. I'll come and see you in the morning, OK?"

"How are you going to get home?"

"No problem. Bob's outside with the car. After he picked you up in the ambulance his shift was over."

"Janet, what about Gordon? Supposing they don't let me out?"

I must have sounded panicked. She patted my hand wearily. "I'll go via yours. He can come back with me tonight. I'll get in touch with Millie. I might even mop your floor. Just chill and get some sleep and don't worry."

She stood in the doorway, and she seemed somehow indistinct, but that was probably because I was drifting off into blessed drug-induced blackout.

I got home on Sunday afternoon, armed with a bag full of painkillers and dressings, and instructions on looking after my injuries. Bob and Janet took me in their car and returned Gordon at the same time. He sat on my lap in the back, occasionally looking up at me anxiously and licking my unbandaged hand.

Millie was hovering in the doorway. "Mum, look at you! Talk about walking wounded."

"We'll leave you in charge now, OK, Millie?" Janet said. "Don't let her do too much. She's not at death's door or anything, but she's had a shock."

"I'll do my best," Millie said. "But you know Mum. I can't guarantee she'll obey."

"Bob, Janet," I said, "thank you for everything. You have both been great. I'll see you at work tomorrow, Janet."

"What? No, that's crazy!"

"Crazy or not, if I'm not actually on the way out, that's where I'll be. I haven't got court tomorrow, have I? But we have work to do." I gave her a meaningful look.

She sighed. "You're your own worst enemy."

I managed a feeble smile. "Aren't we all? I may not stay a full day. Will that satisfy?"

"I suppose."

Indoors, Millie made me recline on the sofa and brought me a cup of tea. "Don't spill it," she warned, frowning. "So, what on earth happened? You were going to that party."

"I did go, but I didn't stay long. I just had an accident, that's all. Gordon had peed on the floor. I wasn't wearing shoes. I slipped, dropped my tea. Luckily, as you know, Janet came to my rescue. What about you? How was your evening with Tiffany?"

She sat on the edge of the armchair opposite me. "It was OK, and we did some work. But I'm worried about her. She's all over the place, really tearful, can't concentrate. Convinced her dad will be found guilty. I don't know why. She's just that sort of person, I guess. Anxious, a bit of a pessimist. Anyway, I'm going to get on by myself today. Being with her yesterday, trying to keep her on track, I didn't get as much done as

I wanted." She got up, sighing. "I'll be glad when this lot's over. Get my life back. I'll make us something to eat in an hour or two, Mum. And I'll take Gordon out. Don't work too hard."

"No. Just some odds and ends to sort out." I patted the thick file on my lap. I'd made sure there was no name visible on it. "You go and get on in peace, love."

I got up early on Monday morning to make sure I had plenty of time to sort out changing the dressing on my neck and make myself look less of a wreck. Though I wouldn't have admitted it to anyone, I felt unsteady – but only physically. I'd spent some of the night giving myself a stern telling-off for being so wobbly, and now I wanted to get back to my case with fresh determination. Richard, frankly, could go hang. He was no longer in my life, so he wasn't going to influence it any more than I could help.

As I was choosing a scarf to drape round my neck and conceal my injury, my phone buzzed with a text from Janet: "Interesting brown envelope arrived by courier. Addressed to you."

When I arrived at chambers she waved me into her office. "What sort of time did you get here?" I asked.

"Early. Wanted to clear up a few things. Like deciding how to reassign some of your workload. Because," she eyed me meaningfully, "I think you're not as chipper as you're pretending to be and will probably not last the day." I opened my mouth to protest but she waved me to silence. "Whatever. So anyway, I was here to take delivery of this." She handed a brown envelope across the desk. "I think the chap on the motorbike would just have poked it through the door and scarpered."

I stared at it. "I wonder."

Wordlessly, Janet passed over a letter-opener. I slit the seal and let the contents fall on her desk. There were several sheets of paper, and something in a plastic wallet. On the top was a brief letter with the Palace Chambers heading.

> *Dear Anna,*
> *This was all I could get out of them.*
> *Yours,*
> *Clive.*

"Yes, oh yes," I whispered. "Some useless stuff here, I guess, but if I am not mistaken this disc is a copy of the pub's CCTV footage. It had better be for the right date, or I shall have very strong words."

In some respects Hartington Chambers, although it looked fairly modern from the outside, was traditional. There was a waiting area for clients with a coffee machine and squashy chairs; on the walls hung legal cartoons, and in a small alcove a shelf with crusty legal tomes such as *Halsbury's Laws of England*. I had little idea if they were often consulted since most of my colleagues did their research online, as I did. The rear of the building was nineteenth century, refurbished superficially but retaining some uneven wooden floors, short flights of stairs, and a maze of small rooms in which the uninitiated often found themselves aimlessly wandering. This was one reason for our unusual arrangements: normally Janet and her minions would have occupied a good-sized room where they could all be in constant contact when last-minute alterations needed to be made, such as when a case overran, the barrister attending couldn't get to his or her next case, and someone else had to be found at the last minute. But in our building such a room simply wasn't available, at least not in a suitable location. How Janet kept such tight control over the other clerks was just another example of her capabilities, and a mystery to me. However, a short way down the cream-painted, soft-carpeted corridor that led away from the reception area there was a small room with a computer, a screen, and a stack of chairs. Janet summoned Elizabeth, and we armed ourselves with coffee. We took down three chairs and closed the door. Elizabeth, seeing the bandage on my hand and the dressing on my neck, raised her eyebrows in mute enquiry.

"Just a stupid accident," I murmured. "My own fault. Nothing to worry about." I parked myself in a chair. "We have a disc," I told Elizabeth. "Delivered this morning by an unknown hand. Janet will do the necessary, and then we watch. Three pairs of eyes will be enough, I hope."

Janet was already busy with the computer. "What time setting?"

"Well, we know Leaman was in the pub by eight thirty. We also know that Sergeant Winter was dead by nine thirty. So let's be as certain as we can – run it from eight to ten, Janet." I turned to Elizabeth. "Better prepare yourself for a long morning."

She smiled. "Maybe a productive one, though."

I nodded. "It had better be." A thought struck me. "Janet, do we need to watch two hours of footage of the side of the pub as well as the back?"

"Not really – the alley is a dead end. There's a high wall and barbed wire. Tell you what, though. We'll watch the two hours of the back of the pub. Later on I'll make sure the alley is covered. You can be getting on with other things, and if there's anything to report I'll let you know. I don't think you're up to four hours of this."

I frowned. "I'll be fine. But OK, let's do that. And thanks."

We took a break halfway through for more coffee, but apart from that watched in intent silence. The only movement in the back yard of the Duke of York for that evening was the landlord – once to empty something into a wheelie bin, then to snatch a hasty cigarette, leaning on the side wall in the darkness.

Janet switched off the computer. She was smiling faintly. "OK? Seen enough? If anyone wants me, I'll be in here. They'd better not want me."

I got up. The painkillers were wearing off, and my head was throbbing fiercely. I had a spell of dizziness, but it passed. "I'll be in my room."

At my desk I took another dose of painkillers with a swig of water, opened up my computer, and tried to work. Just before one o'clock Janet put her head round the door. "Just to let you know," she said, deadpan as ever, "no one in that alley for the time specified apart from a couple of horny teenagers and a few rats. Oh, and an old chap peeing on the wall where the alley meets the road, and it definitely wasn't our client."

"Thank you, Janet. So, as we thought, Leaman didn't leave the pub. Remind me to send you a bottle of something."

She grinned and vanished. "I prefer red, if that's OK," her voice came from the corridor.

It was, I thought, the lid well and truly nailed down on the coffin containing the case against Leaman. Now the burden of proof rested squarely with the prosecution. Could they prove their case beyond reasonable doubt? I thought not. Weariness descended on me like a bag of wet builder's sand. I put my coat on and collected my bags.

Janet looked at me approvingly as I stopped by her door and waved half-heartedly. "Good. Showing sense at last."

At home, I changed into something baggy and comfortable, made myself a sandwich, and flopped on the sofa. Somewhere around the middle of the afternoon I awoke with a jerk as the files that had been on my lap slid to the floor with a thump. At the same time my doorbell rang.

I got up with a muttered groan and padded to the door, remembering to adjust my scarf so that my neck dressing was covered. Everything was hurting: the skin of my neck and jaw stung and burned, and my cut hand throbbed. Time for more painkillers.

I opened the door to find Rachel on the step.

"Anna, are you all right?"

"Yes, well – no – but how did you know I might not be? Sorry, I'm not making a lot of sense – I just woke up. Come in, though."

"I can't stop. I've left Michael with Jonathan, and he has a meeting at the hospital. Michael, that is! But I had to see if you were OK. John Sutcliffe told us."

"What did he tell you?"

"He was worried. He rang you and got no answer. Later he tried again and spoke to someone who was picking up Gordon."

"That would be Janet, my clerk."

"Well, she told him what had happened, and he told us. Anna, I'm so sorry."

"It's hardly your fault! Look, don't stand on the doorstep. Come in, even if just for a moment."

She came inside and I closed the door. "I had absolutely no idea of any connection between you and Jenny Preston," she said. "I'd recently met her at antenatal and she seemed nice, so I invited her. I feel awful. Responsible."

"You aren't," I told her firmly. "There's no way you could have known. I freaked out a little when I saw Richard, came home, and had a stupid accident. But it's not your fault."

She bit her lip. "Look, I really can't stop. But I would like to come and see you if it's not a nuisance. Are you free tomorrow?"

I nodded. "Actually, I've decided to take a day off, so I'll be here. I went to chambers this morning because there's always work to be done, but but I realize I am probably suffering from a degree of shock, so a day of no work will probably be a good thing. Yes, do come tomorrow."

"Elevenish?"

"Perfect. And Rachel, don't go blaming yourself. It was just an unhappy coincidence."

She opened the door and stepped out. She turned to me, her face uncharacteristically anxious. "You're burned, aren't you?"

"Scalded."

"Yes." She hesitated. "I could ask Michael to look at it if you like. It's his area of particular expertise."

"Certainly not! It's not too bad, and they did a good job at the hospital. I wouldn't dream of wasting his time."

"Well, if it gets worse…"

"Rachel, go home. I'll see you tomorrow."

"I brought my own teabags," she announced the next morning. She had run the distance from her place to mine and was dressed in her usual close-fitting black gear and running shoes, but she didn't seem at all out of breath. "It's filthy stuff, tastes like ash, but I'm being kind to my new son or daughter and restricting my caffeine intake." She inhaled, closing her eyes and smiling. "I'll have to make do with the smell of yours."

When we had settled ourselves, she said, "How are the injuries?"

"Stinging. Throbbing. Aching, in the case of my back. Pounding head. But painkillers help, and nothing seems to be septic. How did the party go after I left?"

She shrugged, took a sip of her tea, and pulled a face. "OK, I guess. I'm a novice in these matters. But people ate and drank and chatted and wished Michael a happy birthday, so I suppose it was all right. I wanted to do it for him, but I'm glad it's over."

"Is Jasper right? You'd rather be a hermit?"

She grinned. "Not all the time. I'd want the right people around at my beck and call, naturally. What about you? Do you go out a lot?"

I sighed. "I did once. But things are different now."

I wondered if she'd follow this up with some question about Richard and why I'd felt it necessary to avoid him; but Rachel, as I found many times afterwards, often came at things sideways, adopting an unlooked-for direction.

She leaned forward. "You know what I'd really like to know?" she said. I raised an eyebrow. "How you came to be where you are now. What it's like to train for the Bar. To the outsider it all seems so closed and specialized, arcane even. I suppose that's part of the glamour."

I laughed. "Forget the idea of glamour," I said. "Unless you think a scratchy grey wig and a voluminous black gown are the height of fashion. But I think that's the impression a

155

lot of people have. It's all an illusion, though. What do you think of when you think of a barrister's day? Worn stone steps up to venerable old buildings, polished oak, ancient leather? Swaying a jury by the sheer power of your rhetoric? The reality is more like starting out in the dark of a winter morning to catch a train to some dump you'd never choose to go to, courthouses whose architecture reminds you of a Victorian jail or a sixties school, a great deal of waiting around, witnesses who don't show, cases which collapse after you've done a lot of work to prepare, cranky judges, ungrateful clients, terrible vending machine coffee, and waiting too long to get paid. Absolutely not glamorous."

"So what's the appeal?"

"Well, at first I guess I *was* seduced by the glamour, as you call it. The idea of defending the innocent, of using my knowledge of the mazes of the law and my arts of persuasive oratory to achieve a particular result. In the beginning, I absolutely loved every aspect of my work. You couldn't keep me out of court, even when I was not involved in the case. I haunted the Old Bailey, the Royal Courts of Justice, the Appeal Court. I drank it all in. But that was London, and I only had that heady life for a year or so."

"Start from the beginning," she said.

I took a deep breath. "I had a very easy life, I realize now," I said slowly. "Kind family, good education, support. I did a degree in law, then the BPTC."

"The what?"

"Oh, it's a year of training to be a barrister. I was lucky – I had a scholarship from my Inn. You know about the Inns of Court?" Rachel shrugged. "Well, perhaps you don't really need to. I worked hard, though. Did mini-pupillages that year." Catching her look, I said, "After the BPTC – the Bar

Professional Training Course – if you're lucky you get taken on by a chambers as a pupil, two sets of six months each, when you follow senior barristers around, being a dogsbody and learning by observation and emulation. But before that, while you're still training, you can get shorter taster periods, which are good experience. I was only twenty-two when I was called to the Bar – ridiculously young and I knew nothing of life's realities, certainly not at first hand. My pupillages taught me a lot, though. I followed some amazing barristers, and I learned a few dodges. After that I was even luckier to be offered tenancy straight away at the same chambers. Some people have to wait a long time. It's nerve-racking, as well as expensive."

"They must have thought well of you, then," Rachel said.

"Who knows? I'm sure there were others just as good, or better. Like I said, I worked hard, I was super-keen and always available. I didn't mind the grotty jobs. I did pro bono work when I could – that's work for nothing. I threw myself into everything. I remember it now: the ambience of the Inns, like a little medieval London hidden in the modern city, its own cloistered world; and the parties! There was a lot of heavy drinking going on in those days. My Inn was notorious for it. But for me it was only for that short time; it all came to an end in 1997."

"What happened in 1997?"

"I got married. Do you want a refill?"

She got up and stretched. "Maybe in a minute. What I need now is the loo. Occupational hazard, as I'm sure you remember."

While she was gone I refilled the kettle. It was strange, remembering the days when, it seemed to me, I was a different person – enthusiastic, energetic, optimistic, loud, cheerful. And that didn't end with my marriage, not then; what ended was my life in London's law circles with the opportunities it offered.

"So," Rachel said as she plumped back down on my sofa and accepted a steaming mug of her peculiar-smelling tea, "how did you meet Richard?" She frowned momentarily. "That's if you don't mind talking about him."

I shook my head. "I don't want to see him. Or speak to him, if I can avoid it. But the manner of our meeting has its humorous side." I stretched out my legs and took a sip of coffee. "You see me as I am now – forty-three, slightly too well padded, short, blonde – maybe even the occasional stray wisp of grey. Imagine how I was back then – in my twenties, slim, blonde, just as short, but young and fresh-faced, even with an air of innocence. Totally deceptive." I smiled at the thought. "I enjoyed the contrast between how I seemed and what I said. People didn't expect this girlish creature to speak as she did, and about such terrible things – sad things sometimes, hilarious things, and often rather sordid things. My clients' unusual sexual preferences. And so on."

"And did you have it then, your fabulously commanding voice?"

This made me laugh. "I believe I was working on it," I said.

"Because," Rachel said, "you probably don't realize how unexpected it is – so powerful, and coming from such a small person!"

"So I've been told. Anyway, I was invited to a dinner party. I dressed appropriately, certainly not in any brazen, cleavage-flashing way. For some while I held my peace. But I couldn't help but notice the very good-looking man with the warm brown eyes and shock of coppery hair some way up the table who kept giving me quizzical looks. But then something came up in conversation regarding the law and my opinion was sought. Here was my moment to be a shocking little show-off. I can't remember exactly what it was I said, but it involved my client's interesting private habits, and I didn't mince my words. Of course I kept confidentiality – it was all anonymous. I remember a few gasps and sniggers around the table, and Richard laughing.

"Afterwards he said it was the contrast – the demure, almost childlike outward appearance and the plain-speaking, uninhibited use of language – that bowled him over. He said I was like a plummy, foul-mouthed schoolgirl, and he found me hilarious."

"What about you?"

"Oh, well, I was bowled over too! Good looks, energy, ambition, charm, and never taking no for an answer. That was Richard. The only drawback was that he wanted to go back to Brant. He was in London for a meeting with a potential client. He had it all worked out – how his business would thrive where there was less competition, where things were cheaper, and he'd already bought some derelict properties. I was sorry to leave London, but Brant was familiar to me. I'd grown up here; my parents and two of my brothers were here. And I would have followed Richard anywhere, then.

"So we got married after about eight months of travelling up and down from Brant to London, and I moved down here, and we occupied one of his semi-renovated properties. I started practising at Hartington Chambers as a junior, and for that short time we were happy. We didn't have much at the beginning, but Richard worked very hard and was beginning to succeed, and I tried to make my name with every case that came my way: road traffic accidents, divorces, parents fighting over custody of their children. Some petty crime. Even inquests and courts martial – I wasn't fussy. Apart from work we didn't go anywhere, no holidays or weekends away, just a bit of socializing and a lot of sex. So yes, I was happy, and I suppose he was too, for then."

"And then it all went to pot," Rachel murmured.

"How did you know?"

"Just the way you're telling it," Rachel said calmly. "But I don't know why."

"Ah," I said softly. "The *why* was Millie."

"Are you sure you don't mind me knowing all this?" Rachel said.

"No, it's OK." I took a deep breath. "We both wanted children – eventually. Him more than me, I suspect. He had no family and seemed keen to found a dynasty! I was more lukewarm about it. Children would cramp my style, restrict my upward rise, ruin my figure. I was a long way from being ready. Then Millie happened, far too soon. We accepted it and came round to the idea, in time. I carried on working, determined to keep going till the last possible moment. Anyway, I was in court and late for another appointment. As usual I was wearing my high-heeled court shoes. There was a blood-red carpet which didn't lie properly. My heel caught and I toppled over. I was seven months pregnant."

"Oh dear."

"Oh dear, indeed. That night I went into premature labour. It was awful. So much pain, so much blood. Anyway, not to over-dramatize, Millie was born, almost eight weeks early, and she wasn't well. They whisked her away pretty quickly, because I was even more unwell, though at the time I wasn't completely aware. Later they told me I had an unsuspected genetic condition which meant my body's connective tissue was weak. I couldn't understand this; clearly I hadn't inherited it from my mother, who gave birth to almost full-term triplets naturally, and then fifteen months later had me. Well, I bled and bled. In the end there was serious alarm. The normal measures they use to stop excessive bleeding post-partum weren't working. I was out of it: Richard had to agree or I could have died. I had to have a hysterectomy. So that put paid to the dynasty." I paused and Rachel stayed silent. "I had a sick baby. They were worried about her breathing, her kidneys, her heart. She had infections. Nobody knew if her brain was affected. And I was ill for some time. It was horrific. Richard was good – I must give him his due. When they finally let us out – me first, then Millie – he looked after us. But I was also afflicted with post-natal depression, probably not helped by my weakened physical state and all the horrors the three of us had been through. Yes, he tried to be an attentive husband and father, and he's always been a good dad to Millie, even now, but I'm fairly sure that awful time was when he started on the first of his many infidelities. The way I was, I wasn't much use to him. He just got what he needed elsewhere, I suppose."

Rachel pursed her lips. "Did you know about all that, at the time?"

"Kind of. Or very soon after. But I put it to one side. Once Millie was out of danger, once she started finally to thrive, I concentrated on work, and Richard put most of his energies into building his business. But I suppose I did know at some level, and maybe that killed off something in me."

"Your trust in him, I imagine," Rachel said with some acidity.

"My belief in us as a unit. Anyway, it's all in the past. We soldiered on amicably enough, for Millie's sake and for the sake of domestic peace. But something had definitely gone. Perhaps it was never there in the first place. Perhaps it's all an illusion. What do you think, Rachel?"

"What's an illusion?" she asked softly.

"Oh, I don't know. Domestic harmony. The possibility of people understanding each other. The whole marriage and family thing."

She shook her head, smiling faintly. "You're speaking from your own bitter experience, Anna. But it's not an illusion – it's an uncomfortable reality. I can't speak for you, or for anyone else, and no set-up is perfect. But it can work, and it can bring joy as well as frustration. I have daily evidence of that. And in your case, whatever else went wrong, you have Millie, who seems to have survived her bumpy beginning."

I drained my cup and put it on the small table at my side. "You're right. I hadn't realized I was storing up so much bitterness. But seeing Richard, obviously prospering, looking so sleek and smug, with someone so young, beautiful and adoring – not to say fertile! – stirred up the sludge, I suppose."

"No surprise."

The phone rang in the hall. "Who still uses the landline?" I muttered. "I hope it's not Dad with some emergency. No, I reckon that'll be Geoffrey. Excuse me, Rachel."

It was indeed Geoffrey, who had been alerted by John and was ringing to see how I was doing. I reassured him. He didn't ask about the case – deliberately, I thought.

When I returned to the living room, Rachel said, "Your mobile buzzed while you were out."

"Oh." I scrolled down and found a message from Janet: "Just wanted to see if you are OK. Also, Elizabeth and I, having reread your defence statement, agreed this is why we pay you so much." I chuckled and texted back: "Why have I not noticed the millions in the bank? You are very droll. Thank you and Elizabeth for your confidence."

"Something funny?" Rachel asked.

I sighed, sobering. "Not really. Just a tiny spark of merriment in a pretty dark place. My clerk has a unique sense of humour. I can't say much, but right now I'm involved in a case which has tested my conscience."

"I thought barristers flushed their conscience down the toilet every time they donned a wig."

"Ha, that's harsh! But you know what, there's some truth in what you say. Typically we love to win. Sometimes what's right goes out of the window. I thought I'd long since come to terms with the contradictions that are part of the system, but this case has made me wonder." I paused, thinking. How much could I tell her? Very little. "There's been a conflict," I said slowly, feeling my way, "between Anna the lawyer and Anna the Christian. There may also be an impact on Anna the parent, and that's the hardest part."

She frowned. "Sounds scary."

I nodded. "It might be. It's like, I don't know, walking a very narrow path in court heels, an overgrown path where thorn-bushes are threatening to take over and try to scratch you at every turn."

"I have been praying for you, you know," Rachel said. "As I said I would."

"Thank you. I know others do too. It may be all that's keeping me on that rocky little path."

"Are you back at the abbey?"

"Yes. I didn't go yesterday, obviously."

"And?"

"It's good. A homecoming. But also probably another reason why my conscience is troubled."

Rachel was quiet for a moment, I supposed digesting what I had said. Then she seemed to veer off at a tangent, in a way that I was beginning to anticipate. "I was thinking about what we talked about, oh, a while ago. And you said something like the more you have, the more you have to lose. That love makes you vulnerable. You were right. And I knew it, didn't I? Because of my dad. If I believed in fortune, I'd call Michael and Jonathan, Jasper, Dulcie, this unknown little person" – she patted her stomach – "hostages to fortune. But I don't, and I don't think you do either. I believe – or I tell myself I do – in God's providence and care, even though often circumstances make me – not doubt, not really, but I do wonder – and the only conclusion I ever come to is that all God's ways are unfathomable to human understanding." She flashed me a smile. "It used to be a simple equation. Just me and my work, my focus, my obsession, if you like, driving me on and defending me from the terrifying reality of my humanity. Because loving someone is very alarming. You've given them power over you, opened yourself up to hurt. I saw that in Eve Rawlins, though I didn't really understand at the time. When it came to me that I loved Michael, which took a while – because, you know, I can be extremely dense! – I was fearful, in denial. What if he didn't feel the same and I lost him and all that went with him? Even when I knew he loved me, when we were married and parents, living side by side, and I had daily evidence that his love was deep and true, that I could depend on him, there were still moments of fear – not that either of us would change, but that death would rob us of what we most prized. And I know that will happen. As a human arrangement, one day we will be lost to one another." She wrapped her arms around herself, as if in defence against such cold thoughts. "I wouldn't change a thing. It's been worth it. But it still creeps up on me sometimes, that knowledge, that shudder of terror."

"Yes. I remember you saying something about that. But even when you thought yourself invulnerable, you weren't," I said.

Rachel smiled wryly. "No. It was an illusion. Shattered by a woman wielding a kitchen knife."

I pondered. "And of all human loves, the love for your child leaves you most open to hurt."

She nodded. "Yes. As Jonathan grew inside me physically, he grew as an idea in my mind as well. He made his own space. And now that space can never be closed, even if – God forbid – he should die before me." Momentarily she closed her eyes against imagined anguish. "You know about that. You have a space in your heart and mind and life that is Millie."

I smiled and sighed at the same time. "Yep. A big, unwieldy, intractable space. Sometimes, I think, filled with rampant all-devouring weeds." I felt a strange urgency, a need to express thoughts that were still coming together. "But Rachel, thanks to you and others I am remembering what I used to believe more actively than I do now. I've had time to think the past couple of days, and I have to ditch my tarnished self-image. I can't let what Richard did to me affect me any more. I have to go forward with what faith I can muster. I have to remember there is One who defends us daily, who loves and provides infinitely. I know it's impossible for us to comprehend fully; our minds are limited and our love is narrow. But his is not. And we can depend on him infinitely, because he died and rose and defeated death for us. I used to know this with everything I had, and I want it back. Of course we still fear death; we always will, as human animals, both our own death and that of those we love. But we have to remind ourselves that it isn't permanent for those that are his. We still have to go through it, just as he did. But we'll come out the other side – rejoicing, I hope."

"Yeah. Wise words. But hard to keep in sight!" She smiled, and those icy eyes kindled. "I think I need a refill. I haven't talked this much in ages."

We chatted on for a while, mostly about inconsequential things, and then she said she had to get back home. As she hesitated by the front door, she said, "I hope that case of yours pans out OK. Will you have to speechify in court?"

I shook my head. "Much as I still relish the opportunity of speechifying, especially these days when oratory is not often required, I am hoping that this won't come to trial. Better that way – to avoid any miscarriage, to keep the whole thing as low-key as we can, to avoid a media circus, not to mention the waste of money and court time. But no one really knows what's going to happen. It's not my decision. I've done what I can. Now we can only wait."

Something about my conversation with Rachel, something about Rachel herself, sparked a train of thought in me that was unusually optimistic, almost buoyant. Perhaps it was the trajectory of her story from hard and narrow and self-absorbed to a warmer and more outward-looking life. I had said I needed to ditch my self-image which, though I had described it as "tarnished", was probably in a direr condition than that: more like crumbling at the edges. The bitterness I harboured was toxic and would not only eat away at me but also poison other aspects of my life.

I had recalled to myself and Rachel the hopeful, energetic young thing I had been, and now I found more memories resurfacing from those days. In my second year as a law student I had joined a guided tour of the Inns of Court that someone had organized for us. My memory dished up images of London's incessant racket suddenly reduced to a distant hum as we moved into a world of film-set quaintness, often lit by the dull glow of gas lamps. I remembered gaping up, with the others, at the majestic Gothic Revival that is the Royal Courts of Justice; later, when I passed them nearly every day, I ceased to notice – it was all just a blur of fountains, gardens, squares, and cobbled lanes. But I recalled with clarity the dining hall of Middle Temple where, so our guide informed us, the first performance of *Twelfth Night* had taken place in 1602, possibly in the presence of its author. It may have been this extraordinary thought that led me to choose Middle Temple for my own Inn: I, a nineteen-year-old rookie from the shires, would breathe Shakespeare's air. Did I think some lingering magic of his might aid my own oratory?

I had been back only a few times since leaving London almost twenty years before, and I wondered what, if anything, had changed. In my mind, despite the interjections of my more cynical self, it retained at least some of its glamour, if only in bleak contrast with the realities of the present. In 2012 a piece of legislation known as the Legal Aid, Sentencing and Punishment of Offenders Act had significantly reduced cases eligible for legal aid, all in the service of saving money. The legal profession ground its teeth, claiming that cuts to funding meant that fewer people could gain access to legal advice. For the criminal barrister in particular, income was greatly reduced. I thought of the barristers' strike that had taken place the year before in protest against these and other measures, and I wondered what had truly been achieved. Was I mad even to consider the lure of London? The same restrictions would apply; but would there be more scope? Was it even feasible? Why was I even thinking in such ways? I thought about the case I was even at that moment defending: committed as I was to seeing the case collapse, I acknowledged a twinge of disappointment not to have the opportunity to stand up in court. With a shudder I even wondered what there was, once Millie was at university, to keep me in Brant.

FIVE

When I changed the dressing on my neck the next morning it looked, I thought, slightly inflamed. Blisters had formed, but I assumed that was to be expected. Perhaps the antibiotics were taking their time to bite. My mood of the previous day persisted, and I did what I could with a new dressing, draped a scarf apparently carelessly, and went to work. The Leaman case was, for the time being, in the hands of someone else, but there was work to do, and no doubt a backlog, despite the heroic efforts of Janet to disperse my share of incoming cases among my colleagues. At the very least there would be paperwork to square away and routine e-mails to answer. I hailed Janet as I passed and swept into my room.

Perhaps she noticed something unusual; I didn't normally breeze in exuding expectant confidence. Perhaps I was even humming. I had barely hung up my coat, pulled up my chair, and opened my computer when she sidled in. For some reason Janet rarely simply walked; she either stomped or slithered. That day she was serpentine, an impression strengthened by the narrowness of her eyes.

I looked up. "What?"

She didn't answer, but, to my surprise, came closer and leaned over the desk, frowning. "There's something wrong."

"With what?"

"With you." Then she sniffed.

"What are you talking about?"

She pulled a face. "Anna, that's gross."

"What is, for heaven's sake?"

"Take off that scarf." Matching her frown, I did so. "You need to look in a mirror. Your dressing is wet. I think your wound is weeping, and I have to tell you it smells."

She was right. I covered it up again and went down the corridor to the washroom. Gingerly I peeled the dressing away and found that the redness had intensified, and the blisters had spread and burst. It was not a pleasant sight.

Janet came in after me and closed the door. "Have you got a clean one?"

"No. I just changed it before I left the house."

"You need to get that seen to."

I bit my lip. "I've got a lot to get through. Maybe at lunchtime."

"Don't leave it. The work will still be here when you get back."

I turned to her. My light mood had crashed, and I felt foolish tears prickle my eyes. "You've already done a lot of covering for me."

She shook her head. "A few more hours won't make much difference. To be honest, I don't think you gave yourself long enough to recover."

I heaved a sigh. "And to think I was feeling better this morning than I have for a long time. I was even thinking I might have a go at resuscitating my London career."

"What?"

"Never mind. You're right. I'll get myself back to the hospital. Sorry."

As I left she was shaking her head.

Luckily when I got to A and E the same young doctor who had treated me on Saturday evening was again on duty, and he remembered me. I had to wait some time to be seen, and sitting on that hard utilitarian chair, in a row of similar chairs, surrounded by drab walls, a scuffed, stained vinyl floor at my feet, I felt misery return along with stinging pain and an alarming level of dizziness. Finally I was admitted to a cubicle, the curtains were drawn round me, and the doctor peeled the dressing away.

"Oh dear. Not what we hoped to see." He dropped the dressing into a bin and hunted in a set of plastic drawers. "Here." He tore open a paper package and handed me a large, square, gauzy cotton pad. "Hold this on the wound. I'll be back in a minute."

I was left alone with increasingly dark thoughts for what seemed a lifetime. I was sore, light-headed, queasy, and bored. I berated myself for thinking even for half a day that I could ever again shine on any stage. How vain, how stupid.

The curtain was eventually flung aside, and the young doctor stood back. "Here we are, sir. Thought you should see for yourself." He turned to me with an air of triumph. "Got the top man to look at you, Ms Milburn."

To my horror, Michael Wells, distinguished as a doctor only by the identifying lanyard round his neck, walked into the cubicle. There was a faint smile on his face. "Hello again, Anna." He turned to the young doctor. "All right, Jason, I'll go on from here."

When we were alone he pulled up a chair beside me. "Right. Let's see what's going on." He gently took the wad away from my neck. "Hmm. Yes, I see."

I felt utterly mortified. "I hope you don't think I asked to see you."

"I know you didn't," he said calmly. "How could you have known I was even in the hospital today?" He fished in his shirt pocket, put on a pair of glasses, and examined my neck intently, not meeting my eyes. "My impression is you are not the sort of person to demand special treatment. Anyway, Jason did the right thing. Burns are something of a particular interest for me. And I was here. So you don't have to complain."

"I'm not complaining!" I protested. "I am simply—"

"Keep still please." He pulled some gloves from a dispenser on the wall and put them on. Gently he probed my increasingly painful wound. "I imagine that's very sore."

"It is."

"Well," he said, "thankfully it's not as bad as it might be." He peeled off the gloves and threw them in the bin. "I'll get them to give you a different kind of dressing. What antibiotics are you on?" I told him. "OK, perhaps we need to revisit that. And it might be a good idea if you got the nurse at your GP surgery to change the dressing daily. And don't get it wet."

"So I can't wash my hair," I said dully.

"Perhaps not, just for a few days till it subsides," he said gently. "It needs looking after. As do you. A burn injury, even a relatively minor one, especially when it's on or near the face, can deliver a shock. Don't push yourself too hard, even if that doesn't come naturally to you. It'll be the quickest way to healing."

I nodded. "Not that I'm especially vain – at least not in that way – but what about the possibility of scarring?"

"Do as I've suggested, and it should be fine." His voice was serious, but there was amusement in his eyes. I realized he was well versed in dealing with difficult women, on top of a long career of tending to injured people.

I tried to smile. "Thank you. I'll do my best."

He pulled back the curtain. Then he turned back to me. "I should thank you too," he said. "Rachel has enjoyed your meetings. She doesn't have many friends; not those who can cope with her – how shall I put it? – *direct* way of speaking."

"Neither do I," I said. "She's a remarkable person. And for some reason she makes me feel more, I don't know, positive."

"I think she'd be glad to know that," he said with a smile that lit up his dark eyes. "She is under the impression that normally she has the effect of terrifying people."

This made me laugh despite myself. "I guess that doesn't surprise me. But I am made of stern stuff."

As he left I heard him chuckle quietly. Once again, I thought, *Lucky Rachel*.

I went back to chambers, more to report to Janet than to do any work. She followed me into my room. "I've got a new dressing," I told her. "A different type of antibiotic. I saw a very senior plastic surgeon – my friend Rachel's husband. He said it's not too bad, as long as I look after it." I picked up a pile of files from my desk. "I'll take these home and look at them. And I'll see how I feel in the morning. I won't come in if I feel unwell. OK?"

She nodded grudgingly. "I suppose. Chambers won't fall apart if you're not here, you know."

"I know. We'll only fall apart if *you're* not here." A thought struck me. "Janet, wouldn't you like a nice, shiny assistant? I know you've got what's-her-name, the mouse, but couldn't you use a new addition?"

She bristled. "What for? Don't I have a whole bunch of them at my beck and call?"

"Yes, you do. I just thought maybe someone lively and keen, some bright young thing, to take the edge off the boring stuff."

"Hmm." I could tell she was not convinced.

She followed me out of the door and down the corridor to her own office. She paused in the doorway. "What did you mean? Earlier, when you said something about resuscitating your London career."

"Oh, forget it. It's not going to happen."

She scowled. "You're not thinking of leaving, then?"

I raised an eyebrow. "I thought you said you could manage without me."

"Don't annoy me – I'm dangerous," she said. "I have the power to send you to the worst Magistrates' Courts in the county. I can give you the dreariest cases and hold back every cheque."

"So you can. I am contrite."

"No, you're not. For goodness' sake, go home. Some of us are busy around here."

I took the rest of that day off, and the next, only leaving the house to go to my GP surgery, where a young nurse furnished me with a clean dressing. The rest of the time I lounged on the sofa in my pyjamas, trying to deal with the papers I had brought home, more than once falling asleep and waking to find everything on the floor. Millie, when she was not at school, was attentive, bringing me cups of tea and sandwiches, seeing to Gordon, doing the small chores that keep a household ticking over. To my surprise I was tired, and even when I had spent much of the day nodding off I slept all night as well. Eventually the effects of the accident began to wear off. The new dressing had something in it which facilitated healing, and my wound gradually became less sore as the inflammation subsided.

By the afternoon of the second day I managed to put together some comments on the papers I had brought home. I e-mailed them to Janet, feeling moderately pleased with myself. That evening I dragged myself up from the sofa, took a long bath, careful not to get my neck wet, and cooked a meal for the two of us.

"You look a bit better, Mum," Millie said.

"I want to get back to work," I groused. My enforced idleness hadn't improved my temper.

"I'd *love* to have several days off just to sleep," Millie said. "You're such a workaholic."

I was loading the dishwasher when the phone rang. "Anna, it's Rachel. How are you?"

"Oh! Hello. Better, thank you. Determined to go back to work as soon as possible."

"Michael told me he'd seen you in the hospital. I was concerned that you'd got worse." She hesitated. "I didn't want to bother you at home in case you were asleep. So I went to your chambers."

This was a surprise. "Did you?"

I heard her quiet laugh. "Bit of an impulse really. I was shopping at that supermarket where we met. Do you remember? Where I left my credit card on the table. It's just on the other side of the square from your chambers so I went in and had a word with your clerk."

"You met the redoubtable Janet! She didn't say."

"Yes. She's quite formidable, isn't she?"

"Ha! I wouldn't be surprised to find people say that about you."

"They do. I don't *feel* formidable. Any more than you do, I imagine."

"Hmm."

"I liked Janet. I thought she was, I don't know, different."

"That she is."

Again Rachel hesitated. "We had a good chat, actually. And she said something… well, I don't know how to put it, and it isn't my business anyway, but…"

Light dawned. "Was it about some foolish throwaway remark of mine involving my going back to London to polish up my rusty career?"

"Something like that. She seemed worried. She didn't exactly say so, but it's clear to me she admires you tremendously."

I hooted with laughter. "Now that I don't believe. Janet admires no one, least of all me. Why should she?"

"She has every reason, I'd say," Rachel said quietly. "But whatever you believe or don't, it's obvious she doesn't want you to go. And nor do I."

For a moment I couldn't answer her, I was so amazed. Then I said, "Oh. I didn't know I was so popular."

I heard her laugh. "I don't know about popular, but you have two admirers at least, and I'm sorry it's just Janet and me."

"Well, I'm not sorry at all," I said. "And thank you for the vote of confidence. But you should know it's your fault I was thinking in those terms in the first place."

Now it was her turn to sound surprised. "My fault? How come?"

"After you went home the other day I felt really positive, thought I could somehow retrieve that person I had been, full of energy and enthusiasm, up for conquering the legal world. Very naive. Even my Millie is wiser."

"I understand that," Rachel said. There was a hint of strain in her voice. "For all that I've gained, I know I've also lost something. I wouldn't swap, wouldn't for a moment go back, even if it was possible. But I sometimes think about the old Rachel, horrible though she was, and I feel a twinge of regret for that single-minded self-belief that I had, the sheer *dash* that I brought to surgery. It's all an illusion, though."

"Yes, I know. And in my saner moments I'd far rather have two such admirers – no, *friends* – than dazzle at the Old Bailey. Not that I ever did, actually. But I thought I might."

Now we were both laughing. "Well, that's a relief," Rachel said. "And I was wondering if you'd come over for supper one day. Don't worry – I'm no chef, but it'd be Michael cooking."

I was touched. "Yes, I'd love to."

"Saturday? If she hasn't anything better to do, Millie would be most welcome too."

"I'll ask her, but I imagine she has plans. She usually does."

"That's OK. See you Saturday, then – about seven? Oh, I'm to ask you if there's anything you dislike."

"Very little. And thank you."

I went back to work on Friday feeling a little drained but otherwise improved. I worked at my desk all morning, then I tapped on Janet's door. "I'm going out to buy myself some lunch," I announced. "Can I get you anything?"

She shook her head. "I brought my own." She had her

phone in one hand; with the other she tapped the lid of a large purple lunchbox which almost matched her jumper.

"By the way," I said, as nonchalantly as I could manage, "I thought you should know I won't be going to London any time soon. Or ever, come to that."

She didn't answer, just looked at me over her sparkly glasses and nodded knowingly.

"Unless," I added, as if having an afterthought, "I get headhunted for some high-profile case and I just can't say no."

She put her phone down and folded her arms. "As you're feeling so full of yourself, I have a nice job for you. Monday morning, nine thirty. Minor fraud, Tuxton Magistrates. You'll be defending, and it won't be a walkover. I'll leave the instructions on your desk. It'll do you good to do some proper work."

I was horrified. "Nine thirty? But Tuxton's forty miles away! And the parking's impossible! Janet, you are a sadist."

"You need to come back down to earth," she said with an evil grin. "You're getting far too many over-the-top ideas. Not to mention all the other barristers covering for you while you attend to higher matters like murder. *Plus* all this attention-seeking falling-over stuff." She picked up her phone again and dialled, dismissing me and grinning broadly.

I shook my head. "Why ever do I put up with you?"

"Because you know I'm right."

Saturday evening with Rachel and Michael was a small oasis for me. It was a fine spring evening and I decided to leave the car at home. As I came to the outskirts of the city and strolled down to the riverside path in the twilight there was peace, and a soft breeze that carried with it a faint scent of the country. I breathed it in, remembering the village where I'd grown up, surrounded by fields and woods, and realized that I missed it.

Michael was an attentive host and an excellent cook, and since I wasn't driving I had several glasses of wine and became, as I liked to think, quite eloquent – but with hindsight I was probably garrulous. Nobody seemed to mind. In fact both Rachel and Michael laughed at my witticisms and seemed fascinated by my stories. I declined the offer of a lift home, and as I walked through the darkness back into the city I felt a sense of well-being that had been missing for a long time. My back still ached, my neck, though better, still stung when I moved suddenly, but somehow it didn't matter.

On Sunday morning I went to the service at the abbey. People I knew, including John Sutcliffe, greeted me warmly, asking after my health. I seemed to be in a kind of bubble, but I was in no hurry to burst it. Then, one of the verses of the final hymn shook me a little, reminding me of a sterner reality. "The Lord is King! Child of the dust... The Judge of all the earth is just." I shivered, an image of a judge I knew appearing unbidden before my eyes, red-faced, black-browed. I thought of all the judges I knew, all the Silks, all the advocates, busily interpreting human laws, when in the end there was One who would dispense perfect justice to all of us "children of dust". I felt much of my insouciant mood drain away. It seemed a heavy responsibility in that moment, as much for a grubby fraudster as for a murderous destroyer, to do a good job, to try at the very least to approach the notion of justice served. I had spent the weekend preparing the case for Monday morning, and I would do my best in court; but I went home sobered.

On Monday I got up early. My daily visit to the nurse at the surgery would have to wait till after the Tuxton case was over. If it wasn't too late, I would call in on the way home. A shower was difficult with my dressing, so I had a quick bath, dressed carefully, and swathed the inevitable scarf round my neck. I checked that I had everything I needed in my briefcase. I called up the stairs to Millie, who answered groggily. "Mil, you need to get up. I don't have time for Gordon this morning. Please, at least let him out in the garden and feed him."

She appeared at the top of the stairs, her hair all over the place, her eyes glazed with sleep. "Where're you going so early?" Her voice was slurred.

"I told you. Tuxton. You'll have to sort yourself out this morning."

"I always do," she said sullenly.

"Whatever. I'll see you later. Have a good day."

Her only answer was a sceptical grunt as she vanished back into her bedroom.

The Monday morning traffic was as heavy and ill-tempered as I'd expected, but thinned out when I joined the A road beyond the suburbs and into more rural regions. I opened the window an inch or two and was rewarded with birdsong. I took the slip road into Tuxton and then spent a frustrating twenty minutes trying to park. Eventually I found a space in a supermarket car park half a mile from the courthouse and trudged through the streets with my heavy briefcase and a bag containing my court shoes.

I did my best that morning. My client, an unprepossessing, red-nosed man in an eye-catching checked jacket, was found guilty – as he almost certainly was – but I managed to get his sentence reduced and afterwards he shook my hand in pathetic gratitude. As he was led away, I felt again that strange sense of foreboding. What of the altogether more serious case of the murdered police officer? We had heard nothing more from the prosecution, and I imagined tense discussions at Palace and perhaps hard questions being put to the investigating police team. Whatever the outcome, much as I wanted to succeed, to get Leaman off for what I believed were the right reasons, I wondered if in this case, as in many others, anything like justice would be achieved.

I was changing back into my walking shoes and thinking about stopping somewhere for lunch on the way home when one of the court clerks put her head round the door. "Ms Milburn – there's a phone call for you. You can take it in my office."

It could only be Janet, because who else knew I was here? She also knew that I always switched my phone off when I was in court. As I followed the clerk down the corridor, briefcase and bag in hand and coat slung over my shoulders, I wondered if, finally, there was news from Clive Stephenson, and I felt my heart hammering high in my chest.

It was Janet, and she sounded uncharacteristically tense. "Is your case done?"

"Yes, fifteen minutes ago. We lost, but—"

"Never mind that now," she interrupted. "I've had your brother on the phone."

"Which one?" I asked stupidly, as if it mattered.

"Alastair. He's been trying to reach you all morning. When he couldn't, he rang here. He knew I'd know where you were. Anna, you've got big family trouble. Your mum's gone missing."

People say all sorts of things about how they feel when they get bad news – they go cold, they feel faint or numb, their scalp prickles. Nothing of the sort happened to me; I simply, for a moment, stood dumbfounded.

"What? What did you say?"

"Look, Anna, I don't know any more. Ring your brother."

As I hung up, the clerk gave me a sympathetic smile. "Is everything all right? Can I get you a coffee perhaps? A nicer one than the machine can offer?"

"Thank you," I said distractedly. "Perhaps that would be a good idea."

Once she had gone I sank down into a chair and dialled Al's number. Kathryn answered; her voice was cold, but I barely registered it. "Just a minute. I'll get Alastair."

There was the sound of voices from somewhere, but I couldn't identify them. Then Alastair answered. "Anna, found you at last."

"I was in court, Al. Sorry you've had a job getting hold of me. What's happened?"

He spoke calmly, but I could hear fear in every syllable. "Dad rang me before eight this morning. He put Mum to bed in the normal way and had an early night himself. Poor man's worn out."

"I know." The clerk came back with a china cup and saucer and two biscuits. I nodded my thanks and she went out, closing the door quietly behind her.

"He got up this morning and found the front door open. When he went to get Mum up, she wasn't there. Her green coat and her huge bag were missing, but her shoes were still in the hallway."

"So she's gone out in her slippers."

"He hunted all through the house, the garden, the shed,

just in case. And all through the village. He asked people, but no one had seen her. When he got home again he found a note. She'd tried to tell him where she'd gone, but it was gibberish, completely incomprehensible."

"Al, this is terrible. She hasn't been out by herself in years. How will she cope? What was she thinking?"

"We never know that, do we? Do you have any idea what might have been in her handbag? Would she have had any money? Anything to identify her?"

"All there was in that bag was a pack of tissues and a comb, Al." I heard him swear softly. "Look, what's been organized? Where is everybody?"

"I'm at home, and so is Kathryn. And Sam. The other children we packed off to school – they would only get in the way. They are understandably very upset, and we didn't want them making it worse with Sam. You know what he's like when he's anxious, and he's fond of his grandma. Dad is at home, in case she turns up, and Ronnie and Tanya are with him. We informed the police as soon as we knew and they're looking for her."

"I'll come straight to yours. Be there in about an hour."

"All right. Please, drive carefully."

When he'd hung up I drank my coffee as quickly as possible without risking another scalding. I was barely thinking – or perhaps my thoughts were whirring so fast I couldn't catch them as they passed. The caffeine took effect, and I thought I should let Millie know. Obviously she would be in classes now, so I sent her a text. Almost immediately I had a reply. "Oh, no! Nothing much on this afternoon, just revision. I'll come now. Tiff can drive me." I sighed deeply and put the empty cup and saucer on the edge of the desk. Millie would be useful: she could soothe and distract Sam and keep her cousins calm when they came home from school. It was going to be a long day.

Driving to Alastair's, I remembered to pray for my mother's safety. Prayer, as I knew, could achieve many things, the majority of which we mortals are not equipped to understand. But for me, at the very least it served as a reminder that I had no need to bear everything alone, and that it was anyway useless to attempt it. I thought of my mother, the mystery of her dimming thought-processes. I couldn't begin to fathom what it was that had, so suddenly as it seemed, made her get out of bed, put on her coat – did she put it on over her nightdress? Would Dad have left her clothes for the day ready, and did she put those on first? She'd remembered her bag, though its contents would have been of no use to her, but she hadn't remembered her shoes. Perhaps they weren't there; perhaps only her slippers were handy. At least she hadn't gone barefoot. But where was she going? Clearly she'd had some plan, because she had tried to leave Dad a note. Somehow that she had thought of him was a comfort. Maybe she was not so locked into her own tiny world as we all imagined, and the years of relying on one another had carved a habit so far unconquered by her illness.

Lord, keep her safe, our dear, vulnerable mother. Keep her from harm, from roads and rivers, from anyone who might wish her ill. Please let someone find her before she becomes disorientated and distressed. Please bring her back. I'm sorry I seem to remember you only when I need something. Please keep me from that pernicious unthinking habit of coping with everything by myself. I need to create better habits, ones where you are there from the beginning.

Alastair and Kathryn's house was on the other side of the river from mine, on the outskirts of the city, so thankfully I was able to avoid the centre. I parked in the road by their driveway and walked up to their front door, which was open. I left my files in the car.

I'd caught sight of Al in the small front room which served as his study. He was on the phone and waved when he saw me. Otherwise no one seemed to be about, so I called up the stairs. Soon Sam came bounding down and enveloped me in a hug. "Auntie Nanna! Millie's here, Millie's here!" Millie came down the stairs behind him. "Hi, Mum. You OK?"

"As far as we can be, love. Where's your aunt?"

"No idea. There's some sandwiches in the kitchen if you're hungry. We are, aren't we, Sam?"

Sam grinned and grabbed Millie's hand. "Yeah. But I don't want a sandwich. I want cake."

"OK, let's see if there is any. Come on, Mum."

In the kitchen I sat on a high stool and kicked off my shoes. I rubbed my feet with a sigh of mingled pain and relief. Millie found a plate for me and piled it with sandwiches. She put the kettle on without asking me if I wanted anything – she knew me well. Sam was rooting about in the larder and emerged with a look of beaming triumph, holding a blue and gold tin in both hands. "Cake."

"You sure your mum isn't saving it for something, Samuel?" Millie said. Her tone was stern but Sam giggled: he wasn't fooled.

"No, she isn't," a voice came from the doorway – a voice that sounded as if it had blown directly from the Arctic. "Help yourself. Hello, Anna."

My sister-in-law was leaning on the doorframe, her arms held down by her sides, her hands clenched. Normally

I maintained civil relations with all my brothers' wives, though I wouldn't have called any of them friends, even after so many years. But today the very air smelled hostile – a clear sign that for Kathryn I was a traitor.

"Hello, Kathryn," I said, deliberately keeping my voice low and even. "Has there been any news?"

"Not that I've heard." She turned away from me. "Is that tea you're making, Millie? Yes, I'd love some, thank you." We all watched in silence as Millie poured tea for herself and us, and made a cold drink for Sam, who was obliviously munching cake. Mug in hand, Kathryn turned back to me, and I saw she was preparing her weapons.

"So," she said. "In court today, weren't you? So Alastair said. Defending? Not that evil man, I hope?" Her voice was brittle.

"No, it was a fraud case, in Tuxton."

"I see. But you *are* going to defend him, aren't you?"

I saw Millie frown; I turned to look Kathryn in the eye and saw her flinch. "If you are determined to have this conversation," I murmured, "despite the other pressing concerns we have today, could we please not have it in front of the children?"

Millie didn't let me down. She took her cousin's hand, the one empty of cake. "Come on, Sammy, let's go and watch a film in the other room. I'll bring your drink."

When we were alone, I said to Kathryn, "Yes, in answer to your question, I have accepted the brief. Do you have a problem with that?"

I saw her fists clench and unclench. "You know perfectly well I do – and why."

I sighed. "But Kathryn, it's my job. I don't pick and choose. It's the cab rank rule, apart from anything else."

"The what?"

"I'm sure I've mentioned it before. I'm obliged to accept a solicitor's instructions if I am the next barrister available and sufficiently qualified – whether or not the client or the case is personally repugnant. As they are. Surely you know that."

"Frankly, I don't seem to know anything any more." I heard her voice tremble, and I felt a wave of pity. "But I don't buy that stuff about you having to do it. I'm sure there are ways to refuse. Aren't you head of chambers?"

"Not exactly – there's no such person in our set-up. But yes, I am the senior. And you're right, there are ways to avoid the rule, but they are narrow." I paused, watching her, preparing my words. "The fact is, I'm not permitted to allow my opinions about the character, reputation, conduct, guilt or innocence of any potential client to colour my judgment. But I did choose to take this client on, quite apart from that, and I did it with good reason."

She took a step forward, her face flushed. "How *could* you?" she demanded. "What possible reason could outweigh what he did to Sam? And all the other heedless children. Not to mention Liam's parents – his friend who died."

"Kathryn, please. You're Sam's mother, and of course what happened to him is dreadful, for you and Al and all the family. As Sam's aunt, it grieves me too."

"How can I believe you? You use all that skill with words to defeat me, but I just can't believe a word you say. If you had any real feeling for Sam, or for us, you would have turned that monster down flat."

I shook my head and spoke quietly. "I'm afraid there are other considerations, and I can't really discuss them while the case is ongoing. I wish you had more trust in me."

"How can I? The evidence of your selfishness is right in front of my eyes. It's always been the same, ever since I've known you. What Anna wants, Anna gets, and to blazes with anyone else's feelings. You use all those barrister's tricks to argue black is white. And everyone thinks you're so very wonderful. I don't know how you get away with it."

"Kath, enough."

My eyes swivelled to the door. Alastair stood there, Sam at his side, his eyes round and anxious.

"Mum, why are you cross?" he said, his brow furrowing.

Kathryn turned to look at him, her mouth open in a soundless wail. Millie, coming up behind Sam, took her cousin's arm.

"Hey, Sambo," she said soothingly. "You know what grown-ups are like – they're always off on one. Come on, let's go and finish your film." She gave us a reproachful shake of her head and led Sam away.

Alastair came into the kitchen. He held Kathryn by both elbows. I saw she was shaking. "This isn't helping, love," he said gently. "Especially not today." To my dismay Kathryn was crying, trying to swallow her tears and failing. She shook him off, ran out of the room and up the stairs. A door banged.

Alastair leaned on the worktop, momentarily closing his weary eyes. "I'm sorry, Anna. But you understand."

"Only too well, bro." I slid off the stool, crossed the room and gave him a hug. "No news, I assume."

He shook his head. "I was just on the phone to the police. They are actively looking. Nobody's seen her. All we can do is wait."

"Did they say anything about getting it on the news?"

Alastair nodded. "There should be something at six."

"It's horrible feeling so helpless. I want to go out there

myself and look. I just don't know where 'out there' is." I paused, thinking. "Al, would it be best if I wasn't here? For domestic peace?"

He shrugged. "Possibly. But as far as I'm concerned you're welcome to stay."

"Thanks." I bit my lip. "There are things I need to do. I ought to go home at some point and see to the dog. I must speak to my clerk as well and give her the latest. She's been covering for me a lot lately." I unwound my scarf. "See this?"

Alastair frowned. "What have you done?"

"It's a scald. Had an accident with a cup of near-boiling tea."

"Good grief, Anna! That must have been painful."

"It was. But it's healing. Look, how's this for a plan? I'll go home, walk and feed Gordon, ring chambers. I'll have my phone so you can contact me if you need to. I'll catch the news at home, then I'll come back and bring a takeaway for everyone. You can tell me what you like. I'll have to come back to fetch Millie anyway. I feel we should be together in the circumstances. But at least this gives you and Kathryn some time to talk things through if you want to."

He shook his head. "I've tried, believe me."

"I'm sorry it's caused so much trouble."

"It's OK. We'll weather it." He gave a weary smile. "Yes, I think your plan'll do nicely. Obviously I'll call you if anything changes."

"The only thing is, Al…" He raised a querying eyebrow, and I lowered my voice. "Millie doesn't know I'm defending Leaman, and I'd much rather she didn't. I don't want her hearing something she shouldn't."

"Understood."

At five to six I switched on the television. After a number of seemingly banal items of local interest, suddenly an image of my mother flashed on the screen. It was some years out of date, and she looked noticeably different, which was frustrating, but no doubt they had asked my father for a picture and he probably couldn't find anything more recent. The woman in the photo was smartly dressed, her hair well cut, her smile broad, and it was clear she had all her mental faculties intact. How was anyone to recognize my mother as she had become? I imagined her in her favourite coat, slippers on her feet, her huge bag clutched to her chest, her empty smile. Inevitably, I also imagined her in the river, or run over by a speeding truck. A treacherous idea flashed through my mind: horrible as it was to contemplate, would it be better than her vapid current existence? Would it give my father some freedom? I shook my head, as if to banish my unwelcome thoughts. I knew for my father that such freedom would be bought with too high a price. I switched off the television.

I put Gordon in the car and drove back to Alastair's, stopping on the way at a fried chicken takeaway where I loaded up with a vast quantity of carbohydrates and saturated fat, much to Gordon's fascination. Alastair and Kathryn's fifteen-year-old twins Katie and Megan, and nine-year-old William, were home from school and they all greeted me with subdued voices. Only Sam was his usual ebullient self. We sat round the big dining room table and Al dished out food. I had never known a gathering so quiet in this house. Kathryn said almost nothing and picked at her meal. Alastair tried to talk to his children about their day, but no one was particularly forthcoming. Millie, sitting next to Sam, watched everyone with thoughtful eyes.

The children disappeared as soon as they had eaten. Kathryn vanished upstairs, muttering something about taking a shower. Millie, Al, and I cleared up the debris and loaded the dishwasher, saying little. Sam was in the lounge at the front of the house, listening to his favourite music and singing along. It was odd to hear him carolling childish ditties in his deep voice.

"Have you spoken to Dad?" I asked Al.

He nodded. "Just after the news. He saw it too, of course."

"How did he seem?"

"Dazed. I don't know. Ronnie and Tanya are still there. I suppose he's holding together as best he can, but he blames himself. No surprise."

"Poor Dad. As if he hasn't had enough to bear."

Alastair looked up sharply. "What was that?" A loud scream came from the front room. "Sam?" He dropped the towel he had been holding onto the floor and sprinted from the room, almost colliding with Sam in the hallway.

"Daddy!" Sam shrieked. "I looked out of the window, and I saw Grandma! There's a police car!" He tugged at his father's sleeve. "Come and see!"

Alastair opened the front door. Two police officers, a man and a woman, were walking up the path, and between them, holding on to the man's arm and still clutching her ridiculous handbag, was my mother.

Millie and I finally got away about ten o'clock. We stopped at a park on the way and gave Gordon a quick walk and a chance to sniff somewhere new. As we closed our own front door behind us, Millie said, "I don't think I can go to bed just yet. Too much to process."

I yawned. "I know what you mean. I'm shattered, but I

don't think I'll sleep." I flopped onto the sofa with a groan of weariness.

"Isn't it odd?" Millie said, parking herself in the chair opposite. "I mean, Grandma getting it into her head to just leave the house at seven in the morning. Why would she suddenly think it was a day to get 'little Sam' – *little Sam!* He's nearly as tall as his dad! – and take him down to the river to see the swans? I know she used to do that, because she took me too sometimes, but that was years ago. We weren't even in school."

I shook my head. "And to go prepared as well. That vast bag of hers contained half a loaf. For the ducks."

"I know it's sad, Mum, but it's also a little funny."

"Hmm. Only on the surface, I'm afraid, for me anyway. I'm thinking of that pathetic moment when she looked all round at us, bewildered, and said, 'But where's little Sam?' and he's just as perplexed and says, 'Here I am, Grandma' and she frowns up at him because he's too tall and grown up, and it's not till he sits down that she thinks he's small enough to be the 'little Sam' she remembers. To me that's just sad, not funny at all. Anyway, I'm relieved she came to no harm." I shook my head. "More than twelve hours off our radar. And where was she all those hours? Till that cab driver spotted her and took her to the police station. Which reminds me, we must remember to write to that cab driver and thank him."

"Wandering about, I suppose," Millie said. "Looking for somewhere she recognized. She didn't look too bad for someone who'd been out all day walking around. It's a good five miles from Burrow Bridge to Uncle Al's."

"What amazes me most," I muttered, "is that she had a sort of lightbulb moment when the policeman asked her where she wanted to go and she recited Al and Kathryn's address! It was as if there was some momentary connection in her brain. Most of the time she doesn't even know where she lives herself."

Millie stretched and heaved herself off the chair. "I suppose I should go to bed."

"You did really well today, Mil," I said. "I was proud of you. Looking out for Sam. And the other cousins, keeping them on an even keel."

Millie looked back at me from the doorway, a strange little smile on her face. "I was proud of you too, Mum."

"What? What for?"

"I heard more of your argument with Aunt Kath than you thought," she said. "She was out of order, I reckon. I mean, I understand why, but still. And you were very restrained."

I sighed and sat up, resting my arms on my knees. "I feel for her. And for Al. Parents think about their kids, what they might become – perhaps people who could one day do some good in the world, find a cure for cancer, discover another planet – or at least you imagine they might be decent citizens with homes and jobs and children of their own, and here's Sam, stuck at fifteen for ever."

"Not even that, Mum," Millie observed. "More like five. But you can't just heap all the blame on the dealers."

"How do you mean?"

"Well, I know people say they're predators and all that, but what they're actually doing is making money. So do a lot of people who most people would think of as respectable. Like judges." She rolled her eyes. "Yeah, the dealers don't care what happens to their customers, like they don't have a conscience. And that's all wrong. But Sam and his mate weren't new-born babies. They knew the score. They have to take some of the responsibility for what happened. They took the stuff. They should have said 'no thanks', shouldn't they? Sure it's bad to see what happened to Sam and I know it's going to be like that for ever, but he was an idiot, Mum, face it."

"What you say is true, Millie. Not the bit about judges – in my experience few judges moonlight as drug dealers, if any. But we can't ever say anything like that to his mother. She's very anti-me as it is."

"I know, and she's a bit off with me as well," Millie said. "If you ask me, she's one jealous lady."

"Why do you think that is?" I asked her. "Because you and Sam are almost the same age, and she compares you?"

"Maybe, but it isn't just that," Millie said. She scuffed at the carpet with one bare toe. "She's jealous of you too."

"Hmm, I'm not sure about that. She forgets I almost lost you when you were a baby, more than once. She has three other children, all healthy, a loving husband, and a comfortable lifestyle. Why would she be jealous of me?"

"I suppose," Millie said soberly, "she sees how close you and Uncle Al are. You talk about stuff she's not interested in and she feels excluded. She sees you are a gazillion times cleverer and more confident than she is. I guess that's what you call insecurity. How old is she – in her forties? Seems to me it's about time she got over it."

This made me laugh. "Oh, Millie, you are priceless. Perhaps a bit hard hearted, but refreshingly honest."

"I can't think where I get it from," Millie said with a knowing smirk. "I'm going to bed. Night, Mum. Don't stay up too late or the bags under your eyes will be down to your knees."

She left the room and I called after her, "That's a rather

disgusting thought!" I heard her cackling with laughter as she ran lightly up the stairs.

When she had gone, I wondered just how much she had heard of that altercation with Kathryn. Had Leaman's name been mentioned? I thought not. She had given no sign of knowing facts which I wanted, for as long as I could, to keep from her. Maybe she had heard just the end of our conversation, Kathryn's accusations, her general disgust with me. I hoped so.

A few days later I decided it was about time I visited the nice young nurse at my GP surgery. My back and head still ached at times, but otherwise my injuries were less painful. I called in on my way to chambers, and while I waited I looked through some papers from my briefcase, something that had been shelved while I was concentrating on the Leaman defence statement.

"Ms Milburn? Come in, please." The nurse – Leila, I thought her name was – stood in the doorway of the treatment room and ushered me in. Gently she peeled the dressing from my neck and exclaimed, apparently with genuine pleasure, "That's healing up nicely."

"Does this mean I can wash my hair?"

"I don't see why not," the nurse replied. "Just keep an eye on it, and make sure you dry it thoroughly when you're done."

It was a relief, and I was grateful for Michael Wells' care. When I arrived at chambers there was another piece of good news. Janet hailed me from her office. "All OK with your mum?"

"As well as it can be, thanks," I said. "Safely back home and no harm done, which is a miracle, considering. And my dad's getting over all the stress. He just keeps muttering, 'I didn't know she had it in her.' It's made us all more aware, though. How we need to take time to be there for them, which can only be a plus."

"Not easy with all your busy lives," she observed. "Oh, here's a thing. That motorbike courier was here again, early. There's a letter on your desk."

I raised my eyebrows. "Clive Stephenson, do you reckon? I didn't think all this cloak-and-dagger stuff was quite his style."

She went back to her screen. "You just don't know, do you?"

The note from Stephenson came on the headed notepaper of his chambers and seemed official. He had, he said, on further consideration and after consultation with senior colleagues, decided to drop the case on the basis of insufficient evidence against the client.

I took the letter up the corridor and waved it at Janet. "Seems we did it. Our client will be a free man shortly."

She nodded. "Your expertise has triumphed once again."

I sighed. "I wonder if this might be a pyrrhic victory."

Her face was blank. "What's that when it's at home?"

"A victory gained at too great a cost. Named after some ancient Greek general."

She swivelled her chair round to face me, crossing shapely legs enveloped in black-and-green patterned tights. "I see where you're coming from. But what else could we have done?"

"Declined the brief."

"And then what? Someone else would have taken him on. There might have been a very different outcome. Maybe he'd be in jail as a murderer. With the real villain chuckling into his beer."

"Yes, but with this villain out of action. A more popular outcome, probably."

She made a rude noise. "Popular? Since when did we do *popular*? No. If you rate my opinion—"

"As you know I do," I interrupted.

"We did the right thing. Now we brace ourselves for the fallout."

I smiled, a little bleakly. We had won, as far as it went. But it was not a triumph that made me want to celebrate.

At home that evening, with a swathe of backlog dealt with and an upcoming case prepared for, I closed my files with a small groan and thought about what we might have for dinner. I'd opted recently for far too many takeaways. I scrutinized the contents of the fridge and was not encouraged. A trip to the supermarket would soon be necessary. I managed to get a few items together which would make an unexciting but reasonably healthy meal and sat at the kitchen table with a peeler and a chopping board. I could hear Millie's music pulsing through the ceiling; I knew her exams started in a few days. Despite my occasional nagging – as she would have called it – I wasn't really worried. Millie was bright, diligent, and organized. She also had one particular university in her sights and a set of grades to aim for. I thought it was my job, over the next week or two, to prioritize making things easy for her and feed her with nutritious meals. I must play the mother, not the barrister, for a while.

Nevertheless, as I scraped and chopped, there was an unease pricking at me, and it wouldn't go away. Had I really done the right thing? I wanted to run it past someone, not so much for advice as to clarify my own thoughts. Geoffrey, I knew, wise and knowledgable though he was, would see it only from a lawyer's point of view. I needed someone more impartial, someone on the outside, someone who would listen and consider before volunteering any opinion. Why hadn't I thought of it before? I would give Rachel a ring. We hadn't spoken for some while, and it would also give me an opportunity to thank Michael for looking after my scald. I picked up the phone.

As it turned out, it was a few days before we found a mutually convenient time. Rachel had a number of complex surgeries to attend to, and to help her prepare and avoid stress Michael had taken a week off. I arrived on foot about midday on a day when Rachel was between operations, and I found her, in her running gear, stretched out on the sofa, her eyes closed. It was a fine, balmy day, the front door was open, and I let myself in, calling out as I took off my shoes. I put my head round the lounge door and she opened her eyes and smiled.

"Hello," she said. "Good to see you. I'll get some coffee on."

"You sure this isn't a bad time?"

"No, you're not hard work, not like some!" She pulled herself up in one lithe movement. She grinned impishly and spoke in a low voice. "Come and look at this." I followed her to the door to the kitchen, and we stood in the doorway.

Jonathan was sitting in his highchair at the table, a bright yellow bib tied loosely round his neck. Gripped in his fist was a plastic spoon which he was banging rhythmically on the tray in front of him. He was chuckling and singing as he watched his father, who was standing at the cooker waving a wooden spoon in time with his son, also singing. I recognized – only just, because neither was a wonderful singer – the song as "*Frère Jacques*". Michael looked the part, swathed in a striped apron. From time to time he turned to the hob and stirred, then resumed the show. He caught sight of us grinning in the doorway and looked mildly sheepish.

"Do go on," I said, trying not to laugh.

Jonathan obviously agreed, because he yelled something approaching "More, more!"

Michael turned back to his son. "Hold on, mister impatient, I have to make some toast."

"I'll do it," Rachel said. "I'm making coffee anyway. I'm allowing myself just this one." As she passed, she planted a kiss on her son's dark head and patted her husband's back. "Do you want some?"

"Yes, please." Michael turned to me. "I'm trying to teach Jonathan some French songs. But I only know one."

"He's trying to make him bilingual," Rachel said to me. "French songs at mealtimes."

"There's always the *Marseillaise*," I suggested.

Michael's eyes lit up. "So there is!" He broke into a hearty but slightly offkey rendition of "'*Allons, enfants de la patrie…*'" and then stopped with a puzzled frown. "What comes next?"

"'*Le jour de gloire est arrivé*,'" I supplied. "Sorry, I don't know any more."

"More, more!" Jonathan chanted.

"Anna, I think we should escape this chaos," Rachel said. She had a brimming cafetière in one hand and two mugs in the other. "Michael and Jonathan can eat beans on toast and sing French songs as loudly as they like, but I'm going to close the door." She turned to her husband. "Come and join us if you like, darling. Once you've finished your chores. Bring your own cup."

Michael retrieved toast from the toaster. "You are far too kind to this humble skivvy."

"I know. It's just the way I am."

Back in the lounge, with the door firmly closed, Rachel poured coffee. She looked at me with those piercing eyes. "You said you had something you wanted to run past me. Not sure how much help I can be, especially if it's something obscure and legal."

I shook my head. "No. Those I can deal with myself. It's more ethical. Moral. A matter of conscience. Pricking away at me like St Paul's thorn."

"OK. I'm listening."

I drew a breath, collecting my thoughts. "I took on a case. Defending. I was unsure, reluctant even. Because the client was, is, a known criminal." I saw Rachel's eyebrows rise. "*Known* as in strongly suspected. By all the law-upholders in town, not to mention many of the citizens. Not *known* as in *proved*."

"Why did you decide to defend him – or is it her?"

"Him. Because I was alerted to the possibility of a miscarriage of justice," I said. "That sounds pompous, I know. Once I'd looked at the paperwork supplied by the police and the prosecution, I was even more certain he wasn't guilty of the crime they were accusing him of. Perhaps other crimes, but not this one. And it was a very serious charge. The case against him was ill-prepared, shoddy, full of holes. I think they were in a hurry, desperate to get him banged up and bask in the resulting glory. I can't say I blame them, to be honest. But it won't do. It goes against everything I've stood for the last twenty years. The law may be an ass in many respects, but without it – and without people prepared to put it into practice, regardless of their private inclinations – we're sunk."

"Fair enough."

"Anyway," I ploughed on, "not to make too much of a saga of it, we succeeded in getting the case dropped. No trial." I looked up at her and smiled faintly. "No speechifying. No purple passages to an electrified jury. Ha. There's a pretty myth."

She frowned. "So – aren't you pleased?"

"It's not so cut and dried, I'm afraid. I did what I thought I should, and, as I told my very angry sister-in-law recently, I'm not supposed to turn down cases just because I don't like the client or because the crime he's charged with is especially repugnant. Now this man will soon be free. He is not a nice man, and I'm afraid his wicked career will continue."

"But," Rachel said, "if he didn't commit this particular crime, presumably somebody else did."

"Indeed."

"Sounds like the police need to go back to the drawing board."

"Yes. And there's another thing. I am going to be very unpopular, not least with the police, with whom I have had a reasonably good relationship up to now. I know one officer in particular who will be furious."

"Perhaps he should have done a better job in the first place, from what you've told me."

I took a long gulp of my coffee. "That's certainly what I think. But I'm not going to tell him that. I'm hoping to avoid him until the dust settles."

The door to the kitchen opened and Michael appeared, divested of his apron, with Jonathan in his arms. "All right if we join you?" He put the child down in the middle of a heap of bricks, and he immediately crowed with delight and started stacking.

"You seem to have a very happy little fellow there," I said.

Rachel smiled. "He is. He's very easy to please. But then, he hasn't got much to be miserable about."

I laughed. "That doesn't stop the grumpy ones! Some children seem to run their parents ragged whatever they do for them."

"Was Millie like that?"

"No, she was OK most of the time."

"Shall I make some more coffee?" Michael said. "Looks like you've depleted that pot."

"Please. But I'd better have some of my own peculiar brew. And then come and help Anna with her dilemma. Though actually I'm not totally sure what it is yet."

In a few minutes Michael was back, armed with a fresh pot of coffee, a mug of his own, and another steaming mug for Rachel, who gave him a swift summary of what I had told her. "Have I got that right, Anna?"

"Impeccable," I said. "If you weren't a surgeon you would have made a good lawyer."

She smiled. "Thanks. But I don't think so. I wouldn't have the patience with all the quibbling. Whereas a nice open chest cavity has few moral implications."

Michael leaned back in his chair. "Correct me if I'm wrong, Anna," he said. "Are you wondering if you've done the right thing? You said you felt you were bound to act in the way you have, and for good reasons, but now this man is free to go on doing whatever it is he does. Is that it?"

"In a nutshell." I paused. "But that's not all." I felt a twinge of unease. "Are you sure you don't mind me loading you up with all this? It's just that I felt I needed some input from someone outside the law."

"It's fine, really," Michael said.

"Well, it's strange," I said hesitantly. "I thought I'd got all this straightened out in my own mind years ago, but now it's haunting me and I can't seem to shake it off – the sense that there's something awry in the very system I'm part of."

"Perhaps," Michael said quietly, "the fact that you've recently started going back to the abbey after a long absence has made your conscience more sensitive."

"Oh. I suppose. I hadn't thought of it like that."

For a moment we were all silent, the only sound the clatter of bricks as Jonathan's tower teetered, then crashed. He squealed in delight. Then I said, "Some years ago I read a book by a forensic pathologist. He was retired when he wrote it, but he'd had a remarkable career and some of his experiences were both famous and horrific. Cases he'd dealt with involved multiple fatalities, and many of them resulted in drastic changes to the health and safety laws. I think he was even involved with the aftermath of 9/11 as a consultant. In his working life he was often in court giving evidence as an expert witness, so he saw the workings of the court at first-hand, without being himself part of the system. And some of his remarks were damning."

Both Michael and Rachel leaned forward.

"Such as?" Rachel asked.

"Well, he cited a case where an old, experienced – and, by the sound of it, wily – defence barrister tried, with all the aggressive eloquence at his disposal, to twist the evidence of the expert witness in order to exonerate his client. I don't think he succeeded, but he might have. I know there have been cases which should have been won but which were lost through poor advocacy, and vice versa – whatever the facts happened to be. That's the thing – we barristers are often just that sort of person, argumentative, confident, competitive

– or we wouldn't have chosen the profession in the first place or have survived in it. So you have the defence and the prosecution equally determined simply *to win* – and sometimes the truth is a casualty. I hold my hand up to that charge; if I'm in court pleading my case, I have to be very careful not to give in to the overwhelming desire to come out on top. My godfather maintains to this day that it's what he saw in me when I was a mouthy child in contention with my brothers."

"But what's the alternative, Anna?" Michael asked.

"In some European countries the judge has a more pivotal role," I said. "Obviously that too has its pitfalls. There's a lot more to it and things are changing – slowly – but I'm trying to explain a highly complex subject in easily digestible terms. Sorry if that sounds patronizing."

"No, I'd have to do the same," Rachel said with some irony, "if you were my patient and I had to tell you what was wrong with your heart."

"Changing the subject entirely," Michael said, "how's your burn?"

"Clean and healing," I said. "And that's another reason why I wanted to come round today – to thank you for your timely intervention. It's lovely to be able to wash my hair again. The nurse said that would be OK."

Michael waved a self-effacing hand. "You're more than welcome. I'm glad it worked. So where were we?"

"More or less done," I said. "I'm sure you'll be relieved! It's not an easy one to figure out, and as I said I thought I'd dealt with all these issues as a green law student years ago. And to be even-handed, there are many senior barristers, with loads of experience, who firmly believe the system we have is the best in the circumstances. They think the idea of opposing arguments, plus a judge, and a jury drawn from ordinary citizens, is the likeliest way to see justice done. And maybe they're right for the most part. But in this case I had my doubts that a jury of Brant citizens would be sufficiently impartial, however the judge might have directed them to lean only on the evidence."

"I see why you feel uncomfortable," Michael said.

I sighed. "And there are personal things involved as well, but I don't want to go into those, not now." I paused, just as Jonathan was placing a brick on top of yet another precarious-looking tower, his little brow furrowed in intense toddler concentration. I continued. "Normally my working life doesn't throw up moral conundrums. The sort of thing I usually do is straightforward, even dull. This is the first high-profile crime I've had any dealings with for a long time."

Michael shifted in his chair. Rachel, cradling her empty mug, looked at him with narrow eyes. "Any thoughts, O wise one?" she said.

"Nothing beyond the obvious," he said hesitantly. "In every life situation, especially the ones that seem intractable, we have the recourse of prayer. I pray before every operation, but it's not the same as Anna's dilemma, because I'm just praying for good decisions and a steady hand. No, she needs, I suppose, to pray for guidance of a different kind."

"Yes. I do need to remember that," I said. "Look, I didn't come here expecting answers – that would be unfair and unreasonable! I'm just grateful to have had the chance to offload it and clarify things in my own mind. So thank you both for being such good listeners." I smiled. "Any more coffee in that pot?"

Rachel topped up my cup and we spoke of other things.

Jonathan abandoned his bricks and leaned on the sofa where his mother sat, looking up at her with his intent blue gaze, so like her own, if softer and less challenging. She gathered him up, and he leaned into her shoulder and put his thumb in his mouth. "Are you weary, little man?" she said softly.

Michael heaved himself out of his chair. "I'll take him up." He took Jonathan from Rachel's lap, who gazed at her husband appreciatively. "You might hear some more French songs, if you're very lucky," he said.

"We wouldn't mind," Rachel said darkly, "if only you had a repertoire of more than two." She reached up and stroked Jonathan's back. "Sleep well, sweet Jonny."

When they had gone I said, "Something I've meant to tell you, Rachel, and I keep forgetting. Seems my Millie and your Jasper have met."

"Really? He hasn't said."

"It was a while ago. They didn't know each other before, as far as I'm aware, but he played the gallant knight one evening when Millie had to help a friend who was very drunk and sick in one of the local clubs. Apparently he offered them a lift home."

"He's a good chap, Jasper. Full of mad ideas these days, but you expect that at his stage in life."

"Where is he at university?"

"Porton. My old stomping ground."

"Oh! How odd. That's Millie's first choice, if she gets the grades. But he's ahead of her."

"He's coming to the end of his second year. Philosophy and something."

"It's a long way from Brant – a hundred and twenty miles or so, isn't it? He seems to be here often at the weekends, though."

"Ah, well, that's not because he's pining for us. He's in the university swimming team, but he still belongs to the club here, and if there's something special on he'll come back for it. He has a rattly old car but manages to make short work of the distance. I shudder when I think of his driving – it's a good job Millie declined his offer of a lift."

I laughed. "Millie's still learning. But she has a new friend with a fancy car and gets to drive that sometimes. Far too fast." Thinking about Tiffany Leaman, and all that went with her, brought me back to current reality, and I shivered. "I should go and leave you in peace," I said.

Rachel got up. Her eyes sparkled with mischief. "You must come round for supper one Saturday when Jasper is home. Bring Millie. They can renew their acquaintance."

"Not," I said sternly, "until her exams are over. Frankly, I can't wait. She is extremely volatile. Crotchety. Stomps round the house sighing and glowering when she isn't actually revising. It can't come soon enough." Rachel came with me to the door. "I've been meaning to ask you," I said, "what do you make of this leaving Europe thing? Seems utterly hare-brained to me."

She nodded. "I'm sick of all the news coverage. So much hype, so much that is completely false, especially some of the wilder claims. It's been a bad campaign from all sides. Who knows? I wonder about free movement, free exchange of ideas. And what might become of our home in France if it all goes belly-up. It's a worry, certainly."

"How has it come to this?"

She shrugged. "I have no idea."

I was surprised that evening to take a call at home from Clive Stephenson. "Off the record, Anna," he said. "That's why I'm ringing you at home, as a friend. Be prepared for a backlash. You aren't very popular right now with the boys in blue."

"I'm not surprised, Clive. But thanks for the warning. Presumably you've been in touch with Steve Bryant?"

"Yes," Stephenson said heavily. "He is furious. On the surface his ire is directed at you, but I suspect he is even more annoyed with himself, because he has made a hash of this case, and his SIO hasn't minced his words. Between you and me, he's due for a severe reprimand. So he's humiliated, and therefore dangerous. However, I think he is being given a chance to redeem the fiasco. They're letting him keep on with the investigation, and I dare say he still nurses the hope of catching Leaman in his net while he goes about other business."

"Wouldn't he be better off trying to catch a murderer? Apart from anything else, it'd go a long way to restoring his reputation."

"Let's hope that's what he does. I should thank you too. For alerting me to a possibly embarrassing situation for my chambers."

"No problem, Clive."

I hadn't long put the phone down, and was thinking about supper, when Millie came flying in. I hadn't seen her since the morning; she'd gone straight from school to Tiffany's.

"Mum, guess what! They've let Tiff's dad out of prison!"

I tried to sound amiably neutral. "Oh, have they? I expect Tiffany's pleased."

"She's over the moon. She always said he was innocent." She frowned suddenly. "Funny though, you'd think her mum would be chuffed as well, but she seemed, I don't know, underwhelmed."

"Is he back home?" I felt suddenly cold, as if a wind from Siberia had swirled through the house. "Did you meet him?"

"No," Millie said carelessly. "Not yet." She paused at the foot of the stairs, swinging her bag, and gave me a look; a tiny smile that was strangely knowing. "But I expect I will, at some point. I'll be back down in a mo, when I've dumped this lot." She started up the stairs.

"How did your exam go this morning?" I called after her.

"Not bad," she called back. "I'll tell you all about it when I come down."

I set to peeling potatoes, and I thought about that look of hers. Millie was no fool. She was also more than capable of keeping things to herself, and away from me. To give her credit, sometimes that was to save me disquiet; perhaps every child of separated parents has that choice to make. But at other times she hugged her secrets to her chest simply to have a life that I knew nothing of. Something about what she had said, the tiny markers of nuance and emphasis, gave me the growing conviction that she knew, perhaps had always known, about the reputation of her new friend's father. If I was right, she would understand completely the anguish of her aunt and uncle; no wonder she had said nothing. How much had she heard of Kathryn's accusations? I felt a sudden sweat break out on my face. Did she also know of my own involvement? I couldn't ask and she almost certainly wouldn't tell me. It was the worst bind, and I felt panic rising up inside me, threatening to steal my breath. I wanted to snatch her away and hide her somewhere; but there was absolutely nothing I could do – and no one I could tell.

Except one – and that night, lying in bed, weary but twitchy with anxiety, I poured out my fear. *Lord, I am afraid. Afraid I have put my child in danger. Perhaps it was never as direct as that. What danger do I really think she is in? Just to be in contact with a bad man, to be in his shadow, vulnerable. I feel so totally helpless. I can't forbid her. I can't tell her why – she'd disdain my every argument. But she is naive. She's young enough to believe that nothing will happen to her. But it could, and it's because of the work I do, and the decisions I've made. Dear Lord, please, defend her.*

SIX

I should have known.

If Millie came at something sideways, asking a question in apparent innocence, my every sense should have been alert; but I was preoccupied, as usual, with my work. I was rereading a memoir by an august QC whose career had been dedicated to civil rights issues and whose passion was the defence of the average citizen against the formidable might of the State and allied powers. I had just read a description of a walk to the cell where a suspected terrorist was being held, running a gauntlet of police officers – with dogs – who made no attempt to disguise their expressions of hatred and contempt for the defending barrister. In their eyes, although the trial had not yet been held, the defendant was guilty, he deserved to suffer the law's full rigours, and in defending him the barrister was regarded as a traitor.

I had not had to run such a gauntlet, and now with the collapse of the case I had no need to face those who, I was certain, regarded me in just those terms, but I felt deeply uneasy. Since Leaman's release things had gone very quiet, as far as I was concerned. But I knew that the police, and others, were angry and frustrated. The public perception of Leaman had not improved, and my stock was low because of it. The investigation to find the murderer must have been ongoing; I knew nothing about it. I went on with work as it came in and did my best, but I was distracted. Although the weather was fine, with the promise of summer, a dark grey cloud of uncertainty and worry hung over me. I put the book down with a sigh. I agreed with the author that our adversarial system was probably the best way to ensure that the innocent got an even break, as long as the rules were fairly applied; but what of the slippery criminal?

Immersed in my thoughts, I went into the kitchen to make some coffee and found Millie rooting around in one of the drawers.

"There's so much rubbish in here!" she muttered.

"What are you trying to find?"

She looked up, her expression a studied blank. "Oh, it's nothing important – I was just wondering if my passport was here."

"Are you thinking of taking a trip, then?" I asked.

"Maybe," she said airily. "Last exam tomorrow – hooray! – and then I'm free. Well, there are things going on at school for the next few weeks, and I might sign up to some of them, but I don't actually have to. So, maybe…"

"Whose idea was it to take a trip?" I asked.

"Oh, you know, just people at school, talking… nothing concrete or anything. Ah! Here it is. I might as well keep hold of it now I've found it."

If Millie was being mysterious, it was nothing new, and probing on my part would be counterproductive. I set it aside; she would tell me, or not, but it would be in her time.

The next day's developments drove everything else out of my mind – for a while anyway. I had barely settled at my desk when there came a tap on my door, which was open, and Janet sidled in. It was always interesting to see what the day's get-up was, and today was no exception: a shiny gold top teamed with black leggings and black ankle boots sporting a silver and gold trim, with a turquoise scarf knotted at her throat. Only Janet could pull off such sartorial eccentricities.

I raised an eyebrow and said, "Good morning."

She examined her fingernails, which were painted cerise and made her look predatory. "There was an early call for you this morning."

"From?"

"That persistent reporter from the *Brant Herald* who wants to interview you. The one with the little pointy teeth."

"Are her teeth really pointy?" I asked. "Or perhaps it's your shorthand for 'I don't like her and she wants to get her teeth into you'. Hmm?"

She wagged her head from side to side, as if considering. "Maybe a bit of both. I haven't really got close enough to check out her teeth, but it's what she's like. A persistent little terrier. With a nose for trouble. I told her no the first time, but she keeps trying." She perched on the edge of my desk, and I leaned back in my chair with a sigh as she continued. "I've been doing some research. She trained for the Bar – did you know that? Got chucked out, though. Probably got a down on barristers generally."

"She does a once-in-a-while legal column for the paper, doesn't she?"

Janet nodded. "Among other things. She has to do the

other stuff, but my impression is it's the courts that interest her. Sniffing around for a bit of malpractice, a bit of scandal, miscarriages of justice, and so on."

"An axe to grind?"

"Most likely. But she says she wants to get your angle on Leaman – for the readers of her paper, the good citizens of Brant, who don't like him one bit."

"I don't like him one bit myself. But I'm not going public on it."

"I told her that, but she'll be back, or my name's not Janet the Clerk."

"I wonder why she got chucked out of Bar school," I murmured.

"I didn't find that out," Janet said. "Give me time."

The phone rang in her office, and she walked along the corridor to answer it. A few moments later she was back. I closed the file I was trying to read; clearly this morning it was a lost cause. Janet was alight with excitement.

I eyed her wearily. "Not our reporter friend again! What's her name, anyway?"

"Melody Parker, believe it or not. No, not her. It was *Leaman*."

I sat upright. "What? What does he want?"

Janet grinned, her eyes sparkling with mischief. "He wants to come and visit. To thank you personally."

I groaned and rested my head in my hands. "What did you tell him?"

Janet folded her arms. "I told him I would have to consult you. I can fob off a nosy reporter, but this one's beyond my pay grade."

"I don't want to speak to that man ever again if I can avoid it. Is he still on the line?"

"No. I said you were terribly busy and he'd have to wait."

"OK. Choose your moment, ring him back, and tell him that if he's really overflowing with gratitude he can write a letter. I'll put it in a gold frame and hang it on the wall – perhaps don't tell him that bit."

I was due in court that afternoon, but just as I was entering the court car park Janet rang to tell me to turn round and come back, because the parties had settled at the eleventh hour. "Waste of time and petrol," I groused, "not to mention my prep. By the time I get back, there won't be much point coming in to chambers. I'll go straight home. I've got a briefcase full of paperwork, so I can get that done over the weekend. Also, today was Millie's last exam, and I'd like to find out how she got on before she disappears off somewhere to celebrate."

"See you on Monday, then. Have a high old time with your thrilling backlog."

"I wish. Nothing much changes, does it?"

I changed into comfortable clothes and took Gordon for a stroll in the park. There were few other dogs about at this time of day, and few people. Later, when the children were being collected from surrounding schools, there would be dogs accompanying parents to the school gates, and later still, when the working day was over, there would be another influx. As it was, I had the place almost to myself. Gordon busied himself checking out the recent scents, and I ambled along thinking about nothing, which was an unusual privilege. The weather was balmy, with just a ripple of breeze disturbing the leaves, and the trees, some of them well established and tall, were coming into their first flush of full summer foliage, dense and bright. Here the sound of the ever-present traffic dulled a little. I remembered growing up in sleepy Burrow Bridge, even smaller then than it was now, roaming the woods and fields with my brothers in the long school holidays. No doubt I was over-romanticizing the bucolic peace and pleasure of those days; the reality was more likely to include blisters, sunburn, and fraternal quarrelling, but I felt a distinct pang of nostalgia for life in the country.

Back at home I made the most of the weather and opened all the windows on the ground floor, letting in air that was more or less sweet. I made a cup of tea, fed the dog, and settled on the sofa in the front room with a pile of letters and my laptop.

I was making good progress and had reduced the stack considerably, but my eyes were tired, and I wondered whether I should make an appointment to get them tested; much as I might like to deny it, I was at an age where many people found they needed reading glasses. Then I heard Millie's voice through the open window, but not only Millie's: answering hers was a distinctive tenor. Then her key turned in the lock, she came indoors, and there were loud hoots of mingled laughter from the hallway.

She put her head round the door. "Hey, Ma. I saw the car. You're home very early."

"Mm. Case got cancelled. How was the exam?"

"Not too bad, I think. But the main thing is – they're over! I feel like dancing. Shall I?"

"Go ahead. Pirouette round the garden. I'll video you on my phone and post it on social media."

She made a face. "Maybe not then. Oh," she added casually, "Jasper's here too."

Jasper appeared in the doorway behind her, his dark hair tied back with a piece of string, a few wispy tendrils escaping. The bits of him that were exposed – arms, neck, face – were all suntanned.

"Hello," he said, smiling.

"Hello, Jasper," I said. "Home for the weekend again?"

His smile broadened. "Can't keep me away."

"Do you young things want a cup of tea?" I asked.

"No, thanks," Millie said airily. "We're going to drive down to the beach. Tiff's going to join us there later. It's such a lovely day – in more ways than one! Jasper picked me up from school in his terrible car. I only came home to change. Didn't think you'd be here."

"Have Tiffany's exams finished too?"

"No, poor thing," Millie said. "She's got one more on Monday. I persuaded her she could take a few hours off without risking total failure. But she's coming out in her own car so she can go home early and work." She turned to Jasper and slapped him lightly on the chest. "While these two lazy layabouts lounge around in the sunshine and eat ice cream!"

"I hope you've got some money, then," Jasper said amiably. "Because I'm broke."

"You're hopeless," Millie said. "I might have been looking forward to a meal somewhere posh to celebrate the end of exams."

Jasper pulled his wallet out of his back pocket and emptied its contents onto his hand. "Might stretch to a burger from that stall on the beach," he said dubiously.

"Forget it, cheapskate. I don't fancy food poisoning. Anyway, I'm going to change. I won't be long." She left the room, humming under her breath, and I heard her running up the stairs.

"Come in and sit down, Jasper," I said. "Never believe Millie when she says she won't be long."

He sat in the armchair opposite, leaning forward with his elbows on his knees. Apart from his skinny scruffiness he was very like his father. "I'm in no hurry," he said.

I leaned back against the cushions. "Has your term finished already?"

"Nearly. I've got a piece of coursework to hand in by the end of next week. But I felt like coming home and maybe going down to the pool to see some of my club friends. There's a trip coming up in the summer – a competition – somewhere in Belgium. I thought I'd see who was signed up for it."

"Oh. Are you competing?"

"I'm not sure yet. But even if not, I'll probably go just for fun."

"Ah."

After a moment, Jasper said, "Millie tells me she'll be at the same uni as me, if she gets her grades. Which I'm sure she will."

"Yes, so Rachel said. That's quite a coincidence."

He shook his head. "Maybe not so much. Porton has a reputation for the subjects we're both doing. But maybe I can help her a bit – give her the lowdown on options, help her with accommodation, and all that."

"That would be kind."

"Actually," he said thoughtfully, "we might even have a room going spare in our house. I'm pretty sure one of my housemates is thinking of moving in with his girlfriend. It's a terrible dump – the bathroom is disgusting, and perhaps she wouldn't like living with three unwashed men – but it's very cheap."

I was spared the need to respond; as if to prove me wrong about taking ages, Millie appeared, transformed from her sober school suiting, in tiny ragged denim shorts and a loose striped top, her over-large sunglasses perched on her head. She looked carelessly wonderful: slim, fair, and fresh. Somehow I doubted that Jasper had come home just to go to his swimming club.

"Come on then, Sugar-daddy, let's go," Millie said, laughing at her own wit.

Jasper pulled himself to his feet. "Bye, Ms Milburn," he said politely. "See you sometime."

"It's Anna," I called after his retreating figure. The door slammed, and their laughter faded as they went down the path.

What was a mother to think? Were Millie and Jasper an item, or at least becoming more than friends? Was I ever going to be informed? Probably not. I thought about the future, immediate and distant. I had no real doubt that Millie would get the necessary grades. I wondered what she thought of moving in with three third-year men. Had the subject been discussed between them? It would solve a few problems, certainly, but might well create others. I sighed. I expected to be required for a number of duties before Millie left home – mainly money and transport – but for the rest, she would do all the deciding, and anything I had to say would no doubt be discounted. I felt fatalistic about it, but even so a chill feeling made me wrap my arms around myself, as if to ward off the thought of an empty house, evenings that were too quiet, my only child growing up and becoming even more independent. I had no quarrel with her taste – I liked Jasper, and knew him to be kind. But I didn't want to think about my life after October, nor what it would contain outside of work, family things, and the occasional visit to the gym. In a very short time I would be forty-four. Not old – but rather than feel my life becoming fuller with time, I felt my world shrinking, my cup emptying.

Monday started badly. I had just managed to make coffee in chambers when Janet beckoned to me as I passed her office. She was on the phone, gesticulating to me incomprehensibly. I went in and put my steaming cup down on her desk. "What?" I mouthed.

She shook her head and went back to her call. "One moment, please, Miss Parker." She covered the mouthpiece. "I'm sorry, Anna, but it's that reporter again. She's—"

I reached across the desk, and with a sigh Janet put the phone into my hand. "Miss Parker? Anna Milburn. Would you please stop phoning my chambers and annoying my clerk? Have I not made myself clear? I do not wish to make any kind of public statement, whether in your newspaper or elsewhere."

I employed my most formidable court voice, the sort I wished I could have brought out more often to reduce the cocky know-it-alls – those who thought they could play the system – to abject snivelling, and that I had admired in the mouths of barristers in the highest courts of the land when I was a student and a pupil. I had never had much chance to use it, and even when I did criminals usually refused to snivel. It also cut no ice with Melody Parker.

"Oh, Ms Milburn, hello, how are you?" She sounded breathless. Before I had any chance of replying she blustered on. "I am a great admirer of yours – did you know that? Well, you may know that I myself once aspired to the Bar, but – well, that's another story. Anyway, I've always been interested in legal things, and now I have a great opportunity because my editor has agreed to let me do a series on what's going on in court around the city, and associated matters of interest, and—"

"Miss Parker! Please stop there—"

Now she had begun I couldn't hold her back. "But Ms Milburn, wouldn't you like the opportunity to lay before the public the dreadful state the criminal justice system is in, what with all the cuts? Especially after that report that was recently issued. And," she babbled on, "you must know how much public feeling the case against Calvin Leaman has generated in Brant and beyond, so I would just *love* to have your angle on why the case against him collapsed—"

"Miss Parker – stop," I thundered. Finally she dried up. "The case against Mr Leaman collapsed, as you put it," I said, very slowly, as if speaking to someone of limited understanding, "because of *lack of evidence*. Whatever the public perception of him, he was not guilty of the crime with which he was charged. Mr Leaman was my client, and as his defence counsel my job was to defend him. Which I did. However, Mr Leaman is no longer my client, and we have no more interaction. I do not, I repeat *not*, wish to be interviewed. Please make this your last call to these chambers. Good morning." I handed the phone back to Janet, and she ended the call.

"That told her," Janet said. "But I reckon she won't give up."

I frowned. "She may be a nuisance, but she's canny. She mentioned that government report."

"What? The one that nobody took any notice of?"

"That one. The one that starts, 'The criminal justice

221

system is close to breaking point.' The press preferred to run a story on some cooked-up scandal involving a popular TV programme – the imminent collapse of justice merited not a word. The old saying about crime not paying has taken on a new meaning these days, I reckon. There's plenty of money in crime, but precious little for the criminal barrister." I shook my head and heaved a huge sigh. "Do I have anything desperately important on this morning?" I asked.

"You have an appointment at eleven. Nothing too strenuous. You can handle it." She handed me a slim sheaf of papers.

"All right. I'll see this –" I glanced at the name on the front page – "Mrs Albert. Then I'm going to the gym. I feel I have a great deal of energy to dissipate. Negative energy."

"Good idea," Janet said. She turned back to her screen. "Don't take it out on Mrs Albert, though, will you? She's an inoffensive lady who just needs a bit of advice."

"Why would I take it out on Mrs Albert?"

"I hope you wouldn't. But you are glowering."

"Small wonder," I muttered. "It's a great pity a few more of our clients, not to mention employees of the press, can't see their way to being *inoffensive*." I stalked back to my room and closed the door with a deliberate click.

I spent an hour or more at the gym, finishing with thirty lengths of the pool and a tepid shower. Normally I liked my water hot, but I was being kind to my wound. The chlorine had stung it a bit, but I noticed no greater harm done. The exercise left me completely limp and wrung out, like a wet flannel, with about as much combativeness. I bought a sandwich and ate it in the gym café, then drove slowly back to chambers through the sunshine.

Though weary, I was feeling calm as I trotted up the steps. Then I heard my name called.

"Ms Milburn! Please, wait." I recognized the voice, and my stomach tightened. Slowly, hoping I was wrong, I turned by the door to chambers and looked down. I hadn't noticed the sleek black car parked unashamedly in one of the barristers' spaces at the front. Stepping out of it, adjusting his jacket and smoothing down his thinning hair, was none other than Calvin Leaman. Momentarily I closed my eyes, wishing either him, or myself, a thousand miles away.

He advanced, smiling, his hand outstretched. I held on resolutely to my briefcase with both hands.

"Mr Leaman," I said frostily. "I have asked you not to telephone, or to call. Our association is at an end. That is the way I wish it to continue. Please excuse me."

I turned back to the door and started to push it open. But he ran up the steps and stood between me and the entrance. "Please, Ms Milburn, I beg you," he said with a show of sincerity that made my lunchtime sandwich curdle. "I just wanted to thank you in person. You did me a great service—"

"I simply did my job," I said. "Now, please let me into my chambers. I have other clients to see."

"Please, there are other matters—"

I held up my hand. "If you wish to communicate with me, or with these chambers, I suggest you write a letter."

"No, no, you don't understand." Suddenly he whipped around, staring across the square, shading his eyes against the sun with his hand. "Oh dear." He spoke in a low voice, radiating concern. "Have you been harassed by a reporter from the *Herald*? Because if I am not very much mistaken she is sitting at an outside table at that café – see? And she's taking pictures. For your own sake, Ms Milburn, we need to go inside."

I followed his gaze. Very quietly I muttered an expletive. A young woman was indeed sitting at a table across the square. She wore dark glasses, but since I had no idea what Melody Parker looked like it was an unnecessary and, I thought, risibly overdramatic disguise. But she had a small camera in her hand, and as I turned towards her she lifted it to her eye.

"All right, Mr Leaman," I said, as evenly as I could. "Five minutes. And then you leave." I opened the door and stalked inside. Leaman followed me down the corridor, past Janet, whose eyes widened as she looked up. I held open the door of my room. "Do sit down," I said brusquely. "If you have something of interest to say, please say it. And then go away and don't pester me again."

He sank into a chair as I closed the door. "Oh, I don't think I am *pestering* you, Ms Milburn," he said softly. I sensed that all pretence was slipping away. "What I am doing is *helping* you."

"I think you'd better explain that extraordinary claim."

He leaned back in the chair and folded his arms. I remained by the door, my arms held straight at my sides, making a huge effort not to clench my fists. I surprised myself by the strength of my impulse to smash something into his mismatched teeth.

He smiled slightly. "I met your daughter the other day."

"How—"

"My girl Tiffany told me she had a nice new friend," Leaman went on. "And I was pleased for her. To be frank, she's not been the best judge when it comes to friends. Then the two of them happened to be there when I was, and Tiffany introduced me to Emilia Preston. Who was charming, I have to say. Very polite. Fond of Tiffany, who'd already told me how much her friend Millie had helped her. With her schoolwork. I remembered the name Preston from my brief association some years ago with a local businessman of that name. Whose wife at the time, I recalled, was a barrister called Anna Milburn. Anyway, your daughter is very like you, except taller."

I exerted every ounce of control. "So you have met my daughter. What of it?"

"I thought you might be concerned about her having an association with me. Through Tiffany, who is herself obviously harmless. Unfortunately, as you know, the case against me has stirred a lot of people up round here. The police are not happy, for a start. I wouldn't want either of our girls involved—"

"Are you threatening me, Mr Leaman?"

"Of course not!" He raised his voice. "What have I got against you? Nothing! I came here today to thank you! You are very high and mighty with me, and I suppose you have your reasons. But I wanted to warn you."

"About what?"

"Please, won't you sit down for a minute? You make me feel uncomfortable, standing there with a face like thunder."

Reluctantly I skirted the desk and perched on the edge of my chair.

"You got me off," he said. "And for that I shall always be grateful. I didn't do it, but someone did. Like I said to you when you came to see me in prison, I reckon I know who *did* do it. Anyway, the police are sniffing around again. I felt you should know this, because whether you like it or not you have a personal involvement now. I had a phone call late last night, from one of the lads who works for me. Not one of the bad lads, either. Pleasant enough boy, only twenty-one, not very bright, but good for polishing cars and running errands. Paul Fleetwood. Mean anything to you?"

I racked my brain; then I remembered. "The boy who gave your man Priddy an alibi."

At the mention of Priddy, Leaman made a face as if he had just tasted something vile. "He should be *my man*, after all I've done for him when nobody else would touch him. When he came out of jail. Like I said to you, I took him on because I owed it to his dad. Old John. But just lately Vincent has been getting very lippy. Full of complaints. Sour and foul-mouthed. Always putting me down to the other men, pretending it's a joke if I challenge him, but really trying to turn them all against me. He hates me, when he should be grateful." He shrugged. "I don't get it. But I reckon he's lost it. Jealous, full of rage, thinks I owe him something – who knows what? He's mad. That's all there is to it."

I watched him. There was something, I thought, that he wasn't saying. "Are you sure?"

"About what?" he said guardedly.

"I'm wondering if there's something specific that might account for Priddy's antagonism, especially if it's recent."

Leaman shifted in his chair. "Hmm. There was something." He flashed a brief assessing glance in my direction. "Vince is a drinker. I've always known that, but as long as it doesn't affect what he does at work I reckon it's his business if he wants to fry his brain and pickle his liver. I've had to speak to him about it once or twice before. Anyway, about a month ago he came to work stinking of booze and unsteady on his feet. I heard him shouting at young Paul, and I went down onto the floor from my office to see what was going on. The other lads were all standing round listening and smirking instead of getting on with their work. I'd had enough of Vince's little ways and I gave him a right – mustn't swear! Well, I wiped the floor with him, I was that annoyed. In front of his boys. Told him if he couldn't control his drinking and his behaviour he'd be out of a job. Made him lose face, I suppose."

"I see. So what about Fleetwood?"

"Ah. Well, like I said, late last night I had a call from young Paul. He was in a panic. The police have been grilling him again. Went round to his flat, asked him a lot of questions. He told me he'd stuck to his original story, that he and Priddy were at his place that night, the night Sergeant Winter was murdered, and they were playing cards and drinking beer and watching a film till late. I'd never noticed Priddy and Fleetwood being that friendly before, not like Priddy is with the other lads. The few times I took any notice, I thought Fleetwood was scared of Vince, to be honest. He's not a hard nut, not like the others. I spoke to him very nicely, very gently, fatherly if you like. I asked him what really happened."

"And?"

"He started to cry. I mean, loud sobs. And then he hung up."

"What then?"

"I called him back, tried to calm him down. I asked him again: what really happened? He said he couldn't tell me. Because Priddy—" Leaman shook his head. "I never found out what he was going to say. He hung up again, and when I tried to call back it went straight to voicemail. The next day he called in sick. I haven't seen him since." He leaned forward, frowning. "Ms Milburn, that boy is terrified. Priddy's got something on him, threatened him with something. I don't know what. Anyway, I had a word with one of the other lads, one I thought might be reasonably reliable. I asked him to go round to Paul's and tell him that if he's got something to say different to his original statement, if he didn't tell the truth the first time, he should tell the police. I told him they'd want to know, that he wouldn't be in trouble. I guess they already reckon he's lying."

"So did he?"

"I don't know yet. The other boy hasn't got back to me. But you see, Ms Milburn, the whole thing is getting very nasty. I want those girls out of it." He got up, and I also stood. We faced each other across the desk.

"What about Priddy himself?" I spoke reluctantly; the last person I wanted to be beholden to was Leaman, but I had to know. "Are the police grilling him too?"

He shook his head, and when he answered his voice was hollow. "That's just it," he said. "Prettyboy has gone missing. Nobody has seen him, for – I don't know, days. He didn't come to the warehouse. Nobody's seen him in his usual haunts, because I got the lads to ask around." He shook his head, his expression grim. "He's like a wild animal. Unpredictable, but cunning as well. The police are looking for him. For all our sakes, Ms Milburn, I hope they corner him very soon."

He made his way to the door and put his hand on the handle. Then he turned back to me. "You won't ask, I know," he said softly. "But I guess you'll want to be informed if anything happens. You may be right about me; I am not a nice man, not in your world. But I'm a parent, just as you are. I won't come here again, but I'll phone you if there's any news. I can't see the police keeping you in the loop. Why should they? Steve Bryant is royally hacked off with you, as you most likely know. No wonder. He's probably in some pretty deep bother with his bosses."

I would never have thought myself capable of saying what I said then to Leaman. "Yes, please do," I ground out. "You can ring here. I would appreciate it."

I knew I had to talk to Janet. I waited till I heard Leaman's car start up and roar away; then I hurried along the corridor to her office. To my surprise she wasn't there. I went further along the corridor to make myself a reviving cup of coffee, and there I found Janet and Elizabeth Merchant, head to head in some sort of clandestine conference. When they saw me they jumped apart, looking slightly guilty.

"What's this?" I asked. "Plotting? Anything I should know about?"

"Yes," Janet said, recovering her normal aplomb. "And no." Elizabeth merely smiled enigmatically and slipped away to her own space.

I made myself some coffee. Janet was still hovering, eyeing me thoughtfully. "Come to my room for a minute, please," I said. "There are things you should know."

Once she was installed, with the door firmly closed, I gave her the gist of my conversation with Leaman. "I have a horrible feeling things are about to blow wide open," I said. "Miss Melody Parker had a camera. I'm not sure if she managed to take a photo or not, but…"

"But if she did," Janet finished for me, "she could make something out of almost nothing."

"Yes, but apart from that we have a potentially dangerous man out there. Even Leaman's perturbed enough to want his daughter out the way. If that young man Paul Fleetwood decides to change his evidence there could be all sorts of trouble."

Janet nodded. "You need to speak to Millie."

I shuddered. Simply thinking of Millie in the same frame as Leaman and his cohorts sent a cold sensation to every nerve-ending. "I'll text her now. I don't even know where she is – her exams are over and she's enjoying a few days of freedom before the school reels her back in."

I sent a brief text to Millie. "Need to chat – important."

Janet and I sat sipping our coffee in silence. Then my phone signalled an incoming text. "Hey, Ma. Left you a note at home. I'm out with friends for a few days, so don't worry. I've got Gordon with me."

I bit my lip. Was she at Tiffany's? Was Leaman back? Would he warn them? I didn't want to frighten her unnecessarily, but I needed her to be safe. I sent another text. "Need to talk now. Call me."

After a few minutes my phone rang. "What's up?" Millie sounded puzzled, but not alarmed. I heard muffled talk and laughter in the background.

"Mil, where are you? I'm not trying to keep tabs on you, but something's come up and I need to know."

I could almost hear the frown in her voice. "I'm at Jess's. I didn't tell you, because there hasn't been time: Jess and Will broke up. Jess and I are back to being friends. She's feeling down, so we're trying to cheer her up."

I felt a small surge of relief. Then another thought struck. "Is Tiffany with you?"

"Yes. Jasper's here as well, and, guess what, so is Drew Clarke! It's so weird, but Jasper and Drew used to go to the same primary school when Jasper lived in Brant, before he went to London. Drew's a year older, but they knew each other! It's quite a party here."

"Millie," I said urgently, "sorry to interrupt, but this is

important. I'll explain when I see you, but I don't want you or Tiffany to go back to her house. If you need somewhere to go, bring Tiffany to ours."

"I don't get it."

"I know you don't, sweetie. I don't want to go into it all now. You're OK at Jess's. Just don't go to Tiffany's."

"You're being very mysterious, Mum."

"Can't be helped. Do you have what you need there?"

"Yes, I brought a change of clothes and a washbag and Gordon's food. We thought we'd go for a walk tomorrow and get some of the fat off him."

"OK, well, I'll see you when we're both at home. Oh, and Millie? It might be an idea to suggest to Tiffany that she texts her parents. Especially if they don't know where she is."

"Hang on." Millie's voice died and I heard mumbled talk. I waited. Then she came back. "Mum, I'll call you back in five."

"Is she OK?" Janet asked.

"Yes. She's at her friend Jess's. Jess's family have a huge rambling old place out near Thripp's Ford – they'll hardly notice if there are several uninvited guests. Your Drew's there too, apparently."

Janet's immaculate eyebrows raised a notch. "Is he? That boy pops up everywhere. He's got my car as well, I dare say."

My phone rang. "Mum, this is weird. Tiff rang her dad, and she said he's acting strange. He wouldn't say why, but he told her not to come home for a while, till he tells her it's OK. Seems he's sent her mum away as well. Gone to her sister's or something. What's going on?"

"I hope nothing. We're probably being clucky and paranoid. I'll tell you when I see you."

"All right, Mrs Mystery. Don't get too lonely without me, will you? See you soon."

When I'd rung off I turned to Janet. "This is awful. I have this very unpleasant sinking feeling."

Janet shook her head. "Don't let your imagination run away with you. Millie'll be OK at her friend's. If this nutter's out there bent on mayhem he'll be after Leaman, won't he? If he's after anyone at all. We don't know that he is. You said nobody'd seen him, so he's lying low. Our kids aren't in danger, Anna. He doesn't know who they are, let alone where they are. Brant's a big place."

"He knows Tiffany, I imagine."

"They're all together. Presumably this Jess has parents."

"Yes. They're sensible people."

"Well, then. You won't achieve anything by worrying. Why don't you get some work done? There's plenty I can pass your way without you even leaving the building."

I had to smile, despite the leaden feeling in my gut. "You're a terrible bully."

She slid off the chair and stretched. "It's a good job I am. This place would go to pot otherwise."

I dealt with a number of unchallenging items and left anything needing thought or research for another time. I was in no mental state for deep concentration or balanced legal opinions. At six I closed my laptop and stuffed my feet back into my shoes.

Janet was still in her office, but she too was closing down for the day. I leaned against her doorframe. "See you in the morning."

She frowned as she looked up at me. "You look awful," she remarked. "Pasty. Kind of colourless."

"I feel colourless, believe me."

"That burn's not bothering you again, is it?"

"No, not at all. I know it still looks a bit red, but it seems to be healing up nicely."

She nodded. "Good. Look, if you find you're getting screwed up thinking about Millie and worrying, especially as you're going to be on your own tonight, do you want to come and have supper at ours? Nothing fancy."

"Thanks, that's kind. But no, I think I need to be at home. Just in case that errant daughter of mine shows up."

The house felt stuffy and airless after the warm day. I opened most of the windows and looked out at the back garden. The grass needed mowing. Feeling restless, I got the mower out of the shed, plugged it in, and gave the strip of lawn a shave. I'd left it too long, and the result was straggly and yellow. Perhaps, I thought, I should take more interest in the garden, since gardening was reputed to be good for health, mental as well as physical. I never seemed to have the time for anything but the barest maintenance, but perhaps I should take in some of the gardening programmes on TV. Millie would no doubt make some acid comment about my middle-aged interests, but I couldn't escape the fact that I *was* middle-aged. Or nearly, I corrected myself, remembering with little enthusiasm that I had a birthday approaching with merciless speed.

The house was quiet – too quiet, with not even a shambling dog puffing and wheezing in his basket. I made myself some supper and poured a large glass of wine.

Despite my disinclination, I found myself thinking about Calvin Leaman. There was something about him that nibbled at the edges of my mind, something that reminded me of someone else, in a way that made me squirm. Irritated, I looked in my diary. True to her word,

Janet had loaded me not only with the backlog I had dealt with earlier but also with what looked like a full day in court the next day. With a small sigh I opened my briefcase and located the relevant files. There was nothing very exciting, nothing I couldn't handle. It would, at least, pay the bills, provided the cheques came in; it might even take my mind off Millie. To my dismay Leaman came back to haunt me, and I realized with a shock why he made me so uncomfortable. It wasn't simply what I thought I knew of him, my disgust at his reputed shadowy dealings; it was that he reminded me of Richard.

Of course they were not at all alike, superficially. Richard was a good-looking man, trim, well dressed with no hint of bling; he had a good head of hair and a perfect set of teeth, expensively cared for. But there was an air of – what? I could hardly pin it down. A whiff of slyness, a knowingness, that set me on edge, and I wondered uneasily – not for the first time – how far Richard, in his business dealings, had bent with the wind. Had he ever slipped to the wrong side of the law when pursuing some business interest, some profit? Well, then as now, he was hardly going to tell me about it. It was clear from our first meeting that he was ambitious, and he had certainly succeeded in almost every venture. But, busy building my own career, I knew little or nothing of his associates. If he had been less than honest, did that make me complicit, simply because I hadn't taken the trouble to find out? The thought made me cringe.

The buzz from my phone came as a welcome interruption, and Alastair's warm, lazy tones just as welcome. "Hey, squirt. How's it going?"

"Oh, you know, bro, as ever, all work, no play," I countered, keeping my voice light and neutral.

"Well, that might be about to end," he said, "if only for one fun-filled evening."

"Now I'm worried," I said.

"You should be. I have been deputized, as always, by our idle, good-for-nothing brothers, to do something about your birthday."

I groaned. "Oh dear. I should be thankful, I suppose, that it's you. Mark and Ronnie wouldn't listen to a word I said."

"Quite. They are pitiless."

"Senseless, more like. Look, Al, there are things going on. Plus the scare over Mother going missing. All that. Work is – well, there are problems. I really don't want anything over the top. I'm relying on you – convince them. I'm not in a fit state for Mark and Ronnie's imaginative birthday treats. So-called."

"Understood," he said. "How about a quiet dinner somewhere nice? Do you know the Lime Tree? Back of the abbey, I'm told. Discreet, expensive, quiet. Probably a favourite haunt of the Dean and Chapter. I'll pre-empt the brothers and book a table for – what? Ten? Will Millie come? Will you bring anyone?"

"No idea about Millie, and she isn't here right now. I could ask Geoffrey, I suppose. Yes, the Lime Tree sounds nice, Al. I'll get back to you soonest. You guys all OK?"

"Mm, more or less. Sam hasn't yet got over the scare of Grandma going walkabout. You know what he's like when he's anxious. But I think you may be about to get an apology."

"Oh? Who from?"

"Kathryn. She's been very quiet. Possibly thought better of all that stuff she said about you. I didn't say a word, and that's probably been eating away at her as well. She knows what I think."

I sighed. "I'm on her side, Al. And yours. If she only knew it."

"Yes, I know. Keep me posted, OK?"

Lying in bed, I thought about the next day and the cases I had to deal with. I was due at the Brant Magistrates' Court at eleven, but I knew from long experience that the chances of any case beginning on time were slim. I thought of the Crown Court and the phenomenon of "floating trials" that caused such misery to all concerned: having waited weeks, even months, for their case to be heard, a defendant or a complainant could find it deferred at a moment's notice. This had always been so; trials notoriously overran or folded unexpectedly. But now several cases would be scheduled for the same day, even though there was no way they could all be heard in the time available, just in case a trial resolved. Inevitably some poor souls were sent away for another unspecified length of time, their lives on hold as they waited for justice. Justice! I wondered whether any of us, with the best intentions, were in a position to assure our clients they would get anything approaching that airy chimera.

I thought of all the recent developments: the legislation that had led, in some cities, to newly refurbished courtrooms, supplied with all the high-tech equipment you could wish for, standing empty, languishing for lack of trained people to run them. There was no lack of cases, especially now when more and more allegations of historical sexual abuse were filtering through. The "floating trial" was just one consequence of the massive backlog.

I wondered about the future of the criminal Bar, to which I had once aspired, but which now simply didn't pay me enough to live on. Sometimes, in darker moments,

I wondered if the system which everyone, innocent and guilty, relied on without really thinking twice about it, was indeed, as that report had asserted, at breaking point. Small wonder that barristers like myself were compelled to diversify, to take on every kind of case that came their way. My work now bore no resemblance to what I had thought it would be when I decided, all those years ago, and with the most impeccable ideals, to go into law. Even allowing for my youthful naivety, the changes that I had seen were all, it seemed to me, for the worse.

The next morning I went into chambers before court to check my e-mails, just in case something had changed at the last minute. Nothing had; but there was an e-mail from Melody Parker. I unplugged my laptop and stalked down the corridor. Janet looked up enquiringly.

"Tell me what you think of this," I said, barely containing my disgust. I planted my laptop in front of her.

Janet read the brief message. "Oh dear. Seems like Ms Parker is determined to pursue you, one way or another. Didn't I say she wouldn't let go?"

"You did. And now, since I have so high-handedly declined to give her an interview, she, so she says, will have to draw her own conclusions regarding recent events and people's motivations. Meaning, chiefly, mine. About which she knows nothing."

"Since when did the press need to know anything about anything to make a story of it?" Janet observed. "This," she tapped the e-mail on my screen, "is just covering her back. If I'm not mistaken she'll have written that article already, with the full backing of her editor."

"Pandering to their smug, ignorant, prejudiced

237

readership," I spat, "reinforcing the image of us as overpaid out-of-touch cynical fatcats, immune to any notion of truth. The hypocrisy is sickening."

"Nothing new, then," Janet murmured. "That'll be in this evening's edition, I expect. Not on the front page; that's reserved for the politicians. And they're getting worse by the day." She looked up at me, her expression almost sympathetic. "Better get a coffee before court," she said. "You won't get one at all there, or if you do, it'll be undrinkable slop."

"How right you are. Well, here's to another day trying to shore up the crumbling edifice. If it runs late I'll go straight home from court."

She gave me an enigmatic look. "All you can do is your best."

"Huh. Spare me the platitudes."

The day was busy and so provided welcome distraction. I was able to restore disputed property to a widow; I dealt with two custody cases, trying as always to build around myself a carapace against the grief and hysteria these situations so often generated. I tried, unsuccessfully, to keep a foolish young man from being found guilty of a relatively minor sexual harassment offence.

It all took time, and by the end of the afternoon I had had enough. I said goodbye to the court staff I knew there and made my way home. Knowing what the traffic would be like, I'd left the car behind; lugging my heavy briefcase and extra files, I took a bus and walked the last part.

I was in the shower, washing away not only the dirt of the day but also, I hoped, some of its weary frustrations, when I heard the front door slam and voices in the hall. I towelled down, put on a bathrobe, and went to the top of the stairs. Millie appeared from the kitchen, an anxious-looking Tiffany hovering behind her.

"Give me a minute," I said. "I'll get some clothes on."

I dressed quickly and ran a brush through my still-damp hair, then ran downstairs. Millie and Tiffany were sitting at the kitchen table, and Gordon was snuffling in his water-bowl. The girls were strangely quiet.

"Hello," I said. "You OK? Have you eaten? There's not much in the fridge, but we could get a takeaway."

Millie didn't answer. She reached into her capacious bag, planted on the floor by her chair, and brought out a folded newspaper which she laid on the table. "Mum, you should take a look at this."

A shudder ran through me. I muttered something rude and inappropriate and saw Tiffany's eyes widen. "Sorry." I turned to Millie. "So she wasted no time. Where is it?"

"Middle pages. Are you telling me you knew about this?"

"Not knew, strongly suspected." I unfolded the paper.

"Now where have I heard that before?" Millie said bitterly.

I turned the pages and looked across at her. "It's what I wanted to talk to you about," I said. "But you've got there before me. I'd never have expected you to buy a newspaper."

"I didn't. Jess's mum came home from work this evening and showed it to me. She buys the local paper on her way home. It came as a real shock."

"Yes. I'm sorry you had to see this before I had a chance to explain things." Her face was closed, but I knew she was upset, prepared to do battle. I found the centre pages. My heart sank. "Oh. This is worse than I anticipated." I looked at the two tense faces across the table from me. "Have you both read this?" They nodded. I took a deep breath and read. The left-hand page was dominated by a photo of me and Leaman on the steps outside chambers. Beneath, Melody Parker had given vent to her self-righteous indignation on behalf of "the good citizens of Brant" who, she said, would want to know what "local businessman Calvin Leaman, recently acquitted of the murder of Detective Sergeant Miles Winter, 34" was doing in cahoots with his defence counsel. Ms Anna Milburn, however, had "resolutely declined to give her views on the case. We shall all have to use our own interpretation."

None of this, I thought, could be regarded as news at all, let alone of interest to those "good citizens", whoever they were; but on the facing page, with by-lines from several reporters, including Melody Parker, was a full-page spread about the problem of drugs in the city, and a long diatribe from the editor, a predictable rant masquerading as responsible journalism and full of righteous dismay. There were even grainy photographs and quotations from people who had been tragically affected by drugs. Thankfully I saw nothing there about Sam, but I wondered, with a shudder, how long it would take Ms Parker to make that connection, especially if she had the ear of some members of the Brant police.

I closed the newspaper. "I hope you take all this as it is," I said. "Making something out of very little. Self-righteous cant."

Millie's lips tightened. Tiffany looked on the edge of tears. "Sure, we know you can't believe everything you read in the papers," Millie said. "But we didn't know anything about this. It's not so bad for me – I'm kind of used to you and your work and the secrets you have to keep. But it was a shock for Tiff."

"Of course," I said, gently, smiling at Tiffany. "What the paper has done here, putting the court case on the same page as articles about drug-dealing, is designed to confirm suspicion and prejudice without overtly accusing anyone. It's a dishonest, hypocritical tactic."

I saw Tiffany swallow. "Are they saying my dad is a drug-dealer? Millie thinks so," she said, her voice muffled by her attempt to hold back tears.

I summoned up all I knew of diplomacy. "So it would appear, I'm afraid."

"But he's not, is he?" She looked at me pleadingly. "He imports cars and boats. I've been to his warehouse and seen them."

"Yes, that is his business," I said. I took a deep breath: how far to go? Was it really my responsibility to disabuse this child? "Some people," I said carefully, "think your father is, or has been, also involved in drugs rackets. It has never been proved against him."

Tiffany's eyes were wide, and she said nothing, but a tiny strangled sound escaped her.

Now Millie weighed in. "That's all very well," she said, "and horrible for Tiff. But what about you? You told me you met Mr Leaman years ago, but nothing about any recent involvement."

"I couldn't," I said. "You know the restrictions I work with, Millie. The case was ongoing; I couldn't say anything. And I wanted to keep you out of it too. But the case is over. So now I can talk about it, up to a point."

Millie tapped the folded paper. "This describes you as his defence counsel. Is that right?"

"Yes. It never came to trial, though. The police investigation, and so the prosecution's case, was unsatisfactory. Things not done, things assumed, avenues not explored, evidence ignored, corners cut. When I pointed this out to the prosecution, they dropped the case."

Millie was not done. "Why did you take the case on? OK, you've told me about the cab rank rule, but is that it? Didn't you know there'd be all this in the press?"

"I was prepared for something, yes. But I couldn't have predicted the level of interest, the unsubstantiated vitriol. I was doing my job."

"Mrs Preston," Tiffany broke in, "is it true, though? About my dad being a drug-dealer? It's so awful." A tear ran down her pale cheek.

"I don't know, Tiffany," I said. "Nothing has ever been brought against him. But I'm afraid he has that reputation, and that's no doubt why some people are so angry with me for taking on his defence."

"Including Aunt Kath," Millie said quietly. "I knew there was something going on, the day Grandma went missing. Now I understand." She was looking at me speculatively, her anger seemingly dampened. "So why didn't you turn it down, Mum? Avoid all the fallout?"

I took a deep breath. "Because, even before the majority of the papers were delivered to me, I was inclined to think they'd got the wrong man." I turned back to Tiffany. "Whatever else your dad may or may not have done, he didn't murder Sergeant Winter." I would have gone on, but at this point Tiffany broke, sobbing, her bowed head in her hands, her shoulders shaking.

Millie moved her chair sideways and put her arms around her friend. "Hey, Tiff," she soothed. "Don't get upset. It's rubbish, I know, but at least that bit of it's over. Your dad isn't in jail, and no one's accusing him of anything. Maybe one day he'll explain all this to you himself."

I found a box of tissues and silently handed them over. After a while Tiffany's sobs subsided and she looked up tearily, sniffing and trying to smile. "I'm sorry," she said. "It's just… I've been so worried. On top of exams as well. I didn't know any of this about my dad."

"No need to apologize," I said. "It's perfectly understandable you should be upset."

"What I'd like to know," Millie said, frowning, "is why we are banned from Tiffany's house."

"It was Mr Leaman who wanted to keep you both out of harm's way," I told her. "We know that he didn't murder Sergeant Winter, but somebody did, and that person is still at large. Mr Leaman thinks he knows who it is, and he's worried that he might come after him. I don't know all the details, but it seems there's bad blood between them. So we thought it best if you two were well out of the way."

"Who does he think did it?" asked Tiffany, wide-eyed. "Is it someone he knows?"

"Yes. Maybe you know him too, Tiffany. A man called Vincent Priddy."

At this name Tiffany uttered a small scream and covered her mouth with her hand. "Oh!"

"You know him, then."

"I met him once, when I was little. I've never forgotten it…"

"Go on, Tiff," Millie urged. "What's so scary about him?"

"I remember my mum and I went down to Dad's work, the warehouse," Tiffany said slowly. "I don't know why we went. Normally I wasn't allowed there; Dad said it was dangerous for a small child. For some reason my mum needed to talk to my dad while he was at work. I wasn't supposed to get out of the car, but I was only five, I didn't understand, I just thought it would be fun to go and say hello to Dad; so I broke free of Mum and scampered into the warehouse. And the first person I saw there was this guy who to me looked like a fairy-tale ogre – broken nose, missing teeth, scars across his cheeks. He was also very hairy – bushy beard, straggly eyebrows. I'm sure he didn't do anything apart from appear in front of me – he may even have smiled, but that just made it worse somehow – and I screamed the place down. My dad came running from wherever he was and scooped me up. It was obvious Priddy hadn't harmed me and I told Dad that when I calmed down, so he didn't have a go at him, but he tore my mum off a strip for letting me get away. I heard some angry words, and that upset me even more."

"No wonder you remember him so vividly," I said.

Tiffany nodded. "For a while afterwards I had nightmares about him too. It wasn't his fault, though, was it? He can't help how he looks. But my dad has always been very protective towards me and I think he was annoyed with Mum for ages." She sighed. "They don't really get on, you know, not even after all this time."

"Well, it happens," I said drily, and Millie shot me a look.

Tiffany frowned. "Why does Dad think Priddy is the one who killed the policeman?"

"It's a bit of a saga, but it's to do with how Priddy has been behaving lately. He may be mistaken – nothing has been proved. But it seemed wise to get you two out of the way."

"What about my dad?" Tiffany said, clearly alarmed. "Isn't he in danger?"

"He didn't seem too bothered when he spoke to me," I said. "I imagine he can take care of himself. Try not to worry, Tiffany. Stay here with Millie for a while and we'll see how it goes."

"It's very kind of you to have me," Tiffany said in a small, childish voice.

"It's no trouble, is it, Mum?" Millie said.

"None at all. Now, shall we ring out for a takeaway? What do you like, Tiffany?"

We settled on a Chinese, and Millie took over the ordering. Tiffany asked if she might take a shower, and Millie lent her some clothes, far too big, but adequate for now. "Perhaps in a day or two we can ask your dad to bring some of your own things," I said.

While Tiffany was in the bathroom Millie came down and sat at the kitchen table with me. "Have you told us everything, Mum?" she said sternly.

"No, and I can't. There's too much going on that doesn't concern you, either of you. Besides, I don't think poor Tiffany can handle any more shocks, poor girl. If there's something I think you should know, and it's something I can divulge, I will tell you, I promise."

"All right," Millie said grudgingly. "You're right, though: Tiff has had quite a sheltered life up to now. She's not very streetwise. I'll do my best to look after her." She was silent, then she said, "It's weird, though, don't you think? How she didn't suspect *anything* about her dad. I mean, she clearly thinks he's wonderful."

"I'm more surprised she hasn't heard people gossip," I said. "Like at school, for instance. But you haven't heard anything about Calvin Leaman either, have you?"

She shook her head. "I knew there was someone you all blamed for Sam," she said. "But you were all very secretive. And as for gossip at school, maybe people have said something, but I haven't heard it, and anyway the school is very strict about stuff like that – verbal bullying. It's made me wonder, though."

"Wonder what?"

She shifted in her chair. "Well, how much I really know about my own father. I've always just assumed he is a normal, honest businessman. But maybe I'm wrong. You wouldn't tell me, would you? He could be an international arms dealer for all I know."

I smiled. "I don't think he's that," I said. "I suppose we can never know everything about a person, however close they are to us. Sometimes we just have to trust. You don't really know what I do day by day, do you?"

She rolled her eyes. "Of course I do. You tell me what you've been up to, all the boring cases you've sat in on. You've described to me all the odd people that work in the courts. Especially judges. Anyway, Mum, I don't have any doubts about you."

"You don't? Even though I didn't tell you about the Leaman case?"

"No, because I see you every day, and you may be annoying and nuts but I know you are honest. Some things you just know."

"Thanks for the vote of confidence," I said.

"The thing is, Tiffany thought she knew all about her dad," Millie said thoughtfully.

"We can all have blind spots."

"Yes, and I suppose Tiff's a bit naive, isn't she?"

I left it at that.

That night I had a muddled dream which somehow featured Atticus Finch. Normally my dreams simply fly away from my conscious mind on waking, and remain, if at all, as meaningless rags and tatters. This was no different, except that it caused me to wake in the middle of the night. I hadn't yet got round to changing the quilt, and with the weather warming up I was too hot. I threw the covers off and lay for a moment, feeling as if I was steaming.

Reluctantly, I got up and stumbled across the landing to the bathroom. I went back to bed, now fully awake, Atticus Finch refusing to leave me be. I remembered – how could I not, after so many viewings, such intense scrutiny? – how someone asked him why he was defending Tom Robinson, and his reply: "Because I could not hold my head up in this town if I did not." And yet many citizens of Maycomb, perhaps even the majority, were violently opposed to his defence of Robinson. Here was a white lawyer, against the word of a white woman, defending a black man. My own situation was hardly parallel; but my sense of honour, such as it was, certainly didn't seem to be shared by my fellow citizens. Finch and I were traitors, disloyal to our tribe. I thought of his self-control – when told of Robinson's death, when spat on by Ewell – and how it had faltered only when he believed his son had killed Ewell. Could I muster that level of self-mastery? I doubted it. And all the while young Jem was watching his father, learning in his own time how to be a man of honour. Did my daughter ever watch me? Did she listen to my reasons? Or was she simply too wrapped up in her own life, with all the self-absorption of youth? I thought of Atticus Finch facing the prospect of his young son on trial, and then sitting by his bedside all night. I tried and failed to bat away the creeping sense that my own child was in danger, and in the unforgiving darkness and silence of three in the morning I asked myself an unanswerable question: what could I do to defend her?

SEVEN

The hate mail started to arrive a few days after the photos of myself and Leaman, and the articles about drugs in Brant, had appeared in the *Herald*'s centre pages. It turned out that an e-mail had been sent to the chambers address, and Janet had got to it before I saw it, and summarily deleted it. When more arrived, such that she could defend me no longer, she told me about that first one.

"I think it's just two or three nasty people," she said. "Not a whole bunch of them. One message isn't enough for them – they have to keep going." She was watching me closely as she said this, almost as if she were watching for signs of – what? Panic? Self-disgust? An inability to cope?

"I wonder what it is they are trying to achieve," I said. "Other than venting their spleen, that is."

Janet shrugged. "There are some weird people in this world. You only have to hear Bob going on about how some folk like to abuse paramedics when they are trying to do their job. It's unbelievable. And it's not just a question of ranting and swearing – some ambulance staff have actually been attacked."

I waved a hand towards her screen. "You might as well delete all of them. I've seen 'traitor' often enough, not to mention all the other insults. They're not very imaginative, are they? Oh, and if anything comes in the post, just hand it over if it's addressed to me. There's no reason why you should have this in your lap. I'm the one that's taking bribes from criminals, betraying her profession, family, and country, not you."

"You don't seem too bothered," Janet said.

I shrugged. "So far they aren't actually issuing any threats, are they? I read some old barrister's memoirs a while ago, and he actually got death threats for defending innocent men because everyone believed them to be terrorist bombers."

"Really?"

"Yep. You can understand the wave of hysteria and fury that swept the country when ordinary people were blown to bits while having a quiet drink at their local. But as I'm sure you remember, those guys spent years in jail, and they didn't do it. The defending barrister got into the habit of checking under his own car, just in case. There was a lot of anger."

Janet was silent for a moment. "What would you do if there was a threat of violence?"

I gave a derisive snort. "I don't know. Would I get any joy if I reported it to Detective Chief Inspector Bryant, do you reckon? Anyway, to be honest, I'm more worried about a nutcase on the loose somewhere in this town. For all their efforts, the police haven't seen or heard a whisper of him so far. That bothers me more than a few misguided citizens venting."

I spoke more casually than I felt; it was my pride speaking. When letters arrived in the post over the next few days, their tone became darker, the accusations wilder.

My mere appearance in a photograph with Leaman had led some to assume that we were collaborating in crime. One letter claimed that I was myself a dealer in illegal substances and that Leaman and I had cut a deal. Melody Parker had a lot to answer for. I had no particular armour against such madness except for the low expectations born of experience. It was nevertheless depressing that such unhinged people felt it their right to abuse someone who had at least done her best to serve her city for the past two decades.

Arriving home that evening to hoots of youthful laughter, after a day when several letters had come to chambers in the mail, deepened my sense of isolation. I felt somehow dislocated, as if I existed in a foul-smelling bubble while the rest of the world went on in careless glee. I tried to quash the spurt of irritation I felt on seeing my daughter and her friends appear so carefree when they may well have been in real danger. My back to the front door, I stood in the hallway and took a deep breath to compose myself. At that moment, briefcase in hand, court shoes pinching, head throbbing, all I wanted was to go to bed, close my eyes, and deny all reality.

The kitchen door opened. Tiffany stood in the doorway, wearing one of my aprons, clutching a wooden spoon. Behind her at the table Millie and Jasper were mixing something in a bowl; all of them were laughing. Tiffany looked at me, and perhaps something in my expression sobered her.

"Oh, hello, Mrs Preston. Are you all right?"

I dropped my briefcase. "No, not really, Tiffany. And please, just call me Anna. I haven't been Mrs Preston for two years."

She flushed, and I immediately regretted my sharp tone. This girl was a sensitive soul; she had none of my daughter's combativeness.

"Oh, sorry," she said. "You look tired. Shall we make you a cup of tea?"

I did my best to soften my tone. "Thank you, that would be nice."

"We're making you dinner," Tiffany said. "I'm not sure how it's going to turn out. It's Jasper – he likes to experiment."

"Whatever you're making, I'm sure I shall eat it with relish."

Millie appeared. "Hey, Mum. I ordered some groceries online. I used your card – hope that's OK. There wasn't much in the freezer."

I flopped into a chair at the table. "Whatever."

Jasper spoke soberly, but his eyes were still full of merriment. "Hello, Ms Milburn. I hope you don't mind me gate-crashing."

"Not at all. And please, it's Anna."

Within a few minutes a cup of tea was put in front of me. I drank it, watching Millie and her friends argue amiably and somehow, out of apparent chaos, half an hour later produce a meal that was interesting, nutritious, and edible. Millie opened a bottle of wine, and the atmosphere at the table became convivial, almost like a family meal. I realized that this may have been something Millie missed, when I was so often too busy working to bother with cooking.

Millie took a last lick of her spoon. "Ah! Pudding. What a rarity that is!" She looked at her friends, then back at me. "We've been doing some baking this afternoon. I've discovered that Tiffany, as well as being a wonderful artist, is a really good cook! We made some cakes and I was allowed to ice them, but Tiff's are loads neater. And then Jasper turned up and we decided to cook dinner together."

"We made a pretty terrible mess as well," Jasper said. "As you can see. But before I go home we will clear it up, every last fork." He looked at me with a small frown. "Did you have a difficult day today?"

"You could say that." I stretched and sighed. "But coming home to a good meal has helped enormously. Thank you, cooks." I turned to Millie. "I hope you haven't cleaned out the bank account with your grocery ordering."

"Oh, no," she said innocently. "I just restocked the steak, truffles, and champagne. We can't run out of those, can we?"

"Ha, ha."

I went to my room and closed the door, dimming the laughter from the kitchen. They might not have thought of themselves as children, but when I left they were flicking foamy bubbles of washing up liquid at each other. Jasper was trying to load the dishwasher and ducking the onslaught; it was miraculous that no plates were broken. In the quiet of my own space the sombre mood of the day returned. I lay on my bed, phone in hand, and dialled Geoffrey's number.

His warm, rumbling, familiar tone brought tears to my eyes – a sign, if I needed one, that I was feeling vulnerable.

"How nice to hear from you," he said. "How are things?"

"Well, since you ask, things have been better," I said. "But my chief reason for ringing – apart from the pleasure of a chat – was to ask you if you would like to come to my birthday dinner."

"That would be delightful," he said. "But don't you have anyone more, er, appropriate to ask?"

"You mean someone tall, dashing, wealthy, besotted?"

"Possibly." There was a hidden chuckle in his voice, an amusement I would normally have shared.

"No one of that description exists," I said tartly. "You'd be the first to be informed if such a creature appeared on the horizon in all his glory. No one could be more appropriate than you. It'll be just eight – the brothers and their wives. Unless Millie wants to come, which I doubt; she has other fish to fry. I'll ask her this evening – Al will need to know. He's thinking of the Lime Tree. Have you been there?"

"Actually, I have. Sampled it with John Sutcliffe a few months ago. It was nice. Discreet, sophisticated."

"Oh dear. I hope the trying trio behave. One never knows once they've downed a few bottles of the house best."

"I'll try to be a moderating influence," Geoffrey said. "So what is it that's not going so well?"

"Ah, that." I took a deep breath. "I suppose you don't take the *Herald*…"

After giving Geoffrey all the unsavoury details of my inadvertent appearance with one of Brant's most notorious citizens, he was aghast.

"This is absolutely disgraceful," Geoffrey said. "Have you reported it?"

"Ha! Who to? The police? I'm not exactly their favourite person these days, am I? No, I just have to weather it, Geoffrey. Hope they get tired of their unpleasant game. But I'd appreciate your prayers: I'm feeling battered."

"You are always in my prayers, Anna," Geoffrey said soberly. "But I will redouble and focus them."

"Thank you. So you'll be my gallant squire to the birthday bash?"

"Glad to."

"I'll let you know the time when Alastair's booked the table. Will you find your own way?"

"Oh, yes, it's close enough – I'll probably walk. Anna…"

"Yes, Geoffrey?"

"Try not to let this horrible business get you down. Remember – you've done nothing wrong. On the contrary."

I sighed wearily. "I'll try to keep that in mind."

Although Geoffrey's reassurance offered some comfort, I still couldn't shake the gloom and decided to ring Rachel. We hadn't spoken for a while, and I thought perhaps I should tell her something of what was going on, especially now that Jasper was a frequent visitor. But before I had a chance to key in her number, I heard Millie call me from downstairs. I heaved myself off the bed and opened the door. Millie was looking up at me from the hallway.

"Jasper's going home, Mum. Wanted to say goodbye."

Jasper appeared beside her. "Your kitchen is spotless, Ms Mi – Anna. Just a little damp in places."

"That's OK, Jasper. Thanks again for cooking. Can I suggest – look, I was just about to ring Rachel. Does she, or your dad, take the *Herald*?"

"I don't think so."

"I wonder if you could still get a copy. I'd like her to read those centre pages."

"I could stop at a newsagent's on the way home," Jasper offered.

"No, take ours," Millie said. "Newsagents usually bin the unsold copies. You can bring it back when your parents have read it."

"Good idea," I said. "I'll ring her later. I could do with talking to someone sensible. And Jasper – please take care. I wouldn't want your association with us to get you into any trouble."

He smiled. "Don't worry. I'm sure I can look after myself."

He ruffled Millie's hair, and she made a rude face. "Bye, Mills. I'll give you a ring, maybe tomorrow."

Jasper left, and we stood there in silence, thinking our own thoughts, me at the top of the stairs and Millie at the bottom, listening to the throaty rattle of his car's engine as he drove away.

As it turned out, Rachel rang me before I had the chance to call her. "Anna, this coverage, so-called, is despicable," she said. Her voice was quiet, but full of seething fury. "There should be some comeback."

"If I try to defend myself it will just make it worse," I said. "I have to maintain a dignified silence."

"Maybe you do, but doesn't this scandal-rag have a letters page? I've a mind to send something stinging to the editor."

"Thank you, but really, it would just fuel the fire."

I heard her sigh. "If you say so. But it really shouldn't go unchallenged."

"I do say so," I said. "But I didn't want you to read those pages just to get some sympathy. Your prayers would be very welcome right now. I need as much prayer as I can get at the best of times, and these aren't."

"Aren't what?"

"The best of times. I am worried, to be frank. I want you to warn Jasper. My recent client Calvin Leaman is sufficiently concerned for the safety of his daughter to ask me to give her houseroom for the time being, as she and my daughter are friends. Tiffany is staying with us, more or less in hiding."

"From what?"

"No, from whom. General fallout as well, I suppose, but specifically Leaman's deputy. A man called Priddy, Vincent Priddy: according to Leaman, at best a loose cannon, at worst a lunatic. Suspected of being the real perpetrator of the policeman's murder."

"Good grief. Where is he, this Priddy?"

"That's just it – nobody knows. He's vanished. They're searching for him. But he could be anywhere. Maybe I'm being paranoid – I truly hope I am, Rachel, believe me – but until they catch him I'll be looking over my shoulder."

"Why would he be after you?"

"I don't suppose he is. I think he's after Leaman. But I got Leaman off, or so the theory goes, so that potentially puts me in his sights. Yes, it's all totally irrational – just like the piece in the *Herald*, and just like all the hate mail I've been getting – but rationality is precious and rare, apparently."

"You've been getting hate mail as well? That's dreadful!"

"Well, I'm coping. But that's not it, Rachel. As you know, Jasper's been very friendly with Millie and Leaman's daughter Tiffany. From what I can gather he's been spending a lot of time with them. At the very least, will you please tell him what I've told you, and warn him?"

I heard her take a breath and left her to digest what I'd said. "Well, I can try," she said finally. "And of course I'll tell Michael, and he can talk to Jasper. Normally Jasper will listen to his father. But Jasper can be stubborn. Also, from what little he's said, and the fact that he's been here every weekend recently, and not only at weekends, not to mention that he swans around whistling and generally looking very pleased with life, I'd say he's smitten."

"Really? But as far as Millie tells me they're just friends."

"Maybe not. Your Millie is enough to dazzle any young man – bright, beautiful, full of vitality."

"I suppose. But Tiffany is always there too, isn't she?"

"Is that so?"

"No… since you mention it. I guess I wouldn't know. I'm at work all day."

"Quite. Besides, Tiffany may have ideas of her own."

I frowned. All this, in the circumstances, I could do without. "Such as?"

"Your clerk – Janet. She has a son, I believe."

"*Drew and Tiffany*? I don't believe it."

"Why ever not?"

"Anyway, Tiffany is supposed to be keeping her head down, not gallivanting around town with Drew Clarke!"

"You're at work. The girls have been keeping their heads down, as you put it. But they have had visitors, I believe."

"Jasper told you all this?"

"In a way. What he didn't say I guessed."

"Oh, boy. I guess I've been too preoccupied to notice the obvious."

"I'm really sorry this has happened, Anna. It all seems so unfair. I truly wish I could help."

"You can, by praying for the girls.'

"I will. And Anna? Don't forget to pray for yourself too."

It wasn't especially late, but I felt something huge and smothering descend on me, weighing me down. All I wanted was to sleep – to court oblivion for a while, to be released from thinking, imagining, fearing. I decided to take a shower and go to bed early.

On the landing I met Tiffany, who was coming out of the bathroom, swathed in an old dressing gown of Millie's that was far too long. She saw me looking, eyebrows raised, and giggled. "Yes, I know," she said. "I look ridiculous. Millie's so much taller than me!"

"I understand what it's like to be the shortest person around," I said. "Hence the excruciating high heels."

"Oh, Anna," she stumbled over my name, and blushed. "I forgot to say. I rang my dad, and he said he'd bring some of my own things round in the morning. I hope that's all right."

"Yes, fine," I said, though the thought of Leaman anywhere near my house made me extremely uncomfortable. "But he'd better not hang around. None of us can be too careful until that man is caught."

"Yes, he knows." She bit her lip. Her freshly scrubbed young face registered anxiety and doubt.

"Anyway, I have to be out early," I said carelessly. "I doubt I'll see him."

As with many things, I was wrong about that.

I was up very early. By the time I heard the first sleepy mutterings from the girls I was washed and in court clothes, even though I was due in court probably for the briefest of hearings in the afternoon. Flicking through my diary, I saw that in a few days I was to prosecute a minor fraud in a court about forty miles away. Otherwise the diary was more or less blank, which gave me time to prepare. I downed a slice of toast and two cups of coffee. I was brushing my teeth when Millie's bedroom door opened and she ambled out, barefoot, hair everywhere.

"Hey, Mum. You're early."

"I'm going to chambers to do some prep," I said. "Mr Leaman is coming here at some point with a bag of Tiffany's things."

"I know." She looked as if she wanted to say more, but apparently changed her mind. "We'll see you tonight, then."

"Mm. What are you doing today?"

She shifted from foot to foot. "I don't know. We're feeling like we want to go out. Like we're prisoners. It's nice weather, we don't have school till Monday, we could go to the beach – or anywhere."

I considered the options. "I don't see why not. Actually, it might be a good idea to get right out of the city. Tiffany's got her car here, hasn't she?" Millie nodded. "I'll leave it up to you. Just be careful."

"Maybe we could go to that forest park," Millie said, brightening. "Take Gordon. And a picnic. I'll see if Jasper wants to come."

I wanted to ask her what the deal was with her and Jasper but thought better of it. Instead I merely said, "I hope Jasper isn't neglecting his uni work. Didn't he have a deadline for something?"

She looked at me, eyes wide, as if I were stepping into forbidden territory. "He submitted that," she said coldly. "You don't have to bother about Jasper. That's up to him."

"Right. Well, I'll see you later. Enjoy your moment of freedom." I picked up my briefcase.

The doorbell rang, sounding unnaturally loud and intrusive in the morning quiet. I felt something lurch inside me. "Already?" I muttered. I glanced at my watch: it was only ten to eight.

"You'll have to answer it, Mum – I'm still in my PJs!" Millie hared back into her bedroom, and I heard her speaking urgently to Tiffany.

I plodded down the stairs, took my black jacket from its hook, and opened the front door. Calvin Leaman stood with his back to me, a bag in his hand. He was looking up and down the street.

"Mr Leaman. You are very early."

He turned to face me. He looked grey and lined, his eyes hooded, as if he hadn't slept.

"Good morning, Ms Milburn," he said. "I see you are ready to go out."

"I am going to work," I said curtly.

"I see."

"If you give me Tiffany's things I will leave them inside for her."

He shook his head. "Please. I know you don't want me around, and I can't blame you. But I have to come in. Just for a moment. I don't want to hang around on the doorstep. And there are things I must tell you. I could have rung, but I was coming with Tiffany's things anyway. Please, Ms Milburn."

I felt as if the jaws of a trap were screaming shut. The last thing I wanted was this man in my house, but it seemed my choices were limited. "All right. I suppose," I said reluctantly. I stood back to let him in and closed the door behind him. "Tell me what you have to say, and then let me go out. You can speak to Tiffany once I've gone. She's not even up yet."

He nodded. I had the sense of something crumpled and cracked; it was as if some of this man's habitual self-belief, his arrogance, had leaked away. "It's very good of you to shelter my girl," he said, almost humbly. "I'm really grateful."

"Tiffany herself is no trouble," I said, my tone as haughty as I could make it. "Obviously I don't relish the circumstances."

"No, I understand that. I don't suppose you relish having me here either. But you need to know. I'll be brief." He cleared his throat. "The lad I told you about – one of my young workers? The one I asked to go and see Paul Fleetwood?" I nodded. "He came round to the house last night. He'd done what I asked. Apparently Paul's in a terrible state, terrified of Priddy, and the lad has nowhere to go. He has a sister in the city, but the sister has young children, and Paul doesn't want any trouble to come to her. The other lad spoke to him, tried to make him see sense, and to cut the thing short, he got Paul to agree to talk to the police. He even offered to take Paul in for a few days, to his own flat, till the dust settles, which was good of him. Anyway, he put Paul in his own car and took him down to the nick. Spoke to the man in charge: I think you know him. Bryant."

"Yes. So?"

"Paul retracted his earlier statement. Said he'd lied to keep Priddy off his back. All the time he's pleading with Bryant, asking for police protection." Leaman shook his head. "Prettyboy's put the fear of I don't know what into him. But then, Vincent's not someone to cross if you can avoid it."

"What else? What exactly did Paul say?"

"Chiefly, that he'd given Priddy a false alibi. They weren't together, playing cards or whatever. He doesn't know where Priddy was that night. But not only that: he told them that Priddy had boasted about nicking my watch."

"I see."

"So now, obviously, they want Vincent for that policeman's murder. At least they want him for questioning. I never doubted that he did it – he's got it in him, and he's, I don't know, he doesn't think, he's impulsive, full of rage." He shook his head. "If he was sneaking around the warehouse and saw someone in the yard, why not just lie low? But no, Vince has to whack him. Idiot."

"Let's hope the police are stepping up the search. They've got another chance to get things right."

"Yes. It beats me why they haven't found him yet. Where can the fool be that no one has any idea? He's got to go out some time, surely! He has to get food at least. And he's got a very distinctive face." Leaman gave a bark of hollow laughter.

"Could someone be sheltering him?" I asked.

"He hasn't got anyone that I know of," Leaman said. "He's alienated a few people in his time." A sound came from upstairs, and he glanced upwards. Immediately his expression transformed. "Hello, Tiffany love! How're you doing?"

"Hi, Dad." Tiffany ran down the stairs and threw her arms around her father, hiding her face in his jacket. "I'm OK. Are you OK?"

"I'll leave you to it," I said. I edged towards the door.

Still holding his daughter, Leaman looked up. "I'll keep you in the loop, Ms Milburn," he said quietly. "And next time I'll just ring."

I was coming back from the fraud case the following week when I saw it. I'd gone straight to the court without going to chambers first, and I'd had a successful morning; the detailed preparation I'd done over several days, involving minute checking of accounts, had paid off. A charity worker had been accused of embezzling funds, and was, I believed, obviously guilty. The defence based their case on ignorance, which is no defence at all, and I demolished it. The worker was convicted, and the charity trustees were jubilant. Whether or not they'd get their money back was another matter.

I drove back to Brant and parked at the back of chambers, but instead of going straight inside I decided to get some lunch and do some shopping. Feeling better for a sandwich and a cup of coffee, I ambled through thronged streets. This was a rare treat, to have a spare hour and not be racing from one place to another, loaded down with files. I came across a street market with stalls selling summer clothes, tourist tat, and fruit and vegetables. I bought a bag of apples and crunched one as I strolled.

I passed an outlet for electrical appliances and on impulse went in. Our television was old; I'd been thinking of replacing it. Perhaps now was a good time to compare prices. If I had a baseline I could do a bit of internet research as well. The walls were lined with various sizes and makes of TV, all switched on, but showing just an image, and no sound. The early afternoon news was apparently about to begin.

As soon as the newscaster – a tall, slim, Asian woman in a blue dress – mouthed something I couldn't make out, an unmistakable image flashed on the screen. Though I had never met Vincent Priddy, never seen a photo of him, and had only heard descriptions, I was certain this had to be him. It was no surprise when, seconds later, his name flashed up on the screen. I wondered where this picture had come from; who had taken it, and when? It showed a man of middle years, but aged by his facial scars: oblique stripes across both cheeks, as if he had been clawed. His hair was wiry, over-long, grizzled brown, and his eyebrows jutted wildly. His nose had obviously been broken at some point and allowed to set by itself. He was unsmiling, his dark eyes half closed, and another, smaller scar added a twist to his upper lip. He looked like a man who had been in many fights.

"Something I can help you with, madam?" A shop assistant had materialized at my elbow.

"Uh, what?" I stammered. "Oh, no thank you, I'm just browsing."

When I looked back at the screens, the face had gone. Some other piece of news had replaced him.

I left the shop, any thought of buying a new TV now far from my mind. Despite the warm afternoon a chill settled on my bare arms, and I slung my jacket round my shoulders. I felt a wave of nausea, and interpreted it as sheer fear. Why was Priddy's face on the local news? What had happened? What had I missed? Where were Millie and Tiffany? Then I remembered: safely, I hoped, at school, attending a course of lectures and seminars based around citizenship.

I hurried back to chambers, and by the time I got there I was out of breath. Janet looked up at me from her desk, her expression inscrutable.

"Janet," I gulped, "I went for a wander round town. I just saw Vincent Priddy's face on a TV screen, on the local news. They didn't have the sound on, so I didn't find out why he was there. What's going on? Is it just that the police are looking for him and have gone public?"

She shook her head. "You're not going to like this, Anna. Let me come to your room so we can talk with the door closed."

I sat at my desk, and she planted herself in a chair opposite. "This is between you and me," she said. "I'm not supposed to know either. I imagine the whole story will be on the evening news. I'm not clear on the details, but what I do know is that Paul Fleetwood is in hospital, and I only know because Bob was on the crew that answered the call." She bit her lip. "According to Bob, the lad's in a bad way."

"What happened?" I whispered.

"Bob said he looked like he'd been mauled," Janet said. "A neighbour rang 999 when he heard a commotion. Paul's flat's in a dodgy part of town; people are wary of interfering. But this neighbour heard yelling and screams and loud noises, late last night it was, and then someone running down the stairs; someone in heavy boots, he said. It was dark; he heard a powerful engine revving, but when he looked out of his window he didn't see anything. Then he heard a sound like someone sobbing and moaning. He opened his door onto the landing and there was Paul, curled up on the floor, his arms round his head, blood everywhere."

"Good grief."

"The odd thing was Paul was clutching a suitcase, and Bob said when they got there they had the devil's own job to get it out of his hand."

"Yes," I murmured. "He'd have been getting ready to go to his friend's place. Shame he didn't go sooner."

Janet frowned. "What?"

"Sorry, I didn't tell you. You know Tiffany Leaman's staying at my house, out of harm's way, we hope. Well, her father came by the other day with some fresh clothes for her and other things, and he told me that Paul had been persuaded to change his evidence. What he told the police would have put Priddy firmly in the frame for Winter's murder. What Leaman told us was true – his watch *had* been stolen, and it was Priddy that took it."

Janet whistled. "And they still haven't found him."

"No. It's a complete mystery. Is he that canny that he can avoid detection so long?"

"Search me. Maybe now they've asked for the public to be alert they'll track him down. But if it's him that's done this to Paul I hope the police are warning people not to have a go. The man's lethal."

That evening Millie, Tiffany, and I gathered round our old TV at six o'clock for the news. Once again Vincent Priddy's unlovely face filled the screen. In solemn tones a reporter said that the police were looking for Mr Priddy to assist with their enquiries in the ongoing investigation into the murder of Sergeant Miles Winter. In addition, Mr Priddy was wanted for questioning following a savage attack on Paul Fleetwood, a co-worker who had originally supplied Mr Priddy with an alibi. This attack was being treated as attempted murder. Priddy's whereabouts were currently unknown but it was believed he was still in Brant. If anyone saw him they were to contact the police immediately, but on no account were they to approach him.

"I wonder how that poor young man is," I wondered.

"Perhaps I could try to find out," Tiffany ventured. "My dad might know. I'll ring him. While I'm doing that I'll make us all a cup of tea, shall I?"

"You're a treasure, Tiffany," I said.

"Yep, every home should have one," Millie agreed lazily.

Ten minutes later Tiffany returned with three mugs of rather weak tea on a tray and distributed them carefully. "I spoke to my dad," she said. "He went up to the hospital to see Paul, but they wouldn't let him in because he's not a relative. He did get to chat to Paul's sister, though. Things don't look too good, I'm afraid. They're really worried about him."

Millie gasped and looked up at her friend. "What're you saying, Tiffany? That there's a chance he could die?"

"Oh, I hope not!" Tiffany looked as if she might cry.

"We all hope that, Tiffany," I said gently. "I shall pray for him this evening." The television was now showing a politician beamingly recommending the idea of Britain leaving the European Union, and I switched it off. "Beyond that, there's not much we can do. Now I will give you both a shock: since Millie has restocked the fridge and freezer,

I will cook us some supper. For a change. You can tell me what you would like, and while we're eating it I want to hear all about this citizenship thing you've been doing at school."

Millie groaned. "It'd be just your sort of thing, Mum. But actually rather serious and heavy, wasn't it, Tiff?"

"Oh, I liked it," Tiffany said, brightening. "And tomorrow there are some people coming to talk about careers."

"Any idea what you want to do?" I asked her.

"No, not really. But I don't want to go to university. I don't think I'm clever enough. I might do something at Brant College where Drew is. He's doing Business Studies, isn't he, Millie? But then, he's clever as well. Maybe I'll work for my dad in his business."

I smiled feebly. Which business was she talking about? But what, really, did I know? What did any of us know? No criminal activity had ever been proved against Calvin Leaman; and just lately I was learning, to my cost, how a reputation could be so undeservedly lost in the face of misreporting and malicious bias.

At one time the *Brant Herald* had been a respectable newspaper: it actually purveyed news rather than whipping up the prurient credulity of some sections of the public with manufactured scandals. I had allowed myself to feel some relief that the hate mail, both by e-mail and post, had begun to peter out. I should have known that Melody Parker, backed by her timeserving editor, wouldn't let a story die if there was an ounce of life to be wrung from it, however obvious its departure from fact.

I hadn't, of course, forgotten the paper's campaign against me and my former client, but I was busy and put it on a high shelf, hoping it would gather dust and become invisible. But on the day of my birthday dinner, this was revealed as pure wishful thinking.

Alastair had booked the table for nine o'clock – on the late side, but the restaurant was popular and he'd left the booking until he'd heard from Mark, who always made things difficult. I decided to splash out and buy an outfit for the occasion. I hadn't had anything new for some while. I was pleased to find something that suited and didn't cost the earth – a dress that hid the bulges, in a pleasant shade of blue-green. It fitted, I didn't hate it, and if Millie said it made me look like some variety of vegetable I would ignore her. I hesitated over the shoes: comfort or height? I opted for comfort, considering that I sacrificed this on court days. Whatever shoes I wore, my brothers would tower over me; I would have to stand up to them, as always, by other means.

Thinking about my brothers, I smiled to myself as I dressed that evening. Complain as I often did, especially about Mark and Ronnie, an evening with the triplets was bound to be challenging, argumentative, and above all entertaining. Inevitably, on the relatively rare occasions that we were together, the sparring and jostling for supremacy that characterized our childhood was revived.

I took a taxi to the restaurant and met Geoffrey at the door. He gave my arm a gentle squeeze and planted a fatherly kiss on my cheek. "You look dazzling, my dear. Happy birthday."

"Dazzling, eh? Thanks."

Alastair, Kathryn, Ronnie, and Tanya were already inside, perched at the bar with a row of drinks. There was a flurry of greetings, hugs and kisses, and birthday wishes.

"Let's take possession of the table," Ronnie said, his voice booming as usual, "since it was so difficult to acquire. So

Al tells me." He looked around. "Quite posh here, isn't it? Should I behave?"

"You'd better," Geoffrey said with mock severity, "or I shall have no compunction in asking the management to eject you onto the street."

Ronnie pulled a face. "Yes, Headmaster."

A waiter guided us to our table, nicely situated in the bay window overlooking the cobbled square. The back of the abbey loomed, visible as a mounded silhouette in the soft evening darkness, surrounded by antique streetlamps.

"Nice view," I said as I settled into a chair. "Any chance of a drink, boys?"

Alastair took my order and went back to the bar, returning with a glass which he placed in front of me.

"Thanks," I said, and took a sip. "No sign of the metropolitan contingent?"

"Mark and Lesley are coming up by train," Alastair said, "to avoid the matrimonial dickering that always seems to precede a celebration – whose turn it is to drive." He glanced at Kathryn. "Seems I'm the sober one tonight." Kathryn raised her glass to him in salute. "So if they caught the right one, they are probably walking up from the station now. Mark wanted me to meet them there with the car, but I told him the exercise would do him good."

"He's rich enough to take a cab," Ronnie said. "Just too tight."

"That's why he's rich," I countered. "He doesn't spend every last halfpenny like you."

The door of the restaurant opened, letting in a cool breeze. My oldest brother, ushering in his wife before him, closed the door with a bang. "Aha, my delightful family!" he crowed. Heads turned at adjacent tables, but Mark, as ever, took no notice. He joined us at our table, and more hugs and handshakes and greetings were exchanged. My drink was already soothing my nerves and deadening any social embarrassment I may have felt. With my brothers I knew I might as well just go along with whatever transpired. Causing mild mayhem was an art form with them.

Mark signalled to the waiter and ordered drinks for himself and Lesley, who was already head-to-head with Kathryn, exchanging news of offspring.

I proffered my own empty glass. "While you're at it, bro, you can fill this up for me."

The talk grew louder as the drinks flowed and only subsided momentarily when the waiter approached and asked us if we were ready for our first course.

"Are we?" Mark said, looking round the table. "Hadn't we better order some wine? What's everybody eating?"

This caused more arguing and delay, but eventually Mark demanded the wine list and made a selection. There were moments when his high-handed approach was useful. Our starters arrived and were consumed. Ronnie was telling Mark about some deal he had secured, and Mark was putting his own financial spin on it, dealing out advice whether or not it was wanted.

"I'm going to the ladies' before the next course," I announced. "Push your chair in a bit, Ronnie."

"What's this?" Mark said in mock-horror. "Surely our undersized sister isn't getting just a trifle tubby!"

I pulled a face at him. "Get lost, string bean. At least I've got all my hair."

I was washing my hands at the basin when Kathryn slid in. She was elegant as always in a close-fitting blue number but I thought she looked strained, older than her years.

"You all right?" I asked mildly.

"More or less." She hesitated, then she said, "I read that piece about you in the *Herald*."

"Ah, yes, that."

"It's all rubbish. But still upsetting. People saying nasty things."

"It happens."

She looked at me and seemed to take a breath. "I said a few of those myself not so long ago. I was out of order; I realize that now. I'm sorry, Anna."

I patted her arm. "Forget it, Kath. It was a difficult day. We were all tense. And I do understand how it is with you and Al and Sam."

"I know." She held out her hand, and I took it. "Friends?"

"Of course."

That was one of the few positive things that happened that evening. The wine was emptied and replenished, our main courses arrived and were demolished amid appreciative comments, apart from Mark's; he preferred to believe that nothing originating from Brant could compare with the capital's offerings. Mark unfortunately tended to become even more belligerent when he'd had a few drinks. "I hear you've been in the news, small sister," he said.

Lesley pinched him. "Mark, give over. It's the poor girl's birthday."

Before I had a chance to retort, Ronnie leaned over the table and spoke conspiratorially, but still far too loudly. Ronnie was never much of a whisperer. "Funny you should mention the *Herald*," he said. "Because if I am not greatly mistaken, I recognize the back of that head over there. Table on the far side. Don't you, Al?"

We all looked. "No," I said. "Who is it? And why do we care?"

"See if he turns round," Ronnie hissed.

The waiter brought our desserts, but we all ignored him, our eyes trained on the far-side table. After a moment, with an expansive gesture, and amid general laughter, we caught the man's profile.

"Oh, great," Alastair muttered.

"Who is it?" I repeated. I thought perhaps my voice was slurring; my brain certainly wasn't at its crispest.

"I hate to cast a damper," Alastair said, addressing me, his voice low. "That's the editor of the *Herald*."

Ronnie made as if to rise from his chair. "Shall I give him a piece of my mind?" he growled.

Tanya tugged at his sleeve, and he slumped back down. "Remember, darling," she said, "it was him that gave you that nice write-up after the gallery show."

He glared at her. I recognized the signs of over-drinking. "You think I'm going to toady to that snake when he's persecuting my only sister?"

"Ron, dear," I murmured. "Thanks for the thought, but it'll only make matters worse. Anyway, I don't want to be the cause of wrecking your career. Let's pretend we don't know who he is and get on with these calorie-laden confections."

Despite my brothers' valiant efforts to the contrary, things were not quite so bullish after that. I kept a discreet eye on the editor's table, noting that when he paid his bill it was presented to him with much smiling and jesting by the restaurant manager. Clearly he was someone of consequence, at least in this establishment. Perhaps he was a frequent customer. I watched as coats were collected and draped over ladies' shoulders by attentive men. The party were obliged to pass near to our table on their way out; first two women, expensively dressed and wearing an eye-hurting display of jewellery, then two men, smartly suited. The editor was the last to leave, and as he came level with us, with just my two brothers and their wives between me and him, he caught my unwilling eye, smiled knowingly, and waggled his fingers in a parody of acknowledgment. I gave him my most baleful stare in return.

When the door closed behind them, Mark, for once exercising a shred of tact, leaned towards me. "What on earth have you been up to," he hissed, "to fall foul of him?"

"Let's not go into all that now, Mark," I said heavily. "Not on my birthday. We were having a perfectly pleasant time till we realized he was here."

"I saw him a while back," Alastair said quietly. "And I know he's been watching us – as covertly as he can. But you're right! It's your birthday, and people with birthdays get presents." At this there was a general easing of tension as people fumbled in bags, bringing out brightly wrapped parcels which they put on the table in front of me.

Lesley presented me with a fat package wrapped in silver. "This is from Dom and Lolly," she said. "They send their love and best wishes." Why did Lesley invariably look smug when talking of her children? I hoped I never did. When she asked after Millie – almost as an afterthought – I did my best to avoid any show of maternal partiality. To be proud of your children is one thing; to parade their supposed across-the-board perfection and general superiority quite another.

We made the best of it; we ordered coffee and brandy and someone paid what was undoubtedly a painful bill. I hoped it wasn't Alastair. He'd get the share promised by the other two eventually, I supposed, but only by continual harassment that was foreign to his nature. Ronnie always claimed he was broke, and Mark's hold on his purse-strings was legendary.

We gathered outside the door, putting on coats and jackets. The evening was mild, but it was late and a fresh breeze brought with it a slight chill. Mark looked at his watch, then declared they must run if they were to catch their train. With hurried kisses and goodbyes exchanged, they were gone, Lesley almost running to catch up with her husband in her foolish shoes. Alastair and Kathryn, and Ronnie and Tanya soon followed, leaving me and Geoffrey. He waited with me till my taxi arrived.

"Goodnight, my dear Anna," he said. "I hope your birthday wasn't too bruising." He chuckled softly. "How different those boys are from my Charlie. So competitive!"

"Probably comes from there being three of them," I said. "I guess I'm used to it."

He smiled, then sobered. "And as for the other thing," he said diplomatically, "try not to let it get you down. Remember – you have friends. Me included, of course, but One in particular."

"Thanks, Geoffrey." I sighed. "I can't promise, but I'll try."

Two days later, when I went into chambers I found the previous evening's edition of the *Herald* neatly folded on my desk. Seeing the florid font of its title, the over-decorated *H*, I felt a cold prickle run down my arms. *Not again.*

Janet appeared in the doorway. "You've been relegated," she said with her usual succinctness.

"What?"

"No longer the scandal queen at the centre. Some other poor sap's getting it in the neck. Probably some failing hospital, or some management type with his hand in the till, or some banker buying a yacht with his latest bonus. All very self-righteous."

"Nothing new there," I muttered. "It's taking me all my charity not to wish something humiliating on that editor and his toadying minions, especially Miss Melody Parker. So am I not there at all?"

Janet gave a little humourless laugh. "Oh, you're there all right. Just on the gossip page, that's all. Demoted. But with their usual nasty way of doing things."

I turned the pages and found an unflattering picture of a tousled woman, head flung back, laughing and lifting a brimming wine glass in one hand. "He must have taken that himself," I murmured. "It's a terrible shot."

"Where were you?" Janet asked.

I told her.

"Ah yes, you said. The paper's very coy. Talks about 'a select local restaurant' and a 'rather rowdy party'. He's got a cheek, hasn't he? Since he was there himself."

"That's a gross understatement," I said sourly. "That man, his underlings, his horrible paper, are shameless. I wonder if I can sue."

"That's not the worst of it, though," Janet said. "Look what's next to the photo."

"It's a picture of the hospital."

"Look at the caption."

"Oh, boy. 'While certain of our professional classes enjoy the good life, an innocent young man, caught up in the seamy criminal side of our city, fights for his life following a vicious attack.' I know that's not true."

"How come?"

"Because Tiffany heard from her father. She told me last night. He's in touch with Paul Fleetwood's sister. The lad's badly knocked about, but he'll recover, thank God. 'Fighting for his life' indeed."

Janet shrugged. "You surely don't expect honesty from the *Herald*, do you?"

I sighed. "No. But I hate that it's sunk so low, and people believe it. Do you think the barrage of hate mail will resume after this?"

Janet pursed her lips. "You might get away with it. What with all the nonsense our politicians are spouting, maybe the loonies won't notice you." She turned to leave, then looked back. "Oh, by the way, we should have a Management Committee meeting."

"What, another one?"

"The last one was a while ago. I've put it in your diary, and I'll tell the others. You should chair this one. Things to consider, diktats from on high – in other words, the Bar Standards Board – and they want to know what we're doing about our maternity policy. Who'd ever have thought that was such a burning issue?"

I sank into my chair and closed my eyes. "I can't wait."

That lunchtime I left chambers and walked across the square, through the streets, past the restaurant where we'd recently celebrated, and across to the abbey. I entered by the great west door and breathed in its familiar scent of old wood and candlewax. Apart from a straggle of tourists it was empty. Someone was practising in the organ-loft on a very quiet stop, the music thin and reedy, barely registering on my conscious ear. I slid into a pew somewhere in the centre of the nave, leaned back, and closed my eyes. A dull headache was throbbing at my temples; I probably needed something to eat. I unfolded the copy of the newspaper that I'd brought from chambers and laid it on the bench beside me. When I'd decided, ten minutes before, to come here, I'd vaguely recalled a story in the Old Testament where something similar had happened. What was it? A king, taking a letter into the Temple. Hezekiah.

There was a Bible in the rack in front of me and I hunted through it till I found it: 2 Kings, chapter 19. The Assyrian emperor had written a boasting letter, claiming that no country, certainly not pitiful little Judah, could hope to stand against the might of the Assyrian army. Hezekiah, one of the few faithful kings, knowing he could not of himself hope to withstand so mighty an enemy, had taken the letter into the Temple and placed it before the Lord. There he prayed that God would act to save his chosen people in the face of Sennacherib's insults. And God, through the prophet Isaiah, promised to put a hook in the emperor's nose and a bit in his mouth and take him back by the way he'd come. *How I'd like to see that happen to the editor of the* Herald. *I shouldn't be desiring revenge, I know. But it's hard not to.* I read on. That very night the angel of the Lord swept through the camp of the Assyrian army and 185,000 soldiers were killed.

I didn't desire death and destruction for anyone; there was enough of that in the world without my adding to it, and Hezekiah's world was very different from the one I knew. I murmured an apology. But then I prayed: *I'm not a king, and no army is threatening me. I'm sick of being persecuted, even if it's only by this weaselly little rag of a newspaper. But that's not my real worry. I'm scared, Lord. For my daughter, and her friends. I'm going to leave this with you, just like Hezekiah and his letter, because the whole issue is far too big for me even to encompass, let alone seek an answer. I'm going to trust you to bring about a righteous outcome and defend the innocent. And if I have to act, help me to know what to do. Thank you.*

EIGHT

I was working late, poring over some papers I had spread out across the kitchen table for easier reference. Head throbbing, I knew I should go to bed but doubted my ability to sleep. Just as I was thinking about making a cup of tea, I heard a soft footfall outside the door. Millie came in, a wide fleecy scarf wrapped around her thin cotton pyjamas, her hair ruffled, her eyes heavy.

"Hey, Mum. You're up late."

"Earning a crust, I hope." I gave her a wan smile. "Couldn't you sleep?"

She slipped into the chair opposite me. "No. I keep thinking about that man." She shivered.

"What, Priddy?"

"Yes, him." She leaned forward. "Mum, do you really think he might be after us – me, you, Tiffany, her dad?"

I shook my head. "Sweetie, I have no inkling as to this man's psychology, his motivations. What is he thinking? Is he thinking at all? What do any of us know?"

"Tiff's dad thinks he wants revenge on him, but I don't know what for, and neither does Tiff. The thing is, if the police are after him for the murder of that policeman, what has he got to lose? He could do anything, couldn't he? Go mad in a shopping mall, take a hostage, throw himself in the river. Whatever."

"I know. And one thing I've realized, over and over, is that you can't count on anyone being rational. Which makes guessing what someone might do, especially someone you don't know, next to impossible."

"Yeah. I suppose it's a bit easier if it's someone you do know." She looked at me speculatively. "Do you reckon you know me well, Mum?"

I smiled. "That's a funny question." I thought for a moment. "Yes and no. No, I don't know half of what goes on in your head, and you're changing rapidly because it's that stage of your life, and anyway you like to keep things to yourself a lot more than you used to, which is natural. But at some deep level I know you well. You're part of me, and I've seen you grow and change, and I've noticed things through the years which you may not even be aware of yourself – the bits that are like me, the bits that are more your father, or his mother, or great-uncle Sid – and the bits that seem to be uniquely you."

"Hmm. I didn't know there was a great-uncle Sid." She digested what I had said, chewing her lower lip. "There's something I thought I might tell you, though."

I felt a small chill. *Now what?* "Go on, then."

"I've decided not to take up Jasper's offer of a room in his flat in the autumn. Assuming," she added hastily, "I get my grades and go to the same uni. I'm going to accept the place in halls. I really like Jasper, but you only get one chance of getting a place in halls, and I reckon it's the best way to make friends at the beginning, because everybody else is doing the same. I can always hang out with Jasper if I want to, but he's only got one more year to go, and I've got three."

"Good," I murmured. "That's wise."

"Also," she went on, her voice strengthening, "I reckon we women need our girlfriends. I don't know about men's friendships – they seem really weird to me – but you need your girlfriends when things get tough. Or when you just want to relax and hang out and do silly things and talk."

"Did anything in particular bring you to that conclusion?"

She nodded. "Yes, sort of. I've watched Jess lose her sanity over Will, who's nice enough but just a boy when you get down to it, and sometimes they're on and sometimes they're off and she's in a state and crying on our shoulders and then he comes back and she's away again with no thought for her mates." Millie looked up at me, her expression all scorn. "I never want to be that girl," she said, her voice low. "The sort that moons over some bloke and makes herself ridiculous. The sort that treats her friends like agony aunts and dumps them when the guy deigns to reappear in her life. It's so undignified. Sometimes I think Jess has no self-respect."

I opened my mouth to comment, but she was ploughing on. The thought, not especially welcome, crossed my mind: *How like me she is sometimes.*

"Whereas," Millie said, "Tiffany, who I wouldn't have thought of as a friend at all a few months ago, has been unbelievably loyal. She's not the brightest – I mean, I love her, she's great, but she's a child in some ways – but she's always there, faithful. I didn't know this till after, but she turned down seeing Drew because I was feeling less than brilliant."

"That's a thing, then, Tiffany and Drew?"

S. L. RUSSELL

Millie shrugged. "I don't know. It could be. Just like, in a different way, Jasper and I could be. All to play for, no guarantees. I know she likes him, though. And he'd be lucky to have her, which I never let him forget."

"Well, thanks for bringing me up to speed. I have to be honest, I'm glad you've decided to stay in halls for your first year. As you say, you can always be friends with Jasper, or more than friends, if it works out. But to live in his flat might restrict your other potential friendships."

"Yeah. That's what I thought." She fell silent.

"Not to mention living with three men might have its disadvantages. I don't know them – maybe they're paragons – but young guys aren't often models of cleanliness. You might end up having to wash their dirty dishes just to get something to eat out of."

She smiled. "I thought of that. I'm not the tidiest, I know" – she flashed me a complicit grin – "but I am keen on basic hygiene. The thought of sharing a bathroom with three guys was almost enough in itself to sway my decision!"

I took a breath. "But you know, Millie," I said slowly, "I take on board what you've said, and I agree, the spectacle of one of your usually sensible friends losing it over some boy is pretty sickening – especially if it's some self-important fool of a boy whose attractions you totally fail to see. And now, for you and your friends, really isn't the time to be thinking about any degree of permanence; there are too many other things to do, to experience. But a good, long-term relationship with the man of your choice can also be life-enhancing. Not to mention there'll come a time when all your friends are disappearing into cosy domestic situations where you are only a visitor."

"Oh, I don't write it off for the future," she said. "The very distant future, that is. But I wouldn't have thought you'd be too keen to recommend anything like marriage."

"Why? Because my own didn't work out? I hope I can see beyond that. Well, most of the time."

"Mum," she said, uncharacteristically hesitant, "can I ask you, now that I am a bit older, did you tell me all the truth, you know, why you and Dad got divorced?"

I'd been expecting this, in some way, at some time, over the last two years, simply because my daughter is no fool; and because it wasn't unexpected, I'd given thought to what I might say and how I might phrase it, as it seemed important to get it right, as far as I could. "No, not entirely," I said. "You were told the truth, but not all of it, to save you unnecessary distress. We told you that things had gone wrong over the years, that we felt it best to part, but that we were still reasonably friendly, and both your father and I were still equally your parents and dedicated to your welfare."

"All rather bland, and didn't actually tell me anything," Millie commented. "That bit, for example – *that we felt it best to part*. Seems to me those few words hide a whole lot of unsaid stuff."

"I see you've thought about it," I said, raising my eyebrows. "Did you think that at the time?"

"Not really. Too busy processing the shock, and all the changes. But since? Yeah. So, Mum, I've been upfront with you. Want to tell me what really happened?"

I pondered, and she watched me struggle, saying nothing. In the end I said, "You have to understand I can't speak my mind, not completely. I hate it when separated parents criticize the other partner to their kids. It's horrible for the children; their loyalties are already conflicted. Richard Preston is no longer my husband, but he is and always will be your father. So no, I can't tell you everything, and anyway some of it is our business and no one else's. But I can tell you the facts, and you'll have to draw your own conclusions. Fair?"

"Sure. I get it."

"There probably was a lot of drifting apart. He was working on building his business, I on building my career. We were very busy. Found time for you, but not so much for each other. Here's a fact, untainted by my interpretation: one evening he came in from work, slouched in the doorway of the kitchen where I had papers spread out over the table, just like now, and said, 'I want a divorce.' I was stunned."

"You hadn't seen anything coming?"

"No. If you'd asked me, I'd probably have said we no longer had much in common, except you. But with hindsight, I'm pretty sure he was already seeing Jenny. Clearly he'd decided he wanted something more fulfilling than our convenient arrangement. But it was still a shock – a derailing shock, for a while."

"Wow. I didn't know that."

"No. How could you?"

"But Mum, looking back, at the beginning, did you really love each other then?"

"Yes, I thought so. It seemed quite a match, to us and all our friends – two ambitious young people, keen to achieve. We were hasty, I suppose. And I did that thing you speak so scornfully of – threw in my London life, which I loved, to live with him here in Brant, because that's where he was setting up in business. No doubt I was starry-eyed. But I think, at the time, so was he."

"Do you think," she said slowly, and I sensed that a question was coming that I had long dreaded. "Do you think it was me, coming too soon, being so sick, taking all your time, that made everything go wrong?"

I leaned over the table, scattering papers, and took her hand. "Sweetie, listen. Never think it was your doing. What happened when you were born happened to us all – me, your dad, and you. None of us had a choice. We got on with the situation as it was. We were both very worried – it was probably more worrying for your dad because I was ill as well. Maybe that did have an effect. But what it also did was to strengthen our knowledge – his as well as mine – of how precious that little life we'd made was. Made together. That can't change, however many other children your dad has. He is sometimes forgetful, I know; he's a busy man with many things on his mind. But he's a loving father, and your dodgy start makes him that bit more protective. Never doubt that, OK?"

She pulled her hand away and folded her arms. "No, I know Dad loves me," she said. "And of course I love him just because he is my father. But that doesn't blind me to the fact that he's been a bit of a cheating rat, to be honest."

"What?"

"I'm not stupid, Mum," she said. "And Jenny talks to me, when I go over there, when Dad is busy and it's just the two of us. Even she reckons she wasn't the first."

"Oh." I was flummoxed.

"Well," she said with a grin, "I didn't know at the time, and you didn't tell me. All honour to you; you didn't slag him off once. But," she said, sobering, "it's all right for him. There he is, nice new wife, younger, beautiful, who adores him, who's about to have a baby, making him feel like some kind of hero. But what about you? You live here –" she waved a hand around our modest kitchen – "you work all hours, and you don't have some loyal hunk backing you up. Why not? How can that be fair?"

"Fairness doesn't really come into it," I said faintly. "And as for *why not*, I haven't looked for it, and it hasn't come my way."

"So he tells you he wants a divorce, and you just cave in and let him get away with it? You didn't fight for the life you had?"

"No." I laughed, but without humour. "I figured if he didn't want me, I wasn't hanging around. It's called pride, darling. And you have it in spades."

"Yeah, I suppose. And there are some weird set-ups, I know. From what Tiffany tells me, there's not a lot keeping her parents together either. Mrs Leaman is nice, but she seems... I don't know, she seems in awe of her husband, almost timid, but at the same time she's very attached to her things, like her car, her jewellery, her whole lifestyle. And it's almost like she's abandoned Tiff, just scuttling off to her sister's at the first sign of trouble. How weird is that? But it can work, Mum, can't it? A permanent relationship, I mean. Drew says his parents act as if they think the other one's an idiot, but they're still together. And Jasper says his dad's like a different person since he married Rachel."

"That's an interesting household, for sure."

"Jasper takes all the credit for it, you know. Getting his dad and Rachel together."

"Does he?"

"He calls it 'The Jasper Wells Dating Agency'. Silly boy. Apparently he was friends with Rachel first, and then he says it was his idea to invite her to their place in France to recover from all that awful trauma and her injuries, and *then* when he saw his wicked plan was working and his dad was smitten, he says he had to put him straight when he was in a state, etc."

"Jasper seems close to his father."

"Oh, he is. He told me about when his parents split up. He hated having to go to London to live, not because he didn't get on with his stepdad – he says he's OK – but because he was worried about his dad, thought he'd be lonely. He even bought Dulcie for him – he was only twelve at the time. They are nice, the Wellses, all of them. And Jasper is genuinely pleased his dad is happy."

"Not jealous of Jonathan?"

"No, he adores him. And I think Jasper knows how much he is loved, however many more kids his dad has." She shot me a look. "As you say is the case with my father, though there I am not quite so convinced."

I laughed. "Millie, you are priceless."

"Am I? I thought I was just honest." Her eyebrows twitched. "A chip off the old block, as they say."

"I must quiz Rachel about that story when I see her. Get her take on it," I muttered, almost to myself. "Oh, but Millie, I'm pleased you've decided to stay in halls. In fact, I'm delighted you've told me all this stuff. It makes me realize what a wise young lady you are becoming."

"Huh, yeah, sometimes. But I'm also eighteen. And I want to be nineteen, and twenty, and thirty. I want to have a life." Her tone had changed, panic entering her voice. "What do you think, Mum? Is this guy really a threat? Am I going to be affected by some stupid quarrel we know nothing about?"

"*No*, Millie, no," I said earnestly, suddenly jolted back to reality. "That can't happen. We have to believe we will be defended. I have prayed for protection. Yes, we need to be careful, but we – and Tiffany – will be all right."

"I hope you're right, Mum. I hope prayers are answered. Seems to me there are no guarantees. There's a girl in my year at school, my age, Andrea. We've hardly seen her for months. She's got some hideous cancer, and the treatment's almost as bad as the disease. What about her? Is she going to make it to nineteen, twenty, thirty? Nobody knows. Even if she recovers, her whole life's been on hold. And there'll always be that threat, won't there?"

"Poor girl. Horrible for her. Devastating for her family. I'm not saying all will always be well, Millie. Things do go wrong. We have to live with, and for, what we have now. And speaking for myself, I have to trust God."

She didn't comment, just took a deep breath and smiled a little awkwardly. "Yeah. Well, I think I'll go back to bed. See if I can get some sleep. You should too, Mum." She pushed back her chair and went to the door.

"Tiffany's asleep, I take it."

"Yeah. You know, I have to look out for her. There's something innocent and harmless about Tiffany, despite everything. I don't want her to get hurt, but somehow I feel it's inevitable."

"What about Drew?"

"What about him?"

"Is he solid? Will he be a support for her, if there's fallout? And when you're not around?"

She paused, considering, standing on one socked foot. "I think so. It's too soon to tell. But if he ever treats her badly he'll have me to reckon with."

"Scary."

Again, that faint, awkward smile. "Thanks for being honest with me, Mum."

"You have been too, and I appreciate it. And Mil, what

you want for yourself, I want that too. With every fibre of my maternal being. A life, a future. Choices. The prayers continue. It's all I know to do."

I wasn't expecting to be in court on this particular day. Janet, knowing my predicament, had been straining every muscle to keep me close to Brant and available to drop everything. But that morning she presented herself at my door, bearing a cup of coffee and smiling apologetically.

"OK," I said warily. "You need me for something."

She put the cup down on my desk. "Sorry, but it's you or nobody. Everyone is busy, out of town, or down with this virus that's going around."

"Tell me the worst, then."

"Elizabeth Merchant just called in. Her trial, the one she's been prosecuting here at Brant Crown Court, is in a real state."

"Nothing new there."

"No, but it's a big one for her. It involves a defendant who doesn't speak English. They'd organized an interpreter, but the interpreter hasn't shown up and no one can track him down. On top of that, at the last minute two of the jurors have called in sick. Basically the trial is going to overrun. It should have been reasonably open-and-shut – Elizabeth was confident she had it all sewn up for a conviction."

"Frustrating for her, but sometimes I think the term 'open-and-shut' should be banned. It's almost inviting chaos."

"I know. But the bottom line is she can't be at her case this afternoon. This one really should be straightforward. Please – will you take it?"

Returns are a part of life. Trials, by their nature, go

wrong. If we didn't take returns the system would be even more crazy than it is. We don't have to do them, but we often do, out of a sense of duty, and of professional courtesy. I liked Elizabeth, and I wanted her to do well at her trial, even if it meant last-minute stepping in.

"All right," I said. "When is it?"

"Three o'clock. You'd have to leave by twelve at the latest. It's in Northampton."

"What? How long does that give me to look at the papers?"

Janet looked at the clock on the wall. "Hmm, about two hours. But like I said, it's not complicated."

"Famous last words," I grumbled. "Go on, then. I'd better make a start. Northampton, indeed."

Janet was right about one thing. The case was straightforward, and no doubt Elizabeth had accepted it on that basis, even though it was some distance from Brant. Like the rest of us, she needed to make a living, and at this stage of her career she also felt the need to make a name. I didn't want to be so far from home – not as things stood, not at the moment – but I felt there was little choice.

By four fifteen the case was wrapped up. As I gathered up my files and prepared to leave, thinking of the drive ahead and how I could avoid the rush-hour insanity by taking a different route home, one of the office staff called me. "Ms Milburn? Urgent phone call for you."

I frowned. "Did they say who they were?"

"Your husband."

My husband? That set the alarm bells ringing. I followed her to her office. She indicated the phone on the desk and I picked it up.

"Anna?" Richard's voice, strained and relieved at the same time. "Found you at last. Your mobile's switched off. I've had to run around and contact your chambers clerk to find out where you were."

"Hadn't you better tell me why you're calling?" I spoke calmly, but dread was rising up, threatening to choke me. There could only be one reason he was calling: our daughter.

"It's Millie. She rang me about twenty minutes ago. Anna, wherever you are, you need to get home. She wasn't panicking exactly, but she's worried. I didn't really understand what it was all about – some long, garbled tale about a man and a car. But you need to speak to her, urgently."

Despite the warmth of the afternoon, I felt a wave of cold wash over me. "If it was so urgent, couldn't you have dealt with it?"

"No, that's just it. I would have but I'm at the hospital. It's only because I slipped out to get some coffee that I found Millie's voicemail and called her back."

"Why are you at the hospital?"

"Jenny's in labour. I can't leave, not now."

A surge of sheer fury made me grit my teeth. Maybe I was being unreasonable, but it seemed to me that he was setting his unborn child above the welfare of his existing daughter. But this wasn't the time for an argument.

"Right. Well, I'm on my way. Bye, Richard."

"Anna, please." He sounded fraught. "Let me know what's going on, soon as you can. Once the baby's safely born, I can be more use."

"I will."

I ended the call, thanked the clerk, and raced out of the court to my car. As I started up, I mentally prepared a way back that would avoid the worst of the major roads. I left the city and started eastwards on less crowded routes – or so I hoped.

I'd been driving for about fifteen minutes when my mobile buzzed. I'd left it on the passenger seat, and a glance told me it was Millie's number. A few hundred yards further on I came across a place to pull off and park, and I swung in.

I paused to breathe for a few seconds. My palms were sweaty, and I felt unusually hot. Fumbling, I found Millie's number.

"Millie? Are you all right?"

Simply hearing her voice flooded me with relief. "Yeah, just about, Mum. I couldn't get you, so I had to ring Dad."

"I know. He called me a while back."

"My little brother's on his way, apparently. So Dad couldn't help."

To my dismay I thought I heard tears in her voice. "What is it? What's happening? And where are you?" I said urgently.

"Don't panic – we're safe for now," Millie said. "But Mum, where are you?"

"I'm on my way home, but I could be a while. It's rush hour, and I got sent on a case to Northampton. Hadn't you better tell me what's going on?"

"Yeah, OK. Brace yourself, Mum. Tiff and I decided to go to the shop on the corner after our session ended, about three thirty, maybe later. Just for a few snacks. We got to the gate and Tiff suddenly grabbed my arm, really tight. Mum, I've never seen anyone so scared. She was pointing across the road. There was this old black car parked there, really weird-looking. I've never seen anything like it before – dusty and beaten up. There was someone inside, but we couldn't see who it was, not clearly. All I could see was they were wearing a black hat. But Tiff recognized the car. She went really pale, Mum. She said, 'I know that car.'"

"Go on, Millie. Bottom line."

"Well, Tiff said that car has been in an outbuilding at the Leaman place – I mean, for years. Mr Leaman used the building as a garage and a place to put junk. Ages ago he let Priddy have a go at – what? Restoring it, I think she said. He's mad about cars. But he hasn't been doing much with it, and it's just been there in that outbuilding, more or less forgotten. But Tiffany recognized it straight away. That's why she was so scared – because who else would it be, sitting in the driver's seat, *outside our school*?"

"Oh, Millie! Did you speak to your headteacher? Does she understand how serious this could be?"

"I was going to, Mum, but we couldn't track her down. So we asked her secretary and she said she was in some meeting, not even in the building. Tiff was getting very twitchy, and I didn't want to take the time to explain things to the secretary.

"But there's more. Obviously we didn't go to the shop. We went back into school, but when we couldn't find anyone to tell, Tiffany rang her dad. He called us back a bit later, and said he'd been to that old garage, and not only was the car missing but there were signs someone had been there. It was dirty and disgusting, with loads of litter, and bits and pieces of clothing as well. Mr Leaman was so furious with himself, Mum, letting that man hide under his nose. But how could he have known? Priddy is obviously cleverer, or maybe just sneakier, than anyone's given him credit for. No wonder the police couldn't find him – it'd be the last place they'd look. The only thing Mr Leaman was relieved about was sending Tiff and her mum away. The thing is, if Priddy wanted

292

to harm Mr Leaman, he could have, couldn't he? He was right there, on his property." She paused, as if gathering her thoughts. In the silence I heard a car horn sound. "Except," she went on, "if I remember right from being at Tiff's, that outbuilding is sort of hidden away, on the other side of what used to be a tennis court. That's probably why Mr Leaman didn't suspect."

The implications were clear enough. "Yes, if he wanted to harm Mr Leaman directly, presumably he had opportunities. But if he's been outside your school, it seems to me he has another game in mind."

"Mum, that's so scary," Millie whispered.

"The police need to know, Millie."

"They do know. Mr Leaman rang them straight away. He said he had some trouble at first persuading them that he didn't know about Priddy and that old car. I suppose he managed it in the end. What do we do now? How long are you going to be?"

"I'll be as quick as I safely can. I can't answer for the traffic. Won't Mr Leaman come and help?"

"Oh, Mum, that's another thing! He was coming down to school to get us as soon as he'd spoken to the police, but when he got to his car he found every tyre had been slashed! He's had to get someone out to replace them."

"OK, Mil," I said, my voice quavering. "Is that car still there outside your school?"

"No. As soon as whoever it was saw Tiff and me running back inside he reversed and turned the car round – nearly hit an old lady with a fat little dog – and roared away."

"Right, here's what to do. Stay at school as long as you can. Wait for someone to come and get you – whoever can get there first."

293

There was a silence. "Mum, it's too late. We're already on our way home. We thought – Tiff thought – Mr Leaman couldn't get to us yet. Dad's at the hospital. You're miles away."

It felt as if some malevolent hand had reached inside my chest and squeezed my heart. For a moment I couldn't breathe.

"Mum?" Millie's voice trembled.

I steadied myself somehow. "All right, sweetheart – tell Tiffany to drive carefully. When you get home, make sure everything's locked up tight. I'll get to you as soon as I can. The police know what's happening. Try to keep calm."

"OK." She sounded relieved. "Don't break the speed limit, though. Oh, and I don't want to use up my phone battery till we get home, just in case. But I'm worried about Jasper. He was going to come over this afternoon."

"I'll ring Rachel. She can tell him to stay put."

"And Mum, Tiff said you and her dad probably need to be able to talk to each other, so I gave her your number. I know you aren't too keen on him, but I thought it might be a good idea. I hope that's OK."

Great. "Yes, of course."

After I ended the call to Millie, I tried to compose myself. Eyes closed, I breathed deeply, consciously unclenching my fists, trying to achieve some measure of control. And in this extremity I remembered to pray. My prayer was garbled and full of fear, and I just had to hope and believe that God understood. *Armies of angels*, I pleaded. *At both ends of our street. Please.*

I started up the car, and was about to pull out onto the road, when I remembered about ringing Rachel. Sighing at my own muddled brain, I switched off the engine and phoned her.

"Hello, Anna – nice surprise," she said after what seemed a long wait.

"Maybe not so nice," I said grimly. "Rachel, listen. Is Jasper there?"

"No, he went out about half an hour ago. I think he's probably on his way to your house. Why?"

I told her what Millie had told me. "Rachel, I'm afraid that Jasper might be putting himself into danger, and it's really nothing to do with him. I'd hate any harm to come to him."

For a moment she was silent, then she said, "Me too, Anna. But if he was here, and I told him what you just told me, my guess is he'd be out of the door like a rocket. He'd want to be there with Millie and Tiffany, whatever the danger. Nothing I could say would stop him. We just have to hope he's already there. I can try his mobile, but I don't think it will help."

"Are you on your own?"

"Yes, just Jonny and me. Michael's operating this afternoon, but I can call his secretary and get him to ring me as soon as he's out of theatre."

"Do that," I said. "Right now I need to get back to Brant."

"Of course," she said sombrely. "Not a lot I can do. But I'll pray – safety for all our children."

My brain was evidently recovering from shock, because before I pulled away I rang the number I had for Steve Bryant's direct line. It went straight to voicemail. Biting my lip, frustrated, I called the Brant police and asked for him.

"DCI Bryant is out on a case," a bored voice told me.

Rage and panic building, I blurted, "This is urgent. My name is Anna Milburn. DCI Bryant knows me. It concerns the safety of two, possibly three, young people."

"Ms Milburn?" The voice sharpened. "One moment."

After what felt like a lifetime another voice came on the line. "Ms Milburn – it's your case DCI Bryant is dealing with. I'll give you his number."

I dialled Steve Bryant's number, and he answered almost immediately. "Steve – Anna Milburn."

I heard him exhale. "Have you been in touch with your daughter? We're almost at their school to pick them up."

"They're already on their way home. I told them to stay put, but it was too late. Sounds like Tiffany panicked. And another friend, Jasper Wells, is on his way to join them. I was too late to warn him as well."

I heard him curse. "Where are you?"

I told him. "As soon as I get off the line I'll be on my way, as fast as I can."

"Wait – do you buy it?" he asked abruptly.

"Buy what?"

"Leaman's story. You must have got to know him. That he didn't know Priddy was holed up in his garage."

"For heaven's sake, Steve, does any of that matter now? We need to get to those children! But for what it's worth, Leaman's been convinced all along that Priddy murdered your colleague." Bryant grunted. "Look, Steve, Leaman's no friend of mine, whatever the *Herald* would have you believe. But our kids are friends, and that's why his daughter's with mine, and we have to get to them."

"All right. I'll tell my driver to turn around and head straight for your place. We followed up what Leaman told us – gave him the benefit of the doubt, though there's not a copper in Brant who's happy with that."

And, I thought sourly, *you have to get it right this time, pal.*

"What you can't know," Bryant went on, "is that we found the car. The one we think Priddy was driving. Abandoned down by the viaduct. Engine steaming. Full of rubbish. And no sign of Priddy. So he's on his feet now. We'll get him,

Anna." His tone softened. "Don't think I can't understand. I'm a father as well. You must be at your wits' end."

"Yes. Look, Steve, the sooner I get going, the better. Just keep those kids safe."

"Do my best."

As I pulled away, I wondered about that. From what he was saying, Bryant was still as hostile to Leaman as ever, unwilling to take his word. I shook my head in disbelief. The evidence was stacked up against Priddy now, but it was as if Bryant, and perhaps the majority of his colleagues, were incapable of believing that Leaman wasn't involved. Maybe there were reasons for that, in the history I didn't know; nevertheless, I was astonished that Bryant was still running the investigation when he had made so many blunders, cut so many corners, played – so it seemed – fast and loose with procedure. Maybe he had already been subject to a severe reprimand, as Clive Stephenson had suggested. Maybe they were now keeping a closer watch on him. At that moment I couldn't have cared less, and I dismissed him from my mind: right then there was no space for anyone but Millie.

A few miles from Brant my phone buzzed again. Millie. This time it took me a mile or two to find somewhere safe to pull over.

"Millie?"

"Oh, Mum. Thank goodness!"

She sounded so frightened that my stomach seemed to shrink in on itself. "What is it, Mil?"

Her voice sank to a whisper. "We're home now and we think he's here."

My stomach lurched. "Priddy?"

"We didn't get a close look. But someone is round behind our shed."

"I'll call the police again. They're probably already there. Is Jasper with you?"

"Yes. It was Jasper that spotted him. He thought he saw someone at the back. A shadowy figure... Mum, I'm so scared. Who else would be sneaking around our garden? But how did he know where we live?"

"No idea. Hang in there, sweetie. I'll ring DCI Bryant."

I could hear my heart thundering in my ears, and my hand shook as I phoned Bryant's number. "Steve? Anna."

"We're just turning into your road. What's up?"

"I just heard from Millie. I think he's found us, Steve. There's someone in the garden."

I heard him mutter something. "OK, Anna, don't panic. I'll call for backup."

I almost screamed. "Can't you get the kids out?"

"We don't know enough yet. We don't even know if he's armed, Anna – just get here. We've got it covered. Give me your daughter's number. We'll do everything we possibly can to keep them safe. And drive carefully."

I gave him Millie's number, ended the call, and threw my phone down onto the seat. It felt as if something was stuck in my throat. *Help, Lord, help.* I fought for control, breathing slowly. *Come on, Anna,* I told myself sternly. *Get a grip. You're no use here.* I decided to brave the motorway, and for once my luck held – if luck it was. The next junction was about two miles away, and when I joined the carriageway I saw that I had bypassed the worst of the rush-hour traffic. Being able to drive at seventy was a welcome distraction. In ten minutes I had left the ring road and was crawling closer to home.

As I approached the road that ran parallel to mine, I sensed rather than saw the commotion ahead. I parked at the kerbside and walked briskly, breaking into a run as I came to the end of our road. Why was I in such a hurry? What good could I actually do? But I knew I had to be there, to be close to my child, whatever happened next.

An ambulance was parked at the corner of the road. I halted momentarily, feeling a sudden new wave of fear. Was it there on standby, automatically called in case of need? Or was someone already injured? I came up behind the police cordon, and a uniformed constable held an arm out to stop me. A crowd of people had gathered, staring, muttering, peering forward. Why were they there? At first I recognized no one, then I thought I saw one or two neighbours. An elderly couple had bulging shopping bags: clearly they were being prevented from entering their own house, for their safety. But others must have come simply to stare. "My daughter's in there!" I said to the constable. "That's my house you're staking out. I'm Anna Milburn. Let me talk to DCI Bryant."

"Hold on, madam." The constable spoke to a colleague standing near him, and the young woman disappeared into the crowd.

A moment later she returned. "This way, Ms Milburn."

She threaded her way through, and I followed closely. "Guv, Ms Milburn."

Steve Bryant was standing on the other side of the cordon, a loud-hailer in his hand. "Anna, I'm going to try to talk to our man."

"Where is he?"

"We aren't certain. We managed to get round the back, but there was no sign of him." His voice lowered. "Look,

Anna, try not to panic, but we think he's already inside. The glass in your French window was smashed. We tried your daughter's number but there was no answer. I'm going to try to get him to talk to me. Persuade him he'll be better off not doing anything rash."

At this moment I heard a loud crash from the direction of my house, followed by the sound of glass falling, tinkling. The crowd shifted and muttered uneasily. Over their voices we all heard a piercing scream. It was unmistakably a girl's voice. Just as I saw Steve march forward into the empty space in front of my house, Calvin Leaman careened round the corner, panting, red-faced, forcing his way to the front of the crowd. A police constable tried to restrain him, and I heard him bellow, "Get your hands off me! WHERE'S MY DAUGHTER?" All heads turned towards him, mouths open.

An eerie silence seemed to descend, blanketing us all. In the midst of it we heard Steve Bryant's voice, distorted by the loud-hailer. "Vincent Priddy! If you're there, come out before you get into more trouble. Just show yourself, walk out wherever you are, come towards me, hands where we can see them, and no harm will come to you." The echoes died, and in the silence I heard a squeak. My gaze flew upward, and I saw Millie's bedroom window, always stiff, slowly begin to open. There was a jagged hole in one of the panes, and more glass fell. Nothing was said; nobody moved. Then there was a shuffling and a shoving, and the curtain flapped. The window swung wide, and visible behind it I saw three familiar faces, pale, hollow-eyed: Tiffany, Jasper, and Millie, with Gordon clutched in her arms. The man behind them was in shadow, but there was no mistaking the light reflecting off the blade of the long knife in his hand.

For a brief moment the world, the road, the hedges, the

lampposts, all seemed to tilt. The tarmac swayed up towards me. My legs turned to wet paper. I heard myself groan. Then I felt a hand take me by the elbow – a warm, strong, steadying hand – and I found I was upright. My eyes were swimming, unable to focus.

"Anna." A deep voice, one I knew. I blinked the tears away. Michael Wells was standing beside me, his hand still firmly gripping my arm. "Hold on." I looked up at him, seeing his face drawn and lined as never before.

"Oh, Michael," I said. My voice was very faint, as if I was hearing it from a great distance. "You're here."

He nodded grimly. Then he looked away from me, his eyes searching the front of my house. "What's going on?" he asked quietly.

"That man has our children," I choked out. "And a knife."

I saw Michael close his eyes briefly. He said nothing.

I looked out again into the road and saw Bryant lift his phone to his ear and speak into it, listen, then speak again. Then he hurried back to the cordon, took Calvin Leaman aside, and muttered something to him urgently. I saw Leaman nod; he looked dazed, as if someone had punched him in the head. He ducked under the cordon and walked unsteadily forward a few paces. He stopped just across the road from my front door, only metres away from where Michael and I stood, pressing against the barrier. I saw Bryant say something to a constable, and then both of them looked surreptitiously towards the other end of the street, where another barrier had been set up.

I nudged Michael. "Look."

His eyes narrowed. Out of nowhere appeared shadowy figures in black, with helmets, masks, firearms clutched across their chests. I counted five or six.

"How far away do you think they are?" I whispered.

Michael's voice was low, barely audible. "Fifty metres?"

It all felt completely unreal. The afternoon sun was waning, slipping down behind the houses. It wouldn't be dark for several hours yet, but there was a weary quality to the light that signalled another day ending. An ordinary day for most, I supposed. The tarmac was its usual black unremarkable self beneath my feet; those same feet were recognizable in my old brown driving shoes. Michael was a solid figure beside me, tall, in his work clothes, his white shirt open at the neck. All seemingly ordinary; and yet everything was surreal, as if it were some cardboard film-set, with reality hidden behind. Somewhere in that reality my only child was threatened with a knife. I knew it, but I couldn't comprehend it.

But things were happening. Several policemen were herding the crowd back, and we were pushed along with them. "For your own safety, madam," one of them muttered to me.

I sucked in my breath.

My front door was opening. Out onto the front path, stumbling, came Millie, still clutching the dog, and Jasper close behind. Behind them we saw Tiffany, held back by a bare arm across her throat. Priddy marched her forward. The knife was in his other hand, held down for now. He was only a little taller than Tiffany herself, and he walked crouched, his back bent. His head appeared over Tiffany's shoulder, dark eyes under massive brows darting from right to left, his wild hair straggling across those scarred cheeks and round his neck. He growled something to Jasper, who opened the gate. Then all four of them were standing in a line, with Tiffany still in Priddy's grip, her face bloodless, her eyes squeezed shut.

Leaman, on the other side of the road, just a few metres away, started forward with a strangled cry. Priddy raised the long-bladed knife and pressed its point against Tiffany's neck. "Better stay where you are, Cal," we heard him say. His voice was gruff, but in the silence we heard every word. "Better listen to me for once, 'less you want your little girl hurt, eh?"

I saw Leaman take a breath, his hands clenched at his sides. "What do you want, Vince?"

"Just for you to listen for once, Cal. Like you never do."

"You talk, then. I'll listen. Just let the kids go. They've done you no wrong."

Priddy laughed, a wheezy gleeful parody of humour. "Come on, Cal, give me some credit. I ain't that stupid. Soon as I loose my grip on this sweet little neck, the coppers'll let rip."

"Just tell me what you want, Vince."

Priddy's roar startled us all. From the quiet, almost restrained way he'd been talking to Leaman, suddenly he bellowed. "Just my rights, you stinking cheat! You promised me way back. You promised me a fair cut. You said I could run the show. You said I'd have more money than I knew what to do with! But you've held out on me all these years. You've looked down on me, you've told people I can't be trusted, you've used me. Worked me into the ground. You'd rather deal with Billy Telfer! That weak slimeball!"

"I'll make it right, Vince." Leaman held out both hands. "Just let the kids go."

Priddy shook his head. "It's too late, Cal. I'm going to get sent down for that copper. It don't make no difference what I do. I've got nothing to lose. But you – you've got plenty. You've hurt me, and now I'm going to hurt you."

It was as if time itself hung suspended. I felt a nudge, a draught at my back, and suddenly Rachel was there. She slipped an arm round Michael, and then she found and gripped my hand.

I had glanced towards her; now we all heard a scream, and our heads whipped round to the tableau at the gate. Horrified, I saw the long knife rise, the sun flashing off the blade. Leaman surged forward with a desperate roar. We saw an arm flail, then came a screech, a spurt of bright blood and a moan that was all my own. Immediately I heard a sharp crack, the knife flew into the air, and Priddy staggered and fell, clutching his shoulder, howling. Then, all of a sudden he was surrounded by armed police.

Among the pandemonium Michael ducked under the cordon, brushing aside the constable with a gesture of impatience. He strode forward and came up level with his son as Jasper began to crumple, his knees buckling under him. Michael put an arm around Jasper's back, holding him upright, and took his hand, which was dripping blood. I heard Rachel gasp and mutter something. Michael marched Jasper towards us. The lad's face was milky-white, his eyes glassy. "Rachel, you drive," Michael said. "I'll be in the back with Jasper. I need to ring ahead to the hospital."

Bryant came up. "Sir, what are you doing?" he demanded. "This young man's a witness—"

Michael turned on him. "He is my son, and I am a surgeon," he said, his voice oozing barely controlled fury. "If I don't get him to the operating theatre right away he risks losing his thumb. He's holding the ends together right now. See? Now, let us pass." Bryant, bewildered, backed away. Rachel raced off to where, presumably, she'd parked her car, with Michael striding behind her, holding Jasper up. Then they were gone.

What happened next was a blessed anticlimax. Gordon, escaping from Millie's arms, scampered towards me and sat at my feet, his stump of a tail wagging wildly. I looked at my daughter – my living, unharmed daughter. She was standing in the middle of the road, holding a weeping Tiffany, and Calvin Leaman had his arms round them both.

By the time Richard arrived, the road was empty, innocent, normal; the gawkers had gone, the first stars were appearing, shyly winking in the dusky sky. Priddy, still cursing, had been driven away, first to the hospital, then... I didn't care to imagine. The black-armoured team vanished into a van, the cordon was taken down. The spare police officers left.

We piled into my front room: the two girls, Leaman and myself, Bryant, and a female constable. Bryant took brief statements from the girls. "I'll be back," he said. "I'll need more detail. But for now I'll leave you alone to recover." He nodded curtly and left.

"I'm taking Tiffany home," Leaman said. "Thank you for taking her in, Ms Milburn. If she'd been there when Priddy was hiding out in my garage, I hate to think..." he tailed off, shaking his head. "So, thank you. I appreciate it." The girls said tearful goodbyes, clinging on to each other. "Come on, Tiff. Time to go," Leaman said gruffly. "You'll see Millie soon. Let the dust settle. Anyway, I need to call your mother."

Leaman took Tiffany by the hand, and almost pulled her down the front path. They nearly collided with Richard on the pavement. Frowning, he shouldered past them and came in at the open door. "Millie? Are you all right?"

Millie slid off the stool she'd been perching on. "Dad? You came. Yes, I'm OK. It's all over. You missed the drama." She smiled weakly.

Richard stood in my kitchen, his hands on his hips. I watched from the doorway. "You sure you're OK?" he asked Millie. "Your mum said there was some crazy man threatening you, or something."

"There was, Dad, but he's gone. Don't worry. Look, you've got enough to think about right now. I'll tell you the whole story sometime soon. When we can all sit down quietly." She put her arms round his neck and hugged him, smiling. "What news, then? Is my baby brother with us? Has he got hair? Has he got all his fingers and toes?"

Richard beamed. "Yes to all those questions," he said. "I came as soon as I could, Mil. I had to stay for a while, till they were settled, till Jenny was asleep. You understand."

"Of course I do, Dad. So, what are you going to call him, remind me?"

"Ben. Benjamin David Preston. Eight pounds, four ounces."

"Congratulations."

How gracious my Millie was being, when all I wanted to do was give Richard a firm shove out of the door. I didn't want him here, in my house, in my life. There was no longer any room for him. I stood with folded arms, leaning against the doorframe, and Millie caught my look.

"Dad, go back," she said. "To the hospital. That's where you should be, with your wife and baby. We can catch up later. I need a shower and my bed."

"Are you sure?"

"Yes, Dad. Anyway, once they are home, I'll be round to give him a cuddle."

"All right, sweetheart." Richard planted a kiss on top of Millie's head. "I'll see you soon." I stood aside to let him pass. He nodded, smiling faintly. "Anna."

When he'd gone, I said, "Did you know all along the baby was a boy?"

"Yes, they knew at the scan."

"You didn't say."

"I didn't think you wanted to know, Mum."

"Hmm. Maybe I didn't." I sat opposite her at the kitchen table. "Millie, did you tell Bryant everything?"

She frowned. "Sort of. Well, what I told him was true, but it wasn't everything, no."

"What did you leave out?"

She bit her lip, and her eyes welled with tears. "The fact that it was my fault Jasper got injured."

"What? Jasper put himself between Tiffany and Priddy's knife – we saw it."

Now tears were running down her pale cheeks. "Yes, but Priddy wouldn't even have got into my room if I hadn't done what I did."

I stretched over to the worktop and fetched down a box of tissues. "Here." She dabbed her face. "What did you do, Mil?" I asked softly.

She swallowed. "Well, we knew he was in the garden, and we could see he was hunting round, trying to find a way in. So we barricaded ourselves in my bedroom, put furniture up against the door. Jasper even had the idea we could escape out of my window if we had to, down onto the porch roof. He was full of ideas like that. Then we heard a loud crash, and the sound of glass breaking. I reckoned he'd broken a pane of the French doors at the back – I don't know what with. Maybe he'd found something in our shed. And then I remembered."

"What?"

She let out a moan. "I remembered that we'd left Gordon

in the kitchen! I couldn't bear for him to get hurt and told Tiff and Jasper we had to get him out. You'll say I was crazy to put Gordon ahead of our safety, but the thought of that man hurting him to get at us…" For a moment she dried up, her eyes wild. "They tried to talk me out of it, but I started to drag the chest away by myself, so they helped me. I thought I could get downstairs, grab Gordon and race back before he got in and found his way around. But when I got to the kitchen door he was there. Rooting around in the drawers."

I frowned. "What?"

She shook her head. "Mum, he was looking for a knife. Didn't you realize? The knife he threatened us with, that was one of ours. I don't think it's one you use much."

"Dear Lord," I muttered. "So what then?"

"It was a horrible moment," Millie said. "I kind of froze. That man, our knife in his hand, and a look on his face – I can't describe it. I called Gordon and picked him up. Then Priddy made me take him up to my room. By this time Jasper and Tiffany had come to find me. They were already on the stairs. Priddy was well chuffed. He had three hostages now, not just one. Anyway, he made us all go back into my room. Then he smashed the window and made us stand there where you could see us." She shivered. "He didn't need to break the window. I think he did it to make a point, to scare us. And he was so angry, Mum. He said he was going to cut something off Tiffany – her finger, or her ear – just to get back at Mr Leaman. He wanted to do it right where Mr Leaman could see, to torture him, I guess. He threatened Jasper and me too, said he'd cut us if we tried anything. He said he didn't care any more what they might do to him." She paused, then she added, "You know what happened after that."

She looked up at me, her eyes full of misery, and when she spoke again she sounded about five years old. "So you see, if I hadn't gone down for Gordon, we might have escaped somehow. If Jasper loses his thumb, it'll be my fault. He won't be able to play the piano or anything." Her face crumpled, and she put her head in her hands and sobbed.

I leaned across the table and took her hand. "Millie, Millie, listen. Jasper will be all right. His dad will patch him up. He did an amazing job on Rachel's cut hands, and she can still do delicate operations. Don't worry. Maybe you were rash, but I understand you couldn't leave Gordon at that man's mercy."

She lifted her tear-streaked face. "You may understand, Mum," she whispered, "and maybe even Jasper might. But won't they all hate me now, the Wellses?"

"That's as unlikely as Priddy walking free." I shook my head. "Look, sweetie, why don't you go and have a warm shower and put your PJs on? I'll get you something to eat and a hot drink and you can go to bed. It'll be the best thing. You can ring Tiffany before you go to sleep, if you want. My bet is she'll be doing just the same."

Before I went to bed myself, fortified with sandwiches and several gins, I looked in on Millie as I had done countless times through her childhood, to make sure she was covered up, or just to watch her as she slept. Sleep had smoothed out her worried frowns and made her look like a child again; her ancient teddy bear was even back on her pillow. I felt exhausted, my legs as unwieldy as tree trunks, my eyes going in and out of focus. *Thank you, Lord. Thank you for that multitude of warlike, fiery, invisible angels. That great army. We couldn't have done without them. Thank you for standing between our children and injury or death. Please be beside Jasper as he recovers, and surround him with your healing and blessing. Thank you, Lord.*

A few days later I left Millie asleep and went to work, a little late so I could wait in for the glazier who was due to mend the broken windows. I'd managed an unsatisfactory job myself with cardboard and a few bits of wood I had found in the shed. Janet had already heard about the drama via Drew and Tiffany. She asked me if I was all right, and if Millie was all right, but since she offered no comment on her son's friendship with Tiffany, beyond a quirking of her flawless eyebrows, I also said nothing. I had slept badly the last few nights and felt old. Luckily I had a quiet day – probably thanks to Janet's intervention – and spent it at my desk, dispatching a mail backlog and downloading articles from the internet for later study.

Arriving home late that afternoon, I found the house empty, quiet, and surprisingly tidy. *This is how it will be in the autumn when Millie's gone.*

There was a note on the kitchen table held down by a peppermill, but before I had a chance to read it my mobile buzzed. I fished it out of my bag from under a stack of files.

"Hi, Anna." Rachel. "How are you feeling?"

"All right, I suppose. About twenty years older, but maybe that'll wear off, in time."

"Everybody's here. Come and join us."

"Everybody?"

"Hmm, well, almost. Jasper's home, bandaged, his hand immobilized. At the moment he's lounging on his bed, lapping up all the attention. He says he's 'entertaining visiting dignitaries'. In other words, Millie and Tiffany. But Jonathan is also up there with them, as some kind of chaperone. I am

310

nodding off over a heavy surgical tome. Dulcie and Gordon are asleep at my feet. Michael is on his way home from the hospital. The only person lacking is you."

I felt a physical weight lift from me. *Perhaps I am not alone after all.* "Give me five minutes to change and I'll be right over."

"Great. I'll put the kettle on."

When I arrived, the doors and windows were all open, and a large mug of steaming coffee awaited me on the kitchen table. Rachel stretched out her long legs and flexed her shoulders. "I think I am descending into a sort of pregnancy-induced mental torpor," she said. "I can't understand a word of this." She flapped a hand at the chunky book which lay open before her, its pages black with diagrams and graphs and unpleasant-looking body-part cross-sections.

I slid into the chair opposite and took a welcome sip. "How's Jasper's hand?" I asked her.

"Well, these things aren't completely predictable, as I know very well." She traced a barely visible scar across the palm of one hand with the fingers of the other. "But mine was a more complex injury, which came out all right, and we had the same surgeon." She smiled, clearly remembering.

"I was wondering about that. Obviously at the time of your surgery you were just Michael's patient and there wasn't any emotional connection. But how can a father operate on his son? Isn't that just too difficult?"

"Yeah, there is that, but Michael wanted to do the job himself. What he did, though, was to get a colleague to assist, as a precautionary measure. Honestly, I don't know how he does it; maybe he kind of compartmentalizes things. Perhaps he had to try to forget that the damaged hand was his own son's. You can ask him yourself." She shuddered. "I just tried to imagine what it would be like if it was me and Jonny, if he had a heart problem. I don't think I could do it. On the other hand, could I trust anyone else?"

I downed half my coffee and felt revived. "I sincerely hope you'll never have to find out. So, has my daughter told you everything? How Priddy found his way to them because of her devotion to her dog?"

Rachel laughed. "Yes. It was the first thing she did – like a confession."

"She was worried you'd all be angry with her."

"What nonsense."

"That's what I told her." I caught her glance, ice-blue and sparkling with amusement, and in that moment I had the strongest feeling that this infant friendship would become a lasting blessing.

"But you know," I said slowly, "I'm wondering what it all means."

She frowned. "What exactly?"

"Why all this happened. Where God was in it. How far what I did, my decisions, precipitated events. I suppose I'm processing."

"Hmm. Well, if you come to any conclusions, please let me know. I'm in a bit of a fog myself."

"Because it could all have come out very differently."

"Yeah, I know. Horrible to contemplate. You'll have to consult my husband, I think. He's a lot more spiritually aware than I am. Sees connections, God's hand, all that. Not to mention he is much better versed in Scripture than me. I am a baby compared to him. He'll probably quote the Psalms at you."

As if summoned, Michael strolled through the back

door, pulling off his tie and throwing his briefcase onto the nearest chair. "It's so good to be home, I might just burst into song," he said with an unexpected air of theatre.

"Tough day at the office, dear?" Rachel enquired, one eyebrow raised.

He slumped into a chair next to me and rested his head in his hands. "The office was what it was," he said. "Nothing but meetings and paperwork."

"Tea? Coffee? Or are you starting on alcohol?" Rachel heaved herself out of her chair, and I saw how her unborn child was stretching her loose white shirt. She ran a careless hand along the back of her husband's neck as she passed.

"Coffee. Then alcohol. Am I cooking?"

"So you said. But if you are too demoralized and exhausted we can always send out for a takeaway."

"No, I'll do it. Just fill me with caffeine and I'll be a new man."

"I think I am rather fond of the old one," Rachel said.

"You only *think*?" Michael tried to look shocked. "Is this the beginning of the end?"

"Please. I can't go through all that again."

This made me laugh, and I nearly choked on the dregs of my coffee. "All what?"

Rachel put a mug down in front of Michael. "Best not to ask." She grinned.

"How many am I cooking for?" Michael asked.

"Seven, if you include Jonny." She looked at me. "That's assuming you don't have a better offer, Anna."

"I can't think of anything better," I said with feeling. Sensing they might want to speak privately for a while, I got up. "I'll go and touch base with the kids," I said. "Make sure they aren't up to mischief."

Michael laughed. "That chunky dressing will cramp Jasper's style for a while, I think. Just as well."

"Oh?"

He shook his head. "I don't think for a moment that Millie and Tiffany would have any trouble fending off unwanted attentions," he said. "But I am not so decrepit that I can't remember what it was like to be twenty with surging hormones and unmerited self-belief."

Rachel's eyes widened. "Do tell."

He drained his cup and got to his feet, chuckling. "Not a chance."

I needed no directions to Jasper's bedroom: loud music and shrieks of laughter led me to an innocently open door. Jasper lay on his bed, propped up on pillows, and beside him, quite unselfconscious, my daughter lolled. His bandaged hand was strapped to his chest, but his uninjured left arm was round Millie's shoulders.

Millie waved a languid hand. "Hey, Mum."

I leaned against the doorframe and looked around. The room was full of stuff – piles of books, a keyboard, music, clothing tumbling off chairs, a quilt on the floor. "Where's Tiffany?"

"Here I am." Tiffany's muffled voice came from the other side of the bed. She sat up, ruffled and flushed, her hair sticking out in all directions. "Just having a bit of a fight here." I heard a child giggle and crow, and walked around the end of the bed. Jonathan was sitting in Tiffany's lap, pulling at the ends of her hair, pummelling her cheeks, generally having huge fun at her expense.

"Looks like you are all none the worse for your adventure, if we can call it that," I observed. "How are you, Jasper?"

"I'm OK, thanks, Anna," he said, his smile so like Michael's. "Holding court, as you see. Like some Eastern potentate."

"Better make the most of it," Millie said tartly. "While we are all bowing down to the great hero."

"Hey!" Tiffany protested. She got to her feet with difficulty, dusting down her top. She bent and picked Jonathan up. He had found the remains of a biscuit on the carpet and was solemnly munching, spraying Tiffany with crumbs. "Ugh, monster, you are making me sticky," she complained. She turned to me. "Millie likes to scoff, but I think Jasper *is* a hero," she said. "If it wasn't for him, I might actually be dead." She shivered.

"I agree, Tiffany. What Jasper did was very brave, whatever my cynical daughter thinks."

Millie stretched and wriggled upright. "Yeah, I think he was brave too. But he's so smug with it! What is it about men? They're so full of themselves!"

Jasper gave her a hard shove, and she fell off the edge of the bed onto the floor.

"Ow!"

"That's what happens to people who don't show the appropriate level of besotted admiration," he said sternly. "Only the mindlessly adoring are fit to share the hero's bed. You should know that."

Millie got up and tugged down her rucked-up shirt. "You'll be on your own, then, love," she sniffed.

"Here," Tiffany said. "Take this crumby, sticky, grubby child, Millie. I'll take a turn with the hero." She sniggered. "Am I adoring enough?" she asked Jasper.

"No," Jasper said. "You're just pretending. You've spent *far too much* time with Miss Emilia Preston. But, on this occasion, I'll graciously relent." He patted the space beside him. "Come and snuggle up."

Tiffany planted herself on the bed with a bounce of springs.

"This scene of decadence is too much for me," I said. "I'm going back downstairs. Just to let you all know that Michael is cooking, and I think I just heard a cork pop. Behave yourselves."

A voice hallooed from the bottom of the stairs. "Anna, if you're coming down, can you bring Jonny?"

"Gladly." I plucked the little boy from Millie's arms. As I turned to go I heard Millie say, "Budge up, fatty", and I left the three of them squashed together, one on each side of Jasper, giggling helplessly.

The table was cleared, the dishwasher stacked. I was replete and felt I had had a drop too much to drink. But the atmosphere lent itself so effortlessly to comradely chat and laughter that I sensed something hard and tight begin to unwind somewhere deep inside me.

"It's nearly the summer holidays," Millie observed sleepily, leaning on the table with one elbow. "What are we all going to do with the endless weeks of freedom and self-indulgence?"

"We're going away," Tiffany said hesitantly.

"What?" Millie sat up. "Away where? You never said."

Tiffany wrapped her arms around herself in a typical gesture. "We were just talking about it last night, at home. Dad said we all need to recover. Him included. Well, maybe him most of all. He *was* in prison, after all. That can't have been very pleasant. And I know he's concerned about this referendum that's coming up soon, and what it will mean for his business.

He needs to think and make plans, I guess. But he's thinking about me too. I know we are joking about it, but for a minute there… you know, Millie, it *was* horrible. Anyway, Dad has an old friend with a huge villa. It's in Sardinia, and there's a path which leads right down to the beach, and a pool, and a terrace overlooking the sea. His friend says there's room for all of us. We'll probably be away for most of July and August."

"But Tiff," Millie said, looking aghast. "What about, you know, you and Drew?"

Everyone's conversations came to an abrupt end. We saw Tiffany's fair-skinned face suffused with a ruddy blush. "Ah, well," she stammered. "Dad said, if I liked, and if Drew could rustle up the airfare, he could join us there for a week or two."

"Wahay!" Millie hooted.

"I think maybe," Tiffany said, "Dad wants to check him out. You know what dads are like – overprotective."

"Mine isn't," Millie observed. "But Tiff, that's great. Just think – beach barbecues, long romantic walks, topping up your tan in that spotty bikini…"

"Except I won't be lying in the sun," Tiffany said. "You know I always burn and look like a lobster. Anyway, one thing I've managed to get Drew to do. If he wants to come to Sardinia, he has to give up smoking that pipe."

Rachel, Michael, and I were having difficulty suppressing laughter. Tiffany's prim and haughty expression was utterly comical.

"Yeah," Millie said. "Made him look like an old man."

"It wasn't so much that," Tiffany said. "It was the smell. He kept it in his pocket, and sometimes it wasn't properly out. He stank of old tobacco and singed trousers."

We gave up the effort and cracked up.

The young ones went back to Jasper's room. Rachel took Jonathan upstairs for his bath and bed. Michael and I sat in the lounge with a cafetière of coffee, the French doors still open, though the evening was darkening, a breeze making the thin curtains billow, letting in the scent of roses and cut grass.

After a brief silence, Michael said, "Rachel mentioned you were wondering what it all meant – what has happened, why it happened that way."

"Yes," I said. "I'm not sure I'm clear-headed enough to articulate it after all our eating and drinking. But I can't help looking back and wondering how far what I decided – sometimes small things, or so they seemed at the time – made big differences. I guess just saying 'yes' to the Leaman brief started things off in a particular direction, and after a while it all took on a momentum of its own."

He shifted in his chair, gazing thoughtfully at his mug. "Your work inevitably involves moral dilemmas at times, I imagine. Rachel and I have an easier time of it – we just mend people's bodies. But for you it's different. As a person of honour, and even more as a Christian, you have a tricky path to tread."

I nodded slowly, thinking. "When I first started out, I wanted to be a criminal barrister above all. Young Anna loved the drama, the cross-examination, the old courts, the frantic pace, barristers getting instructions just hours beforehand, the whole grand theatre of it all. But when I came here to Brant I had to specialize elsewhere, just to make a living. Apart from defending Rachel's attacker – which wasn't much of a defence at all, not even a mitigation – this brief was the first crime I've been involved in for a long time. Leaman asked for me, for reasons of his own.

My reasons for taking it on were complicated, and I hope they were honourable, but there was also that frisson, that thought that perhaps I could once more stand up in court and argue my client's case. It didn't come to that, and it was right that it didn't. But…"

"But what?" Michael prompted.

I sighed. "I have to confess that employment tribunals and motoring offences and child arrangement orders, all important in their own way, are not very exciting. And they make up a lot of my working life, among other things. I wanted to be an eloquent advocate, but what I am is a combination of counsellor, handkerchief-supplier, psychiatrist, social worker – even surrogate parent at times. Maybe I am foolish, but there is still, lurking somewhere in the depths, a memory of the glamour and drama of a criminal trial. It's all nonsense, I know that. But perhaps we need a bit of nonsense to keep us going." I smiled a little sadly. "All I wanted, when I was a foolish, ignorant child, was to be like Atticus Finch."

"That's no bad ambition," Michael said. "Even for non-lawyers. But tell me, when you were offered the Leaman brief, what else could you have done?"

"Oh, I had options. They just didn't feel… right, somehow. But things could have panned out very differently. We could be looking at a very much worse scenario, right now." I shuddered.

"But we were all praying," Michael said. "Weren't we? Weren't you?"

"Yes. I prayed for armies of angels at each end of my road. But it doesn't always work out, does it?"

He shook his head, smiling faintly. "No. And I grant you it's a great mystery. Inevitably there are huge chasms in our understanding. Faith has to fill the cracks."

"Rachel said you would probably quote the Psalms at me."

"Did she? Actually, I was thinking of a verse from Isaiah."

"Go on."

"I can't quote it verbatim. I'm not that Scripture-literate! Hold on, I'll get a Bible." He got up, crossed the room and took a Bible down from a bookshelf, flicked through it, and looked up at me. "Here it is: 'You, Lord, give perfect peace to those who keep their purpose firm and put their trust in you.' I suppose we can try, and keep on trying, hard as it is. But there *is* a psalm I can think of. Fifty-five, somewhere in the middle. You might look it up."

"I will," I said. "As you say, keeping one's purpose firm is a challenge, but right now 'perfect peace' is a lovely idea."

A voice called from upstairs. "That sounds like my cue for persuading Jonathan it's sleep time," Michael said. "He's probably had far too much excitement."

"And Tiffany mentioning the referendum has reminded me," I said. "Among all the excitement we've all been subjected to recently, we mustn't forget to vote. For what it's worth."

Michael shook his head. "We have to believe it's worth something."

"Of course. Now, I must get my errant daughter and go home," I said. "It's been such a good evening, Michael. Thanks."

"Our pleasure," he answered, his face suddenly serious. "You're most welcome."

Later, as we were thinking about going to bed, Millie passed me on the landing on her way to the bathroom. "It's nice that Tiff's going to get some downtime," she said. "I'll miss her, but I'm glad she'll have some time with Drew as well. I know

I take the mickey but Drew's all right really." She hesitated, as if she had something else to say. "Mum, Jasper wants me to go to France with them, to their house, when they go for the summer."

"Does he? And what do Michael and Rachel think of that?"

"Oh, he said they're all for it."

"Wow, that's incredible. Well, what do you think? Do you want to go?"

"Yes, sort of. What do you think I should say?"

"Millie, this is unlike you. Normally you know your own mind very clearly. And if you don't, mine would be the last opinion you'd seek. What's going on?"

"I'm a bit worried, that's all." She looked suddenly defensive. "I don't know what Jasper wants. Am I a mate? Does he want me to be his girlfriend? Not sure I can cope with that – you know, close quarters and no one to consult. No girlfriends, basically."

"Rachel would be on your side. She would help."

"I know. And she's good at straightening Jasper out. But she's pregnant, and tired, and she's got a toddler to look after, and I don't want to load her up with my stuff." She stared at the floor, biting her lip, and I suddenly saw her as young and naive and uncertain. Which she was, except that normally she would never have admitted it, nor allowed me to refer to it. Perhaps the events of the past few days had rocked her off balance more than she wanted to acknowledge. "I'd feel happier if you came too." She caught my expression. "You don't have to look so astonished."

"But I am! I'm speechless. I thought you'd be delighted at the chance to get away from an interfering parent who's always trying to cramp your style."

"I guess… maybe just at the moment I'm feeling a bit insecure. Things have been weird, though, haven't they? Was it just a few days ago that a man with a knife was threatening to cut bits off Tiffany? That there were all those armed policemen in our road? Sometimes it's like I dreamed it. I suppose it's more of a little wobble." She frowned. "That woman police officer, she offered us all counselling. Did you know that? I said I was OK, but maybe I should have accepted it. Maybe I need it." She heaved a sigh. "I keep thinking about the autumn too, being on my own in a strange city, not knowing anyone – well, except Jasper. Not knowing where to go, getting lost. I never thought I'd say this, but I sometimes feel I'm just not grown up enough."

"Millie, Millie." I put my hands on her shoulders. "You'll be fine. Everyone feels anxious when life is going to change so radically. But I'd bet my barely existent pension you'll find friends in very short order. Yes, these last days have been enough to shake anyone, me included. And I can tell you I often feel unequal to what gets thrown at me. But you muddle through somehow. One thing did occur to me, though. I wondered if that crazy man said anything – Priddy, I mean. How did he know how to find you? Where we lived?"

Millie pulled a face. "Yeah, well, I didn't tell you everything, Mum. Like how he boasted and threatened poor Tiff – it was horrible. The things he said about her dad, the things he was going to do to her – and nearly did. He found us because he followed Mr Leaman, in the car, at a safe distance, that time he brought Tiffany's clothes and stuff." She shuddered. "I *hate* the idea of him sneaking around, following people, turning up at our house. I hate remembering it. It makes me feel sick."

I wrapped my arms around her, and she leaned into me.

I felt her tremble, and for a moment I hated him too. "It'll pass, Millie," I said softly. "It *will*. Not that you'll ever forget, but it'll lose its power. Maybe you should take up the offer of counselling; I'm sure it's not too late. As for going to France, why don't you sleep on it? And if you aren't sure of the deal with Jasper, just ask him."

"Won't he think I'm weird?"

I shrugged. "Maybe. But it's probably better to be upfront."

"Hmm." She made no move; something else was on her mind. "I'm worried about you, too, Mum."

"Me? Whatever for?"

"If I go away, you'll be alone."

"That's all right. I'm going to have to get used to it, aren't I? In October you'll be gone. It's normal, love. Kids grow up and move on."

"Yeah. I still wish you were coming, though. And don't laugh."

A few days later Rachel rang. "Anna, my bullish stepson has been conspiring. It's something he has quite a talent for."

"What's he done?"

"He wants Millie to come with us to France when we go. And we'd love to have her. She'd be company for Jasper, and if I am very selfish I have to say she's also a big help with Jonny. But what we'd really like is if you came too."

"Rachel," I said, frowning. "Wouldn't that be a huge imposition?"

"No, it would be fun. Please say you'll think about it."

"Well, I… don't know." To say I was nonplussed would have been an understatement.

"Do you have any holiday plans?" she asked.

"No. I haven't even booked any weeks out."

"Work isn't everything. Even if you just came down for a week or so it would do you good."

"But," I blundered on, "don't you just want to be with your own family?"

"I can be with them any time. Please come, Anna. I would really like it."

"Are you sure Michael is in favour?"

"He definitely is. He likes you. Says you are interesting to talk to. At the moment I don't have a lot of conversation – my brain's turned to mush. I am more of a liability than an asset."

"I suppose I could see if I can get a few days off…" My voice failed me.

"Good, hurrah, that's settled. We can loll in the garden with a book and a bottle. Doesn't that sound just a bit enticing?"

I had to agree. "More than a bit."

After she'd rung off I felt dazed. How had things changed so much in such a short time? Then I remembered Michael telling me about a psalm – fifty-five, was it? I took up my Bible and looked it up. In the middle I found words that seemed strangely resonant. Here David was speaking not as a king but as a soldier, but his words might apply to anyone baffled by the battles of everyday life. They certainly applied to me, these past days. "… I call to the Lord God for help, and he will save me. Morning, noon and night my complaints and groans go up to him, and he will hear my voice. He will bring me safely back from the battles that I fight against so many enemies." That was just what he had done. Brought me back safely from the field of battle. *Thank you, Lord.*

Before I could contemplate days of idleness and self-indulgence, there was something I could not neglect. A day or two before I was due to drive down to France – Rachel and family, with Millie, had already gone – I drove to Burrow Bridge, unannounced. I wanted to see how my parents were coping before my father had a chance to make things look more serene than they were.

I found them both in the garden, sitting side by side on deckchairs in the sunshine.

"Hello, Dad. No, don't get up." I bent to kiss his cheek. "Mum." She held out her arms, smiling, and I hugged her. "I'll get another chair." I fetched one from the shed and sat with them. "I thought I'd call by, see how you are." I looked around. "The garden looks good," I said with some surprise.

"Your brother came over and cut the grass," my father said.

"Who, Alastair?"

"No, Ronnie, believe it or not. And Tanya weeded the borders. Actually," he went on, with a little quirk of his eyebrows, "those two have been here quite a lot lately. Helping. It's been nice, hasn't it, Nan? Seeing a bit more of Ronnie."

"Yes," my mother said vaguely, still smiling. "Good boy, Ronnie."

"Maybe," I said, "he saw how it was, when Mum went missing. I wanted to ask you, Dad – what about help? You know I'm going to be away soon, for about ten days or so."

"Yes, Millie told us. That'll be good for you, love." He leaned over and patted my knee. "You work much too hard. You all do."

"You're a one to talk!" I said.

"Well," he said thoughtfully, "I won't say it hasn't been hard at times. But we're all right. Our carers are regular, and Ronnie and Tanya and Alastair and Kathryn are at the other end of a phone. We're all right, aren't we, Nan?" My mother nodded and smiled. He turned back to me, lowering his voice. "I made her promise," he said, "never to go wandering off again. I don't know if she'll remember. But I told her she'd given me a proper fright, and she seemed to understand. Well, who knows? But anyway, darling, you must go and take a break. It'll do you good. Have fun and forget about us for a while. We'll be just fine."

A few days after we'd watched the Perseid meteor shower from the garden of the Wellses' French house – something they tried to do every year, they said – Michael came back from a shopping trip to the local supermarket and put a folded English newspaper on the table in front of me as I lounged under an umbrella, sleepily pretending to read.

"I thought this might interest you," he said. "I'm afraid it's not today's."

I sat up. It was a warm day, but a fat cloud was covering up the sun, and the humidity was high. I had as much energy as a well-fed slug, but it didn't seem to matter. It had been a couple of weeks since I'd even looked at a newspaper; the referendum had continued to dominate the headlines and I was tired of all the hullabaloo and posturing. I unfolded the paper and was confronted with a long report about an enormous haul of cocaine recovered from a boat in the North Sea, a hundred miles off Aberdeen, and photos of two middle-aged Turks who between them had been given forty-two years in prison by the High Court in Glasgow.

"Good grief," I muttered.

Michael had gone into the kitchen to put away the perishables; now he came back out with two glasses on a tray. "You need to keep hydrated," he said with a smile.

"Thanks. This is extraordinary. Over *five hundred million pounds'* worth. The biggest haul ever." Michael sat down opposite me as I read on. "It says here it was an international operation. A tip-off from the French, cooperation from Tanzania to allow the boat to be boarded, an investigation involving Guyana, Spain, the Canary Islands, Denmark, Norway, and the US. That's some coup. I wonder where the drugs would have ended up."

"Everywhere, I imagine," Michael said. "Here, England, elsewhere in Europe. There's a big market."

I looked up at him. "Do you think our friend…?"

"Leaman?" Michael shook his head. "I wonder."

"Michael, you've lived in Brant a long time. You must have heard things about him. Do you think the talk was true? How come they never caught up with him? Or is – was – he just a small link in a vast chain? Is he still involved? Was he ever? What do we actually know?"

He shrugged. "We, you and I, don't know anything, do we? Not as a proven fact."

"Hmm. I know one devastating effect, though: my nephew Sam, who will always be a damaged child because of what he took, because of what someone, maybe Leaman, maybe someone else, supplied."

Michael sighed. "Yes, that's certainly a fact, and a very tragic one. What do the police know, do you suppose? To have used considerable resources over a period of years they must have had strong reason to pursue him."

"Mm. Well, I don't plan to call up DCI Bryant to find out. Not that he'd tell me."

"In that case we'll have to accept we'll probably never know. Does that bother you?"

"I guess not. There are so many things I don't know I

would lose what's left of my sanity if I worried about this one. It'll just have to go into a very large box marked 'Unsolved Mysteries.'"

A smile lit up Michael's face. "And hidden at the back of a dark cupboard."

I grinned back. "In the attic."

"Of a derelict house."

"In a forest in Finland."

"That should do it."

Rachel leaned out of the open window in one of the upstairs rooms. "What are you two laughing about?"

I wiped my eyes. "Absolutely nothing at all."

BOOK CLUB QUESTIONS

1) Which aspects of Anna's character did you most (or least) relate to?

2) What do you think informed Anna's decision-making? Do you think she was right in the decisions she made?

3) How would you describe Anna's friendship with Rachel?

4) In what way(s) do you think Tiffany's family background might have affected her?

5) How do you think the events of this story change Anna?

6) Which was you favourite scene?

7) Did you find it easy to empathise with the characters? Was there someone in particular you did or didn't like?

8) How did you feel about the faith element in the story? Did it enhance, detract from, or make no difference to the plot?

9) How satisfying was the ending? Would you have changed anything?

10) Did you take anything of value from this story? If so, what?

If you have a question or comment for the author, tweet @SueLRussell or visit her website, www.slrussell.net.

S.L. RUSSELL'S *THE HEALING KNIFE* IS OUT NOW

ISBN: 978 1 7826 4303 6

e-ISBN: 978 1 7826 4304 3

'A gripping contemporary tale told with a rare elegance'

C.F. Dunn, author of *Fearful Symmetry*